Alison Joseph was born in North London and educated at Leeds University. After graduation she worked as a presenter on a local radio station, then, moving back to London, for Channel 4. She later became a partner in an independent production company and one of its commissions was a series about women and religion, the book of which was published by SPCK. She has since given birth to her third child and worked as a reader for BBC Radio Drama. She is once again living in North London and is currently working on her third crime novel featuring Sister Agnes.

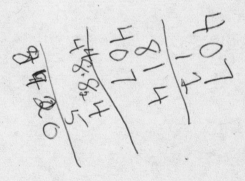

Also by Alison Joseph

Sacred Hearts

The Hour
of Our Death

Alison Joseph

HEADLINE

First published in 1995
by HEADLINE BOOK PUBLISHING

First published in paperback in 1995
by HEADLINE BOOK PUBLISHING

10 9 8 7 6 5 4 3 2 1

ISBN 0 7472 4894 X

Typeset by CBS, Felixstowe, Suffolk

Printed and bound in Great Britain by
Cox Wyman Ltd, Reading, Berks

HEADLINE BOOK PUBLISHING
A division of Hodder Headline PLC
338 Euston Road
London NW1 3BH

ACKNOWLEDGEMENTS

I wish to thank Gill and Tony Waldron and Dr Lucy Mathen for their help with this book. Thanks are also due to the press office at Church House, Sarah Dobson IBVM, Marian Joseph, Dr Jill Bartlett, and Stephen Joseph for the public transport information.

Chapter One

'You!' called a sharp voice behind her. 'Just where do you think you're going?'

Agnes turned, slowly, reluctant to face yet another irritation in what had proved to be so far a very irritating day. Framed by the swing door, the dirty beige of the hospital corridor behind her, stood a grizzle-haired woman of indeterminate age wearing the stiff grey of a senior nurse.

'I'm looking for Mrs McAleer, and I believe she's on this ward.'

In answer, the nurse indicated a sign on the door which said, 'TB on ward. No unauthorised visitors.'

'And?' Agnes said.

'You can read, can't you?'

'I assume parish visiting counts as authorised,' said Agnes sharply.

The nurse took in Agnes's smart, short haircut, the crisp white shirt and the silk black jacket with matching trousers, and allowed a shadow of doubt to pass, sneer-like, across her face. 'Parish?' she said.

'I'm standing in for Father Julius, who has the flu, and I've a long list of patients to see, Kathleen McAleer being

1

one of them, and I'd prefer not to waste any more of my time,' said Agnes, biting back anger at having to justify her presence to this small-minded woman who appeared to view any human contact as an obstacle to the efficient administration of her wards.

The sneer became open hostility. 'Dear Father Julius,' she breathed. 'Do send him my best regards, and say I hope he comes back to work *soon*. And as for Kathleen McAleer – ' she smiled her superiority – 'well, you'll see.' With a whisk of apron she was gone.

Agnes approached the curtained bed that the nurse at the desk had indicated with some apprehension. From within came a peculiar low moaning, recognisably female, punctuated by strange, guttural noises. Agnes put her face close to the curtain.

'Um . . . it's Sister Agnes . . . I'm visiting from St Simeon's,' she said, raising her voice above the noise.

'Oh, thank goodness,' came a light voice, and the curtain was flung back by a young nurse. 'I'm trying to get her feet into the slippers, but she takes it better from you people.' The nurse turned to leave.

'But – what . . . Takes what better?'

The nurse turned back, clearly anxious to get on with more pressing tasks. 'Well, the usual man, he takes her up to the day room for a chat. I suppose she was religious before; anyway, it seems to comfort her.'

'Before what?'

'Don't you have notes on your patients? The second stroke, what else?' and before Agnes could ask anything else, she'd hurried off.

Agnes looked at Mrs McAleer. She was a woman weary with age and illness. Her skin was grey and papery, her mouth was moist and slightly ajar; but her eyes were glassy bright and at this moment regarded Agnes with a look of utter malevolence.

'Er . . . right,' said Agnes cheerfully. 'The day room, is it?'

'Kkkkk . . . Bbbbb . . .' came the reply.

'Oh. Um . . .'

'She can't talk, can she?' someone said. Agnes turned to see a woman with shiny white hair and a bright pink satin bedjacket sitting up in the next bed. 'She were all right for a while after the first one, but last week, another it was, I told them, they said it would finish her off at her age, seventy-nine next month, but it didn't, not Kathleen, I said, not her, and I was right, weren't I, dear? But she can't talk, not now. Probably not ever,' and the woman burst into a brittle shout of laughter which stopped as suddenly as it had begun. Kathleen stared blankly at her neighbour. 'Don't bother with the slippers, dear,' the woman continued. 'She hates them, don't you, dear, she told me, that was before, she said, I won't wear them, I won't. That geezer brought them in, her nephew or someone. Bugger the slippers.'

Agnes saw that Kathleen had begun to rock to and fro. She was making a strange wheezing noise and it was only then that Agnes realised she was laughing too, and saying, at intervals, 'Bbbbb.'

'That's it dear, eh?' her neighbour said. 'Bugger the slippers.'

3

Kathleen was still rocking and saying 'Bbbb . . .' as Agnes pushed her wheelchair gently to the day room. They sat in its frosty shabbiness and looked out through the grubby, wide, metal-framed window over the rooftops of London, the Thames, and beyond that the glittering towers of the City itself.

Agnes turned to her charge. 'Well,' she said, and paused. Again there was an unmistakably hostile gleam in the eyes. 'I'm here instead of Father Julius.'

'Kkkhhgg.'

'You were on my list.' It sounded like a lame excuse, and Agnes wondered why she felt like apologising to this tiny, crippled, speechless woman.

'McAleer? Is that an Irish name?'

Kathleen grunted and turned, pointedly, it seemed to Agnes, to look out of the window. Agnes heard the door swing open, and a sharp voice said, 'Where are her slippers? She shouldn't be out with no slippers. I might have known,' added the grey-haired starchy sister from before, seeing Agnes.

'Hello again,' said Agnes.

'Take her back and get her slippers.'

'She doesn't want to wear them.'

'What on earth do you mean? She's got to wear them.'

'She doesn't want to – do you?' Agnes turned to Kathleen, who stared glassily, open-mouthed.

'It might have slipped your notice, but she has suffered a CVA and therefore can't speak. "Doesn't want to wear them", indeed. Now take her back and get them. Do you hear?'

4

Agnes stood up. 'Oh, bugger the slippers. And I don't have to take orders from you.'

The nurse gave Agnes a frozen look. 'We'll see about that,' she said, and left sharply. Agnes sat down and looked at Kathleen who once again was rocking to and fro, wheezing with laughter, her face a cracked grin of merriment, repeating, 'Bbbb . . . KkkBbbb.'

'Well,' said Agnes. 'What did Julius talk to you about?'

Kathleen stopped laughing and looked out of the window.

'Why don't you want me here?'

Kathleen turned back to her slowly. 'Bbbb . . .' she said.

'You're not expecting words of comfort, then? Solace from your faith? That sort of thing?'

Kathleen spat out a guttural response. 'But,' added Agnes, 'you used to believe?'

'Bbbb . . . Gggg . . .' Kathleen said, looking levelly at Agnes.

It was as if Agnes had suddenly acquired a new language. 'Might that mean, Bugger Off?' The mask of hostility melted just slightly. Kathleen turned away once more.

'OK, let's go back to the ward. I'm sorry to intrude. Julius must have been mistaken to give me your name.' Agnes stood up to go – and then a thought caught her and she sat down again. 'A long time ago,' she began, 'when I still lived in France – yes, I know I still have a French accent even now – I very nearly gave up too. I was married to a man – a violent man . . .' She broke off and

5

looked at Kathleen, who quickly looked away. 'Of course,' Agnes said, 'it's nothing compared to what you're going through. But what I mean is, there are always times when God's love seems like a bad joke, or at best, like some fairy tale you tell children so they can believe the world's a good place. Against all the evidence.'

Kathleen was looking out of the window. Agnes stood up and took the brake off the wheelchair. 'Only,' she added, as they began to trundle their way back to the ward, 'that's it, isn't it? That's the Number One question. Why, when these awful things happen in the world, or happen to us, do we continue to believe? Why the hell should we? But that's the whole point. I'm not explaining myself very well,' she said as they arrived back by Kathleen's bed, and Agnes sat down opposite her again, looking for some kind of response in the despairing face. The hostility, at least, had gone. 'Anyway, I'm sorry to intrude. Julius will be back next week, I hope.'

She stood up to go. The lady in the next bed looked up from her magazine. ''Ave a nice fag, did yer?'

'What?' Agnes said.

'A fag. That's what the usual geezer does. Takes her up to the day room for a smoke. Missed out, did yer, Kath? Never mind, that 'orrible old nephew of yours might run to a packet of ten.' She settled back to her magazine.

'Well, I wish Julius had told me,' fumed Agnes as she strode from the ward, consulting the next name on her list. 'Wasting that woman's time, and mine, when all those

6

words of comfort on faith in the face of adversity could have been replaced by a couple of Silk Cut. And I'm already running late. I was hoping to be back in the office by lunchtime.' Agnes continued to stride angrily along the corridor, up in the lift, on to the next ward.

What she was trying not to think about – the main cause, in fact, of her annoyance – was a letter that had arrived that morning in their little office and had been handed to her by Julius with a look that was supposed to be neutral. It was addressed in the bold, italic script of her ex-husband, Hugo Bourdillon, and it enclosed a large photograph of Hugo standing next to a rather beautiful woman.

'Good God,' she said, reading the note. 'He's remarried.'

'Oh yes?' Julius replied, vaguely.

'She's called Gabrielle, and he's having a wonderful honeymoon in North Africa. How extraordinary.'

'The third Madame Bourdillon. I wonder how long she'll last.'

'Oh, who cares,' she'd replied, throwing the letter in the bin, and, on impulse, slipping the photograph into her bag.

Who cares? she thought now. Me, the first Madame Bourdillon. Who am I to care? It was all a long time ago. She took a deep breath and went through the swing doors of ward A12, to visit a sentimental old soul who wanted to talk about her husband, dead these last seven years but still very much with her, and did Agnes think the Virgin Mary was watching us, because she didn't mind the angels looking down but women are so much more critical, aren't they?, and she'd hate to think of her seeing the dust over the door frames.

Meanwhile, Kathleen was being wheeled along once more by a cheerful nurse. 'There we are then, dear,' she burbled, 'they'll be ready for you in a minute.' The nurse parked her outside a sign saying 'Ultrasound', and wandered off, leaving Kathleen in the deserted corridor. Kathleen could hear distant cries, and from a nearby office came the sound of typing. She thought how strange it was that she could hear perfectly normally, and yet she inhabited a world without speech; like those windows, she thought, where you can see out but no one can see in. Like on – what was the word? – those vehicles, ambers . . . ambergris . . . ? Flashing lights on the roof, sirens. Ambulate. Ambush. Language for her had become a high wall, a sheer surface that was impossible to scale. Words, she thought. Words. She tried to say the word 'Words', just to see. 'Bbbbb,' she heard herself say, just as the nurse returned.

'That's right dear,' chirped the nurse, wheeling her a little further along the corridor. 'Just a few minutes now. There's some students there – you don't mind, do you?'

'Kkkhhh,' said Kathleen, spitting throatily. It was unbearable to her that her body, ugly with illness, should be viewed by a party of keen, scrubbed youth. 'Ggghhh,' said Kathleen, biting back tears of rage.

'That's right, dear,' the nurse replied and, parking the

wheelchair just in front of an open door, wandered off again.

Kathleen found herself wishing she were dead. It was, for her, a novel thought, and she briefly wondered what that nun woman would make of it. The typing stopped suddenly, like a life cut short. The corridor was deserted. Then, in the silence, Kathleen heard footsteps clop sharply along the corridor behind her, coming nearer. She was aware of her pulse quickening, of there being, in the midst of her despair and confusion, a kind of terror. She tried to see the approaching person, twisting with difficulty in her chair, as the footsteps were right behind her; Kathleen turned just in time to see that the door which had been open was now pushed to, leaving a gap of a few inches. There was a strange noise coming from within, a sort of breathless panting; then she heard voices, shouting, a cry, a scuffling noise, followed by a loud thump. Then silence.

Kathleen knew suddenly, with absolute conviction, that something very bad was happening. She continued to stare at the door. A new noise had started up, a quiet dragging, rasping noise. Suddenly, in the doorway, at ground level, a prostrate foot appeared, medium sized, wearing a woman's black court shoe. It began to twitch violently, and Kathleen watched it, feeling a sympathy with its anguished convulsions. Gradually they abated, until the foot lay still. Kathleen, knowing she was seeing death, felt only envy. She gazed upon the foot, and in her mind the words of the Latin mass that she'd learned in Donegal all those years ago came to her. 'Sanctus, sanctus,' she found herself muttering; to herself or out loud, she was no longer sure. A soul released. And whether it was to be united in glory with all the saints, or whether it had simply vanished into nothingness – she envied it.

A glimpse of movement within the room made her remember to be afraid. Instinctively she struggled to turn back in her chair, taking up a slumped position. So that when, a few moments later, someone stepped carefully over the foot in the doorway and proceeded briskly along the corridor, Kathleen, peeking through eyes which appeared closed, saw everything; but the murderer, if murderer it was, saw only a comatose old woman asleep in a wheelchair.

Chapter Two

The staff canteen was unappealing. The fluorescent light made the macaroni cheese, floppy on its plastic plate, seem even greyer. Agnes replaced her tray quietly and left. It was three o'clock, and she hadn't eaten since breakfast, but there were limits. She'd have to grab a sandwich between reporting back to Julius and returning to her usual work at the safe house for young runaways.

At the hospital's main door, the porter asked her to sign out. 'St Simeon's?' he asked, reading her name upside down. 'So you're the one they're looking for.'

'What do you mean?' asked Agnes wearily.

'Professor Burgess sent his people down to look for you,' the porter replied. 'Said it was urgent.'

Agnes waited. No more information was forthcoming. 'Yes, well,' she said, 'I've been working non-stop since this morning, I haven't eaten for hours and whatever it is will just have to wait until Julius is back.' She picked up her bag.

'All right, all right, no need for that. It was a death, that's all. A sudden death up in the teaching staff. They said she was one of yours.'

'One of mine? Whatever can they mean by that?'

The porter shrugged and turned to deal with an elderly man who was inquiring about wheelchairs.

Agnes walked slowly to the exit. The revolving doors flashed with April sunlight. She put down her bag and stood facing them for a long moment; then picked up her bag again, turned with leaden feet and stomped back to the lift. 'Third floor, Room 3018,' the porter said.

The way to Rooms 3010 onwards was barred by a hastily placed sign saying, 'Cleaning in Progress.' Agnes stepped carefully round it and went on her way. She knocked on Door 3018 which was opened a crack by a dishevelled young blonde woman. 'Sister Agnes,' said Agnes. 'Sorry about the delay.' The door opened just wide enough to allow her in.

Inside, crammed into the office, there was a small crowd. The dishevelled young woman hovered nervously; behind her a middle-aged man and two younger people, one male, one female, were bent over something. Without looking up they made way for Agnes, who saw, laid out on a makeshift bed, the body of a woman. She was in her late thirties, perhaps early forties, thought Agnes, with strong, good-looking features; her eyes were bright blue and staring blankly, her dark brown hair was well-cut. Her clothes were of good quality, from the smart office jacket to the black court shoes. Agnes moved closer and made to close the eyes but her hand was grabbed by the older man. 'No, you fool, what the devil do you think—'

'Sister Agnes, parish visitor. You called for me.'

The man looked at her blankly. 'Of course,' he said.

'Only, we haven't quite finished.' He was still holding Agnes's hand, and suddenly he became aware of this, and shook it in greeting. 'Burgess, Professor of Surgery,' he said abruptly, and then returned to looking at the body.

'Who was she?' asked Agnes gently.

'Miss Sullivan. Gail Sullivan. One of the secretaries.'

'Administrators,' butted in the young blonde woman. 'I'm a secretary. There's a difference.'

Her remark went unacknowledged by the professor, who continued talking to the two young people at his side. 'At this stage we can only eliminate causes of death; no one single cause will be apparent. We can guess at cardiovascular disease, maybe a brain haemorrhage, embolism, that sort of thing. Still,' he added cheerily, 'if you're good we'll allow you into the post mortem.'

The young man and woman straightened up, nodded to Agnes and left. Agnes saw their shocked, wide eyes and subdued demeanour, and wondered whether the post mortem would be that much of a treat.

'Yes – ah – right. Funeral,' the professor mumbled at her. 'One of yours, I gather.'

'One of my what?' asked Agnes sharply.

'Parishioners – didn't she attend at St Simeon's?' He turned for corroboration to the secretary, who nodded nervously.

'But I'd know her,' Agnes began, but was interrupted by the professor. 'Yes, yes, we're sure she did.'

Agnes said, 'But surely there are relatives? Family? They must have views about the funeral?'

The young woman shook her head. 'We don't know

anything about her. She'd worked here about two years. Personnel have checked her details, but under next-of-kin on her form she never wrote anything. You know, some people keep themselves to themselves . . .' Her voice tailed off and she stared awkwardly at the floor.

'Did she just collapse at her desk?' asked Agnes. 'Who found her?'

'She was found in the library, dead. Those two students came to tell me,' replied the professor. 'You see, it's the old library – no one goes there now. She was still warm, though,' he added.

'Well,' said Agnes, 'I'll check with Father Julius. I'm sure we can arrange something if needs be.'

'Good,' said the professor warmly, as if dismissing her. 'I'll wait to hear from you.'

At the doorway, Agnes hesitated. 'Surely . . . surely in cases of sudden death you have to call the police – don't you?'

The professor's manner cooled sharply. 'With all due respect, Sister, that is hardly necessary in a teaching hospital of this size and reputation – ' he dwelt on the word 'reputation' – 'with all facilities available . . . I really don't think the police need to be involved, do you? We'll send the post mortem results to the coroner, as usual.'

Agnes smiled warmly, and said with all the sincerity she could muster, 'I'm sure you're right, Professor. I'll let you know about the burial.'

She would have been happy to leave it there, particularly with her hunger reminding her that it was now nearly four o'clock, if the professor hadn't said, 'Burial? Don't you mean cremation?'

There was a strange urgency in his voice. Agnes replied, 'Some Catholics prefer burial. We're crazy enough to believe in the resurrection of the body, and so we don't take any chances.' What was intended as a quip had an odd effect on the professor, who stared at her, blinking, his face shadowed with sudden fear.

'Anyway,' Agnes added, her voice deliberately light, 'I'll let you know what the options are. And if there's anything we can do to help, do feel free to call on us.'

Burgess seemed to wake from a dream, and his voice when he spoke was calm again. 'Thank you, Sister,' he said as she left. 'Thank you for your help.'

Agnes's puzzlement stayed with her. 'I mean,' she said to Julius half an hour later as she devoured a smoked salmon and cream cheese bagel in their office, 'it was like he was haunted, just because I mentioned the resurrection. And anyway, I'm sure she never came here.'

'He had just experienced the death of one of his colleagues,' said Julius, sipping on honey and lemon. A tall man, he was hunched over an ancient electric bar fire. A huge knitted scarf was wrapped several times around his neck and his soft white hair was uncombed. 'You'd feel pretty weird about death if you were him. And no doubt you painted some ghastly gothic picture of the resurrection for him, complete with the day of judgement and the mouth of hell.' Julius's blue eyes twinkled.

Agnes dabbed some cream cheese from her nose. 'No,

Julius, it was guilt. That's what it was,' she said with sudden certainty.

'Well, well, Agnes – ' he pronounced it the French way, 'An-yes' – 'you're the expert on guilt and so you are. Though why you have to see it in all of us—'

'And you should be in bed with that cold of yours,' said Agnes sharply.

'I would be, if there was anyone else to man this office. Or should I say, woman? And now with this mysterious funeral that's been foisted on us—'

'Off you go, then. I'm staying here now, you go and get well for tomorrow.'

'Why?' said Julius, puzzled, standing up to go. 'What's happening tomorrow?'

'I'm going back to St Hugh's medical school to ask a few questions.'

Julius, one hand on the door handle, placed his other hand over his eyes and sighed. 'If you're about to go off on one of your quests again, I'm going to develop Post Viral Fatigue Syndrome and take to my bed for at least a month.'

The cushion that Agnes had aimed at his head thumped softly against the door as he closed it behind him.

Chapter Three

The professor was looking most peculiar. The door to his office was ajar, and Agnes, peering in, could see him in profile, sitting absolutely still, his face blank, the strong features set in granite. He stared straight ahead. After a long moment she heard him say, 'It's difficult. I hope I can give you what you want.' An answering voice told her he was not alone. She knocked, loudly. Without moving, and with visible reluctance, he said, 'Enter! Oh, it's you,' he added, as Agnes appeared in his line of vision. 'Can I move now? This is my portrait-painter, Mr Alexander Jeffes,' he said. 'Commissioned by the medical school to create my likeness to join those of my distinguished predecessors in the main entrance hall. I can only say, I am honoured to be judged worthy.'

Jeffes bowed. The gesture was flamboyant and delicate, and faintly ridiculous. He was in his forties, Agnes thought, with long thick black hair swept back, greying at the temples. She saw he was rather good looking. He wore black jeans and a large black cashmere sweater that had seen better days; through its various holes peeped a maroon silk shirt.

'I'm Sister Agnes,' she said. He bowed again, and she met his eyes which were bright with amusement. She wondered why he was putting on an act.

'Sister?' he said.

'From the church down the road,' the professor broke in gruffly. 'Helping us with this sudden death palaver.'

Jeffes had not taken his eyes from Agnes. 'Don't you wear, you know . . . medieval dress, whatsit?' he said.

Agnes smiled. 'Sometimes. It depends.'

'Much more interesting.'

'What – this, or the habit?' said Agnes uncertainly, aware of the painter's appraising gaze.

'I like folds of fabric,' he said. 'Still,' he went on, waving an arm towards her, 'on you this is OK too.' The gesture was at once both summary and dismissive, as if in those few moments Agnes had been recreated as a painting and now discarded. Oddly uncomfortable, she turned to the professor.

'I've checked with my priest,' she said, keeping her voice business-like. 'We have to be as sure as we can be that there are no other relatives. Then we can do your cremation. I need to talk to Personnel—'

'Fine, fine,' said the professor. Alexander had produced his sketch pad again and was scratching away in a thick pencil. The professor took up his pose once more. 'Mrs Holtby will look after you,' he said, waving towards his secretary's door. As Agnes left the room, Jeffes did not look up.

'I can't imagine that Personnel could release the file just

18

like that. Have you requested it in writing?' Perhaps, thought Agnes, Mrs Holtby was not the 'looking-after' type after all. A brisk woman with a crisp grey perm, she seemed to be someone to whom life's obstacles were all too painfully clear. She wore a pale blue Crimplene suit finished with a thin leather belt that seemed insufficient against her portly frame, which balanced on sharp heels.

'Perhaps I could just ask them?' said Agnes. Mrs Holtby sighed heavily, and wrote a name on a piece of paper.

'Gillian Taylor,' she said, handing the note to Agnes. 'Room 3027, the other side of the building. But I doubt you'll have any luck.'

On the threshold Agnes paused. 'When the body was found . . .' she began.

Mrs Holtby sighed dramatically and shook her head. 'I'm not one to say told you so, but she had only herself to blame.'

'What – who . . . ?'

'I mean, we should know better than anyone, those of us lucky enough to count ourselves part of the medical profession.' She smiled at a spot just behind Agnes's head.

'I'm sorry, I don't quite—'

'Good health. It's all about lifestyle, isn't it? We know that better than ever before. Sensible living leads to better health. Whereas she . . .' Agnes waited. 'Well, for a start, she smoked. And, do you know, she had three sugars in her coffee, Pamela said. Three! I mean, I might allow myself a little as a treat, but I cut down on other things. I'm quite strict with myself these days. Even the professor said the other day, Marjorie, he said, you should let yourself go a little.' She smiled fondly.

'But, surely,' said Agnes. 'To die in your thirties takes more than a bit too much sugar and the odd cigarette.'

'Late thirties, in her case. And it's not just what you eat, is it? A careless attitude, that's what kills you. Smoking, the odd drink here and there, it all leads on, doesn't it? People who are careless about one thing are going to be careless about other things. Over-indulgence, that's what they say. Do you know,' she said, opening the door for Agnes, 'I always look at people's fingernails. You can tell a lot about someone from their nails.' Her mouth formed a brisk smile. 'Room 3027.'

Agnes waited until she was inside the lift before examining her nails. They were short, clean, ordinary. As the doors opened again she saw a face she recognised. A young woman passed the lift and was heading for the stairs. Agnes had caught up with her before she realised that it was one of the two medical students who had been looking at the body with the professor.

'Um – excuse me,' she blurted out.

The girl looked at her blankly. 'Yes?'

'We met yesterday. Briefly. The body – um – you were . . .'

The girl's surly expression made communication difficult. 'I'm Sister Agnes,' she went on, 'I'm helping with the funeral.'

'Good for you,' said the girl, and started up the stairs.

'It's just – I wondered whether – you see, I need to find out about her before I can be authorised to do the funeral,' said Agnes, trying to keep up with the girl's brisk pace.

'Well, don't ask me,' said the girl.

'You found her, didn't you?'

'So what if I did?' The girl stopped, turned and faced Agnes. 'How can that help you? Now, leave me alone.'

Agnes stared at her for a moment. 'OK,' she said, quietly. 'OK.' The girl turned and continued up the stairs. Agnes listened to the clopping of her heels fade. It was an extreme response, she thought, for someone trained to deal with the realities of death, day in, day out.

The Personnel form, when she found it, was not very informative. Gail Sullivan was thirty-eight, had joined the medical school nearly two years earlier as a secretary, had been promoted to an administrative assistant six months ago. A few days off sick here and there. An address in Stockwell which Agnes committed to memory. Her previous job had been as a secretary at the Leeds General Infirmary, whose reference was, if not glowing, at least adequate. Agnes walked slowly along the corridor, thinking. She passed the library, paused, went back, hesitated, and then went in. It was a dark, wood-panelled room. A note on the front desk explained that it was the old reference library; the main library was located in the new academic centre. That explained, thought Agnes, why it was empty, unable to compete with the shiny desks and ultra-fast information systems of the new building. She sat at a desk behind shelves weighed down with dusty old books listing symptoms, treatments, drugs, to copy down the Stockwell address into her diary. While she was thus occupied, she failed to notice Kathleen McAleer passing the door, waving her good arm wildly and being soothed by the nurse who wheeled her along.

'Which two students?' asked Mrs Holtby sharply.

'The two who found the body in the library.'

'What on earth do you need to know their names for? Haven't they got enough on, with their exams and so on, without you bothering them asking unnecessary questions?'

'Then,' said Agnes, 'I shall ask Professor Burgess. Though I'm sure he's seen enough of me for one day.'

'I can't imagine he'll tell you,' sniffed Mrs Holtby. 'Now wait, you can't just walk in . . .'

Agnes knocked loudly on the adjoining door and, without waiting for an answer, strode in, shutting the door firmly behind her to drown out Mrs Holtby's protests.

'I'm so sorry to bother you again, Professor,' she began, mildly surprised to find that Alexander Jeffes was still there, 'but I wondered whether you wished to attend the funeral yourself. It seems it'll be a lonely affair.' The professor was at his desk, the painter beside him, and they were poring over some papers, which Agnes would have assumed were merely some sketches if the professor hadn't hurriedly closed the file as she came in.

'Oh, er . . . well, I expect someone will represent the hospital. Just let my office know the date, time and so on.'

'Thank you so much, Professor. I thought, perhaps – those students – I'm sure they're much too busy, but just in case they feel somehow involved – what were their names again, you did introduce me—'

'Mark Henderson and that Hart girl you mean? Julia

22

Hart. Final years, exams and all that. I doubt they'll be too bothered. Doctors, after all. And bright ones, expect to do well, him especially. Now if that's all . . . ?'

As Agnes closed the door behind her, she felt the two men exchange glances.

At London Bridge she caught the Tube to Stockwell and emerged into the fading daylight. It was drizzling, and the puddles were rippled with dirty yellow under the street lamps. Agnes wondered whether English law allowed for an individual to arrange a private post mortem. She wondered how on earth she might acquire the body from the hospital in time to do her own. She thought of contacting the police, but what would she say? All she knew was that that Julia woman was avoiding something, and the professor was behaving very strangely. Even if it did turn out to be a sudden death, Agnes felt she had to put her own mind at rest before the funeral.

She walked past tower blocks which seemed to have been dumped right on top of the shabby Victorian terraces. Some of the houses were being restored to their former glory, but Number Thirty-six Montgomery Crescent had rotten windows, peeling paint, and two bells. She went up the three front steps and rang the bell for Flat A. There was no answer. The windows looked well locked; an area so used to break-ins would know better than to allow access to a complete amateur like herself, she thought. Smashing a window would only draw attention to herself. She turned away, thinking she'd have to come back another time, and headed back to the Tube station. As she turned the corner of the crescent, she saw a young man who

looked just like that student, the boy, what was his name?
Mark Henderson. It looked remarkably like him. Surely, it
was. She watched him go up the steps and let himself in
with a key. Agnes watched as a light went on at the first-
floor window, then went on her way.

'We could pretend,' she said that evening, pacing Julius's
little office which was at the side of St Simeon's church.
She still wore her raincoat, which was damp from the
evening rain.

'Pretend a cremation? You're a crazy woman, Agnes,'
Julius replied, sitting quietly, watching her.

'Yes. Burn an empty coffin, put the body in storage
somewhere.'

'Oh yes. I'm sure no one would mind. "Can we borrow
your freezer for a few weeks, just for a body that Agnes
needs to keep a while" . . .'

Agnes paused, took another sip of coffee from a mug
on her desk, paced again. 'But what if—'

Julius smiled. 'There you go again, with your "What
ifs". What if life turned out to be different from what it
is . . . ?'

'You're not being very helpful, Julius,' she said.

'Look, Agnes, I agree with you, it's all rather odd.
Some woman drops dead, and this Professor Burgess
decides she's one of our parishioners, even though we've
never heard of her. Gail Sullivan?' He shook his head.
'Maybe he is trying to use us to solve a problem. But in
that case, tell someone in authority. Or wait until the
coroner has a look.'

'But—'

'Agnes, just because you saved your wretched ex-husband from jail last year, doesn't mean you should go around seeing murder here, there and everywhere.'

The little leaded window behind him glinted in the light from the lamp on his desk. He looked up and met Agnes's eyes. He sighed. 'I suppose – there's always your friend Jim Lowry.'

'Detective Inspector Lowry in Gloucestershire?'

'Yes. He must know people who'd store a body for you.'

'You're right.' Agnes reached for the phone, then looked at her watch. 'I'll phone him in the morning.'

'That poor professor doesn't know what he's taken on.'

'"That poor professor" is behaving very strangely.'

Julius sighed again. 'Honestly, Agnes, I must be as crazy as you are. Depriving that woman of a decent burial—'

'Only postponing it, Julius.'

He stood up, put on his coat, picked up his keys. As they went to the door, Agnes took his arm. 'You know, Julius, you're my only true friend in the whole world.'

Julius patted the hand that lay on his arm, and sighed. 'I know, I know. That's just the trouble.' Arm in arm, they went out into the street, the church steeple silhouetted behind them in the London night.

The next morning when Julius arrived for work, Agnes was already on the telephone.

'So you think – yes, I thought you'd say that. But if I phone the police, what do I say? Remember how long it took you to believe me last time? . . . OK. Yes, the post mortem's tomorrow, I think, but – yes, but what if I don't trust their results? . . . Fanciful? Now, listen Jim, I was right last time, wasn't I? . . . Good. Ah ha, now you're talking. Yes, a private post mortem . . . That's more like it. And they've got freezers? . . . Not ghoulish, Jim, just practical. Great. You've got my number here. You're a true friend, Jim.' She rang off.

'You're doing rather well for true friends,' said Julius, handing her a cup of coffee. She grinned at him, and the phone rang again. He answered it and handed Agnes the receiver.

'Darling!' gushed the voice. 'It's me, darling, Athena. Guess where I am?'

'Um – Paris?' hazarded Agnes, surprised at the wave of pleasure she felt at hearing that voice after so long. 'Barcelona? Gretna Green?'

'London, darling. I've acquired a pied-à-terre, charming little place it is, in Fulham.'

Agnes smiled. 'So who is he, then?'

'You do spoil things, don't you? "He" happens to be an art dealer – a tall, gorgeous, sexy . . .' She broke off and giggled. 'Super-rich – yes, you are,' she said to someone in the background. 'Fortyish – you *are* . . .' There was more giggling, then Athena came back on the line. 'Listen, darling, this is hopeless. Lunch – today? On me? Great. Do you like fish? Charming little place just off the Old Brompton Road. On the corner with Keyes Street,

26

you can't miss it. One o'clock? See you there.'

Agnes hung up. Julius looked at her. 'True friend Number Three,' he said drily. 'Athena Paneotou, your partner in crime-solving in Gloucestershire last year. And don't tell me, True friend Number Two is Detective Inspector Lowry, who, as I guessed, is indulgent enough of your whims to help you organise a private post mortem on your so-called murder victim, instead of having the sense to tell you to phone the police.'

Agnes laughed. 'My true friends know me better than that.' With a swish of raincoat she was gone.

'No, Cook,' Julius murmured to the door as it closed behind her, 'Madam will not be lunching at home today.'

Professor Burgess paced his office. 'Now look,' he said angrily. 'When I handed this business over to you people, it was precisely to avoid this kind of fuss. And now you come here talking about adverts in the press and all kinds of nonsense.'

Somewhere a clock chimed ten. Agnes sat quietly. 'It's up to you. I can always phone the police, get them to trace her relatives.'

'There's no need for that, as I've already said. It's only right that her parish priest is dealing with it.' The professor paused by the window, looking out at the grey morning. 'And of course, we'll see to it, I mean, financially – donations to the Church, that sort of thing. Just let us know.' He turned to face her. 'The post mortem's tonight, I mean, this afternoon. You'll have the body tomorrow.'

Agnes fiddled with a biro on the desk. 'One has to be

considerate, Professor,' she said. 'What if you'd lost contact with a daughter or niece, and it turned out she'd died and had been buried by strangers with indecent haste—'

'Cremated . . .'

'Cremated, yes – all I'm saying is, I have to be quite clear that we're doing the right thing. It'll take a few days, I hope, Professor, no more than that.'

'It had better do, Sister.' He turned back to look out of the window again.

Leaving his office, Agnes headed for the drinks machine by the staircase. An untidy young blonde woman was bashing a button marked 'Hot Chocolate'.

'Stupid bloody machine,' she remarked to no one in particular. ''Ave to start bringing me thermos in.'

Agnes recognised the secretary who had greeted her in Mrs Holtby's office on the day the body was found.

'Try "Black Coffee",' she suggested helpfully. 'It tastes disgusting, but at least it works.'

'Ooh, no, I couldn't. Ugh. Rather 'ave nothing at all.' The young woman looked at Agnes while she did battle with the machine. 'You're that Catholic whatsit, in't yer? You were 'ere when—'

'Yes, that's right,' said Agnes, taking a steaming hot plastic cup from the machine and looking at it with distaste.

'Poor girl. Just when 'er life was looking up an' all.'

'Did you know her well?'

'As well as anyone. Which ain't saying much. Maybe white coffee with sugar?'

'Here, let me try. So, when you say her life was

looking up . . .' Agnes put a coin in the slot and pushed a button, which provoked a whirring and sloshing noise. The young woman stared at the machine uncertainly.

'Yeah,' she said. 'I reckon she'd fallen for someone. Not much to go on, mind. She weren't one for joining in.'

The machine finished its work. Agnes handed a frothing cup to the girl, and made a face. 'Best I could do, I'm afraid.' The girl shrugged, took the cup, and headed off down the corridor, with Agnes at her side, to her office. The door said 'Registry Administration', and there was a list of four names. 'Which one of these are you?' asked Agnes.

'Dawn. Dawn Scott.'

'There's no Gail Sullivan here.'

'No. She was here, till she was promoted to Pharmacology, down the corridor.'

Dawn put her drink down and moved her typewriter into a business-like position. Agnes perched conversationally on the edge of the desk. 'So, what was she like?'

Dawn paused to think. 'Quiet. Bit boring, really, though you don't like to say, do yer? You know, if we went for lunch, the girls and me, she'd never come with us, ever. Not even Christmas.'

'Where was she from?'

'Dunno. She didn't talk like – you know, like us. Maybe a Northerner. I think she mentioned it once.'

'Was she lonely?'

'Maybe. Though she seemed OK. Liked her new job, was thinking of training, you know, to be a pharmacist.'

'And what made you think she was in love?'

'Dunno. She just seemed, you know, sort of happier.
Last time I saw her. Like, she was wearing make-up; she
never used to. And she smiled more. Like I said, it's not
much to go on.'

Agnes threw her empty cup into the waste-paper bin.
'Oh well, it's been nice talking to you. If anything occurs
to you – 'she scribbled her phone number on a bit of
paper and handed it to her – 'you can always ring me.'

Walking down the corridor, Agnes found herself
designing a business card in her head. She imagined thick,
cream card, and the words 'Sister Agnes' in a delicate but
square typeface. She wondered what else to put. Her name
would be enough, surely, and then a phone number? No
need for anything so blatant as 'Private Investigator'. But
maybe a fax number, that would be nice. So much more
elegant, she thought, than these scrappy bits of paper. She
found she was passing a door bearing the name, 'Gail
Sullivan, Pharmacology Assistant'. She opened it gently
and went in.

It was a plain office with the bare, glossy walls of the
institution. There was nothing on the two empty desks to
indicate that anyone had ever worked here. On one desk
there was a typewriter, shrouded in a black cover. The
room seemed too quiet, apart from the faraway sound of
typing from a distant office. Agnes opened a couple of
desk drawers at random; one was empty, the other
contained a meagre stack of paper clips, drawing pins and
staples, and a roll of Sellotape. She became aware of the
sound of footsteps approaching out of the silence. Thinking

hard, she whipped the cover off the typewriter, spread a few sheets of paper on the desk, picked up a pen and started writing a random list of figures. She was thus absorbed when a man entered the room and went to a small cupboard on the wall opposite, ignoring her. He was tall, with a neat ginger beard. He tried the cupboard door, rattled it, found it was locked, tutted loudly in frustration and left the room again.

'It just goes to show,' Agnes was saying to Athena, 'how women are invisible. All I had to do was take on the guise of one of the girls in the office, and he saw nothing amiss.'

'You should be glad you can still pass as a "girl",' laughed Athena. 'Anyway, maybe he was too absorbed in looking for whatever it was in the cupboard.'

'Mmm, maybe.' Agnes took a sip of white wine and surveyed her friend, the extravagant black hair, the loud check suit with brass buttons, and even louder red lipstick. She thought how much better she looked than when she was Hugo's mistress. 'You look well,' Agnes said.

Athena looked up from the menu. 'Do I?' she said.

'Look at you, smugness itself. You can tell me all about him in a minute. Shall we have the halibut?'

'I fancied the lobster, actually. Well, he's lovely.'

'How did you meet him?'

'It was amazing really. "Across a crowded room" stuff. A private view at a gallery in Bath. Incredible. Of course, I noticed him immediately, because he's so good looking. And he knows loads about art. And he's got this lovely sandy hair, not thinning or anything even though he's forty-eight, really thick and it sort of falls across his face and it's so sweet. And he's got brown eyes, with long eyelashes, so boyish. And his body – mmmm,' she broke off, lost for words.

Agnes smiled. 'And all his own teeth?'

'You! Must you spoil things? No, actually, he had a rugby accident and lost quite a lot. Now he just plays squash.'

'So everything's lovely, is it?'

In answer, Athena leaned back in her chair and stretched. 'Mmmm,' she said, grinning from ear to ear.

'That good, eh?'

'Ze lobstere eez off,' came a voice behind them as the dapper French waiter appeared.

'Oh, no,' giggled Athena. 'I'll have the halibut like my friend here, then.' The waiter took their order and left. Athena said, 'I missed you.'

'I missed you too.' Agnes raised her glass. 'A la nôtre.'

'Cheers. To our London life.'

Agnes sipped her wine thoughtfully. 'It's funny he should be an art dealer. I met a painter recently . . .' Her voice tailed off, and she stared into her glass.

'Well, well,' said Athena. 'And who is he?'

'No one, actually. No one like that, anyway.'

After lunch, they went window-shopping in Knightsbridge. 'So,' said Agnes, as they gazed through a window at a terracotta linen suit, 'how's Gloucestershire?'

'When I last saw it, dull and full of horses. And before you ask, your ex-husband hasn't been sighted for weeks.'

'He's in Tunisia or somewhere.'

Athena took her eyes from the window display. 'Ah, so you're still in touch with him, then?'

'I like that silk waistcoat there – the embroidered one. What, Hugo? No, not in touch. He just sent me a card to say he'd remarried.'

'Remarried?'

'Uh-huh. Wife Number Three.'

'Incredible. What's she like?'

Agnes handed Athena the wedding photo. 'Still,' Athena said at last, 'at least it's not some nineteen-year-old bimbo. I mean, this woman—'

'Gabrielle—'

'She's at least thirty-eight, I'd say.'

'Oh, forty, at least.'

'More his equal. And nice-looking.'

'Is she?' said Agnes, still staring at the window.

'What does she do?'

'He said in the letter she runs her own design business.'

'Rich, then.'

'Oh, I'm sure she is,' Agnes said acidly. 'Trust him to marry money.'

'You never know,' Athena said. 'Perhaps he married for love this time.'

Agnes turned away from the window. 'All this is just creating meaningless desire.'

Athena looked at her. 'You mean, the clothes?'

'Of course, the clothes. I don't need them, I can't

afford them.' She set off along the street, and Athena took her arm to keep up.

'Come to dinner,' Athena said suddenly. 'Come and meet Jonathan. I know, tomorrow night, Friday. Eight-ish. We're a bit disorganised, but you'll get fed eventually.'

On her way to the Tube, Agnes posted a stack of envelopes, all alike, all addressed to various newspapers and magazines. They contained a classified advertisement:

GAIL SULLIVAN; WAS LIVING IN THE NORTH, NOW BASED IN LONDON AND WORKING AS A MEDICAL SECRETARY. AGED ABOUT THIRTY-EIGHT. IF ANYONE KNOWS ANYTHING ABOUT HER, COULD THEY CONTACT BOX NUMBER TWENTY-EIGHT.

That evening she attended mass at Julius's church. She knelt between the pews, soothed by the warm old smell of oak and incense, by the murmur of the litany lapping around her. The disconcerting image of a silk embroidered waistcoat flashed into her mind, but she pushed it away.

Chapter Four

As Agnes walked through the revolving door of St Hugh's that Friday morning, the commissionaire nodded briefly at her. It had taken only a couple of days for the hospital to become part of her life. She wondered if the patients felt the same way about it. She thought of Gail, lying in the mortuary, awaiting the arrival of Julius in his van that afternoon to take her to another uncomfortable far-from-final resting place. There were several questions that needed answers, she thought, before Gail could be properly laid to rest.

She took the lift to the third floor.

'But we've already done that,' the girl in Personnel told her. 'Gillian asked me to get the forms from the DSS as soon as Gail – as soon as she was found.'

'And did the National Insurance people come up with anything?' asked Agnes, looking out across the courtyard to the new building, its windows a watery silver in the thin sunlight.

'They can only tell you where she worked, if she signed on, that sort of thing. Does Gillian know you want—'

'Oh, yes,' said Agnes with her best smile. 'I'm

35

organising the funeral. And those sick notes, too, we need her GP's address, just a formality.'

'Here you are then,' said the girl uncertainly, handing over two forms and a couple of slips of paper. 'Not that you'll learn anything. She was a quiet one, that Gail. I only met her once or twice myself. When is the funeral, then?'

Agnes looked up from the papers. 'Oh, next week. Thursday. The body's due to be released to us today.'

'Body,' said the young woman. 'Dying like that. One moment you're a person, the next you're a body. Funny really.' She opened her stapler and began, slowly, to refill it. Agnes folded the papers carefully and left the room.

At eleven o'clock, she drifted into the student coffee bar. Standing in the queue, she became aware of someone standing behind her. 'Hello,' a voice said.

'Hello, um . . .'

'Alexander.'

'Yes.'

'Still here, then?'

'I visit parishioners here, some of ours, some from further afield,' she said.

'And there's that funeral, still, isn't there?'

Agnes looked at him hard. Why should he mention the funeral? she wondered. Perhaps the professor had confided in him. 'Allow me,' Alexander was saying as they reached the till, waving a five-pound note towards the cashier. 'Take a biscuit too, if you like.'

'I won't, thank you,' Agnes replied, resenting his easy generosity. 'I overdid Easter a bit.'

'When I was a child, we didn't have Easter. My stepfather preferred Lent.' He reached for some teaspoons.

'There's something to be said for Lent,' Agnes said.

'Oh yes?'

'An antidote to our decadent times, perhaps.' She picked up her tray and turned to go. He followed, sitting down opposite her. She felt irritated, wanting to say, 'Just because you paid for my coffee doesn't mean I have to put up with you.'

'So you really have faith then?' he said.

'What does it look like?'

'I'm sorry, I didn't mean to be rude.' Agnes saw, for an instant, the performance falter.

'It's just,' he went on, 'my stepfather rather spoilt all that.'

Agnes sipped her drink. 'That's a shame.'

'And now my mother's ill . . .' He looked away, scanning the crowded space, his expression suddenly vulnerable. For a moment the mask had dropped, but then he turned to Agnes with a brittle smile. 'Still, no reason to burden you with all that.'

'Oh, it's what we're for,' Agnes replied lightly.

'You're lucky, knowing what you're for.'

'Don't you?'

He shook his head.

'I thought you artists . . .' she went on.

'No, not artist. Purveyor of phoney images to self-deceiving people.' He shook his head. 'It's just coincidence that I also happen to use paint and brushes to do it.'

'But, don't you—' Agnes began, but his attention went

to someone across the room, and he waved.

'You were saying,' he said absently, as the person he'd greeted came to join them. He was a thin man with short dark hair and sallow skin, dressed in an expensive shirt with a high, old-fashioned collar. 'Stefan, good to see you. This is Stefan Polkoff, Professor of Anatomy here, and this is um—'

'Sister Agnes.' She held out her hand, and after a moment Polkoff took it in his own chilly fingers.

'Shall we go?' he said to Alexander.

Alexander got up. He hesitated, then said quietly to Agnes, 'It was nice to talk to you.' Then he was gone, the thin man bobbing at his side.

Agnes felt that she'd been discarded for the second time. She was irritated by his constant performance, his rudeness. And yet— 'My mother's ill,' he'd said, as if Agnes was the only one to know. She drained her cup and got up to go. Picking up her jacket she noticed through the clatter and buzz of the canteen the two medical students sitting together, deep in conversation. As she approached their table, Julia looked up at once, registered who she was and cast an urgent look at Mark, who then looked up at Agnes too.

'Hello,' said Agnes.

'What do you want?' he said.

'Why do you keep following us around?' Julia butted in. It was Mark's turn to throw her a warning look.

Agnes said, 'I'm sorry I've been giving you that impression. Really, it's nothing. It's just, I'm arranging the funeral, and I wondered if you wanted to be there.'

'Why should we—' Julia began, but Mark interrupted.

'It's very kind of you, but just because we found her . . . I mean, you must understand, we hardly know the woman . . .'

'Yes, of course,' Agnes replied. 'It was only courtesy to let you know.' And why, if you hardly know her, do you have a key to her flat, she wanted to add. 'I'm sorry to bother you. The funeral's on Thursday, at the crematorium in Landwell Street. I really won't be following you around any more.'

She turned and left, aware of two faces still turned to her departing back, the boy's uneasy, the girl's downright hostile. Once again, she wondered why.

At two o'clock that afternoon, Julius parked his battered white van amongst the huge dustbins and air-conditioning vents at the back of the hospital. Upstairs, on the third floor, Agnes had just marched into Professor Burgess's office. 'She says I'm not to have them,' she said angrily to the startled professor. 'Your Mrs Holtby. She won't release the post mortem papers.'

He sighed. 'There were copies left for you,' he said frostily. 'Wait here.' He reappeared a few moments later and handed her some sheets of paper. 'It won't make much sense to you, I'm afraid.'

'But you can see I must have them. I can't go cremating someone without due authority.'

His manner was guarded. 'Of course. This is your copy. And anyway, I'm sure the coroner will give you the paperwork you need.'

'Thank you, Professor. I don't suppose I need bother you again.'

'I hope not, Sister.'

Julius saw Agnes appear from a doorway marked 'HAZCHEM', and beckon him in. 'This really is the underworld, then,' he said as they set off down the chilly corridor towards the mortuary. 'The realm of the dead.'

They emerged some minutes later carrying a coffin-shaped metal box, which they loaded carefully into the van.

'I'm sure if you hadn't been looking the part they'd never have released it,' said Agnes.

'I'd squared it with the undertakers – it was all above board,' Julius replied.

'It's all a bit Burke and Hare.' Agnes started to giggle.

'Except those two stole bodies and gave them to hospitals, not the other way round.'

'Oh dear, it feels awful, Julius.'

Julius touched her arm. 'As you said, it's just postponement. And it may be you're right – in which case, we're doing the right thing. Now, you're sure this place is expecting us?'

Agnes produced a scribbled map with directions from Lowry's contact. 'It's a forensic laboratory just off the A2 near Swanley.'

They set off, taking the Old Kent Road and finding themselves in what appeared to be an endless traffic jam, until at last the dreary suburbs grudgingly gave way to fields. Agnes directed them to the edge of a light industrial estate, a driveway concealed with rhododendron bushes, a single-storey building in white concrete.

A brisk woman with grey hair pinned into a soft bun greeted them. 'Anne Halliday,' she said, shaking Agnes's hand vigorously, nodding at Father Julius. 'Let's find your body a home, then.'

The metal box was brought out of the van, and a couple of young men in white coats appeared from nowhere and carried it into the building. Agnes and Julius followed, through several sets of swing doors, arriving at last in a small sunlit laboratory, where the box was placed carefully on a bench.

'One of mine,' Dr Halliday said, ushering the two young men out of the lab. 'A favour returned,' she added, turning to Agnes. 'Your friend Jim Lowry has helped me out once or twice. We knew each other in Yorkshire. Still have a house up there, near Whitby. Get there when I can. I like the air. And the beach. Nice pebbles.'

'We're very grateful,' Agnes said.

'You'll be back tomorrow, then? Saturday. That's when I was going to do it.'

'Yes, I'll be here,' Agnes said. 'Julius won't. In fact, I wondered whether he could just have a look at her now.'

'Agnes—' Julius began.

'Burgess said she was one of your parishioners. Perhaps you'll recognise her.'

Julius nodded. Dr Halliday pulled at the catch and lifted the lid, then gently unwrapped the white sheeting at the top of the body to reveal the face. The eyes were closed now, and the skin was yellow and waxy, the brow slightly furrowed. Julius and Agnes leaned over Gail, one on each side.

'The stillness of death,' Julius breathed. He straightened up, rubbing his back. 'I don't recognise her. She may have come to church once or twice. Who knows?' He shrugged. 'They obviously wanted an easy way out.' Carefully, he covered Gail's face again, his fingertips lingering over her forehead for a moment. He sighed. 'It ought to be commonplace, death. After all, we're all going to do it. But whenever I see a body . . .'

Dr Halliday nodded. 'I know. Hundreds of them over the years. All unique. And yet, as you say – commonplace. Seeing a body, it ought to be like looking in a mirror.' She approached the coffin. Over the chest lay a piece of paper wrapped in cellophane. She picked it up and read out, '"Gail Sullivan. Female. Cause of death, pulmonary embolism, thrombosis not previously diagnosed. Query contraceptive pill, contra-indicated." Well, we'll see,' she said. 'I'll show you the way out, it's a labyrinth in here.'

Julius and Agnes came out into the fresh air and breathed deeply.

'Agnes,' he said, 'do you believe in an afterlife?'

'And you asking that, a parish priest?'

'I just wondered what you thought.'

'I'll tell you one day. It's funny,' she added, 'how supportive you're being about my hunches this time, when last time—'

'Last time you were defending that complete waste of time you call your ex-husband,' Julius replied shortly. 'The prospect of seeing him put behind bars has always appealed to me immensely. Whereas this time, an innocent woman has – possibly – come up against some evil. Perhaps . . .' He shrugged again. 'It seems worthwhile, this time. That's all. Go on, say it,' he began, as Agnes opened her mouth. 'I'm a true friend.'

'But you are, really,' laughed Agnes, as they got back into the van.

Athena opened the door in a flash of red lipstick and bare tanned shoulders above a frill of dress. 'Darling! How wonderful! Do come in.'

As Agnes walked in to the hallway she was aware of muted lighting thrown by strange opaque shapes of jagged glass on the walls. From the kitchen there came a tantalising scent, both sweet and spicy, familiar and exotic. Athena showed her into a wide living room. The warm gold of the walls was echoed in the soft rug under Agnes's feet, and the whole room was suffused in light which was thrown from a huge, chaotic lampshade in the middle of the room, a large frame of copper wire hung with swathes of silk in turquoise and terracotta.

'Well,' Agnes said at last. 'It's not how I think of you, Athena.'

'Me? Oh, no,' Athena laughed merrily. 'It's all Jonathan, this stuff. I'm just the mistress . . .' she giggled again, as he walked into the room. He was boyish and clean-shaven, with angular spectacle frames and greeny-grey eyes. He was wearing a crisp white shirt, with the sleeves rolled up, and green linen trousers.

'Just the mistress,' he echoed, placing one hand on

each of Athena's bare shoulders, and smiled a warm smile at Agnes. 'She does go on, doesn't she?' he added.

'Cardamom?' Agnes replied, sniffing the air. 'Fenugreek? I just can't place it.'

He smiled. 'Right first time. Mostly cardamom, with ginger and a touch of cloves. It's Middle Eastern. Has my mistress, as she insists on calling herself, even though I'm not married, offered you a drink? There's some gin somewhere, though I'm not sure about anything to go with it. Maybe a lemon . . .' He wandered vaguely out of the door again.

'Kept woman? Mistress? What's the difference?' Athena mumbled from a Chinese lacquered cabinet in the corner of the room. 'Here we are. God knows how long he's had this,' she said, producing a bottle of gin which was barely a quarter full.

'There's some quite decent Australian Chardonnay in my bag,' Agnes said. Athena looked at her, then nodded.

'We'll forget we found this,' she said, replacing the bottle. 'I can always finish it by myself when he goes to New York next week.'

'So, how do you two know each other?' Jonathan asked, carving a rack of lamb.

'It's a long story,' Athena said. 'Agnes was married to a man who married someone else and she got murdered, his second wife I mean, and he was charged, and Agnes said he didn't do it.'

'And where were you?' Jonathan asked Athena.

Agnes laughed. 'She was my accomplice, weren't you?

44

I seem to remember our crime-solving involved lots of shopping for clothes and eating out.'

'It was a hoot,' Athena giggled.

'This is delicious,' Agnes said. 'Where did you learn to cook like this?'

'From books, mostly,' he replied.

'Jonathan was a Bedouin Arab in his previous life,' Athena added. 'He has an affinity with it all. In fact, left to himself he'd have dug a hole in the back garden and baked the dinner in ashes.'

'That's enough of that,' he replied, leaning over and placing a finger against her lips. She grabbed his hand and bit it, then laughed. Jonathan snatched his hand away. Agnes glanced across at Athena, who looked suddenly old.

'So,' Jonathan was saying, 'what sort of nun are you?'

'Well, my previous order was Benedictine, but last year, around the time of the – the Hugo business, I had a bit of a crisis, and now I'm in a more open order, an Ignatian order. I help run a hostel for young runaways, a safe house.'

'When she's not solving crimes,' Athena said.

'Oh, nonsense, that was just Hugo . . .'

'And now there's this artist . . .' Athena teased.

Agnes said to Jonathan, 'Have you heard of a portrait painter called Alexander Jeffes?'

Jonathan thought, then shook his head. 'Don't think so. But it's not my field. Jeffes, did you say? Actually, the name does ring a bell. Something to do with . . . I'll check it out for you, if you like.'

* * *

It was after midnight when Agnes left. Athena took her down to the front door. It was drizzling outside, and Agnes felt in her bag for an umbrella. 'Well?' said Athena, hopping from one stockinged foot to the other.

'I think he's lovely. Charming.'

Athena stared out at the rain.

'What's the problem?' asked Agnes.

'He has a flat in New York, a house just outside Barcelona, and this place.'

Agnes laughed. 'I don't quite see . . .'

'It's not the lifestyle of someone who wants to commit himself, is it?'

'Well, did you keep on your house in Gloucestershire?'

'Of course.'

'Well, then. You've never been one for slippers by the fire and spending your weekends at garden centres, have you?'

Athena laughed. 'No. No, you're right. I'd better go, he's waiting.' She brushed Agnes's cheek with her lips, then fled silently back up the stairs. Agnes set off, putting up her umbrella against the wet night, thinking of the glowing flat she'd just left; remembering a polished laboratory bench, a dead woman lying there alone. Shivering, she walked up to Fulham Broadway in search of a cab.

Chapter Five

Gail's head was turned awkwardly to one side, and the eyes had fallen half open. Agnes felt an overpowering urge to cover her up again with the sheet that Dr Halliday had just removed. She saw the line of coarse stitches that went from neck to groin. It seemed to her to be hugely inappropriate, this dissection of a dead woman just to prove a point or two, and she was on the verge of abandoning the post mortem altogether when Dr Halliday broke in.

'Thrombosis, you said?'

'That's what they said at St Hugh's.'

'Hmmm.' Dr Halliday began to look carefully at the outside of the body, screwing up her eyes behind delicate half-moon glasses balanced on her rather large nose. As she turned the corpse over it flopped loudly against the bench, and Agnes felt dizzy with the noise. She put her hand to her neck, stared at the floor. A tiny beetle was negotiating the swirling pattern of the lino tiles, plodding towards the skirting board and safety. Gail should have been buried last week, Agnes thought, glancing back at her face, as still as ice. It's not too late to call all this off, she thought, imagining the soul in waiting.

'Look,' said the pathologist. She was pointing at the upper arm. 'Syringe mark, I'd say.'

Agnes, leaning over, saw the tiniest pin-prick in the yellow skin. 'What – what does it mean?' she asked, aware of her pulse quickening.

'Oh, too early to say.' Dr Halliday laid the body down again and began to snip roughly at the stitches. She pulled apart two flaps of skin over the ribcage, and Agnes found herself staring fixedly at the doctor's hands as they worked, as Dr Halliday moved aside the ribs where they had been sawn away.

'When Jim Lowry asked me to do this, I said, I hope it's not some fearful old skulduggery. I say, they've been rather wholesale with the old tissue.' Agnes peered into the cavity that Dr Halliday had opened up, suddenly hungry to know. It seemed to her now that, far from doing Gail an injustice, this was an act of charity. The soul could only rest when the truth had been uncovered, and the truth lay here, in these sticky recesses that Agnes was gazing at, in the flesh which appeared in lines of red and white as Dr Halliday worked.

'All sliced up a bit rough, I'd say.' The doctor lifted out the heart and placed it on a set of weighing scales. It had been sliced through and looked like fresh offal, like the meat in the horse butcher's shop that had been on the corner of her street in Paris when Agnes was a child. There had been a garish plaster horse's head on the sign outside, and the young Agnes, skipping past on her way to school, had convinced herself that the severed neck was still dripping blood. She would always linger as she passed, hoping to catch it splashing on to the pavement.

'Did they say pulmonary embolism?' Dr Halliday was asking.

'Sorry? Yes,' Agnes said.

'That's odd. The lungs have hardly been checked.' She weighed them, then lifted them from the scales, squeezing them between her hands. 'I'll just take some specimens for histology,' she said. She sliced delicately through the tissue and removed some small pieces which she placed in little jars. Then she began to cut the stitches up towards the neck. She glanced at the throat, then something checked her and she peered further in, prodding at the tissue. After some minutes she straightened up again.

'Hmmm,' she said. 'Are you sure you got the right notes? There's gross oedema of the larynx. At first glance she seems to have died of suffocation. Maybe an anaphylactic reaction.'

'Meaning?'

'Some kind of allergy. Very odd. I'll take some specimens from the liver, I think.' Again she placed some neat slices in a jar. 'I must say, I can't make it out. As I said to Jim, I'd hate to unearth some member of one's own profession behaving badly.' She prodded the abdomen of the body, then once more. 'But then,' she added, snipping away at the lower stitches, 'Jim said you were daft as a bat, but that your hunches did tend to prove right.'

'Jim said that, did he?'

'Oh dear. Dreadfully tactless of me. What I meant

was – good God. Oh my goodness.'

Dr Halliday straightened up from the bench. 'Give me those notes.' She snatched them from Agnes, her gloved hands smearing the paper. She shook her head. 'Whatever it says here, it isn't. Brace yourself,' she said turning to Agnes. 'I'm afraid this isn't just one death, it's two. Your what's-her-name here – was pregnant.'

That afternoon, Julius popping into his church to tidy it up for Sunday morning found Agnes on her own in the Lady chapel, absorbed in prayer. There was nothing unusual about that, except that as he tiptoed past to replace the candles at the altar, she looked up, startled, as if she didn't recognise him.

'What is it?' he whispered. 'Agnes . . .'

She shook her head, crossed herself and got up, then stood, contemplating the image of the Virgin Mary with troubled eyes.

'Agnes, what's happened?' he said, taking her arm.

She turned to him. 'Our corpse,' she began, her voice flat. 'Gail. She had – she had a baby?'

'Where?'

'No, I mean, it wasn't – it wasn't born. It was there. I saw . . .' She flopped down on a pew and buried her head in her hands. Julius sat down next to her.

'That tiny life,' she blurted out, 'only just touched down, being wiped out again. And I bet they had no idea, whoever bumped Gail off, that they'd just ended two lives.'

'When you say bumped off . . .'

'Dr Halliday's convinced. She said there are traces of drugs taken orally and injected, so someone wasn't taking any chances. Embolism indeed.' Julius watched the colour return to her face. 'Every time I find myself face to face with the evil of which we are all capable . . .' She shook her head. 'The gift to us is that we can carry life, and then someone goes and does this . . .' She bit her lip and her eyes welled with tears.

'If you'd like to write down its name, we can mention it in the prayers tomorrow.'

Agnes nodded. 'But – what name shall I give it? A murder victim before it's even been born.'

Julius considered. 'It's like the unknown soldier, isn't it? A casualty of a peculiar kind of war.'

Agnes got up to go. 'Perhaps some things have to go unnamed,' she said.

At nine-thirty the next morning, Agnes was standing on the steps of a large Georgian house, fiddling with her keys. 'Which of these bloody things is it – oh, hello,' she said, startled, as the door opened.

'Agnes, isn't it?' A bright-eyed young woman had answered the door, and now stood there eyeing Agnes with undisguised curiosity. She had short, straight blonde hair, and wore jeans and workboots. She was engulfed in a huge multi-coloured jumper that looked as if it was the result of a recycling project.

'Yes. I've come for chapel.'

'They said you might.'

'And you are . . . ?'

'Madeleine. Sister Madeleine,' she added, with a grin. 'They've just moved me down from the Shrewsbury community.'

Agnes smiled back at her. 'Welcome to Southwark.'

The chapel was a simple, wood-panelled room, with high windows and an altar at one end, on which were placed two candles and a vase of daffodils. To the right of the altar there stood a statue, a huge piece of rough-carved stone representing a heavily pregnant woman. Agnes loved that statue. Her first sight of it had been when she'd arrived at this house last year, still in some anguish about her decision to leave the Order that had been her home for more than fifteen years. A nice, grey-haired sister had shown her the chapel, and had explained that some years previously a benefactor had commissioned, as a gift, a statue of Our Lady for this house. The result had shocked and horrified many people, including the bishop, and the sisters had had to protect this earthy, rough-hewn version of the Mother of God, without even a halo to show who she was, from people who wished to see in its place yet another porcelain representation of meekness in a blue dress.

Now, kneeling with the other nuns, Agnes looked at this Mary again. She was fierce like a tigress; huge, heavy, encompassing God Himself. Pregnant. In her prayers, Agnes was aware of compassion for Gail, and for Gail's unborn baby, and her eyes pricked with tears.

Afterwards, coffee was served in the kitchen. Women greeted her, asked after the teenage runaways project, told her the Community's gossip, how Sister Catherine was going to be allowed to attend the Radical Catholic conference in Siena after all; how the ceiling in the top bedroom, which fell down two months ago, still hadn't been replaced. Agnes chatted, laughed, aware of Madeleine watching her, waiting like a suitor. And so when, alone in the kitchen, Agnes began to wash up the coffee mugs, she wasn't surprised to find Madeleine by her side with a tea-towel.

'Hi,' Madeleine said.

'Hello,' Agnes replied, running a bowl of rinsing water.

'How's it going?'

'How's what going?'

'Oh, you know.' She wiped a cup. 'They say,' she went on, 'that you were married.'

'They do, do they? Well, yes, I was.'

'They also say that your ex-husband was accused of murder and you got him off.'

Agnes fished mugs out of hot soapy water and rinsed them. 'They say an awful lot, don't they?'

Madeleine shrugged, and grinned. 'You London lot have interesting lives.'

'Yes, well, these days, I'm rather enjoying having a less interesting life.'

Madeleine looked at her. 'You don't seem the type.'

Agnes looked back at her and smiled. 'Neither do you.'

That afternoon, Julius entrusted Agnes with the parish visiting at St Hugh's again. 'You've developed such an affinity with the place, I didn't think you'd mind,' he said.

Agnes methodically worked her way round the wards,

leaving Kathleen McAleer till last.

'I expect you don't really want to see me in your current state of mind,' she said lightly, pulling back Kathleen's curtain. She was not prepared for the response. Kathleen looked up from some kind of dream, saw it was Agnes and began to wave her good arm wildly. 'Kkkkg,' she said. 'Kkkkkg – ooooooh!'

Agnes sat down next to the bed. 'What is it, Kathleen? What's happened?'

'Lllll – oohhhh.' In frustration Kathleen began to bang her fist against her forehead.

Agnes gently took hold of the hand. 'Shhh. Hush . . . Now listen, if there's something you want to tell me, we just have to find a way. Can you write?'

'Nnnnn.'

'Draw?'

'Nnn . . .' Kathleen indicated her wheelchair, and turned her arm in a circular motion.

'A walk? We'll go for a walk?' Violent nodding ensued. 'Right. Slippers? No? Fine.' Briskly, Agnes set off, pushing Kathleen out of the ward. To the nurse sitting at the desk, who opened her mouth to protest, she said, 'Spiritual emergency, I'm afraid.' Once in the corridor, she said, 'Where now?' Kathleen pointed with great authority towards a sign which said 'To Reception, Lifts, Medical School', and they set off in that direction. Once more at a spot where the corridors intersected, she pointed to a sign which said 'Ultrasound, X-Ray and Medical School Library'. The last three words had been covered with a shabby piece of paper but were still visible.

Agnes and Kathleen continued along the corridor. They seemed to be heading for the Ultrasound department. 'Did you have a scan recently? Was there a problem, is that it?'

'Nnnnn,' Kathleen replied. 'Nnnnn – Kkkkkkk!' The last sound was a screech and she was pointing at a door. It was the old medical school library, the dusty old room where Agnes had written down Gail's details – where Gail herself had been . . . A question was forming in Agnes's mind. What connection could there be between that grisly event and Kathleen's current state? Agnes looked down at her charge, looked at the panic and frustration in her eyes – and let out her breath in a whistle. Kathleen was rocking in her chair, a grim smile across her face, her eyes animated. Agnes crouched down by her wheelchair and took both her hands. She spoke very softly.

'You know?' Kathleen nodded, her eyes shining. 'You know about a death that happened here last week?' Kathleen nodded wildly. 'You saw something?' More nodding. The truth hit Agnes like a blow. 'You saw someone? Do you think – do you think you saw the murderer?' Kathleen was gripping Agnes's hands and nodding furiously. 'But do they know – did they see you?'

Kathleen said, 'Nnn,' released Agnes's grip and took up the position she had assumed at the time.

'So,' Agnes went on, 'it didn't occur to them to register your presence. I see. What did they look like? Was it a man or a woman?'

'Kkkkk.'

'Was it a man?' Kathleen nodded. 'Gggg.' She was

trying to say something else. 'Sssss.' She held up her hand and opened and shut the fingers.

'His hand? He had no hand?'

'Nnnn.' Kathleen made a fist.

'He was carrying something. What? What was it?'

In Kathleen's mind there was an image; a familiar object, she saw them all the time in the hospital, people in white coats wielding them like weapons, only they weren't – not usually anyway. She knew the word, if only she could make that connection . . . she knew it. 'Sssss,' she said.

'Sssss?' echoed Agnes. 'He was carrying a – Sss . . .' She shook her head.

'Ssinj,' said Kathleen.

'Singe? Syringe?'

Furious nodding from Kathleen, who now gripped both her hands tightly, and – laughed. Real laughter, with tears in her eyes. The first word she'd been able to say for an eternity – a shame it had to be murder weapon, really, but what the hell, she thought, laughing again, clapping her hands together with Agnes's in applause for herself.

'We'll do it,' Agnes said softly. 'We'll do it. Come on, let's get back.' Agnes stood up to go, then a thought occurred to her. 'When you pretended to be asleep – I mean, do you think he was convinced?'

Kathleen shrugged. 'It's just,' Agnes went on, 'if I was a murderer, I'd take no chances.' She set off, wheeling Kathleen gently. 'You might be in danger, if they get scared,' she went on, talking softly. 'Have you noticed anyone hanging around your ward? . . . Heavens, they could tamper with your medication, anything. Do you have medication?'

Kathleen made a gesture of throwing something over her shoulder.

'You – you throw it away? How the devil do you get away with it? Oh well, they can't get you that way.' Agnes suddenly had an image of Kathleen being wheeled away for an operation – an unnecessary, deadly operation. She put one hand on the old lady's shoulder. All the same, she thought, anyone thinking that Kathleen McAleer was an easy target would pretty certainly be proved wrong.

'Julius,' said Agnes on Monday morning. 'We need a fax machine.'

Julius looked up from his desk. 'We do, do we?'

'They've got a special offer on at that electrical store on the High Street.'

'And does this by any chance mean that Sister Agnes needs a fax machine?'

'Heaven forbid, Julius, that I would put my own needs before those of the parish.'

'I take that as yes, then.'

'It would be useful, really it would. Just think of the postage you'd save. Not having to wait until the next day for mail—'

'I could receive missives from the Vatican as they happen.'

Agnes looked at Julius. 'The parish council can't afford it,' he said. She continued to look at him. 'How much?' he asked.

'Two hundred and seventy-eight pounds, and I'd go halves,' she answered briskly.

'You know, Agnes, for someone who's supposed to live in poverty, you have mysterious resources of cash – or is it just you don't carry it, like royalty?'

'Thanks Dad,' chirped Agnes, disappearing out of the door with Julius's cheque-book.

'This receipt says three hundred and two pounds,' said Julius, two hours later, sitting on Agnes's sofa bed in her tiny flat. He had found her this home, two dingy rooms, at a time when she needed to escape. Now it was light and airy, its plain white walls offset with antique furniture and the odd work of art, mostly rescued from her marriage. Julius's favourite was a tiny wooden icon of St Francis which was on the wall by her bed.

'Sorry?' said Agnes, from her kitchen, where she was slicing something loudly. 'Oh that,' she added, coming into the room with a plateful of salami. 'I worked out even more of a bargain. You see,' she said, pointing with a greasy finger to a neat little machine sitting on her desk, 'it turned out that if you bought a phone-cum-answering-machine-cum-fax, it was cheaper.'

Julius's mouth was set in a thin line. 'Three hundred and two pounds is not cheaper than two seven eight. Just because your villain of an ex-husband set up some mysterious trust fund—'

'It's nothing to do with that. And anyway, this way I don't need my phone, so you can have that for the parish, I'll donate it—'

'I paid for that in the first place—'

'—and it's not as if you want this thing in your office, spewing out paper every half an hour and making all that noise.'

As if on cue, the machine suddenly sprang to life as a fax came through. Agnes bounced over to it with delight.

'Look, look,' she beamed. 'My post mortem results.'

'I didn't know you'd died, let alone been chopped up.'

'Samples analysed. Significant doses of toxins. Phone me,' Agnes read out.

Agnes dialled Dr Halliday's number at once.

'Ah, yes,' the doctor said, 'you got my fax, then? Right, well, it's very odd indeed. The drug taken orally was penicillin.'

Agnes tucked the phone under her chin to scribble notes on a piece of paper.

'It was a huge dosage, and she must have been allergic to it. Classic anaphylactic reaction,' Dr Halliday was saying. 'But then, even stranger, it was followed up by intravenous potassium chloride. That is technically what this person died of. A lethal injection, it stops the heart instantly. But you see, it's a neat jab, the victim must have been either acquiescent or semi-conscious from the allergic reaction. I don't know what to make of it at all. If she had anything to do with pharmacy, she'd know something about all this – and she'd certainly have known that penicillin was potentially lethal to her. And in such large amounts. It really doesn't make sense. Presumably they sent a fake post mortem report to the coroner, else you'd never have got your permission for burial.'

* * *

That evening, Agnes popped in to see Kathleen.

'We need to talk,' she said, noticing how well Kathleen had begun to look. 'Sorry, that wasn't very tactfully phrased,' she added. 'Let's go somewhere – where do you think?'

To Kathleen, the question seemed filled with possibilities. Where did she want to go. Home, was the obvious answer. Then she thought, what she fancied was a nice pint of ale. And some crisps. Instead of the slops they fed her in here. Down the – what was the word? Crowds of people drinking, smoking. Hubbub. Something like that. 'Hhbbbub,' she said.

Agnes screwed her face up, trying to hear the meaning.

Kathleen tried again. 'Hbub.'

'Bub?'

'Ppub.'

'Pub? Fine, we'll go there.'

It took Kathleen fifteen minutes to get ready, with Agnes's help. Proper shoes, with stockings; a nice frock, fastened with an amethyst brooch. It had been her great-aunt Cecilia's; oh, the stories she could tell about that brooch if only she could find the words. 'Bbbb,' she said, pointing at it and smiling, and as they passed the nurses' desk she waved at the girl on duty, who was so shocked she just sat there and let them pass.

'We'll be back for lights out,' Agnes said as the swing doors shut behind them.

Quarter of an hour later they found themselves in a dilapidated old pub just by the docks.

'You'd think there'd be sawdust on the floor,' said

Agnes. 'There probably was last time you came in here.'
Kathleen laughed. 'What'll you have?'

Agnes bought Guinness, and lots of crisps, and a glass
of white wine, and sat amongst the soggy beer mats and
ashtrays full of cigarette butts sticky with lipstick.

'So. What's next?'

Kathleen raised her glass with her good arm and downed
a mouthful, pleased with herself for managing to get most
of it past her lips.

Agnes said, 'I'll probably get what-for for this, but if
we're working together on this crime, we need to talk
properly.'

Kathleen grinned, then choked noisily on a crisp. Agnes
patted her back, and passed her her glass. Kathleen seemed
to be a new person since leaving the hospital. Her eyes
were bright, and she seemed more upright, less contorted.
She was drinking quite normally now – but Agnes had
spoken too soon, for as she looked up she saw the old
lady's face was twisted with panic, and she seemed to be
choking again. Her eyes had taken on that distant, glazed
look. It took Agnes a moment to realise that it was
something that Kathleen had seen that was having this
effect on her. Agnes turned slightly and followed her line
of vision – and saw a small group of medical students
from the hospital; among them, Mark Henderson. She
gripped Kathleen's arm, and said quietly, 'What have you
seen?'

Kathleen's eyes met Agnes and they were full of fear.
'Yyyys.'

'Which one?'

'Ggggg.'

'The one in a green sweatshirt and jeans, short brown hair – that one?' said Agnes, describing Mark Henderson.

Kathleen nodded.

'You're sure?'

Kathleen made her hand into a fist again, and said, 'Singe.'

'He was the one carrying a syringe?' Kathleen nodded again. 'He'd better not see us. Let's go.'

They downed their drinks and headed out, struggling with the wheelchair against the heavy swing door. Once outside, Agnes peered back in through the window, and saw, distorted by the frosted Victorian glass, Mark Henderson gazing outwards from his loud group of friends towards the door. 'I've done it now,' thought Agnes.

She wheeled Kathleen back to her ward, past the sister on duty who pretended not to see them, and helped Kathleen undress and into her nightie. She seemed cheerful, and Agnes tried to hide her unease. She left the wards and walked back along quiet corridors to the medical school. She tried Dawn Scott's door, vaguely hoping that somewhere she might find a way into a computer system, a set of files, a record of students; details of Mark Henderson. The door was locked, the medical school was deserted. It would take more than this for the hospital to divulge its secrets, thought Agnes, shivering in the chilly corridor. She drew her coat around her and headed for home.

Chapter Six

The morning's post brought a single envelope with a Leeds postmark. It was from a foster-mother in Pudsey, who had seen the advertisement and said that she had cared for Gail from the age of eight to twelve. She'd kept in touch for a while, and knew she'd qualified as a secretary and was working at the Leeds General Infirmary. When she'd moved on they'd lost touch.

Agnes phoned her to let her know the funeral was on Thursday. The woman sounded sincerely upset at the news, but said she'd be unable to come to London at such short notice. Agnes then phoned the Leeds Social Services Department, and they confirmed that Gail was someone for whom they'd arranged foster parents, and thanked Agnes for letting them know the sad news, which they would pass on to her other foster families.

Then Agnes went back to the Registry at St Hugh's, trying to find a way to track down details on Mark. As she wandered along the corridor, wondering who to ask and what to ask them, she saw Alexander emerge from a doorway, look carefully left and right, and then set off confidently down the corridor towards Professor Burgess's door.

She blinked, wondered where to hide – and then he'd seen her.

'Hello. Visiting the sick again?'

'Sort of. How's the portrait?'

'Oh, that. You can see it if you like.' She followed him into the professor's office, where there was an easel set up with the canvas on it. She saw the outline of a man posed against a grid of lines detailing perspective, the light from the window, the angles of the desk in front of him.

Alexander was watching her.

'It looks like – I mean, I don't know anything about these things,' she faltered. 'It looks very clever.'

'Yeah, well, you still need technique to paint rubbish.'

Agnes felt the words come before she could stop them. 'You know, you're worth more than all this.'

Alexander carefully fashioned a sneer. 'Really? Did Our Lady just tell you? "Tell that jaded, world-weary old cynic that he could be something" she said, is that it?'

'It felt like that, actually,' said Agnes, feeling foolish. 'But then,' she added, leaving the room, 'what would you know of inspiration?' She walked through the open door, aware of his eyes burning through her, and once out in the corridor went straight into the Ladies' toilets, only breathing normally when she heard the door swing shut behind her.

'How's the investigation?' asked Julius that afternoon.

'Going nowhere. I have a prime suspect, and no way to track him down. It's pathetic really. My only hope is that tomorrow's funeral brings something out into the open.'

'I feel bad about that poor girl in the lab still. And the parish paying to burn an empty coffin.'

Agnes ran her hands through her hair. 'I know. I feel pretty stupid at the moment too.'

The day of the funeral was damp and grey. Arriving at the crematorium, Agnes realised that there were only going to be two mourners to pay their respects to the empty coffin – herself and Julius. It was optimistic, she thought, to have expected anyone else to appear. But as she took her seat and Julius began to say the words of the service, Agnes heard the door opening and a rustling of a raincoat as someone sat down at the back of the chapel. She waited, her head bowed in prayer, then, after a few minutes, turned to see who it was. Mark Henderson was sitting at the edge of the very last pew. He sat very upright, his face pale, his expression blank. Agnes turned back and tried to concentrate on the rest of the service, her mind working furiously. At the end, Julius played a tape of Bach organ music, and Agnes stood up. She saw that Mark too was getting up to go, and she followed him out of the chapel into the garden. As she drew level with him he turned sharply and said, 'Well?' His tone was harsh.

'Well what?' Agnes replied.

'Why shouldn't I be here?'

'No reason. No reason at all.' Agnes waited.

'Good. I'll be going then.'

'I think, perhaps—'

'What?' He turned, hostile, scuffing the gravel path with his toes.

'Perhaps if – ' she began – 'if there's something about Gail's death—'

'Well there's nothing, OK? Nothing at all.'

Agnes held his gaze. 'Gail was murdered,' she said.

Mark eyed her coolly, but his face was drawn, his eyes dark circles against the pallor of his skin. 'No one killed her,' he said evenly.

'So – so why were you seen leaving the library, carrying a syringe?' The crematorium garden was silent in spite of the birds flitting between the dripping trees.

After a long moment, Mark said, his voice a whisper, 'Who – who sent you?'

'No one.'

'The police.'

'No, of course not. I just found out—'

'Why? Why did you find out?'

Agnes's voice was calm. 'I don't like untruth. I needed to know. And now it looks as if you're—'

'A murderer. Yes, it does bloody look like that, doesn't it? Well, I'm not, so you can bloody well fuck off. OK? Just get the fuck out,' he shouted, striding off wildly across the lawns towards the railings, his arm raised awkwardly across his face as if to protect himself from the chilly drizzle, although in fact, Agnes realised as she hurried to catch up with him, he was crying. He came to a halt where the garden gave way to the burial ground, by endless stone rows of white and grey and granite pink. At Mark's feet was a marble slab bearing only a tiny spray of dandelions and the name 'Elizabeth' in carved square lettering. Mark had covered his face with his hands and

Agnes realised he was openly weeping. She waited for the sobs to abate, then said, gently, 'The baby . . .'

Mark shook his head, still hiding his face.

'Did you mean to kill her?'

Again, he shook his head.

'What was in the syringe?'

The hands came away from the face. Mark stared down at her, his eyes huge with fear. He spoke suddenly. 'Even if you hand me over to them, I'll plead not guilty. OK? That's why the professor decided—' He sat down suddenly on the wet grass.

Agnes sat down next to him. 'Professor Burgess was protecting you? The fake post mortem, all that?'

He nodded.

'Why?'

Mark turned on her. He looked very young. 'The police – if they didn't believe me – we couldn't risk it. And anyway, technically I killed her. She was alive until I administered . . . it.'

Agnes laid her hand gently on his arm. 'Mark, you can trust me, you know. Whatever you tell me need go no further.' She felt him flinch. 'Did you kill Gail?'

Mark looked away, staring out across the ranks of graves. He turned back to Agnes, and said softly, 'Gail killed herself. I just finished what was going to happen anyway.'

'I see. Did Gail kill herself because of the pregnancy?'

Mark nodded.

'And was it your baby?'

He nodded again.

'When did you two meet?'

Mark took a deep breath. 'I got a job in the pharmacy last vacation, to pay the bills. I met her there. I was lonely, so was she.'

'So you got together.'

'Yes. It was a mistake. It dragged on for a while, but then I met Julia and decided to end it. That's when Gail told me she was pregnant.'

'When was this?'

'A couple of months ago. I didn't know what to do, I suggested she have an abortion. She was furious, she said it was against her religion. Then she said she'd never wanted this baby except for the fact it was mine. She waited around for me to change my mind, and I was such a coward I suppose I gave her the impression I might, even though by then Jules and I . . .' He sighed. 'I spoke to my tutor in the end, and he was really supportive—'

'Burgess?'

'No, McPherson. He said I had to get my priorities straight, and it wouldn't make her happy if I just tied myself down to her, not in the long run. And I suppose it gave me strength to tell her, finally, that – that I couldn't. I offered money for the child and everything, not that I've got any. Then it was strange, she seemed to accept it, and I didn't see her for a couple of weeks. But then, last Tuesday, when she – when it happened . . .'

He tailed off, his eyes shadowed with the memory. He took a deep breath and said, 'She asked me to meet her in the old library. No one goes there now – so I was sitting there, and she came in. She looked weird, kind of calm, and she said, "It's all settled now." And she was carrying a syringe. I didn't know what was happening. And then she said, "We're all going to die." And it, like, dawned on me, because she looked so odd – and she said she'd taken the Amytal already, and she'd got twenty minutes, and now I was going to have the potassium chloride, and they'd find us all dead, all three of us, she said, the holy family. I remember her saying the holy family, I don't know why she said that.'

He stopped and blew his nose, then went on, 'And she came at me, and I had her wrist, and I thought, she can't kill me like that, because it only works intravenously, not like from a random jab. And then it was really awful, she began to suffocate. First she was panting, but I thought that was just the state she was in, and the barbiturates. Then she started grabbing at her own neck and choking, as if someone was trying to strangle her. She couldn't speak, her eyes were bulging, it was awful, really awful – and I just wanted it to stop, I wanted it all to stop, so I – I gave her the injection she'd intended for me. I didn't really think. And she grew calmer, and smiled, and held on to me, and I held her, and she died like that, sort of convulsing, but calm. It was very quick.'

'So then you stepped over the body, holding the syringe, and went back down the corridor.'

'I went to find Jules.' Mark looked pinched and cold.

'Did you notice Kathleen – the lady in the wheelchair? She said she saw you?'

Mark shook his head. 'I was in a terrible state. Please,

please don't tell. If anyone found out, my mum's so proud
of me, if she knew . . .'

He was trembling. Agnes felt a wave of relief that
Kathleen was no longer in danger. In fact, she realised,
looking at Mark's drawn face, at the terror in his eyes,
Kathleen had never been in danger. This boy, in all his
anguish, was telling the truth. 'What happened then?' she
said.

'Julia said we must get to the body first, pretend to find
it. So we did. We told Professor Burgess. But – then it
was OK, because he was really nice, and I ended up
telling him everything, I was so scared because I sort of
killed her, only I didn't – and he was great, just brilliant,
not like he usually is at all, Jules can't bear him but even
she had to admit he was great – and he said not to worry,
the hospital would take over everything. And I said she
was Catholic, so he said he'd call you lot in. He said I
should just concentrate on my exams. And it was all OK
until you – until you . . .' He sighed. 'I realised you must
know something, and I got scared. You won't do anything,
will you? Please?'

The boy was shivering. Agnes took the jacket that
hung over his arm and draped it round his shoulders.
'What would I do? You did what you felt was right. Your
only sin is cowardice – hardly a criminal offence, else
we'd all be behind bars.'

'Two lives,' he said.

Agnes thought of Gail, swallowing pills, knowing she
was taking another life as well as her own. 'Yes,' she said
quietly. 'But who's to judge where the blame lies? We all

muddle along as best we can. Here you are, a brilliant career before you, every chance of happiness, a lovely girlfriend—'

Mark made a face. 'Or not. She's keener on that bloody painter at the moment.'

Agnes felt a strange jolting sensation. 'Alexander?'

'You know him?'

'Um, vaguely.'

'He's talked her into posing for him, just when I was going through all this. She's gone all quiet about it, won't tell me anything. And one of our friends said she takes her clothes off for him.'

'That's terrible,' said Agnes, with feeling.

They walked back towards the chapel, across the lawns festooned with arrangements of flowers. Agnes wondered how to bury poor Gail properly now that it was all resolved. She felt relief that there was no one to blame. Just life, she thought. Just a muddle of good intentions resulting in tragedy, just humanity doing its feeble best. At the gate she touched his arm. 'How long till finals?'

'Six weeks – no, five and a half.'

'You'll do it.' He nodded. 'It was her decision that she and her – her child – should die. Not yours.'

'Yes. No one can blame me, can they? Not really.'

'No,' said Agnes gently. Mark awkwardly took hold of her hand and shook it, and then turned and went down the drive, out of the gates. His words rang in her ears. 'No one can blame me.' All our petty wrongdoings, our daily round of meannesses measured out with the cry, 'It's not my fault.' When you think of what we might be, thought

Agnes. So much greater than we are.

She turned to go, passing wreaths arranged in shapes, in hearts, in words. 'Dad', said one. Some expensive-looking orchids, past their best, had fallen on to the path. She picked them up and arranged them into ragged bunches on the grass verge.

'So that's that,' she said to Julius, as they sat in their local Indian restaurant that evening. 'Not a murder at all. A strange and bungled suicide. The pity of it, Julius,' she said, snapping a poppadum in half.

Julius spooned some pickles on to his plate. 'Suspicion is a terrible thing. Still,' he looked up, 'at least now you can join Madeleine and me on the project again.'

'Madeleine?'

'Yes. She's just arrived in London, so they've decided to place her full-time on the project as from next week, now the hostel's expanding. Didn't I tell you?'

'No. You didn't.'

'Of course, I've hardly seen you.'

'Just because . . .' Agnes checked herself. 'I mean, I know I haven't been around much, but—'

'I think your Order felt that, while you were settling in—'

'Settling in? I've been there for months.'

'You know these things take time,' Julius said.

'Hmmm.'

Julius crunched loudly on a poppadum.

'Madeleine, eh?' Agnes said. 'That's nice.' She reached across for the pickles. 'Anyway,' she went on, 'it's all

72

over now. The main thing is that Kathleen is safe, I'll pop in tomorrow and let her know. And,' she added, 'we can bury Gail.'

Julius crunched some more. 'Yes, that's good,' he mumbled.

'So it's over,' Agnes said.

'You just said so.'

'And I'm sorry.'

Julius's eyes twinkled as he looked up. 'I can't think what there is to be sorry for.'

'No, no, I freely admit it. I've inconvenienced a large number of people, I've asked you to support me way beyond the call of duty, I've been headstrong and—'

'Now that's enough, Agnes. All this uncharacteristic humility, it's quite putting me off my dinner. Saved by the arrival of our waiter, I think. And anyway,' Julius added, as dishes of food were arranged on the table before them, 'the pursuit of truth is always noble. Yours was the chicken pasanda, wasn't it?'

'You know, Julius,' Agnes said, helping herself to some rice, 'there are times when I still can't tell if you're being serious.'

'I'm always serious. You should know that by now.'

That night Agnes couldn't sleep. The meal had been delightful, but something was making her uncomfortable. She lay in bed, watching the shadows on the ceiling thrown by the tree outside her window. It must be remorse, she thought; allowing her imagination to run away with her, preventing Gail from having a proper burial. She must contact Dr Halliday, and get everything cleared for a secret funeral. Tell her it was suicide, and that the syringe was just Mark putting her out of her misery. Maybe gloss over that bit, it would be a shame if Mark got into trouble. And it was a bit puzzling why someone who worked in a pharmacy would choose to die in such a way. Perhaps Gail thought she'd suffered so much already another twenty minutes wouldn't make much difference. And, Agnes supposed, she'd have been able to get her hands on penicillin with no one asking questions.

Agnes got up and poured a glass of water. We can invite those people from Leeds to the funeral, she thought, although she doubted they'd come. She sipped her water, gazing absently down into the street outside. A woman in a fake leopard-skin mini-skirt teetered crazily down the street, shouting abuse at the odd passing car. Agnes watched her go, a bedraggled figure against the dim yellow light, the swishing of the tyres on the wet road. Agnes yawned.

At three in the morning she woke suddenly out of deep sleep into acute alertness. Her first thought was of Alexander. She sat up in annoyance and punched her pillows into shape. Now look, she tried to tell herself, this is ridiculous. It's over. Julius will resume his hospital visiting, and I'll work with Sister Madeleine on the project. Alexander can finish his boring portrait in peace. Good, she thought. She closed her eyes, then opened them again. Another memory, of being in Gail's empty office, sitting by a typewriter; of someone coming in and trying to open the locked cupboard. Why should this occur to her now?

She needed to sleep. She needed to prove to Julius, and to her community, that she could be a good team member on the project. It was high time she committed herself to something wholeheartedly. Why was she lying awake, thinking about some stranger looking for medicine? And now another thought came to her. Mark had said that Gail had taken Amytal. But, and now she was remembering clearly, he'd said it was a barbiturate. An obvious choice for a suicide. Yet Dr Halliday hadn't mentioned the presence of barbiturates. Agnes was out of bed in a second and rummaging through the papers on her tiny desk, until she found Anne's fax. 'Presence of penicillin and potassium chloride.' That was the syringe, as Mark had said. But Gail had said she'd taken Amytal, not penicillin.

Agnes paced her room. Typical three in the morning thoughts, she thought. Of course she'd doubted Mark to start with, with good reason. But now she remembered him that afternoon in the graveyard; his tearfulness, his terror that she might hand him over to the police. She was certain now that he was telling the truth. So why was she inventing some terrible complication when it was obvious there was none? Really, she thought, it's quite ridiculous.

The wind blew against the window, waving the branches of the tree like the greetings of familiar spirits. Agnes stood in the chilly room and watched the changing shadows, as if they might be bringing her a message. An idea was seeping into her mind, taking form. A thought just waiting to be caught, held in her mind. The man in Gail's office. 'Oh my God,' Agnes suddenly gasped out loud. 'What if – if someone had tampered with – *mon Dieu*, that would mean that there was a murder. Only, it just hasn't happened yet.'

Chapter Seven

Julius's voice down the phone was tetchy. 'Agnes, it's nine-thirty and we were expecting you here half an hour ago. Don't you think this is going a bit far?'

'I'm waiting for a fax – please bear with me.' There was silence from Julius. Agnes went on, 'I think Gail might have taken pills intended for someone else, by mistake. It's essential I find out who they were meant for, before it's too late. You can see that, can't you, Julius – please?'

There was a brief pause, before Julius said, 'We'll just have to manage without you.' He hung up.

Agnes replaced the handset and stared at it. She ran her fingers through her hair. Almost immediately, the phone rang and she grabbed it.

'Julius—' she began, but was interrupted.

'Sweetie, you're there, how wonderful,' rang out Athena's voice. 'I thought you'd be out scooping up baby junkies from the mean streets.'

'Sore point.'

'You don't sound so good. That's wonderful, because neither am I, let's have a boozy lunch and trade our misery.'

'Athena, I'm tied to a fax machine at the moment—'

'I've never tried that one . . .'

'—but you're welcome to drop round here for coffee, and if you do happen to pass that patisserie on Butler's Wharf, they do a fab pain-au-chocolat.'

'Two days,' Athena wailed, half an hour later. 'He said Wednesday, it's Friday now and he still isn't back.' She took a large bite of croissant.

'It is only two days,' Agnes replied.

Athena looked at her. 'You don't understand. It's not the time, it's what he's doing while he's there. Who else he's with.'

'He's probably working very hard and missing you.'

Athena looked up from her cup of coffee. 'Do you think so?'

'He's probably aching with longing for you, and daren't say because he's terrified you'll propose marriage the instant he says anything nice. And he's probably right . . .' Agnes broke off, giggling.

Athena looked crestfallen. 'You're no help. He's not the faithful type, that's all. Means well, but . . .' She shook her head, then took another large bite of pastry. 'And why are you fed up, then?'

'Oh, nothing so interesting as doubting an absent lover. Just that I've managed to irritate Julius – if you knew him, you'd know how serious that is – and it's all my fault. And also that my suspicious mind has made me believe that someone is about to get bumped off and I don't know who they are or how to go about finding out.'

Athena let out a long, low, whistle. 'Wow. And don't tell me, this painter chappie's at the heart of it.'

'That's just it. Maybe, maybe not. Don't look at me like that. The problem is, I can't begin to ask questions at the hospital, because I can't betray my suspicions to anyone. I don't know who's safe to talk to.'

'Not even Alexander what's-his-name?'

'Certainly not him.'

Athena drained her cup of coffee. 'You always did go for dangerous men, poppet.'

'If you mean my ex-husband, that's different. I was young.'

'You weren't that young when you last had dinner with him.'

'That was seven months ago.'

'I rest my case. And did he tell you seven months ago he was about to remarry?'

'Oh, I doubt he'd even set eyes on her then,' Agnes said airily.

Athena narrowed her eyes at Agnes. 'You're jealous, aren't you?'

'Me? Don't be ridiculous.'

'Of course. And this painter – ah, now I see.'

Agnes spoke quietly. 'I don't need Hugo.'

'You've always needed him as a presence in your life. And now he's not there . . .'

'This Gabrielle could never be . . .' Agnes bit her lip.

'You see?'

Agnes began to tidy the table, stacking plates, crunching up paper bags into a tight ball. 'Well, you can talk,

Athena,' she said, 'where dangerous men are concerned. Or maybe there's no such thing as a safe man.'

'Boring, that's the point, poppet. Boring. Give me the dangerous ones any day.'

'Even if they disappear to New York and don't come back when they say they will?'

Athena grinned at Agnes. 'You know, I feel quite cheered up. Must be this pain-au-chocolat.'

'It is your third, after all. By the way, when your beloved does at last check in, could you ask him whether he's followed up my "painter chappie" as he said he would?'

'Of course. It'll give me something to say to him instead of "Where the hell have you been?" Ooh, look, there goes your fax machine.'

'It'll be from Dr Halliday.' The printer buzzed and whirred briefly. Agnes pulled out the finished sheet and read it off. 'Re-checked my samples for traces of Amytal. Absolutely none. Penicillin is strange choice for a suicide, assuming she knew what she was doing. In answer to your question two, they are both white tablets scored down the middle. Phone me.'

Athena said, conversationally, 'So, where are you going to start?'

Agnes sighed. 'I really don't know. There's a couple of medical students I've met. But hospitals are strange places, Athena. Hermetically sealed, everyone protects each other. I'll talk to Mark, definitely. But the other one, Julia, I dunno. She's sitting as a model for Alexander at the moment.'

Athena threw back her head and laughed.

At a quarter to twelve, Agnes was in the empty office of Dawn Scott. She was idly gazing at some plans for the new building that had been pinned to the wall some time ago. The corners were curling, and the ink marks had faded in patches where the sunlight fell. 'St Hugh's Surgery Wing and Academic Centre', she read. 'Mather and Swann, Architects.' Her gaze moved beyond the plans to the view from the window, where the new building rose up all smooth and bright and, next to it, the building site which, according to the plans on the wall, was Phase Two. Then she heard the click of heels approaching, and a grumbling London accent.

'I'm bringing in me thermos tomorrow – ooh, hello, you made me jump.'

'Sorry,' Agnes replied, making way for Dawn to sit at her desk. 'I wanted to ask you something about Gail.'

'She did just drop dead, didn't she? Only there's all sorts of talk goin' on round 'ere—'

'Yes, she just dropped dead. Pulmonary embolism. One of those things.'

'Poor cow. What did you want to ask?'

'If you work here and you need regular prescriptions, can you get them from the pharmacy here?'

'Ooh yes. People do it all the time. You just get the form from your doctor.'

'And you go to the pharmacy?'

'The hospital staff do. The teaching staff go to Pharmacology, saves them time.'

'That's um – Gail's office?'

'Yes. There's a locked cupboard. She'd store stuff there.'

'Who has keys to it?'

'Only Gail. It used to be two or three people, but there was trouble, weren't there, so then they brought in strict rules. She was allowed to bring stuff across from the pharmacy. Don't tell a soul, but I'd often get stuff off of 'er, fer 'eadaches, that sort of thing. She said it was OK. I dunno.' She grinned at Agnes.

Agnes smiled back. 'One other thing – was Gail good at her job?'

'They thought she was the dog's whatsits over at the pharmacy. That's why she was going to train. Yeah, they rated her.'

'Thanks,' she said. 'Thanks for your time. By the way, these plans on your wall—'

'Oh, they're ancient. Should put the new ones up, really. I like them. I like those little trees down there – and all them people. All busy. Look at this little geezer in the hat, I like him. Wish I could draw like that.'

Agnes looked at the architect's plans, neat straight lines showing a gleaming new building, a vision of efficiency, its forecourt peopled with stickmen. She read the description in the corner.

'I didn't know it was a surgical unit.'

'It isn't. Not any more. They changed it. It's goin' ter be genetics now – all the rage, they say. Well, you've got ter keep up, ain't yer? Gotta go where the money is, eh? They got that pharmaceutical company, Stott, it's called, to put up the money. I'd better do me work now, if you don't mind.'

Leaving Dawn, and finding that Kathleen was in Ultrasound, Agnes went straight up to the canteen for an early lunch. She took her tray to a seat by the window and sat down. From here the view looked across to London Bridge and beyond to the Thames. The tall buildings of the City made blurred, brooding shapes against the drizzly sky. Agnes thought of Julius and Madeleine getting on with their work. Real work. Her fish and chips cooled on the plate in front of her.

'Mind if I join you?'

Agnes looked up, startled, to see Alexander looming over her. To her annoyance she felt herself blush. 'Um – no, yes, do, I mean, no I don't mind.'

'Chips, eh,' he remarked, settling down opposite her with his cup of coffee.

'How's the portrait?'

He made a face. 'Oh, that. It's OK. Listen, I seem to keep being rude to you. I don't mean to be.' Agnes waited. 'That's all,' he added.

'Fine,' she said. 'I accept your apology. Anyway, it was presumptuous of me to talk to you the way I did.'

'I accept your apology too,' he smiled.

'It wasn't an apology.'

'Neither was mine,' he replied.

'Good.' They looked at each other uncertainly across the table.

'The other day,' he said, after a brief pause, 'I wanted to tell you – I wanted to show you what I meant. About portraits. You're not eating,' he added, looking at her untouched plate.

'I'm not hungry.'

Their eyes met again. 'Come with me,' he said with sudden urgency.

She followed him, bewildered, out of the canteen. In the corridor, he turned to her. His voice was uneven. 'You asked me how the painting was – I'll show you.' He set off again, hurrying now, down the corridor. Agnes had almost to run to keep up with him. They reached a staircase and he started down the stairs, emerging two floors down on to the ground floor and a carpeted corridor. 'The seat of power,' he said. 'Here we are,' he added, turning a corner. The corridor gave on to a wide, bright hallway, and Agnes saw that they were in the oldest part of the building, in the original hospital, now the main reception area of the medical school. There were huge arched windows against whose panes pattered raindrops from the trees in the courtyard beyond.

'Look,' said Alexander. The walls were lined with portraits, all of them, it seemed to Agnes, pictures of elderly men. '"Professor James Wilmott, Dean 1936-38",' Alexander read out. '"Dr John Jordan, Dean 1956-59." "Mr Richard Bolton, Professor of Surgery 1899-1910." Look at them all,' Alexander said, his voice echoing between the arches, as he strode from one to the next. 'Look at him. "Dr William Chislett". Look.' He grabbed Agnes by the arm and pointed at the portrait. 'Look at his eyes. Dead. Look at that face. Nice and pink, with neat little glasses. Uniform lighting. Dull,' he cried, dragging her to the next painting. 'Look at him. Neat white collar. No expression, hardly a face at all. And him,' he said, moving on. 'What is this man thinking? Nothing. Who is he? Who is he, eh? No one. Dull,' he shouted, pulling her along, 'Dull, dull, dull, dull, DULL!' he cried, gesturing at the faces on the walls. He was still gripping her arm, and now he looked down at her, pausing to catch his breath. 'You see,' he said, quieter now, 'it's a perfectly admirable way of earning a living. If that's what you want to do. There's nothing wrong with all this, absolutely nothing wrong. If it's what you want to do. But me—' he broke off, chewing his lip, looking up at a bespectacled surgeon on the wall above them. 'Me . . .' he sighed, smiled awkwardly, released her arm, stood there.

She swallowed, and said, 'Thank you for showing me.'

He was suddenly awkward. 'I – I feel things strongly,' he mumbled.

'So do I,' she replied.

'Yes,' he said, vaguely. 'I'd better go now,' he added, turning away from her, then turned back. 'I'd like you to – I'd like to paint you. Maybe. One day. Or maybe not,' he said, now half-way down the hallway, loping away from her, already distant, one hand raised in a half-wave as he disappeared altogether out of the main doors into the showery day. She stood in the wide, reverberating space. From all sides, elderly men in faded frames stared blankly down at her. She turned and went back along the corridor, up the stairs to the first floor, thinking that she must look in on Kathleen, but finding that her feet carried her onwards, past the wards, right through to the main doorways at the back of the building and out of the hospital. Emerging into the gritty air, she breathed deeply. Beyond the dreary housing estates she could see the familiar spire of St Simeon's and, without consciously making a decision, she found herself heading towards it. As she reached the church door, she saw that Julius and Madeleine were just locking it. Julius turned and saw her.

She went up to him, and wordlessly, he handed her the key.

'Julius . . .' she began. She wanted to reach out and touch him, to smooth the lines around his eyes, to bury herself in his funny old cardigan. 'It won't be long,' she said.

He looked at her for a moment. 'I hope so,' he said, then turned to Madeleine and ushered her away, adding over his shoulder, 'Lock up as usual.'

Agnes stumbled into the darkness of the church and went straight to the Lady chapel, where she flung herself on to her knees. In her prayers she saw an image of Our Lady, an admonitory figure with a china-doll face, who pointed an accusing finger at her. Did Alexander really want her to model for him? None of it made sense.

She walked home in an angry sunset, the blocks of the housing estates sharp like paper cut-outs. As she let herself into her flat the phone was ringing. She answered it.

'Darling, it's me.'

'Oh. You sound better.'

Athena giggled. 'He's back. Since lunchtime.'

'That's nice.'

'Listen, before I forget, I asked him, like you said, about your chap.'

'And?'

'He said, that his mate Doug was at the RCA with him, and that he got thrown out for some incident involving attacking another student.'

'What, Alexander – Alexander Jeffes?'

'I think so – hang on.' Agnes could hear consulting in the background. 'Yes, that's right. Hang on.' There was more mumbling, then Athena came back on. 'He also says that, apparently, Jeffes is an odd choice, and – and he wonders who else they considered. And that now I'm to get off the phone as he hasn't seen me for—' There was a loud crash, followed by giggling. 'Sorry, we dropped the phone. Must go. *Ciao.*'

'Hello Kathleen,' said Agnes the next morning.

''Lo,' replied a smiling Kathleen.

'Did you say—'

''Lo,' repeated Kathleen, radiant with triumph.

'Oh no,' groaned Agnes, sitting down on her bed and helping herself to a chocolate. 'Now you can talk I can see I won't get a word in edgeways.'

Kathleen cackled and nudged Agnes hard, indicating the chocolates. 'And the good news is,' Agnes went on, handing her the box and lowering her voice, 'that you're not in danger of being bumped off. There was no murder to speak of – the man with the syringe was – let's just say, a victim of circumstances. On the other hand,' she went on, her voice even lower, 'there are still some questions I need answered. So any more sinister strangers armed with medical hardware, just let me know, OK?'

'Nuts,' Kathleen replied, screwing up her face.

'Sorry?'

'Nnnuts,' she repeated. She pointed at the chocolate box, then swiftly removed her dentures and waved them around before replacing them in her mouth. 'Nuts,' she said again, stabbing her finger at Agnes.

'I see. I'm to eat the nuts.'

Kathleen cackled and hugged the box to her chest.

'Next time I'll bring my own chocolates,' Agnes said, getting up to go.

Once out in the corridor, she set off aimlessly towards the medical school. Penicillin, she thought. Hardly a murder weapon. She walked past doors of shiny uniformity, bold signposts that seemed to sing out a triumphant hymn to all of medicine's achievements: X-Ray, Nuclear Medicine, Oncology, Gynaecology, Obstetrics, Operating Theatres, Intensive Care . . . What have I really got, she thought? What evidence is there that makes it worth upsetting Julius and shirking my responsibilities in order to hang around here instead? A cut-and-dried case of a bungled suicide. The only odd thing is that someone who was interested in pharmacology and who was trusted to handle drugs took a large dose of penicillin to which she knew she was allergic, instead of the barbiturates which she had set aside for herself. The thought occurred to Agnes that maybe the other pills were still inside Gail's locked cupboard. And what else? she thought. A hospital post mortem carried out in haste, with a false report. Professor Burgess's anxious protection of Mark and Julia and his apparent complicity in what must be termed, thought Agnes, a cover-up. Although, of course, if the police had been brought in, Mark would have been charged with murder.

And Alexander, thought Agnes. And now it turns out he's violent. Or was, anyway. Perhaps now he just paints young women and – and wasn't that Julia walking towards her?

'Hello,' Julia said, looking up shyly at Agnes. 'I was just thinking about you. I was just thinking how rude I must have seemed. We were so anxious, Mark and I – and you seemed to know so much, and now here you are . . . I say, would you like a coffee?'

The canteen, mused Agnes, looking around at its comfortable squalor, had come to seem like home. 'You see,' Julia continued, as she brought two cups over to their table, 'how were we to know you'd be sympathetic? Mark told me, about the funeral – sugar? – and how nice you were. He's so much better, back on course for finals and everything,' Julia finished, taking a gulp of coffee.

'So you still see him then?'

'Did he say?'

'He said—'

'It's true, we're not really together, I suppose. Actually, I find I work much better now, it's all a bit hot-house to spend your life cooped up with other medics.'

'That's good. To have an escape, I mean.' Agnes sipped her coffee and looked at the young woman in front of her. She noticed her natural poise, in the way she held her cup, in the way her chin-length auburn bob swung against her cheek. No wonder Alexander—

'And I'm being a model too,' giggled Julia suddenly, charmingly. 'Though I don't know why I'm telling you, all of a sudden.'

'What sort of model?' asked Agnes, knowing the answer.

'That painter, Alexander – he asked me. I get paid, too, so it's not exploitation or anything.'

'Are you sure?' Agnes heard herself ask.

'What do you mean?'

'Well, don't you think, maybe he's . . . I mean, to take your clothes off for someone—'

'What?'

'Oh, I don't know.' Agnes shook her head, thinking that she must sound like a prudish old maid.

'Well, I think it's fun. Hard work,' Julia added, 'keeping still, and I get cold sometimes. But he's a very successful artist, you know. He's already got a buyer for my painting. It's in the style of – um – one of those old masters. Velath, something.'

'Velasquez.'

'Yes, that's right.'

'Do you have to lie on a couch and hold a mirror?'

'Yes,' said Julia, wide-eyed. 'How did you know?'

'Inspired guess,' replied Agnes. 'Oh, look, here's Mark.'

'Oh,' said Julia, as Mark joined them, smiling nervously.

'Just been on the wards,' he said, sitting down, 'getting set up for the viva.'

'I should do some of that,' said Julia. She looked at her watch. 'Better go, see you, take care,' she said hurriedly, leaving in a flurry of coat and bag. Agnes looked at Mark.

'I imagine you're thinking the wrong person just left,' she said.

He shrugged. 'Mmm, suppose so.'

'In fact,' Agnes went on, 'you're just the person I wanted to talk to.' Mark waited politely. 'You see,' Agnes said, 'Gail died from swallowing penicillin. She was allergic to it.'

Mark looked searchingly at Agnes. He opened his mouth to speak, closed it again, then said, 'It's true, she wasn't sleepy. But why did she say Amytal? I remember her saying it.'

'Because that's what she thought she'd taken.'

'But she'd have got the drugs herself, she had access to all that—'

'Well, yes,' Agnes said. 'You see, it's quite obvious that Gail never meant to die from a penicillin reaction. It's also obvious that she wouldn't have taken the wrong drugs by mistake. So, it follows that she picked up a bottle of tablets from exactly the place she had left her Amytal with no reason to believe that it wasn't just that. She was the only one with access to that cupboard.'

'I don't see what you're saying.'

'Something very mysterious is going on, that's all. Those drugs were meant for someone else.'

Mark lifted his large feet in chunky trainers up on to the bench and proceeded to retie their laces. 'What did Julia say?'

'Julia? Oh, I didn't tell her.'

'Quite. She's not very trustworthy at the moment,' Mark said, thumping one foot back on to the floor. 'So it turns out you haven't quite solved the mystery of Gail's death?' He smiled briefly, then fiddled with a double bow.

'Well, no. I wanted to ask you – how one might find out who was getting drugs from the hospital pharmacy, I mean, which members of the teaching staff?'

'It'd be on the records. It's easy if you have access to the computer.'

'And do you?'

Mark looked up from his feet and sighed. 'Well, technically I've stopped working there, with finals and everything.' He swung his other foot back down. 'But I could nip in and have a look, I suppose.'

'Would you be able to find out if . . .' Agnes paused, uncertainly, then went on, 'if penicillin had been prescribed for someone who was allergic to it?'

Mark chewed his lip, frowning. 'Mmm. S'pose so. You'd have to check their medical records and cross-refer it. But,' he went on, looking up, 'I don't see any mystery. I mean, someone puts penicillin in Gail's cupboard—'

'—When she had the key. You see, it couldn't have been her, else she wouldn't have swallowed it.'

'Uh-huh.' Mark looked uncertain, and Agnes could see the hospital working in his soul, his brilliant career in medicine glittering before him.

'I wondered,' Agnes said carefully, 'whether you wouldn't mind having a look? In the pharmacy records.'

Mark made a tiny pile of spilt sugar on the table. 'Dunno. Dunno if I can help. It might have gone out the back door. I mean, if you were going to do something a bit dodgy with a drug, you wouldn't put it through the records, would you?'

'No. I'm sure it's all nothing, anyway.'

Mark prodded the sugar with one fingertip. 'Look, if it means that your mind is at rest, with all this Gail business – I'll check the records for you. Get you a print-out. Tomorrow? Saturday?'

'Fine. And in return,' she said, hesitantly. 'Gail's flat. I imagine, I mean, you're probably the only person who—'

Mark rubbed his forehead. 'Oh, that.' His face darkened. 'All her stuff's still there. I've paid the rent till the end of May, but—'

'If you like, I'll clear it.'

'Would you? Oh, that would be brill.'

'You can bring me the key tomorrow. Where shall I find you?'

'I'm usually at the pool lunchtime. In the new academic centre.'

'Swimming pool?'

'Yeah. Bring your kit. I'll sign you in, if you like.'

As Agnes headed back along the corridors towards the main doors, she found herself remembering a lake in France where she had swum many years ago. She had been Hugo's wife and, in name at least, the lady of the château at Savigny, where there had been a deep, secluded, natural pool. She remembered the cool water in the summer heat, where, naked, she would float for hours, watching the ducks and ducklings, splashing the water over her body, looking, with a peculiar detachment, at the bruises inflicted by Hugo. How inevitable it had become, his violence. How familiar. In the end it had been Julius who'd rescued her, when she was beyond rescuing herself, and had arranged for her to come to London.

Julius. She passed a clock which said eleven-fifty, and thought: it's not too late. She could drop all this so-called investigation here, take up her place with Julius in his office, try once again to be the person he believed she could be. Tears pricked her eyes. She saw Julius waiting with the same faith and generosity he had always had, even as a young curate in Savigny. And she knew that she had to have that pharmacy print-out.

Chapter Eight

The pool was a deep blue in colour, reflecting shimmering ultramarine patterns on to the pine ceiling. Agnes walked down the steps into the water, thinking, if I worked here all the time, you wouldn't be able to keep me away.

Mark was ploughing steadily up and down the length of the pool with a shoal of other people and she joined them, feeling with delight her body stretch into the water's flow, feeling her muscles work against its pull.

Emerging from the changing rooms, she joined Mark on a bench by the snack machine. He looked round, then produced a key and a fat computer print-out. 'This is everyone who had pharmacy prescriptions in the last two months,' he whispered to her. 'Patients and everything. It ends yesterday. OK?'

'That's great,' she said, slipping the key and the pages into a plastic carrier bag.

'That's all I have to do, right?'

'That's fine, Mark. There's nothing else I need. And thanks for the swim, it was lovely.'

Leaving the new building, she shook out her hair which was still damp, and set off back to the hospital, past the excavation for phase two of the building. The newly paved courtyard stopped at some hastily erected boards which said 'Hard Hat Area – Keep Out', and a bit further on 'Mather and Swann, Architects. The Stott Microbiology Wing, St Hugh's Hospital, Phase Two'. Someone was standing by this board, oddly stooped. Looking harder, Agnes realised it was the anatomy lecturer she had encountered with Alexander. Polkoff, that was his name. She saw he was tracing the lettering of the board with his gloved fingers, following the writing over and over again, totally absorbed. Agnes tried to get closer, but then, as if suddenly aware that he was being watched, he set off at a brisk, nervous walk away from her, towards the hospital.

Agnes paused by the board he had been fingering. Under the architects' names she saw a list of all the subcontractors involved with the project: structural engineers, surveyors, builders. She read them all, hoping that some great meaning would take shape, but all she saw were names of companies. She shook out her hair. He was a strange man, that Polkoff. Perhaps sawing up dead bodies makes you that way, she thought, so that you go around searching for meaning in everyday objects. But then, she thought, scrunching her hair to dry it in the chilly breeze, who am I to talk?

Looking across at the hospital, she saw Polkoff, a tiny figure now, disappearing into the same basement door from where she and Julius had collected the coffin a week ago. She waited a moment, then strode across the courtyard and through the parking lot. The door was ajar, and she managed to ease it open and slip inside.

She found herself, once again, in the lowest levels of the hospital, where the concrete corridors themselves seemed to be steeped in the inevitability of death, and where the cold smooth floors were for the passage of corpses, not people. There was no sign of Polkoff, nor indeed of anyone else. Agnes set off aimlessly towards the mortuary, the only part of the basement which she knew. Here there were no bright signs to tell you where you were, only the lettering on doors indicating the laboratories and the names of the people who worked there. As she walked under a concrete archway, the gloss paintwork gave way to dark wood panelling, and she realised she must be in the old part of the hospital again. The doors were made of heavy oak, with ornate frames and polished brass signs. One said, 'Pathology museum. Not Open to the Public'. She tried the handle, and it opened.

She was in a wide, light space. Agnes looked up and saw that the daylight came from windows of cobbled glass in the ceiling, a long way up at street level. Above her there was a gallery, which was accessible by wrought-iron spiral staircases at each corner. She was aware that she was not alone, as she could see moving about among the exhibits the occasional youthful face and white coat of a medical student. Though what, she wondered, would they hope to learn from this grotesque array of abnormality. Parts of organs were carefully arranged in large jars of formaldehyde. Clean slices of lung or heart were displayed to demonstrate their pathology, their tumours, the thickening of muscles, the furring up of arteries. Browsing amongst the cases, Agnes thought of her grandmother's kitchen in Languedoc, where up on the top shelves, between sweet bouquets of marjoram and oregano, would be terrines made from the most recently slaughtered family pig. The young Agnes, secretly clambering over the smooth old wood in her Sunday best, would poke her finger into earthenware bowls and lick the salty pinkish jelly from it.

Agnes noticed a young woman sketching, perched on a tiny stool in front of an easel, on which was a half-finished representation of a skull. Passing her, Agnes found herself in the alcove occupied by specimens of foetal abnormality. Here, babies curled in their watery beds in postures of curious contentment, their waxy skin and clouded eyes the only indication that they had died long ago – or, in many cases, never lived, like the anencephalic with a sweet face but a flattened skull where his brain should have been, who would have died at birth the moment his mother ceased to keep him alive. Agnes was moved with pity for this little person, whose destiny it was to live for nine months and then to die, inevitably, both beginning and ending at once. She imagined him becoming an angel, a funny little cherub scooped up by God to take up a special place in Heaven. Looking around her, at these human forms suspended silently, eternally, in their twisted states, Agnes was reminded of the illustrations of monsters she had seen in medieval treatises. Perhaps, she mused, it's all the same; what we call disease, they call monstrosity.

'I thought it wouldn't be long until I found you here.' The voice made her jump. Alexander was smiling down at her. 'I can imagine this place is your type of thing. It's quite something, isn't it?'

'Y-yes.' He was wearing a pale linen jacket and looked, she had to admit, rather good in it.

'I love it here,' he went on. 'Come and see this,' he said, taking her arm as if it was the most natural thing in the world to do, and leading her to a row of jars containing unrecognisable bits of tissue. 'Look.'

Agnes looked in the direction he was pointing, at a small jar containing a yellowish, furry-looking lump. 'So?' she asked.

'Look closer,' he said.

She looked closer still, staring into the fibrous mass, noticing something that looked like . . . like a perfectly formed molar tooth. Alexander watched her. 'See?' he said.

'It seems to have teeth,' she said, levelly.

'And hair,' he went on. 'Look. It's a teratoma, a cyst. I always come to look at it.'

'So you like the side-show, do you?' she said.

He laughed. 'No, not a side-show. It's more like . . . I don't know . . . When I come here, it makes me feel more human. All this,' he said, indicating the museum with a sweep of his arm, 'is the essence of humanity. This is what we're running away from; yet this is, inevitably, what we are.'

'You mean, none of us is perfect.'

'That's a banal way of putting it, but yes. All this desperate attempt to classify the abnormal, just so we can distance ourselves from it—'

99

'Like the medieval monks who searched amongst what they called "the monstrous" for clues as to the nature of God's true creation – I know.'

He looked down at her. 'You would.' For a second, neither of them moved. Then he said, 'There's another thing you'd like. Eighteenth century rather than fifteenth, but just as potent.' He crossed the floor and began to climb a staircase. She followed him up the spiral steps, aware of the rhythmic swing of his legs ahead of her, of the lithe movement of his body. She arrived, breathless, at the top, and again he took her arm and led her to an alcove in which was a single display case. Inside were two figures, about eighteen inches high, one male, one female. They were perfect replicas of the human body – except they looked as if they'd been skinned alive. Every vein and artery was clearly represented, entwined around tiny webs of bone and muscle.

'Florentine,' Alexander said. 'Sculpted in wax. Priceless. They were used for teaching anatomy.'

'And still are?'

'Well,' he said, 'it's less necessary now. Now people can dissect real bodies. In those days, your Church wouldn't allow it.'

'My Church?' Agnes smiled. 'Well, maybe it was a good thing to respect the dead in that way, not to go chopping people up. Maybe it's something we've lost.'

'So you won't be leaving your body to science, then?'

'I certainly won't. Even if I die of something rare and exotic, I won't have them prodding me after I've gone.'

Alexander laughed. Once again their eyes met, then

both looked away and stood contemplating the anatomy figures again. 'Sometimes,' Alexander said quietly, 'they made the female ones with an abdomen you can open, and there'd be a tiny foetus inside.'

Agnes blinked. The image of Dr Halliday bending over Gail appeared suddenly, powerfully, before her eyes. Alexander was watching her. 'I know,' he said. 'Shocking to us, isn't it?'

'Perhaps it was shocking to them too,' said Agnes, shortly. 'The idea that women carry life has always been a source of anxiety – to men, anyway.'

Alexander was still looking at her closely. 'When I said I wanted to paint you,' he said, 'I meant it, you know.'

'Did you?' Agnes heard herself ask.

'Yes. I did.' She looked up at him. 'Would you agree?' he went on. 'I mean, are you allowed?'

'Allowed what?'

'Well, it wouldn't have to be nude,' he said.

'I should hope not,' she said, lightly. 'I thought your nude models were young, nubile—'

'Boring,' he said, with sudden passion, 'pretty faces for rich buyers. That's not what I meant for you at all. You interest me, it's been a long time since . . .' He looked down at the old polished floor. 'You see, you'd be different. It sounds crazy, but my mother – did I mention—?'

'You said she was ill.'

'She's dying. Cancer. And it's made me think about things, about my life, what it's all for . . . I know, it does sound mad.'

'No, no, not mad at all.'

'Well, I've been thinking about my work – you see, I love the portrait, I just know there's something I could do with it, only I'm not, because of the money, all that. But I thought, maybe, if I painted you, there's something about you—' He met her eyes again, then shook his head. 'I'm sorry, it's stupid, I can't imagine you'd . . . and it'd probably be crap anyway. I've no idea if I can do it. At college they said I was brilliant. It does no good, in the end.' He sighed, and rested his hand briefly on her arm. 'I'm sorry, ranting on like this.' He turned and set off down the stairs, across the central area of the museum and out of the door. Agnes stood there, blinking, then followed him quickly down the stairs, almost colliding with him as he stood uncertainly in the corridor outside.

She smiled at him. 'Look, if you're serious, about painting me . . .'

'You mean, you would? Sit for me?'

She looked up at him. 'Yes. Yes, I will.'

'It'll be a huge risk,' he said, still gazing at her. 'I mean, for me.'

Yes, she thought. A huge risk. I've done it again.

'I've done it again,' she wailed down the phone to Athena two hours later. 'I've said I'll sit for him.'

'My my, you do work fast. I mean, that would be pushing it a bit for me, even when I'm on form.'

'I just knew I had to; he suggested it and I just said yes.'

'That's usually how these things begin.'

'Not nude, he said.'

'Of course not.'

'And really, it's only because I need to find out—'

'Of course. Just research really.'

'And I could still say no. I'm going to visit his studio tomorrow.'

'Yes, of course, it might all seem like a bad idea tomorrow.'

'You don't sound convinced.'

'Darling, I'm about as convinced as you are.'

Agnes hung up, allowing her fingers to rest on the phone receiver. She felt terribly lonely. It was all very well for Athena to greet her news with barely disguised glee, but Athena always forgot one thing, one important, utterly central thing, which was that Agnes was a nun. Unavailable, set apart from relationships like – like whatever Athena was hinting at on the phone. Athena was a great friend, but she would never understand that Agnes did not behave with men the way that she, Athena, did.

She stared out of her window, at the silvery sky over the Thames beyond the tower blocks. She noticed that her windows hadn't been cleaned for months, and, fetching a cloth and cleaning fluid, began to scrub at them. It was the same old badness, she thought, the old badness that had never really left her, that reappeared from time to time, gnawing away, threatening all the composure and peace of mind she had fought for since leaving Hugo. 'If you can see it for what it is,' she imagined Julius saying, 'then you can fight it.' But Julius, she wanted to say, it's not that simple . . . Blinking back tears, she scrubbed furiously at the glass.

The next morning, she joined her community for the Sunday Mass. Sometimes she went to St Simeon's but, she knew if she saw Julius she'd only burst into tears, and she knew what he'd say, and she knew she wouldn't be able to follow his advice, because this afternoon she was due to visit Alexander at his studio in Battersea, and whatever Julius said, she would be there. Now, kneeling before the simple altar, as the priest prepared the communion, she wished her tradition was of the weeping, wailing and gnashing-of-teeth sort. It was the first of May, and sunlight glanced through the high windows, across the pale woodgrain of the pews. She heard the quiet chanting of the sisters – 'Lamb of God, you take away the sins of the world' – against the pounding of her own inner turmoil. 'Lamb of God,' she joined in, 'you take away the sins of the world,' whilst wondering how, in the face of the sacrifice of Christ, she could still have so little will of her own. As the priest called them to the altar rail, Agnes joined in the prayer with tears in her eyes. 'Lord, I am not worthy to receive you, but only say the word and I shall be healed.'

Afterwards, she determined to avoid the coffee and chatting, and was just slipping out of the door when she heard her name. It was Sister Madeleine, standing rather tentatively at the foot of the stairs. 'Agnes – are you OK?'

Agnes stood by the open door, one hand on the doorknob. She felt suddenly irritated that this woman, of all people, should presume to ask if she was all right. 'I'm fine,' she said. 'Got a lot on, that's all.' She turned to go. Madeleine said quietly, 'Julius is very unhappy.'

Agnes said, sharply, without turning round, 'I can't think why.'

'I was hoping you would know.' Agnes had started to descend the front steps, and Madeleine was now standing at the top. 'Can I walk with you a bit?'

'I can't stop you,' Agnes replied, setting off down the street.

Madeleine slammed the front door and hurried to catch up with her. 'He seems such a nice man.'

'He is.'

'Only, you've known him so long, I thought maybe—'

Agnes couldn't help herself. 'Will you shut up about bloody Julius,' she yelled, stopping short and facing her. She saw Madeleine's startled look, and thought, the poor woman's going to cry or something now. She should never have followed me.

But then she heard Madeleine say in a matter-of-fact voice, 'It's you that's wrong with him. And you know it. I wouldn't normally get involved, but I'm supposed to be working with you both, and it makes life rather difficult.'

Would nothing stop her? thought Agnes. 'Right, OK,' she said. 'Julius is sulking about me for very good reasons. Firstly, I'm insisting, on practically no evidence at all, that someone at St Hugh's intends very great harm to someone else, and I'm hanging around the place for days on end, neglecting my duties, even though I'm getting absolutely nowhere. Secondly, I've agreed to sit as a model for a man who wants to paint me, even though – and Julius would be the first to say this – he's about as much like my ex-husband as you could get. So, who can blame Julius for being well cheesed off?'

Madeleine said, 'Julius doesn't know about the painter, yet.'

'No.'

'So in fact, it's you who's pissed off with yourself about that one, isn't it?'

'It's bad enough being a nutcase without people you hardly know chipping in with pop psychology.' Agnes turned to go.

Madeleine said, quietly, 'Why does this painter want to paint you? I mean, why you? Lots of people have interesting faces.'

Agnes turned back and stared at her. 'Well, obviously . . .' she began, then stopped. The woman was right, she had never once asked herself that question. So great was her vanity that it had never once occurred to her to ask why Alexander had singled her out. She looked at Madeleine. Slowly, she began to smile. 'You're right,' she said at last. 'I'm a vain old ratbag.' She laughed. 'Thank you, Sister.'

Madeleine smiled back, hesitantly. 'Oh, um, good. I'm not quite sure what I've—'

'Don't you see – you've made me immune again. Set apart, like we're supposed to be.'

'Oh yes, that. Well I'm glad, if that's what I've done.'

Agnes looked at her with renewed interest. 'Look, I really must go. But – one of these days – soon – we must have a drink or something.' She touched her arm. 'Thanks again. And send Julius my love, really, I'll be in touch.'

She strode off towards the bus stop with a lightened step. 'But only say the word and I shall be healed,' she thought. My vanity blinded me. Now I can see how unlikely the whole thing is. Well, Alexander Jeffes, you're going to find it's not that simple.

Chapter Nine

The bell had the word 'Jeffes' neatly engraved underneath it. Agnes hadn't heard it ring, and was wondering whether to try again when a window opened above her and his voice yelled, 'Hang on, I'll be right down.' She took a deep breath and reminded herself that all was not as it seemed, a strangely comforting thought.

He was wearing a tie whose pattern was made up of brightly coloured teapots. She found this ridiculous, which helped too. His welcome, however, was effusive and sincere, and she followed him up the dank stairs of the warehouse building with a certain nervousness. 'Don't your clients mind?' she asked as they reached the top floor.

'Mind what?'

'The shabbiness – I mean, the cynical rich ones?'

'Oh, no, they love it. They think they're getting the real thing.' He laughed, and threw open a double door which let a flood of sunlight out on to the dim landing. 'Here we are,' he said, closing the doors behind them.

His studio occupied the whole upper floor of the building. Wide windows shed light into the space, which was roughly whitewashed and had swathes of white muslin hanging from huge rafters. In one corner there was a couch covered in a dark pink quilt. A full length antique mirror stood beside it. Under one window there was a sink, its wooden draining boards stained with layers of paint. In the middle of the room, Alexander had placed two chairs either side of a low mahogany table, on which were plates of olives, cheeses, bread rolls and salad. 'Lunch,' he said, watching her reaction. She looked away from the table and surveyed the studio.

'It's a lovely space,' she said, 'but . . .'

'But what?'

'Well, it doesn't look as if – as if an artist works here.'

'That's because no art is done here.'

'You know what I mean. There's not a single canvas visible.'

'Are you surprised?' His voice was harsh. 'Do you think I want them all standing around peering at me? Do you think I like to be judged by the rubbish I produce?'

'But what do you show your clients?'

'Ah, well, then I get them out. Carefully picked according to my sales pitch. A sedate Gainsborough, I think, madam, so becoming. Just choose your style. A soft-focus Impressionist? Certainly, sir. Something like this, perhaps. A nude? Of course, sir. We understand each other, sir, you and I. I paint naked women, you pay me for them. It's all the same. But Art?' He laughed. 'No one comes here looking for Art.' He flung himself on to one of the little chairs, his long legs at awkward angles.

Agnes walked over to the window and gazed out of it.

'So you mean,' she began quietly, 'you know you're worth more than this.'

'So you keep saying,' he said, wearily.

'No. What I mean is, if all this suited you, you'd be quite happy. Painting naked women for good money. It's only because you want something else that you hate it so much. But that's just it, isn't it? At heart, you know you're off course.' She turned round to look at him. He grabbed a bottle of red wine that had been standing, opened, on the table, and sloshed some into a large glass.

'And what difference does that make, then, Pollyanna?' he said, taking a swig. 'I still need the money.'

'Yes. Well.' Agnes came away from the window. She sat down opposite him at the table. He poured some wine into another glass, and handed it to her. She noticed that all the dishes on the table were carefully arranged with sprigs of parsley here, coriander there, slices of lemon. She took a sip of wine. 'And how's the professor?' she asked.

'Oh, as usual. Pompous and deceitful.'

'The man or the portrait?'

'Both.' Alexander laughed, then raised his glass to her before draining it. He refilled it generously, then looked across at Agnes's glass and topped hers up too. 'Did you sort out that sudden death thingummy?'

'You mean Gail Sullivan?' Agnes looked at him hard, surprised by his question. 'The funeral was last week.'

'Right. He seemed rather put out by it.'

'The professor?'

'Mmm. Have some feta cheese, it goes well with the

111

olives.' Alexander took an olive stone from his mouth and went on, 'Funny for a medical man. I mean, to be so anxious about a death like that. It is a hospital, after all.' He smiled across at her.

'I suppose when it's one of the staff it's different,' she said carefully.

'Yeah. S'pose so.'

Agnes was aware that Alexander was staring at her. She carefully cut herself a slice of Brie.

'So are you serious, then?' he said suddenly.

'About what?'

'About me painting you.'

She looked up and met his eyes. 'Yes. Yes, I think so.'

'This may be speaking out of turn,' he went on, 'but one of the things that made me want to paint you – please don't misunderstand this – is because it would be painting a woman who's sexual but not sexual at the same time. I don't mean repressed, or anything, but sort of reined in. Unavailable. It would be safe.' He looked up at her. 'Do you see what I mean?'

She met his eyes levelly. 'Yes. Safe. Of course.'

By the time she left it was already getting dark. He had made coffee, and they'd talked about painting, their likes and dislikes, about an obscure painting in one neglected corner of the Louvre, a Dutch portrait of an elderly beggar woman which, it turned out, they'd both discovered for themselves and come to love. Later, Alexander had offered her a lift home, but she'd refused, looking forward to a long walk beside the river. At his door he'd said, 'We could start tomorrow evening. If you like. Eight o'clock?' and she had nodded, aware that he was offering her his hand in a formal way.

Now, as she paused to look at the grand old towers of Battersea power station, she thought about that shaking of hands there on Alexander's doorstep. It had been a gesture of evasion, she thought, of pretence. Twilight clouds scudded across the muddy sky. She set off again, past the wharves of the fruit and flower market at Nine Elms, seeing Big Ben lit up across the river, hearing, as she reached Blackfriars Bridge, the bells of the City churches chime in echoing waves, calling the straggling faithful to evensong.

She let herself into her flat, exhausted. The muzziness induced by Alexander's wine had gone, leaving a mild headache. She lay on her bed, thinking about his comments regarding Gail's death. So he, too, had noticed the professor's reaction. But why should he mention it like that, so deliberately? And this urge to paint her, it still didn't seem quite right. She remembered what he'd said about his mother dying. Had he been telling the truth? Usually she could tell if someone was lying: years of living with Hugo had given her practice. But Alexander seemed to be hiding behind a mask, and she couldn't yet tell where the mask ended and the real man began.

She wasn't aware of falling asleep, but when she next looked at her clock it said five past two. She undressed in the dark, glancing in the mirror at the outlines of her body silhouetted by the street lamp outside. She wondered what Alexander saw when he looked at her, at this body. She put on the light in the bathroom to brush her teeth, suddenly glad that they, at least, were ageing so well. She looked at her lips, regretting having thrown out all her make-up a few months ago in a fit of repentance, and wondered whether Athena would be free that day to go shopping. She looked at herself again. Perhaps Alexander didn't want her in make-up. She shivered, turned out the light, and went to bed.

When she woke up the next morning, her first thought was, this evening I'm going to sit for a portrait. It seemed so unlikely it made her smile. She thought about the last time she had sat to be painted, in Paris, as an eighteenth birthday present from her mother. When, soon afterwards, she'd married Hugo, he had insisted on hanging the painting in the elegant hallway of their Paris home. Until he'd grown tired of it. She got up and made coffee, wondering where that painting was now.

The weather was grey and drizzly, but she felt cheerful. She began to think that, perhaps, there was no reason to fear wrongdoing at the hospital. Perhaps it had all been tied up in her mind with Alexander, and that in a few days' time she could join Julius and Madeleine on the runaways project again. She picked up Mark's computer print-out. Just match up these names, she thought, check that there really was no ill intent in placing penicillin in Gail's cupboard – maybe see if the cupboard can be opened too, and then no doubt I'll realise that it was just a mistake, and that Gail in her anguish grabbed the wrong bottle of pills.

She strode off to the hospital, as sunlight broke through the clouds. She went straight to Gail's office, which was still unoccupied, and picked up a copy of the internal phone directory. Then, with the pharmacy print-out next to her, she went through all the names listed alphabetically under 'medical school'. After about an hour she had isolated a list of eight names from the teaching staff who had received prescriptions around the time of Gail's death; all of whose drugs might have been placed in Gail's cupboard. She wrote them down. 'Drewett, Graham. McPherson, Parry, Polkoff' – him again, she thought – 'Patel, Thompson and Wright.' She ran her hands through her hair. I could be looking at the name of someone who is in grave danger, she thought. On the other hand, she thought, getting up to go to the drinks machine, I could be looking at the names of eight people who happened to get drugs from the pharmacy then. She hesitated, then tried the door to Gail's little cupboard. It was locked.

The next thing, she thought, standing by the machine and sipping her coffee, was to check what was actually prescribed for each of these people. She finished her drink and walked purposefully along the corridor towards the hospital. As she drew near to Professor Burgess's door, she saw Alexander come out of it and start off ahead of her in the same direction. She was about to call him, but at that moment he bolted into an open doorway. She hesitated. A man was walking towards them. His face was familiar. He walked past the doorway where Alexander was hiding, and as he passed Agnes she recognised him as the man who had come into Gail's office when she was pretending to work there and who had tried to open the cupboard door. A few moments later Alexander emerged slowly from the doorway and proceeded on his way, not noticing Agnes who dawdled some way behind him. He went to the staircase and started down the stairs; she turned to the left and went on her way to the pharmacy.

The dispensing window was open, but she knocked on the door next to it. A young woman in a white coat opened the door.

'Hello, I'm Sister Agnes, I'm visiting some patients here, and there's been a muddle about one of my ladies' drugs,' she heard herself burble. 'The nurse gave me this,' she went on, waving the print-out vaguely, 'and said I could check it against your records.'

'I can't dispense anything to you,' the young woman replied.

'No, no, I just wondered whether you'd have kept a record.'

'Oh. Well, we have a book here. I suppose you can look at it.' The woman ushered Agnes in and led her to a huge book which lay open on a desk, then left her to attend to someone at the window. Agnes saw that the book listed in columns all the drugs dispensed, the date, and who had collected them. She flicked back a few pages to Monday 18 April, the day before Gail's death. There was one of the names, Dr Anthony Wright, insulin retard, 10 units per ml., and beside it, the signature, Gail Sullivan, in neat biro. She ran her eyes down the columns to look for Gail's signature again. Dr Bob Graham, 250mg of tetracycline, 14 April. Dr Mary Drewett, 15 April. And there it was: 100mg of Amytal, Gail Sullivan, with her own signature beside it. A few names down she saw Dr T McPherson, penicillin, 250mg. The signature next to it wasn't Gail's, but something illegible beginning with P, or B, thought Agnes, screwing up her eyes at it. She noticed the same signature over the page, next to a prescription for Miss Amber Parry, Nifedipine, 10mg three times per day.

'OK?' said the pharmacist, coming over to her.

'Yes,' said Agnes. 'Can you tell me who this is?' she said, pointing to the illegible signature. The young woman peered at it.

'Um – no. B – something? You see, I don't get to see them all, as long as they're authorised and sign the book.'

'No, of course. Well, thank you for your help.' Agnes was about to ask for a list of authorised people, but thought better of it. It was crucial at this stage, she thought as she walked from the pharmacy, not to attract any suspicion at all.

She thought again of the list of names, and felt a sudden fear that one of those people might really be about to die. The idea was unbearable. Now look, she told herself, all I know is that someone called McPherson was prescribed penicillin at the same time that Gail took some by mistake. And that someone else picked it up, as they also picked up some drugs for this Miss Parry on the same day. It still does not amount to anything.

She turned suddenly and went back to the pharmacy, knocked on the same door, said to the same girl, 'I'm sorry to bother you again, there was one other thing. There's a locked cupboard over in Pharmacology. I believe it may still have drugs in it, after Gail Sullivan's death . . .'

The woman looked at her blankly for a moment then said, 'Oh yes. We never thought. Only Gail had the key over there. Hang on.' She had a word with a man who was measuring tablets into a bottle, and then, picking up an empty cardboard box, said to Agnes, 'I'll come over with you.'

They walked together along the corridor. Agnes said, 'Do people collect their own drugs, then?'

'What do you mean?'

'I mean, is it normal for the academic staff to sign out drugs for each other?'

'Only if they're authorised. People's secretaries can, if they're repeat prescriptions. As long as we know who they are. But mostly Gail did it.'

'One other question – might any drugs be wrongly labelled?'

The pharmacist looked at her briefly, then shook her head. 'I doubt it. There's a procedure, bottling and labelling. There'd be no reason for it . . . You might put the wrong amount, maybe, if you were really tired, but not the wrong drug.'

They arrived at Gail Sullivan's office, and the pharmacist produced a key and undid the padlock on the cupboard. It looked to Agnes as if it had been untouched since Gail's death. Several bottles of tablets stood in a neat row, with a gap just to one side. Agnes reached for the bottle of pills next to the gap. 'Amytal, 100mg' said the label. 'Gail Sullivan'. Behind it were some painkillers, a bottle of white chalky liquid, and a box containing doses of insulin. Agnes placed everything carefully on a desk, wishing she could fingerprint the lot.

'Dr Wright's insulin is here,' said the young woman. 'I guess he came and got some from us that day.' She looked at the Amytal bottle quizzically. 'S'pose she had sleeping problems,' she said. 'We'll junk this.' She arranged everything in her box. 'Thanks for reminding us,' she said to Agnes. 'We're so short-staffed, this lot could have sat here for months.'

After she had gone, Agnes stared at the empty cupboard. It made her fingers itch to think of the clues it might contain, if only she knew how to get at them. She looked around the room, then left, heading vaguely towards Professor Burgess's office. As she passed it, she saw through the open door the easel and canvas of the portrait and, checking the room was empty, she went in. The portrait was in the form of broad, sweeping brushstrokes, almost abstract. A little detail was sketched in: the lines of the forehead and chin, the angles of the desk. There was a gap by the figure's hands, as if he might be holding something.

Agnes heard footsteps behind her and turned. 'I was just,' she said, seeing it was Mrs Holtby, 'admiring the portrait.'

'It's taking shape, isn't it?'

'Mmm.'

'It will be a tribute to him,' Mrs Holtby went on, stroking the edge of the canvas with a fingertip. 'They don't all get them, you know. Usually only deans these days. We'll miss him,' she went on, her finger tracing the edge of the professor's neck.

'When they chose Alexander Jeffes—' Agnes began.

'Oh, we were lucky to get him,' Mrs Holtby replied. 'Many many artists applied, you know.'

'Famous ones?'

'Well, I doubt you'll have heard of them.'

'It's just our Order is thinking of commissioning a portrait,' lied Agnes.

'I can show you the shortlist if you like.'

'Would you? That would be so helpful for us,' Agnes gushed.

They went into Mrs Holtby's office and she produced a sheet of paper from a file and photocopied it, her every tiny movement carried out with exact precision. She handed it to Agnes. 'There you are, dear. Although, if you choose Alexander, as I'm sure you will, you'll have to wait.'

That evening she changed her outfit three times, increasingly annoyed with Alexander for not giving her an idea of what he wanted her to wear. On the way home from the hospital she had popped into a chemist and bought a lipstick. Just in case, she thought, putting it into her bag with a hairbrush. She had finally settled on the green silk shirt with black trousers when the phone rang.

'Madeleine gave me your love,' said Julius. She could hear the smile in his voice.

'Julius, how lovely to hear you. I had a good talk with her.'

'Yes, she said.'

'She didn't tell you about—' If Madeleine had mentioned Alexander, Agnes was suddenly prepared to be very angry.

'She didn't tell me anything at all, Agnes. She just said you had a chat.'

'Good,' said Agnes, sisterly loyalty intact.

'And what was it you didn't want her to tell me?'

Agnes laughed. 'Oh, Julius. Only that – if you must know – oh dear, it sounds terrible . . .'

'What does?'

'Well, I've agreed to sit for a painter.'

'Still Life with Grapes?'

'Don't be silly. And not nude. Just a portrait. Of me.'

'Uh-huh.'

'What do you mean, uh-huh?'

'I thought it would be something like that.'

'Like what?'

'Like that.'

'You're impossible.'

'Not half as bad as you. Look, you will survive all this, won't you? And come back to us? Only, I keep thinking about Gail—'

'She'll be all right. Dr Halliday's looking after her. And really, I think I'm on to something. I'll pop in tomorrow morning, if you like. Will you be there?'

'Of course. You know me. Always there.'

Chapter Ten

'So what happened then?' Athena asked the next morning, leaning forward on Jonathan's deep sofa and pouring coffee into two mugs.

'What do you mean "then"? That's all there is.'

'All you've said so far is that he did some sketches of you and then you went home.'

'That's all there is. And I'm going back tomorrow.'

'But what was he like? Is he really really creative and artistic, and what was his studio like, and what did you wear?'

'I wore my green silk shirt.'

Athena nodded. 'Good choice.'

'And as to what he's like . . . I don't know. I don't trust him, that's certain. He's play-acting.'

'You mean he's not a painter?'

'Oh, no, he's definitely a painter. He was very absorbed in his work last night, that was honest enough. It's everything else: the hospital, the dying mother . . . I'm not sure about him.'

'And is he really good-looking then?'

'What?'

'Well, you obviously think so.'

'I think nothing of the sort.'

'Sure. But if you were the sort of woman who found men attractive, just occasionally, what would you think?'

Agnes laughed. 'Yes. If I were that sort of woman, then I would have to say, he's very good-looking.'

'And so when you were leaving – what time did you leave?'

'About eleven, I suppose.'

'And—'

'And what?'

'A frisson? On the doorstep, perhaps, as you were leaving?'

'Really, Athena. I can't think what you mean.'

'Yes you can.'

'Well, nothing happened. Of course. Nothing can. Can it?'

'How disappointing.'

'For you, maybe,' Agnes said.

'No, for you. Look at you.'

Agnes took a bite of croissant. 'So I look disappointed, do I?'

Athena eyed her friend closely. 'Hmmm. Dunno.'

'I must get going. I told Julius I'd visit him this morning. Oh, and while I think of it, could you ask Jonathan to look at this – it's the shortlist of painters who went for the St Hugh's commission. I'd be interested to know if he's heard of any of them.'

'Sure. If I see him.'

'Now, that looks like disappointment.'

'What does?'

'That expression you just had then.'

'That one, like this?'

Agnes giggled. 'No, really.'

Athena took a sip of cold coffee. 'Not disappointment, poppet. I'm too old for that. Just – oh, I don't know.' She sighed. 'Just remembering, all over again, that men are very strange creatures. Barely human, really.'

'I wouldn't know, of course.'

'No, of course you wouldn't. Lucky old you.'

Half an hour later, Agnes stood by the side door of St Simeon's, her hand poised by the bell marked 'Fr Julius'. Disappointed, she thought. No, of course I'm not. She smoothed her raincoat and checked that her collar was straight. Then she rang the bell.

'You've got keys,' Julius said, as he opened the door.

'It didn't seem quite—'

'Oh, nonsense, you always belong here.'

'You're very good to me, you know,' she said, following him into the little office.

'It's entirely selfish,' he grinned, gesturing to a chair. 'For the odd day or so that you put in at the project, you're a very effective worker. And you have enormous spiritual resources and a good brain . . .'

'I know. My brilliant analytical mind,' she smiled.

'Did I say that?'

'You know you did. About half a century ago.'

'You're not that old. Now me, I am.' He smiled. 'Anyway, I hate to see it all go to waste.'

'It isn't being wasted. It takes a brilliant mind to fathom out the current happenings at St Hugh's.'

'Hmmm. Agnes,' Julius was suddenly serious. 'What are we going to do about Gail Sullivan?'

'We are going to bury her as soon as possible.'

'And how soon is that?'

'Oh, Julius, I wish I knew. It's all so odd. Gail knew a lot about drugs, she put some aside for herself in a cupboard to which only she was supposed to have access, then took a load of an entirely different drug to which she happened to be allergic.'

'So?'

'Don't you see, Julius? She obviously was so completely sure that nothing in that cupboard had changed she didn't even bother to check the bottle. She picked up the one she expected to see, the one she'd put there.'

'She was upset.'

'But she was a pharmacist, well, sort of. And anyway, then Professor Burgess tries to cover it up, does the post mortem, on his own, with no technicians as far as I can see, and writes a pack of lies about the body – it's all so odd.'

'Maybe the professor didn't want one of his best students upset by police investigations so near exams. It seems fair enough.'

'To lie about the causes of death? It's against the law. The coroner will have been given a false certificate.'

Julius began to tidy a stack of books on his desk.

'The thing is,' Agnes went on, 'I think the penicillin was intended for someone else. And Burgess and Co.

didn't want the circumstances of Gail's death investigated because they intended to harm someone themselves.'

'With penicillin?'

'You know what it did to Gail.'

'But she was allergic to it,' Julius said impatiently.

'Other people might be allergic to it too.'

'But they'd know, wouldn't they, Agnes?' Julius stopped tidying the books. 'You can't force someone to take something that's going to kill them just by leaving it secretly in a cupboard. Can you?'

'No.' Agnes looked at the floor.

'What worries me in all this,' Julius said, more gently, 'is – is the way you're telling stories. Embellishing what is, in the end, just the strangeness of everyday life, with all sorts of extra meanings; seeing secrecy and deception when it's just people going about their business. It's not right, it's not – how can I say this – it's not how God wishes us to be, Agnes.'

'In what sense is it not how God wishes us to be?' Agnes said through tight lips.

'Firstly, it's uncharitable.' Julius spoke fluently, as if he'd rehearsed his words. 'In that you're seeing evil in people that isn't there. Secondly, it's one of the ways we become deaf to God, isn't it? Making things up, telling ourselves little stories the whole time to fill the silence. Because if we allowed the silence in, we'd realise how insignificant we really are.' He looked at Agnes, who was staring at the floor again. 'You know what I mean, we've talked about all this loads of times.'

'When we were friends,' Agnes said very softly.

'Oh, now look, come on . . .'

Agnes looked up at him. 'Bury Gail. Go on. You're right, it's only a story.' Her eyes filled with tears. 'It's just my wilfulness, my overblown sense of my own importance that's leading me to hang around the hospital in the hope that something will turn up to make me look very clever. No, you're right, Julius,' she sighed, getting up. 'From now on I'll listen to the silence and let whatever lies in store unfold without acting in any way to change it.' She looked absently for her coat, then realised she was still wearing it. She walked over to the door. 'But Julius, ask yourself, what is the will of God? I mean, just suppose – ' she paused, her hand on the door – 'just suppose that, by telling a story, we could prevent something really bad happening. Something real, I mean. Who knows?' She opened the door.

'Agnes . . .' Julius began, but she appeared not to hear him.

'Bury her, if you want,' she said, her voice flat. 'Do what you think is best.' Julius heard the outer door slam a moment later. He buried his head in his hands.

She walked blindly towards London Bridge, her face fixed in a mask of anguish, oblivious to the bright sun which made the Thames sparkle between the dingy buildings in flashes of uncharacteristic blue. We didn't even mention Alexander, she thought. But then, we didn't need to. 'Bloody Julius,' she thought, and realised she had spoken his name out loud.

She walked into the hospital and straight up to

Kathleen's ward. She was relieved to see Kathleen sitting up in bed looking genial, and she flopped into the chair next to her.

Kathleen looked at her hard. 'Tough?' she said.

Agnes nodded.

'Men?' Kathleen said, and cackled loudly.

Agnes smiled in spite of herself. 'Sort of.'

'Ah.' Kathleen nodded and patted her arm.

'It's being misunderstood,' Agnes went on miserably. 'Trying to explain something . . .' Her voice trailed off. 'But who am I to talk, eh?' she went on after a moment.

Kathleen patted her arm again. A cheerful young nurse passed the bed. 'She's doing well, isn't she?' she remarked to Agnes. 'We never thought she'd get her speech back so well.'

'It's a question of how much you have to say,' Agnes said, looking at Kathleen. They both grinned. When the nurse was out of earshot, Agnes said, 'Seen anything recently?'

Kathleen said, 'Praps. Odd thing. Lady in – lady out there,' she gestured to the corridor. 'Shouting. Loud, loud.' She leant towards Agnes and whispered, 'Bodies.'

'A lady in the corridor was shouting about bodies?' Kathleen nodded. 'Was she a patient?' Kathleen shook her head. 'A doctor? One of the teaching staff?' Kathleen nodded. 'Staff,' she said. 'Nice dress.'

'When was this?'

'Yyesst.'

'Yesterday?'

Kathleen nodded, then looked up as the lunch trolley

appeared. She looked back at Agnes. 'Muck,' she said loudly.

Agnes left her tucking into fish and mashed potato feeling suddenly hungry. She wandered back to the medical school. All I need, she thought, is proof that that penicillin prescription was intended for someone who was allergic to it. She remembered the name T. McPherson. The strange scrawl next to it, the person who had picked it up instead of Gail – and hidden it, somehow, in her cupboard. She wished she knew what had become of the bottle Gail had taken by mistake. Still, she thought, if I can get to this McPherson's records . . . She stopped and sighed. She hadn't even seen Gail's records; how was she to get hold of anyone else's?

She stood in the queue in the canteen. If I can give Julius just one firm piece of evidence, she thought. Just one.

'Hello.' It was Julia, looking friendly.

'Oh, hello. How's the revision?'

Julia made a face. 'I'm on the wards like a mad thing at the moment, talking crazily to patients about their symptoms. It's for the viva, practice. The patients are amazingly nice about it.'

They gathered cutlery and sat down. 'Still,' Julia said, 'it takes my mind off things.'

'What things?'

'Have you seen anything of Mark recently?'

'I went for a swim with him on Saturday.'

'Did you?' Julia raised an eyebrow, ate a forkful of

salad, then said, 'How did he seem?'

'Fine. Preoccupied, like all you final year people. But OK.'

'Oh. Did he ask about me?'

Agnes smiled. 'No, but why should he? Maybe he's asking your friends?'

'Yeah. Only, it's difficult to talk about with them. Don't know why. You see, Alexander . . .' She sighed. 'I've had it with him. I'm going to call off the painting.'

'Oh?'

'I mean, he must fancy me, really he must.' Julia said heatedly. 'He's seen me take my clothes off, he's had to stare at me naked for hours at a time – but when I actually, you know, suggest that we might – I mean, he is gorgeous, isn't he, only of course you don't notice these things, but he is. So why he doesn't want to – do you think he's gay?'

'I've no—'

'He mentioned a girlfriend once, I'm sure he did. And the way he looks at you when he's painting you – you have no idea. And I can't tell my friends because they disapprove of him. The idea that I might have wanted to go to bed with him – and no one has ever turned me down in my life before.' Her voice was shrill with indignation.

'Perhaps he just wasn't worth it,' Agnes said gently.

'No.' She chewed on a lettuce leaf. 'But I'm glad I saw you. Because, I think there's something suspicious about him. All this professor stuff, the portrait and everything. They seem very – involved, somehow. One day when I was with him he delivered a parcel to the professor, and it was all very sort of hush-hush, like they didn't like me being there.'

'What was it?'

'I've no idea, one of those padded things. And then, after Gail's death, he kept asking me about it.'

'What did he say?'

'What was it like finding a corpse, that sort of thing. And he knows we do anatomy – he's studied it himself, you know, with Polkoff, he said. Ages ago.'

'Oh.'

'But to refuse me – and I was really straightforward about it, I just said, look, we obviously fancy each other, why not? And he agreed that we fancy each other.'

'So—'

'He just said he wasn't into casual sex.'

'That's – I mean, that's fair enough, isn't it?'

'It was an excuse.'

'Oh. When was this?'

'Late last night.'

'L-last night?'

'Yes. Why?'

'Oh, nothing,' Agnes said lightly. 'I imagined all you final years were in bed by ten.'

'Alexander never goes to bed before two. So I called round to the studio. I was sure he'd be pleased to see me, he's always said . . .' She sighed again. 'He could at least have tried to be polite. But he practically shooed me out of the door. Said he was working.'

'Perhaps he was.'

'No, he was just making excuses. Well, that's it. Never

again. Oh, I do hope Mark can forgive me.'

Agnes smiled. 'I have a feeling he's the forgiving type.'

Julia looked at her. 'It's funny, you're very easy to talk to about these things, you know? Perhaps, being a nun, you have a sort of detachment. It must be that.' She looked at her watch. 'I'd better go. I said I'd meet my friend Betsy at the reference library. Only, since Miss Parry was admitted yesterday—'

'Sorry?'

'Amber Parry,' she said, standing up. 'The archivist. She used to do the old library, but she had a funny turn, blood pressure or something. She's over in the wards. So they've reduced the opening hours, short-staffed. Such a nuisance at this time of all times.' She grinned breathlessly at Agnes. 'You've really cheered me up, you know. See you.'

Agnes left the canteen and went straight to the hospital pharmacy. She knocked on the door and was greeted by the same young woman. 'I just need to check your book again,' she said firmly.

'I really think the nurses could talk to us directly if there's a problem,' the girl sighed, returning to the dispensing counter.

Agnes flicked back to the week of Gail's death. The strange signature appeared by two prescriptions. T. McPherson, and Miss A. Parry. Nifedipine. She wondered whether Parry's was a repeat prescription, and turning back a month saw the same prescription, and the same scrawl next to it, alone in a sea of neat biro from Gail and the regular

133

nursing staff. B—P—? She wondered. Polkoff, she thought. It fitted the space, and wasn't that two fs at the end?

Walking home, she allowed herself to reflect on Julia's tale of woe. These young women, she thought, flinging themselves at lovers without a care. She found herself idly wondering whether, if she was young now – and not celibate, obviously – she'd do the same. Surely not, she thought. So undignified.

She let herself into her flat and poured a gin and tonic. As she twisted the ice cubes out of the tray, the image came into her mind of Alexander at dead of night, alone in his studio after she'd left him, working. Being visited by Julia. Rejecting her favours. The ice clinked into her glass and she held it up to the window, watching the cubes swirl and crack against the crystalline darts of light.

Chapter Eleven

At ten the next morning, the phone rang.

'It's not too early, is it sweetie? Only, Jonathan's seen your list, and he wants to talk to you. I'll put him on.'

'Hi, Agnes.'

'Hello, Jonathan. What do you think?'

'I think it's very odd. That shortlist, you know. Did they see everyone?'

'That's the impression I got.'

'I'm amazed, I have to say. Amazed. They could have had Rachel Sutherland? Or Edmund Bray? And they chose Jeffes? I thought maybe he'd been – rehabilitated, so I checked with a friend, but no. Jeffes is considered persona non grata or whatever the expression is. They must know nothing, these people.'

'They seem very pleased with themselves to have got him.'

'Inside job, then. That's what Doug said too. Masons or something, return favours, I don't know. Does this help?'

'Help? Yes. Yes, I suppose it does.'

'Good. Right, well. Call round sometime. Bye.'

Agnes replaced the receiver thoughtfully, then almost at once it rang again. The voice sounded muffled.

'Ag. Lady.' There was a scuffle, then a new, brisk voice came on.

'I'm very sorry. She insisted . . .' There was more scuffling, then the brisk voice said, 'It's Mrs McAleer, she insists on talking to you.'

'That's fine,' Agnes said. 'Perhaps you could put her on now.'

'But she can't. You won't understand a word she's saying. I don't know who you are, I just caught her on the phone.'

'Of course I'll understand her. And don't you think, perhaps, that she has as much right to make a phone call as you do?'

There was a brief pause, then Kathleen came on, her voice excited.

'Ag. Lady. Body lady. Here. Bed.'

'The lady who was talking about bodies is on your ward. Do you know her name?' asked Agnes, realising that she knew the answer.

'Amb, sometin'. Amb.'

'Amber Parry?'

'Yyess.' She was almost shouting.

'I'll be right there.'

Amber Parry was lying with her eyes closed in a bay which housed four beds, only one of which was occupied. She wore a neat floral nightdress with a lace collar, and her grey hair was combed and set. Agnes cleared her throat. The eyes flashed open, an odd, opaque grey in colour.

'I'm Sister Agnes. I'm sorry to bother you—'

'So I should think. This whole business . . . I don't need to be here, you know. When will they let me back?'

'As soon as they consider you well, I expect.'

'I believe they wish to keep me here. I don't know who you are, but I believe—' She stopped suddenly, and stared towards the door, then turned back to Agnes. 'You were saying,' she said, sweetly.

'I was saying,' said Agnes, thinking fast, 'that it's a terrible time of the academic year for you, of all people, to be out of action.'

'Indeed it is.'

'They've cut the opening hours of the old reference library, you know.'

'I'm not at all surprised. It's all very well, turning good old-fashioned librarians into so-called "Information technologists", but in the end, it's the students who suffer.'

'Mmm.' Agnes sat beside the bed.

'But it's not just the library, is it?' Amber Parry went on after a little pause. Agnes waited. 'I was employed here as the archivist. That was in 1972.' She turned towards the door, then back to Agnes. 'Ask them when they'll let me out, won't you, dear?' The conversation appeared to be at an end.

'So – so what actually happened?' Agnes asked. 'Your funny turn, I mean?'

'What do they call it? Hypertension. Highly strung, not that I am. They increased the dose, last month, my blood pressure was up, not surprisingly given the circumstances. All I had was a little dizziness, but next thing I know they've put me in here with no indication of when I can expect to be out again.'

'Um – what's been upsetting you?' asked Agnes cautiously.

Amber Parry looked towards the corridor then back to Agnes. 'Promise you won't tell?' Agnes nodded. 'I know things, you see. I keep the archives for the whole hospital, and the Pathology museum. Keeping the records, someone must do it.' She sighed, deeply. 'History, you see. People used to value it, when I first came here. A sense of the past.' Her eyes glazed over.

'But you found something out—'

'It's the new building, you see. It shouldn't be there. Oh, look! There he goes. Ask him, quick.'

'Sorry?'

'That man, there, in the corridor. Consultant. Tell him I want to know. Go on!'

'Want to know what?'

'When they'll let me out. Quick.'

Reluctantly, Agnes got up and followed a tall white-coated figure down the corridor, just in time to see him disappear through the double doors of the ward. She went back in to Amber Parry, who had closed her eyes again.

'Missed him, I'm afraid.'

'Pardon? Oh, it's you. I'm sleepy now. Thank you so much for coming.'

Agnes hesitated, looking down at the peaceful face. It had become impossible to resume the conversation. She glanced at Amber Parry's locker, on which were two cards, propped open. One said, 'Get well soon. Marjorie.' The other, Agnes was sure, was signed with the same illegible scrawl she had seen in the pharmacy book. She left quietly and went along to Kathleen's bed.

'Well?' the old lady looked up conspiratorially.

'Something's upsetting her, something about the new building. She wouldn't elaborate. Could you – could you befriend her?'

Kathleen tapped the side of her nose with a finger and nodded. Agnes giggled.

Standing by the lift, she decided it was time to find out who this T. McPherson was. Before he had a funny turn and was put on the wards too. There I go again, she thought.

The old reference library was no longer deserted. Students avoiding the squeeze and bustle of the new library took shelter amongst the comfortable old shelves here. Agnes went to the year books and found the university calendar for the London medical schools. There it was, St Hugh's. She flicked through the pages listing the different faculties, until she found, under Microbiology, McPherson. Tom. Born 1953. Professor. Graduate of St Andrews and Edinburgh.

This was not greatly helpful. She read on and found lists of lecturers, numbers of students, degree structure. She checked Anatomy and found Professor Stefan Polkoff. Parry, Amber, was listed as Archivist.

Agnes closed the book and replaced it on the shelves.

She wandered along the corridor, then turned and headed for Dawn Scott's office.

'Hello again.'

'Oh, it's you. Hello.'

'Where's the Microbiology department?'

'Ooh no, you won't find it here. It's moved to the new building. That's what I was saying.'

'But that's Genetics.'

'Same difference, innit?'

'So Professor Tom McPherson—'

'It's 'is train-set, innit? The new building. First lot of dosh pays for the new students' centre. Second lot comes through just as McPherson gets to be Dean. Next thing we know, it's genetics, innit? Clonin' 'orrible monsters, 'alf cow, 'alf baby.' She giggled. ''Alf tomato, prob'ly.'

'Did anybody – did anyone mind him becoming Dean?'

'Mind? Nah. They're all like the proverbial lemmings on a sinking ship, them. Off to the States, Germany, them places. You get more money there, don't yer?'

'And didn't Burgess mind when it was no longer a Surgery wing?'

Dawn shook her head. 'Not 'im. You see, Surgery got loads more space in this building instead, and anyway 'e's retiring. Nah, 'e were really pleased about it too.' Dawn settled back to her machine and began to type furiously. Agnes left her and headed for the new building. Crossing the courtyard, surveying the gleaming windows of the new development, she noticed where the new library and sports centre ended, and the Microbiology department began. She passed the board listing all the contractors, then went in through a shiny double door. The foyer was carpeted and led to a curvaceous reception area dotted with potted plants. There was no one about. Agnes checked the floor plan, and seeing 'Professor McPherson, First Floor', got into the lift. The corridor of the first floor was also carpeted and also deserted. She heard, distantly, a door slam. She walked along, checking doorways, past windows which were still crossed with stripes of sticky tape, twitching her nose at the smell of new paint, until she came to a door which said Professor T. McPherson. She took a deep breath and knocked. The voice from within sounded annoyed.

'Yes?'

She opened the door. There, sitting at his desk, was the man who had come into Gail's office – the man whom Alexander had ducked to avoid. He was well dressed, with an upright posture, a neat, sandy beard, and an expression on his face of grumpy impatience.

'Professor McPherson?' Agnes stuttered.

'Yes?'

'I'm sorry, I was looking for someone else,' she said hurriedly, then closed the door again and fled back to the lifts. Are you, by any chance, allergic to penicillin? she wanted to ask him. Might there be someone who wishes you dead?

'Hopeless, hopeless,' she muttered to herself, descending to the ground floor, striding back across the courtyard to the main entrance of the hospital. The new building rose up behind her like a ship, brand new and cast adrift, with only its captain on board.

141

* * *

That evening, Agnes laid out the green silk shirt and black trousers on her bed. She looked at them. If only, she thought, if only I was the sort of person who could just leave things alone. It was true, something odd was going on at St Hugh's, and it seemed to be connected with the new building. And maybe, someone was in danger. She shuddered at the thought that somewhere in the hospital, someone was intending to harm someone else. Why is it so, she thought, that God has created us with such capacity for evil? We are so frail, she thought. How great is our need for God's love. She knelt beside the bed, finding herself, not for the first time, overwhelmed with gratitude for the Order, with relief that she had found a place there. It was the only way of life she could imagine now, for her, the only possible way to make sense of the world. Life without faith, she thought. It was unthinkable.

And is it Thy will, she asked God, that I should go sniffing round the hospital in search of evil? And if so, what has that got to do with Alexander? She had a sudden, childlike wish for an answer directly from Heaven, a reverberating 'Yes' or 'No' from on high. Lord, protect me from myself, she prayed.

She got up, undressed, and went into the shower. Perhaps, she thought, I should just give it up, leave all these McPhersons and Polkoffs and Parrys to their own devices. She squeezed her favourite expensive shower gel into her palms and spread the fragrant lather over her body, hugging herself under the torrent of hot water. But if I did that, she thought, if I stopped now, wouldn't life be boring? The thought had materialised before she could prevent it, and immediately all its implications fanned out across her mind: that God's creation wasn't good enough for her; that in her mortal arrogance she assumed she could create a universe that was more exciting than the true one; that she was happier with her own illusory chattering than listening to God's silence . . . She turned off the tap sharply and stood in the cooling bathroom as the steam condensed on the mirror. She shivered. Julius was right, she thought. Julius is always bloody right.

Her skin was still soapy and cold to the touch. She turned the tap back on a trickle, just enough to rinse off the rest of the foam. The water was freezing cold but she made sure all trace of the shower gel was gone before she got out of the shower. Shivering, she dressed hurriedly, not noticing that her shirt was buttoned crookedly, and roughly towelled her hair, not even glancing in the mirror. She grabbed her coat and stomped off to the bus stop, her damp hair still sticking up at odd angles in the sharp evening breeze.

'Your shirt's crooked,' Alexander remarked.

'Is it?'

'Fancy a glass of wine?'

'No. Thank you.'

Alexander looked at her, then grinned. 'It's going to be a different painting tonight.'

'Is it?'

'I mean, you're in such a mood it'll change what I do.'

'Good.'

'Well, I'll just get on then.'

He changed the position of his easel just a fraction. 'I'm working on the canvas now,' he said brightly. 'So you can stay there.' He set out brushes, paints, materials, then stood and stared at the canvas for a while. He had arranged the sketches in a row on a trestle table next to him, and he leafed through them for a while. Then he looked at Agnes. 'You weren't slouching like that last time.'

'Wasn't I?' She pulled herself into a stiff, militaristic upright posture.

Alexander sighed. 'Look, would you rather not? Do this, I mean?'

'Would you?'

'Me? No, I'm keen on the idea. Very keen, in fact.'

'Fine. Let's get on with it.'

He made some careful marks on the canvas in pencil. The room was silent apart from his pencil and the occasional squeak of the soles of his shoes. Agnes, sitting fixedly, gazed out of one of the high windows. She could see part of the roof against the night sky, and beyond that the twinkling yellow haze of the urban sprawl.

'That shirt, really . . .'

She blinked. 'Sorry?'

'It's all wrong.' Agnes didn't move. 'You see . . .' She looked up as he came over to her. He stared down at her for a moment, then bent down and, starting at the bottom, began to rebutton her shirt. As he reached the middle button she put her hands on his and moved them away, then continued steadily to refasten it herself. She reached the top button.

'OK?' she said, meeting his eyes.

'No.' He leaned over her and undid the button she had just done up. 'It was like this last time,' he said, loosening her collar. A lock of his hair fell forward and brushed her cheek. They looked at each other, then Agnes turned away to stare out of the window again and Alexander went back to his easel, his shoes creaking noisily across the bare boards.

For a long time Agnes watched the sky grow darker, aware of Alexander absorbed in his work, of his glance alighting on her from time to time. After a while the angle at which she was holding her head made her feel dizzy, but she lacked the will to move, or even to complain.

'That's much better,' Alexander suddenly said, breaking the silence after what seemed like hours. 'You've softened again.'

She remained silent, fixed. He looked at her. 'Or perhaps not,' he added, mixing paint on a palette, dabbling his brush. Outside a scruffy pigeon swaggered along the edge of the roof. Agnes wondered whether these urban birds, after generations of city life, now kept the city's unnatural hours.

It seemed much later when Alexander said, 'I think that'll do for now.' She blinked, stretched her shoulders, gradually turned round, one hand on her neck where it had become stiff. The room swam and she gripped the back of her chair.

'You OK?'

'Y-yes.'

'I kept you sitting too long.'

'No, it's fine.'

'What were you thinking about?'

'Nothing.'

'Yes. That's what it looked like.'

She tried to stand up, but was so dizzy she sat down heavily again.

'You should have told me,' Alexander said, concerned.

'I'm fine, really. What time is it?'

'Quarter to ten.'

'Is that all?'

'Would you like a cup of tea? Coffee?'

'Yes. Yes, I would. Thanks. Tea.' She sat and rubbed her neck, then walked shakily over to the couch and settled down there, propping her head on some cushions. She closed her eyes, listening to the noises of water running, kettle coming to the boil, Alexander tinkering with tea things. Perhaps I should go home, she thought. She heard his shoes, and opened her eyes to see him standing over her. She smiled at him.

He said, 'Why were you so fed up when you arrived?'

'Oh . . .' she sighed. 'It's hard to explain.'

'Spiritual doubts?' he asked, sitting next to her.

'Something like that.'

'About me?'

She hesitated. 'Not directly, no. Or perhaps . . .'

He got up and went to make the tea. 'When we embarked on this,' he began, his back to her, 'I thought it would be difficult. This kind of painting, I mean. But in fact, it feels very – it feels right. It's strange, really,' he added, picking up two mugs and bringing them across to her, 'but I seem to be able to see you. In a way I haven't allowed myself for years.' He handed her her tea. 'Look,' he said, going over to his painting. She got up and followed him. She saw a rough outline of a figure marked out in wide sweeps of pink and grey, with flashes of white where the light fell. It was androgynous, faceless, all detail missing.

'See?' he said. 'This movement here, across your shoulders, the long back, the energy that flows to your face from here . . .' He stopped and looked at her. 'That's what I mean.'

He led her back to the couch and they sat side by side and sipped their tea. 'It won't be empty like the Rokeby Venus,' he said suddenly. 'Did I tell you about that? It's all off now, anyway.' He grinned, sheepishly. 'I'm glad, actually. If I'm doing this – ' he gestured with a nod of his head to the canvas of Agnes '– I can't do both. Heaven knows what's going to become of old Burgess once I give myself licence to paint what I see again.'

Agnes smiled and rubbed her neck. 'I'd better be going now,' she said. She put down her mug and went to get her coat, which was thrown over a chair. On the table next to it was a pile of invoices. On the top was a neatly printed card which said: 'Stefan Polkoff. At Home. Friday 6 May. Drinks from 8 p.m.', followed by his address which was in the fashionable end of Hackney. Underneath she saw the same scrawl that she'd seen in the pharmacy book and on Amber's Get Well card. Agnes could just make out the words, 'Alex – can you come? Stefan.'

She looked up to see Alexander holding her coat for her. 'You can come with me if you like,' he said.

'Where?'

'To Stefan's do. I could do with a companion there, some of his friends are very dull.' She hesitated, looking at her coat held taut in his grip, then slowly turned and allowed him to put it on her.

'OK,' she heard herself say.

'I'll come and pick you up, if you tell me where you live. Southwark, isn't it? It's on my way.'

She found herself scribbling her address on the piece of paper he offered her. He looked at it and smiled. 'Fine. See you Friday, then. Just before nine? We don't want to be early, do we? And we can arrange our next sitting then.'

She walked out into the night, having refused his offer of a lift, assuring him she'd take a cab, but now relieved to be outside, to feel the cold wind against her face, to breathe in the damp air. She walked fast, wondering if there'd be a bus. A police car, sirens blaring, shot past her and she jumped. In its wake the night quietened. She felt lost, as if some force had picked her up from the path she knew and placed her on some completely unfamiliar one. The hand of God? she wondered, imagining briefly a huge gold-plated plaster-cast emerging from the clouds and moving people about. But what would God want with all this? she thought, wondering why she'd agreed to go to a party with Alexander on Friday. Far more likely, she thought, pausing at a bus stop, that God's path is marked out clearly ahead and it's me who's deliberately wandered off into the undergrowth.

She saw a bus approaching, its headlights flickering against the deserted street, its windows bright and misted up. She joined the odd assortment of late-night passengers with an almost audible sigh of relief.

Chapter Twelve

If Julius, next morning, was surprised to see Agnes already at her desk, he didn't show it. He paused in the doorway of their little office, then smiled.

'How nice to see you,' he said, going over to the kettle. Julius's coffee, thought Agnes. Yet another reason to be glad to be here.

'These two boys from East Anglia,' she said, looking up from some papers, 'who've been in the hostel since last Thursday – do we negotiate with their Social Services Department for their return?'

'Well, Madeleine was going to . . .' Julius checked himself. 'Yes, we need to phone Norwich and sort it out with them. Thanks.' He put Agnes's cup of coffee down next to her, his hand resting briefly on her shoulder. The old routine, thought Agnes. I think I'll stay here for ever.

At eleven o'clock, Madeleine sauntered in.

'Hi, Julius . . . Oh, Agnes, hi.'

'Weren't you on the overnight?' Julius asked.

'Yup, quiet night. I slept from four till nine.' She went over to the kettle and made a cup of herbal tea, then sat at her place. Agnes noticed that Julius had squeezed a third desk into the corner of the room. Madeleine sipped her tea and snatched a glance at Agnes, then at Julius. 'Um,' she said, 'that kid from Sheffield. Got a court appearance for shoplifting, I said I'd go with him. Two o'clock.'

'Fine,' Julius said. Agnes noticed he, too, was drinking herb tea, something she'd never known him do. The strong Arabica coffee, whose scent had filled the room, had been made specially for her.

The rest of the morning passed companionably, with phone calls, typing, the odd conversation. At noon, Julius prepared to go out to do some photocopying. In the doorway he paused. 'Agnes – can I put you down for the overnight shift tomorrow? There's a gap on the rota.'

Agnes stared at her fingertips. 'Is there any other time?' She looked up at him, uncertainly. 'It's just – there's a party I've got to go to . . .'

Julius's lips were a thin line. 'Fine. Some other time then,' he said. Agnes watched the door close slowly behind him, then buried her head in her hands, listening to the clacking of Madeleine's typewriter, which slowed down and then stopped. She heard Madeleine say, 'Do you fancy a drink?'

The wine bar was situated in a renovated warehouse on the High Street, and was full of breezy young men in City shirts and braces. Agnes, sitting at a table by the window, smiled as she watched Madeleine jostle at the bar in her short hair, huge earrings and Doc Martens. Eventually she struggled over with two glasses of white wine.

'There,' she said. 'Well?'

'Well . . .' Agnes sighed. 'It's all such a mess, and Julius'll never believe me. I mean, any other shift I could do.'

'Tell him, then.'

'I will.' Agnes sipped her wine. 'It's not just that, though, is it? He's hoping I'll drop all this business at the hospital, and I just can't.'

'What's happening?'

'It's all very odd. There's a man who's become dean and has somehow raised a lot of funding for his own subject—'

'Making lots of enemies?'

'Well, apparently not. Apart from one woman who says dark things about his new building. And then she's had what they're all calling a funny turn – and mysterious prescriptions have been taken out for people.'

'Including her?'

'Yes. Including her.'

'Well, I'm convinced.' Madeleine gulped some wine. 'Why can't you tell Julius all that?'

'Because Julius knows me too well.'

'You two talk in riddles about each other, you know? And anyway,' Madeleine went on, taking another swig, 'what about the painter?'

'Oh. The painter. Yes. Aren't you drinking rather fast?'

'I've got to be in court in forty minutes and it's in Westminster. So, is he still painting you?'

'Yes.'

'And is it OK?'

'Not really.'

'I see. It's his party tomorrow?'

'A friend of his.'

'A suspect?'

'Oh, they're all bloody suspects. You see,' Agnes, said, putting her glass down, 'I came back to work today because I wanted normal life again. But I can't escape, can I? I can't just drop it.'

Madeleine fished a court paper out of her pocket and checked the address. 'But Julius must know that.'

'Doesn't mean he likes it.'

'No. Why don't you do the day shift tomorrow? I'll swap with you.'

'Can I? Thanks.'

Agnes was relieved to be away from the hospital all day Friday. Daniel, one of the hostel team, greeted her as if she'd never been away, and she was soon supervising a noisy breakfast for four kids aged between twelve and fifteen, all of whom had run away, all of whom were brazening out their worry as they waited to hear their fate, hoping that their muttered pleas for rescue had been heard.

She stayed at the hostel in time to fix a supper for the kids, as Friday was one of the days when the local supermarket donated all the food that had passed its sell-by date.

''Ere, Miss, what's these then, these fings off of the beach?'

'Not "Miss", my name's Agnes. And that's moules marinière.'

'Agniz. Funny name. Mool what?'

'Eeegh, looks like bleedin' slugs. You ain't gonna eat them, are you, Mick?'

'Miss—'

'Agnes.'

'Oi, Agniz, Rachel's 'ad two banana trifles already, she's just nicked another . . .'

Two hours later she arrived home exhausted but glad. Glad to have made contact with the hostel again, glad to have put a distance between herself and St Hugh's. Glad for Madeleine's support, she realised. It wasn't all a figment of her imagination.

She wondered what to wear. She was only going to Polkoff's on business, after all; it was important to blend into the background. Nothing fancy then. She chose a grey pleated skirt and a black polo neck jumper and, at the last minute, applied a touch of red lipstick.

'What's all this, then?' Alexander said, when she answered the door.

'All what?'

'Pleated skirt? Very austere. I prefer you in trousers.'

'Tough. Shall we go?'

In the car, Alexander said, 'You must be one of the moodiest women I've ever had the misfortune to meet.'

'I like these Peugeots,' Agnes replied. 'Soft top too. Is it the two-litre engine from the XSi hot-hatch?'

'OK, OK. No more personal comments.' Alexander settled into his seat and started the car. 'Blackfriars Bridge?'

'Fine.'

* * *

Stefan Polkoff lived in a large, early Victorian terraced house with a beautifully restored wrought-iron gate and several burglar alarms. Inside it was graciously decorated in subtle greens and cream with lots of polished wood. A silver samovar stood on a wide mantelpiece in the main reception room, which was comfortably full of guests. Polkoff greeted Alexander warmly, totally ignoring Agnes.

'Alex, come and meet Gilbert. Gilbert, here he is, the boy himself. What you both have in common, my dears, is a morbid imagination and an interest in early nude photography. Let me get you both a drink . . .' Polkoff passed on into the crowd. Agnes watched as Marjorie Holtby arrived, tiptoeing shyly into the room. She went over to her.

'Oh, hello,' Marjorie said warmly. 'Oh dear, I do find these things rather a trial, you know. Is the professor here?'

'No, not yet.'

'He had some meeting to go to first. I said to him, you shouldn't try to fit so much in, but he was preoccupied, something to do with money, it always is.'

'What to do with money?'

'It's this Names business, you know, how they all got involved with these insurance things, and everyone said you'll make pots of money, but in the end they didn't. Something like that. Now there's a pressure group they've set up. Some of them have lost thousands. I do think the professor should have known better.'

'Lloyds Names?'

'Yes, that's it. I'm a bit hopeless about all that, even

when the professor asked me about this company thing, signing these forms, I said, oh, you know best, Robert.' She chuckled girlishly, and then turned to the door as Professor Burgess appeared, booming his greetings.

'Polkoff, old chap. Happy Birthday – you see, I knew, old boy. You can't hide your age from me. And here's Alexander too. My likeness, I see, is taking some time in the making . . .'

Agnes saw Polkoff finishing a conversation with Alexander. She caught Polkoff's words, 'Oh, yes, out of action for a good few weeks. High blood pressure, they say; well, she was on those drugs, whatever they're called.'

'Alexander,' boomed Burgess, 'how about a sitting on Monday? I'll have the morning free, won't I, Marjorie?' Alexander went over to Burgess, and Agnes saw him point out Gilbert.

She wandered into the kitchen and found a Polish recipe book, which she flicked through for a while, sipping at some excellent Alsace wine. When, some time later, she went back into the party, she found Alexander talking to an elegant woman with very high heels and blonde hair in a neat french pleat.

'Oh, it must be lovely to be a real artist,' the woman was saying, flashing some very white teeth. 'Although I do think all this modern stuff has gone a bit far, don't you, what with preserved sheep and then whole houses and – and old vegetables, I think it was last week.'

Alexander saw Agnes and said, 'You look tired. Shall we go?' Agnes nodded, and they gathered up their coats.

In the car he said, 'You didn't want to stay, did you?'

'Me? No. I'm not a party person, really.'

'Why did you want to come, then?' Alexander said.

'Why did you ask me?'

He was silent. After a while, he said, 'I suppose you know Marjorie from that death you were involved in.'

'Yes, that's how I met her.'

'One wonders what became of Mr Holtby,' he said. 'Perhaps she ate him.' Agnes laughed.

They drove in silence for a little while.

'Suicide, wasn't it?'

'Sorry?'

'The dead girl.'

'Um – that's not what I was told,' Agnes replied carefully. 'Blood clot or something. We just did the funeral.'

'There were various rumours circulating at the time. Julia told me. Someone said something about her cupboard, stockpiled with drugs.'

'Well, she was a pharmacist, wasn't she?'

'It made me think. You know, all these pills sloshing around the hospital. It would be easy to make a mistake.' He shot a glance at Agnes.

She shrugged. 'S'pose so,' she said. 'Hadn't really thought about it.'

'Southwark Bridge or Blackfriars again?'

'Oh, Blackfriars, I think. I like the view.'

Half an hour later they pulled up outside her block.

'Well?' Alexander said.

'Well what?'

'Did you enjoy the evening?'

'Yes. Thanks for inviting me.'

'I have to say, Agnes – if that's you enjoying yourself, I dread to think what you having a bad time is.'

Agnes smiled briefly. 'I know. I'm sorry. These days I'm not at my best.'

'What's the problem? May I ask?'

Agnes sighed. 'It's a long story.'

'You're a very private person.'

'I have to be.'

'Why?'

Agnes looked up at him. He seemed anguished, somehow, pleading. She looked down at her fingers, clasped in her lap. 'I'd better go,' she said.

'Will you come to me tomorrow?' he said, urgently.

'For the painting? When?'

'All day if you like. I need to get on with it before it all goes wrong.'

'OK. When do you get up?'

'These days, very late. But if there's a reason—'

'Eleven?'

'Fine.' He bent forward, and she had the impression he intended to kiss her – but instead he leaned across her and opened the door. 'Night, then. Sleep well.'

'And you,' she replied, getting out of the car, pulling her polo neck around her face against the cold night air.

Agnes was woken by the phone. She answered it wearily.

'Morning, sweetie,' came Athena's cheery voice. 'How are you?'

'Athena, it's Saturday morning.'

'You weren't asleep, were you?'

'What does it sound like?'

'Sorry. So where were you last night?'

'At a party. Why?'

'With your painter?'

'Not *my* painter.'

'All right, not your painter.'

'How can I help, Athena?'

'There's serious shopping to be done today. I need your views on a suit I've seen in Harvey Nichols. Lilac linen.'

'It'll have to wait, I'm afraid. I'm spending all day with my painter.'

'Not *your* painter. So how was the party?'

'Interesting, I think. I'm finding lots of questions but no answers.'

'Jonathan's convinced they're all Masons.'

'It's definitely something like that.'

'And you and the painter?' Athena asked.

'There's nothing to say. I don't trust him, but I like him.'

'Join the club.'

'No, I don't mean like that. He seems to need – it's like he's asking for – something, I don't know. Something spiritual. Don't laugh, I'm serious.'

'But he's tricky too?'

'I don't know why he's in the hospital. It seems to be connected to this anatomy lecturer. He says he's having a crisis, his mother's very ill – it's a strange time to take on a portrait like that, isn't it? Oh, I don't know. Can the suit wait? I'd love to see you soon.'

'Hmmm. Perhaps. I'll phone you.'

'I'll invoice you for the cleaning bill on this shirt,' Agnes laughed.

Alexander walked around his easel. 'There'll be no spare money from this painting. It's completely uncommercial.'

'My ex-husband would probably buy it off you.' As Agnes spoke, she realised it was true. At least, it would have been true, if this Gabrielle . . .

Alexander dropped his paintbrush and stared at her. 'Your ex – you mean, you were married?'

'Didn't I tell you?'

'You really are a private person, aren't you? When was that, then?'

'Ages ago. I left him to join my first Order, about sixteen years ago.'

Alexander picked up his brush and resumed painting. 'That explains it, then,' he murmured.

'Explains what?'

'Why I couldn't quite get you before. On this, I mean.' He fell silent, and Agnes was left vaguely regretting having revealed so much about herself. After all, she mused, what has Alexander ever told me about himself?

'I have no such secrets,' he said, suddenly. 'No ex-wives lurking in corners of my past. I did have a great love affair at college—'

'At the RCA?' Agnes heard herself ask.

Alexander jumped at the name. He stopped painting

and put down his brush. 'How do you know I was at the RCA?' He stared at her.

'I mentioned you to a friend. This painting, I mean,' faltered Agnes. 'He'd heard of you. A dealer.'

'What's his name?'

'Jonathan . . .' Agnes suddenly realised Athena had never told her his surname. 'Well, a friend of a friend . . .'

'And he'd heard of me. Funny that. No one's heard of me. And the only thing they'd know about my time at the RCA . . .' Agnes sat quite still. 'Did he mention that? My claim to fame from college days?' Alexander's voice was raised. 'Did he tell you I only lasted two terms at the RCA?'

'Yes,' whispered Agnes.

'Did he tell you why?'

There was nothing for it. 'Some kind of violent incident . . .' Agnes began.

Alexander suddenly picked up a bottle of turpentine and threw it through the window. The pane shattered, the sharp angles of glass dripping oily fluid where the bottle had smashed against it.

He turned to face her. 'I was the most promising painter of my year group, rave reviews at the first shows, all that . . .' He went over to the window, and traced the jagged edges of glass with his fingers. 'I wrecked it. My temper. Quite unprovoked attack, they said. They were right. Poor Christopher, I nearly killed him. Could have been anyone.'

His voice was taut with restraint. Agnes, remembering Hugo's rages, wondered what would happen next.

'My family, you see,' Alexander was saying. 'Can't escape them ever. And now my mother . . .'

He grabbed an empty wine bottle from the draining board and threw it at the broken window, where it smashed, adding green glass to the transparent shards. 'I'll never be shot of them,' he said, hoarsely.

The bottle was followed by a plate, and then a mug which missed the window and crashed in two neat halves on to the floor amongst the shards of glass. 'I could have been something,' he was muttering incoherently, picking up a bundle of paintbrushes. One by one he threw these out of the hole in the window. 'And instead,' he shouted, the last brush flung from his hands, missing the window and rebounding weakly on to the floor, 'turned out of college to face a GBH charge . . .'

Agnes sat quite quite still. 'GBH?'

'Well, malicious wounding in the end. I got done for three years, released after two.'

The storm had passed. Alexander stood in the middle of the broken glass, his hands hanging awkwardly at his sides. Agnes stood up.

'I'm going out for an hour. I'll be back.' When she left, Alexander was standing in exactly the same position.

It was just after four when she returned with olives and wine and bread and cheese, and some new plates. The room was bathed in pink light, and some attempt had been made to sweep up the glass. Alexander was sitting on the floor, his head in his hands. Behind him was her portrait, which had been ripped across several times.

She placed the things on the table, then looked at what was left of her image. He had spent the day working on her face. She saw her own angular chin, the outline where her hair framed her face, her straight neck. Under her neck the canvas was slashed right down to the edge of the painting. She could see where her shirt collar began, before it was lost in the frayed folds of ripped canvas.

She went over to the window and stared out across the rooftops, over the faceless towers of the suburbs stretching out towards the south. The setting sun picked out gleaming windows in flashes of colour.

'I'm sorry,' Alexander said, hoarsely.

She turned from the window. She looked at his face and saw how ravaged he was, how eaten away by some kind of inner force – hatred or violence or anger – that for years and years had been gnawing away at him. She saw, too, that she had been trying to reverse this process – and that she had failed.

'I suppose you'll be going now,' he said.

'If that's what you—'

'Yes.'

'At least you tried,' she said.

'And failed. It's part of my life, failure.'

Agnes opened her mouth.

'Don't say anything,' he went on.

Agnes wanted to go over to him, to take him in her arms. Instead, she walked across the silence to the door.

At the door, she said, 'Bye, then.' He had slumped on to the floor again by the ruined painting and didn't look up. As she left she had the impression that the mutilated portrait, leaning raggedly towards him, was keeping him company, as if he preferred that version of herself to the real thing.

Chapter Thirteen

At ten past eleven on Sunday morning, Agnes was waiting in the little office in the basement of Julius's church. She sat on one of the shabby chairs, listening to birds crooning outside the window, hearing the footsteps overhead on the bare floorboards as the refreshments committee packed up their trolley. At last she heard Julius approach.

'I'll take the Communion to St Hugh's, if you like,' she said. 'Father Matthew, the chaplain, asked us to cover for him this week.'

'Yes, I know,' he said. 'Don't forget Bill Docherty, he was taken in last week with chest pains. He's on Ward A10.'

'Fine.'

'Everything all right?' Julius's tone was deliberately light.

'Yes. OK. I'm not doing the painting any more.'

'Oh. Is that a good thing?'

'Yes,' said Agnes. 'Yes, it is.'

'Good.' Julius paused as he handed her the Host. 'Might you be popping in here next week?'

'I hope so. I'll ring you.'

* * *

Agnes left Kathleen till last.

'Nice hairdo,' she said.

'Like it?' Kathleen tweaked the neat grey curls at the back of her neck.

'Lovely. How have you been?'

'OK. New lady, Amb. Friend. Very very upset. Funny turn.'

'Did you get to talk to her?'

'Lots and lots. Nice lady. Upset.'

'What about?'

'Taking it all away.'

'Taking what away?' Agnes settled down on the edge of Kathleen's bed.

'Job. New – book place. All going.'

'They're closing down the library?'

Kathleen shook her head. 'Job going. And more. New building. All wrong.'

'I hope you're not tiring her.' A brisk young nurse approached. 'She's making great progress but she's not to overdo it.'

'Maybe I should talk to her myself,' Agnes said, as the nurse went on her way.

Kathleen nodded. 'Bodies. Still saying. Bodies. Ask her.'

When Agnes arrived at her bedside, Amber Parry was looking less well-groomed than last time. Her hair stuck out from her head in little tufts, and her face looked grey and tired. She opened her eyes reluctantly.

'Hello, it's Sister Agnes.'

'Who?'

'We talked a few days ago. About the new building,' Agnes went on.

'Who sent you?'

'No one. I just wanted to ask you—'

'Oh, yes, I remember now.' Amber closed her eyes and opened them again. 'What about the building?'

'We were agreeing,' Agnes said, drawing up a chair, 'that it should never have been built.'

'So you know too. Did I tell you then?'

'About the bodies?' Agnes hazarded.

'Of course, proving it is the problem.'

'Yes. What proof would you need?'

Amber Parry pulled herself more upright in her bed and rearranged her pillows. 'It was all so long ago, you see.'

'What exactly have you found out, Mrs—'

'Miss Parry. I don't believe we've been formally introduced. I'm the chief librarian and archivist. At least, I was.'

'Sister Agnes,' Agnes said, holding out her hand. 'I've been visiting our parishioners here, and I think that something is – well, let's just say, things aren't what they should be.'

Amber Parry took Agnes's hand and held it limply for a moment. 'It's very nice to meet you,' she said. 'And you're right, of course. One of the few to realise. Things are all awry.' She leaned towards Agnes. 'You asked me what I've found out. Well . . .' She looked around her and lowered her voice. 'If you look at the archives, you'll see that the new building is built on a church burial ground. Hallowed land. I tried to tell them. It was never – un-hallowed, or whatever you do. There are graves under the foundations. The workmen have been turfing up bones as they dig. Human bones.'

'How do you know?'

'Stefan told me. Stefan Polkoff. It was only a couple of days ago. You see, St Hugh's used to be attached to a church like they all were. The hospital encroached over the years, until there was just a tiny Victorian church in the space between the two buildings. And now they've knocked that down. But they shouldn't have, you see. If you look in the records, you can see. But that horrible old Burgess, and now McPherson, all in it together, riding roughshod over people's feelings . . . Just for that monstrosity.'

She paused and took a gasp of breath. Agnes saw that she was very pale. She put her hand on her arm. 'You mustn't upset yourself,' Agnes said.

'Oh, but I must. Who else is going to – is going to tell . . .' She struggled to breathe.

Agnes got up and looked at her notes which were clipped to the end of the bed. There were various drugs listed under medication. 'Have you felt better since you were admitted here?'

'Better? No. I feel much worse. These new drugs . . . make me hazy.'

'Did they tell you why they've altered your drugs?'

'Said it was because of the old ones being too strong. Unreliable. New ones on the market, or something.' She sighed heavily. 'It's all different, these days.'

Agnes sat down next to her and waited for her breathing to become normal again. 'So your job is at risk?'

'Oh, it's terrible. This McPherson with his precious Trust, all these silly new management ideas. "We don't need librarians any more," he said. "It's a different world".' She paused and breathed in, tearfully. 'But it's not just my job. It's history itself. All these young things in the new library, with their computers and their management training courses. And they're talking about scrapping the museum now, too.'

'What will happen to it?'

'All on the rubbish tip, I suppose. I can't bear to think of it. All those specimens, priceless examples of people's work, early diagnosis. I keep thinking of it all smashed on top of some skip lorry . . .' She was seized with another attack of breathlessness.

Agnes waited, and then said, 'These bones that Stefan said they'd found . . .'

'Oh, they sent them to pathology. No one said anything. It's a cover-up, I think. I tried to talk to him myself—'

'Who?'

'McPherson. But he didn't listen. A rude and arrogant man.'

'That's the impression I got.'

'He said why should he stop the digging just for some old bones. I said, it doesn't matter how old they are. He said, "Miss Parry, we're here to cure the living, not bother with the dead."'

'I've always thought the two things were very much related,' Agnes said.

Amber Parry seized her hand. 'Do you? Yes, so do I. Although, I suppose we're too late now. Too late to stop it.'

'Mmm. And was the closure of the museum his idea too?'

'That's all come about with the Trust, and the new funding arrangements.'

Agnes got up to leave. 'Thank you, Miss Parry. You've been very helpful.'

'Well, it's so nice to find one isn't alone.'

Agnes went out of the hospital and wandered over to the new building. She walked past the boards which announced 'St Hugh's Development. Phase Two. Hard Hat Area', then slipped inside the fencing and found herself on the edge of a huge clay pit. Steel joists lay in heaps at the edge, and various heavy vehicles stood around immobile in the sun, like dozing swamp creatures. Agnes peered into the pit and fancied that she saw, mingled with the landfill and the mud, the stirrings of bodies woken from their final sleep.

It wasn't difficult to track down Julia. She was where Agnes expected her to be, in the new library, hunched over a large pile of books and pages of hastily scrawled notes.

'Um, Julia?'

'Wha . . . Oh, it's you.'

'I wondered if you had a moment.'

'What does it look like?'

'I'm sorry.'

'Is it a short moment? I'm due for a sandwich break.'

'I wondered if you could come and look at Amber Parry's notes with me.'

Ten minutes later, Julia stood by the sleeping Miss Parry and flicked through the pages on the clipboard, frowning.

'I'm not an expert, of course.'

'No . . .'

'But this seems OK. If she'd had a funny turn on the Nifedipine, you'd try something else. Any of these.' She replaced the board.

'And the dosages?'

'They seem normal. What's the problem?'

'She was complaining of feeling hazy.'

'Well, people often do. Hypertension, it's tricky. They'll get the right drug and she'll feel better.'

'I'm sorry to drag you away from your studies,' Agnes said as they went out into the corridor.

'That's OK.'

'Would you expect to keep her on the wards for a few weeks?'

'A few weeks? These days? A few days, more like.'

'Oh. Only, they seem to think she's out of action for a while.'

'Who do?'

'Polkoff. I heard him saying—'

'Oh, him. Weird guy. Always whispering with Alexander.'

'Yes.'

'And he's weird too. Alexander, I mean.'

'Mmm. Shall we have that sandwich break?'

'I'm well out of it, you know,' Julia went on as they settled themselves at a table in the canteen. 'Alexander.'

'Oh yes?'

'There's something going on. I saw him lurking around the pharmacy a couple of days ago.'

'Lurking?'

'Well, you know. Like he shouldn't be there.'

'What was he doing?'

'Watching. That's all. People came and went with their drugs, and he watched them. Then he sloped off.'

'Did he see you?'

'No. I made sure. Mark's been so sweet about it all, I couldn't risk – you know. All that.'

'No. Quite.'

'Some men are just dangerous, you know.'

'Yes.'

'Although, life is rather dull now. Just revision. And Mark. But – I dunno.' Julia sighed, and carefully removed all the tomato from her sandwich. 'How do you know if someone's right for you?'

Agnes laughed. 'I'm really not the person to ask.'

'No. It's just – I'm bored, really.' Julia began to arrange the rejected tomato on the edge of her plate. 'I decided to be a doctor when I was fourteen and I haven't looked back. Until now. I never questioned it, you know. But now I'm bored of revision, I'm bored of all these horrible little boys I have to train with – and to be honest, I'm bored of Mark too.'

'Maybe once the exams are out of the way you can take stock.'

'It's all such a conveyor belt, though. Straight from one year to the next, exams, house years. All this having to conform. But then I think, it's what I've always wanted, I shouldn't grumble, loads of people would envy me, wouldn't they?'

'Yes. I suppose so. By the way, I gather they're closing down the Pathology museum?'

'So I heard,' said Julia with her mouth full. 'But you never know. Since it became the Trust, everything changes all the time. New management teams, all that. I guess they think it's not cost effective, or something.'

'But you must learn so much—'

'S'pose so. But the people who get most out of it are those weirdo art school bods drawing dead babies the whole time.'

Agnes looked at this poised young woman sitting opposite her, at the sunlight catching her auburn hair. She said, 'Mark was in real danger, wasn't he?'

'You mean, Gail?'

'I mean, if the police had been brought in, he'd have been charged with murder.'

'It doesn't bear thinking about,' Julia said.

'A lot of lies were told on his behalf, don't you think?'

'Yes, I thought so at the time, but I guess it helped the hospital too, not to have an inquiry, all that.'

'Do you think – do you think it was characteristic of Burgess?'

Julia looked at Agnes. 'If you're asking, do you think

he's an altruistic man, I'd have to say no.'

'To go to the extent of a fake post mortem?'

'How do you know?' Julia was now staring at Agnes very hard.

Agnes looked at the freckled nose, the frank, grey eyes. She had realised some time ago that without an ally in the hospital, her investigations would get nowhere. It occurred to her that Julia might be just the person she needed.

'Never you mind how I know.'

'You won't – I mean, for Mark's sake, you mustn't tell—'

'I wouldn't dream of it. The only problem is, I don't think that's the whole story.' It was a risk, of course, to share her thoughts with anyone. Mark had said Julia was untrustworthy – but then, Mark had reasons of his own. And at least Julia wouldn't want to see Mark facing a murder charge.

'What do you mean?' Julia asked.

Here goes, thought Agnes. 'Julia – I wonder if I could confide in you.'

'Sure. Yeah. What?'

'I think something very serious is going on. I think that someone's trying to kill someone.'

'Wow. Who?'

'That's the problem. I don't know. I don't really know anything, and I haven't been able to find out because I don't know who to ask. So you must understand, I'm trusting you with this. If the person who's intending to murder gets to hear that we know, we'll never know. If you see what I mean.'

'I have got exams, you know.'

Agnes looked at Julia's expression of utter disbelief.

'I know,' Agnes said, 'it does sound ridiculous.'

'Hmm.' Julia fiddled her knife against her empty plate. 'What's it got to do with Gail?'

'Nothing. It was just coincidence. She took pills intended for someone else. For McPherson.'

Julia screwed up her face. 'So it's McPherson they're trying to kill?'

'Yes. No. Oh, I don't know.' Agnes absently picked Julia's tomato from her plate and began to eat it.

'Why should Alexander want to kill McPherson?'

'I didn't say Alexander.'

'Yes, but he's behaving oddly. He was obviously dead keen to get this job here, pulling strings with Burgess, all that. And asking about Gail's death, and the pharmacy—'

'But he doesn't know anything about Gail's death. Whereas the murderer must have been involved with Gail's death, if only by mistake.'

Julia dabbed at her lips with a paper napkin. 'This is mad,' she grinned. 'I mean, here we are talking about it as if—'

'As if it was real.'

'Yes.' Julia laughed.

'Perhaps it's me that's a little mad. I keep thinking I should just turn my back on it all. But I can't. I can't leave it alone.'

'Why don't we just ask him?'

'Who?'

'Ask Alexander why he wants to kill McPherson?'

'But if he does, then we've blown it. We'll never know. And if he doesn't, he might be involved with whoever does.'

'Hmm.' Julia sighed. 'Hospitals are like that. The whole bloody medical profession is like that, in fact. The more I decide I want to do surgery, the more impossible it seems.'

'Why?'

'Oh, they're all chaps. You look at everyone choosing their firms. Certain bright young men go for certain old boys.'

'Masons.'

'I think so. Yes. We could ask McPherson.'

'Ask him what?'

'If someone wants to kill him . . . No, that's crazy too.'

'We could ask – you could ask him whether he was prescribed anything recently. Penicillin.'

'Now that really is daft.'

'No, you see, if we find out he was allergic to it – I'm sure someone meant him to take the pills that Gail took.'

'Knowing him to be allergic?'

'Yes. Oh dear, it does all sound very far fetched. And now there's Amber's bodies—'

'Oh, those. The bones in the building site. We've all heard. The abbot's curse.' Julia giggled.

'Could you?'

'Could I what?'

'Ask McPherson.'

Julia looked hard at Agnes. She rubbed her nose. 'I've got exams.'

'Yes. Of course.'

Julia rubbed her nose again. 'Oh, bugger it. Come on.' She jumped up from the table. 'Seize the moment.' She strode out of the canteen and down the corridor with Agnes hurrying behind her, until they found themselves in the courtyard of the new building.

'Will he be there?' asked Agnes breathlessly.

'It's Sunday. Oh hell. Still . . .' Julia giggled. 'Come on, let's try. We can always raid his medical notes if not.'

They stumbled through the shiny glass doors and into the lift, then crept along the first floor corridor to McPherson's office. Julia stifled a giggle and then knocked.

'Come in,' said a voice from within. Julia opened her eyes wide in mock horror to Agnes, then opened the door and marched in.

'Hello. I'm sorry to bother you,' Agnes heard her say.

'Um, Hart, isn't it? Going around with Henderson, promising young man. Mark. And you are . . . ?'

'Julia,' Agnes heard through the door which Julia had left ajar.

'Yes. That's right. What can I do for you?'

'I need your advice about a career in microbiology.'

'Ah well.' The voice warmed perceptibly. 'We're always looking for bright young people. And if they're as decorative as you are, so much the better.'

'I was trying to find you before exams, a few weeks ago, but I think you were off sick.'

'Me, off sick? Never. Oh, now wait a minute. For the first time in my life, yes. You do have a good memory, Miss – Miss Hart.'

'Julia,' said Julia. 'Your secretary said you had a – what was it . . . ?'

'Throat infection. Must be the air in here, I'm never ill, you know. Can't hold with doctors.' He laughed, heartily.

'She said you'd even had antibiotics.'

'Some sort of placebo thing, yes. Of course, most of them flushed down the john. Can't be doing with all that. I'm flattered by your concern.'

'Well, I'd be very keen to work in genetics, eventually. It's so exciting, isn't it? The Human Genome Project, all that . . .'

'It's always encouraging to find young people who share one's own enthusiasm. My advice to you is, take your exams, pointless as they may come to seem.' He chortled. 'And then come and see me again and we can discuss your future. Of course,' he added, 'I'll have to call you Dr Hart then, instead of Julia. Lovely name, Julia.'

Agnes heard the scrape of a chair. 'Thank you so much, Dr McPherson.'

'It's a pleasure, young lady. See you soon.'

Julia came out into the corridor and placed a finger over her lips. The two women moved silently to the lift. Once the steel slid shut behind them, they burst into hysterical laughter, until, as they reached the ground floor, Julia said, 'We must leave separately. He may be looking out of the window.' Julia walked out into the courtyard, while Agnes made her way through the building towards the academic centre, emerging to join Julia by the swimming pool entrance.

'Of course,' Julia said, crestfallen, 'we don't know what drugs he took.'

'But you were brilliant. Amazing.'

'It could have been anything. Septrin. Erythromycin.'

'But at least we know he was prescribed something.'

'It might have been penicillin. It might all have been perfectly straightforward.'

'Yes.' The two women sat on the wall, suddenly gloomy. After a moment, Julia said, 'We'll just have to raid the notes. Like I said.'

'But—' Agnes stared at Julia. 'Are you serious?'

'Why not? Sunday night, good time. I must go and do some work, but I'll meet you back here tonight. Nine o'clock?'

'B-but – yes, fine. OK.'

'Good.' Julia grinned, gleefully. 'See you then.'

In the dark, the building site was full of menace. The tall arcs of the cranes seemed to be moving, creeping quietly towards the edge of the pit. A workman's jacket, flung carelessly over a steel pole, swayed to and fro. Agnes hurried on until she reached the library entrance. The student centre was all quiet, and the night lights on the side of the new brickwork shed long shadows across the courtyard. Agnes hugged her raincoat around her.

'Hi.' Julia emerged from the shadows. 'Let's go.'

Agnes followed her into the hospital, relieved to find herself in its bright fluorescent corridors. They took the lift to the third floor, and tiptoed along in silence. Outside the locked door of the Personnel department, Julia produced a key.

'Master key,' she whispered.

'How on earth?'

'Rag week. Jolly japes.'

'Which involved stealing keys?'

'You know what medical students are like. I nicked it from a mate.'

'You didn't tell him . . .'

'Not a word.'

The key turned smoothly in the lock, and the two women were inside.

'Right,' Julia said.

'You've done this sort of thing before.'

'Fun, isn't it?'

'Did rag week involve stealing Personnel files too?'

'Not quite. Here we are.' Julia tried the door of a filing cabinet, which was locked. She opened a desk drawer, rummaged through some keys and picked one out. She tried it in the cabinet lock. The drawer opened with a deafening metal scrape. The two women looked at each other, then both began to leaf through the files.

'"M" – here we are. Mac – McPherson.' Julia giggled as she took out the file and opened it. Like Gail's, it contained a few sheets of A4 paper.

'Right,' Julia was saying, 'medical history. Here we are. Any operations, allergies? Oh my God. There we are. Look.'

Agnes looked. Above Julia's neatly manicured finger were the words, 'Allergic to penicillin.'

'But are you sure it said penicillin?'

'In the pharmacy book? Yes. Positive.'

It was half an hour later, and Agnes and Julia were sitting in the 'Bacchus' wine bar on Borough High Street.

'I hope we didn't leave a trace,' Julia said.

'We should have worn gloves.'

'Nothing was missing, though. We put everything back after you made those notes.'

'Yes. It'll be OK.'

'I must give Rob his key back.'

'Could you . . .' Agnes hesitated. 'Could you hang on to it? We might need it again.'

'True. OK.'

'Though where that leaves everything . . .'

'Well,' Julia leaned back in her chair, 'it means your hunch was right. If someone managed to get penicillin out of the pharmacy in McPherson's name, and it turns out he's allergic to it, then that's something, isn't it? Mmm, nice wine.'

'And it does imply that they're involved in the post mortem cover-up. Because they wouldn't want it to be known that there was penicillin in the wrong place.'

'Yes. So it must be someone in with the hospital.'

'Not Alexander, then,' Agnes said.

'Just what I was thinking.'

Agnes sipped her wine. 'Although – it's still crazy. I mean, McPherson being a doctor. You couldn't make a doctor take the wrong pills, could you? Not easily.'

'Oh, but he's not a doctor. Didn't you hear him? He despises doctors. He probably did a medical training once, but he's not a physician. That's why he's so rude. About medicine, I mean.'

'But not about pretty young women who want to do genetics.'

Julia laughed. 'I'm going to have to get out of that one, aren't I?'

'He'll be chasing you across the country,' smiled Agnes.

'Unless he's been bumped off.' They looked at each other, suddenly serious. 'Oh dear,' Julia said. 'What shall we do now? Shall we warn him? Shall we call the police?'

Agnes ran her hands through her hair. 'And there's poor old Amber Parry. Her drugs were collected by the same person who picked up the penicillin.'

'Who?'

'The signature was illegible. But I think it's Polkoff.'

'I can't see the police being interested.'

'What, in a fake post mortem?'

'Well, yes, that. But then, poor old Mark . . .'

'Oh. Yes. Of course.' Agnes looked at Julia.

'No police, then,' Julia said. 'Not yet, anyway.'

Chapter Fourteen

On Monday morning, walking once again towards St Hugh's, Agnes reflected on her decision to involve Julia in her investigations. She felt annoyed with herself, firstly for not being able to do it on her own; secondly, because her serious quest for truth seemed to have become no more than a jolly jape for a bored medical student. Julia had left her the evening before, hugging herself with glee. 'At last something interesting is going on,' she'd said as they'd left the wine bar. And who was to say, thought Agnes, that in her girlish delight she wouldn't blurt it all out to someone?

On the other hand, it was nice to be believed. When Agnes had explained her reasons, her fears that someone really might be intending murder, Julia, too, had seen that it might, indeed, be serious. And, most important of all, Julia had access to information that Agnes did not. For a start, she had promised to find out how McPherson had been prescribed the wrong drug.

Agnes, meanwhile, had agreed to follow up Amber Parry's concerns, although now, as she approached her ward, it all seemed a bit silly. Bulldozers raking over old graves was hardly the same as finding that someone had tried to poison the director of the new Microbiology department.

Amber was sitting up in bed, her cheeks flushed. As she looked up and saw Agnes, she became animated.

'Thank goodness it's you. I've had a visitor this morning. My friend Caroline from the Pathology department. Apparently the site manager brought her some more bones. And the thing is, these aren't old.'

'What do you mean?' Agnes asked, sitting by the bed.

'Just that. A new corpse.'

'You mean . . . ?' Agnes's head was spinning. She had an image of a shallow grave under the new building, of McPherson, freshly buried, now being dug up. 'You mean, someone known to the hospital?'

'Oh, not recognisable. Not that new. But not old.'

'But how does he know? The site manager, I mean?'

'Well, he's taken the bone he found—'

'Wait a minute. Just one bone?'

'So far. But he's checking for more.'

'And where is it now?'

'That's what I was saying. He took it to the Path labs. I told Caroline I thought we should call the police.'

'Hmm,' said Agnes. She looked at Amber, at her pink cheeks and darting eyes, and wondered whether all this was really based in fact, or whether it was just the flight of fancy of a disappointed woman. 'Well,' she said, 'shall I follow this up? Shall I chase this bone, as it were?'

'We both can. They're discharging me tomorrow, they said.'

'Oh.'

'It's hardly surprising these days. I'm to go home and rest for a week. Not that I shall,' she added in a whisper.

Agnes went straight to the building site. It was now mid-morning, and a small group of workmen were perched on some oil drums, their hands cupped round steaming mugs. Agnes approached them.

'I'm – um – looking for the site manager.'

Heads bobbed in unison in the direction of a Portakabin on the other side of the excavation.

''E's always in there, love,' one of the men said. 'Rain or shine. You won't find 'im nowhere else.' This utterance was received with grunts and nods from the other men. Agnes thanked them and picked her way round the site to the cabin.

Inside, a man was sitting at a makeshift desk, talking on the telephone. He was thin, about fifty, and wore small, neat spectacles and a thick overcoat which rather dwarfed him. He looked up in surprise.

'Right,' he said hastily, into the phone, 'will do. God knows. Right.' He hung up, then looked at Agnes.

'I'm sorry to intrude. I'm from Pathology, just checking about this bone . . .'

'Oh. The bone. Yes.' The narrow eyes surveyed her for a moment. He went on, 'Normally, those men will bulldoze anything without a backward glance. But something's got to them. They're picking over the leavings like old biddies at a jumble sale. That's how they found this one. I had to report it.'

'Why was it different?'

The man sighed and shook his head. 'Probably wasn't. But it still had a trace of . . .' His thin lips showed disgust. 'Not that I know much about it.'

'Mightn't a dog have left it?'

'Oh, probably, yes. But the mood they're in, I had to do something. As it is, they've stopped work. Look at them.'

Through the window, Agnes could see four brooding silhouettes, sitting where she'd left them, hunched on the edge of their great mud pit like fairy-tale giants.

'So this is unusual?' she asked.

He nodded. 'Once they heard it was an old churchyard, they were off. Then they found this.' He leaned back in his chair. 'It's OK, though. Someone will say it's a leg of lamb or something, and they'll get bored of sitting there, and it'll all blow over. Give it an hour or two. It's just a bloody waste of time while we're waiting.'

Agnes stood up. 'Have you met Miss Parry, the archivist?'

'Oh, her. Yes. Came in here a few days ago trying to tell me about some old monks. Nuts, if you ask me. Mind you, typical of that lot to take it all seriously. Any excuse.'

Agnes stood up. 'Sorry to have taken your time.'

He waved at her dismissively. 'Oh, no sweat. All the time in the bloody world at the moment, until that lot of pansies decide to get back on their machines. Still, I'm giving them till three o'clock – and then they might just find that someone else is doing their job.' He laughed emptily, then picked up the phone. Agnes decided it was time she looked at the archives.

* * *

At two o'clock, she met Julia in the canteen as arranged.

'Well?' Julia looked well-groomed and alert. 'Anything to report?'

Agnes sat down heavily with a tired-looking salad. 'I've been doing history. What have you been doing?'

Julia laughed. 'Breaking and entering, I think. Daylight robbery.'

Agnes smiled. 'I'm leading you into bad ways. You're not supposed to enjoy it.'

'I raided the files again, right under their noses.' Julia grinned. 'And it turns out McPherson was prescribed tetracycline.'

'How did you find that out?'

Julia laughed. 'Right. First stop, back to Personnel to get his GP's address. I took my mate Fiona with me, she distracted that girl in there, I grabbed the file and had a quick look. Then off to Lambeth Road Surgery to request a repeat prescription for him, pretended to be his secretary. Of course, it was refused – but I found out what it was. Tetracycline. Are you sure—'

'That it said penicillin?' sighed Agnes wearily. 'Yes, I am. So you've done no revision today?'

Julia laughed. 'You are corrupting me, it's true. So, how about you?'

'Well, I've been sidetracked into seventeenth-century land laws and the abbot's curse. Went to the archives, got locked into a tiny room in the old library stack. You see, Amber Parry told me they'd found new bones on the building site. I mean, fresh bodies.'

'Wow.'

'It turns out to be one not entirely clean bone, currently being investigated by the Path labs.'

'Still.'

'Quite. So then I thought I'd better check out these archives.'

'And?'

'It was lovely, fingering old parchment all morning. And such exciting history. It's like Amber said, that site was church land for years, dating back to a monastery. Then it all changed, there's a gap in the documents. Then in the seventeenth century it's a church, rebuilt in the nineteenth century, and gradually squeezed by the hospital as it expanded. And there is an abbot's curse.'

'Really?' Julia rested her chin on her hands.

'There's some tale of heresy in the fifteenth century. Some abbot was found guilty, although it's thought his enemies wanted him out of the way – and he was murdered, and his arm was nailed to the church door.'

'Ugh.'

Agnes smiled and speared a piece of cucumber. 'Not that it helps us.'

'But the new bone does. If it is human.'

'Two bodies, instead of one.'

'A serial killer.' Julia giggled.

Agnes said, 'Come on, I want to prove something to you.'

'There,' she said, as they both stood over the pharmacy book. 'McPherson. 18 April.'

'There's nothing there,' Julia said.

'What?' Agnes saw a neatly Tipp-Exed line. 'But someone must have come back and – you do believe me, don't you?'

'Yes. Because you can see. The marks under the Tipp-Ex. McPherson. That's clear. And it must be penicillin. It begins with P, and that's two "1"s there.'

'It makes it all the odder,' Agnes said as they walked back to the library, 'that Tipp-Ex.'

'Very strange. I wonder who.'

'We'd be much further on if we knew that.'

'Do you think we should warn McPherson yet?'

'Not yet. You've got to spend this afternoon revising.'

'And all night too, I'm afraid.'

They slipped back out into the corridor, and set off towards the medical school. Julia said, 'There's still Alexander.'

'What about Alexander?'

'He's one of our suspects.'

'Is he?'

'You take my word for it, he's weird. Look, here's my phone number. Let me know when it's time for our next assignation. Ooh, this is fun,' she laughed, then fled up the staircase in a flash of black leggings.

Returning home that afternoon, Agnes found a message on her answering machine.

'It's me, Julius. A man phoned for you. Alexander Jeffes. These are his numbers. He said try the studio first. That's all.'

Agnes stared at the phone, picked up the receiver,

replaced it. So Alexander was trying to track her down. It was easy enough, she supposed, to get St Simeon's number from the phone book. He knew she was based there. She picked up the receiver and dialled his studio.

'Hi,' she heard him say.

'It's Agnes. You phoned me.'

'Oh, yes. I didn't have your number. I hope you don't mind . . .'

'No. Of course not.'

'It's about my mother. It's all rather complicated . . . She's worse, you see, they don't think she's got long now, and—' He sighed. 'She used to be Catholic, before my stepfather – he was very low church – but I think she might want to return to all that . . . and I couldn't think of anyone to ask. Maybe she doesn't believe any more, but when someone's – dying . . .' Agnes heard a choke in his voice.

'Where does she live?'

'Luton. Not far.'

'I can find a list of churches in her area.'

'She's about to move to a hospice, when there's a place.'

'They'll have their own chaplains, probably. Just ask.'

'It's that simple, is it?'

'As I said, once—'

'It's what you're for. Yes.'

There was a pause. Alexander said, 'By the way, I'm sorry.'

'It's OK. I'm used to it.'

'No need to be flippant.'

'I wasn't being flippant.'

'I don't suppose you'd—'

'What?'

'Sit for me again?'

'But you said—'

'Oh, the things I say. You mustn't take me seriously. It was going well, before I wrecked it. But we could start again.'

Agnes watched the spring sunlight turn the old wood of her desk to dappled gold. 'Yes,' she said. 'Yes, I suppose we can.'

'You see,' Alexander said that evening, as he stood by the scruffy sink of his studio pouring out two glasses of chilled white wine, 'I was frightened.' He brought the glasses over to the window where Agnes stood.

'Frightened of what?'

'It was going so well. It reminded me of what – of what I could have been. And then you said all that about the RCA, brought it all back . . .'

Agnes sipped her wine. 'Yes. It was ill-judged on my part.'

He looked out at the urban sunset, at a flock of birds sweeping the indigo clouds. 'It's such a strange time,' he said quietly. 'So intense. I've cancelled clients, I've barely worked at the professor. And now here you are. It seems, somehow, that I need you.'

Agnes held her glass up to the window and watched the dying sunlight refract through the liquid. She was aware of Alexander standing beside her, so close that she could almost feel the soft fibres of his jersey against her cheek. She turned to him. 'Where do you want me, then?'

'I can't keep up,' gushed Athena at lunch the next day. 'One minute it's off, then it's on again – and all this so-called painting.'

'What's so-called about it?' Agnes picked at her lasagne.

'Well, you've obviously both got ulterior motives.'

'Which are?'

'Well, for you, it's because you like chasing murderers.'

'And for him?'

'Ah-ha,' said Athena, and winked.

Agnes felt suddenly tired. 'Look, Athena, he's a man in crisis, his mother's dying, his work's going badly—'

'And he's hanging around a hospital.'

'Yes. There is that. It is a bit odd.'

'And why should he go for you if not—'

'It's spiritual. He probably doesn't meet many people who believe, that's all.'

'Hmmm.'

'Anyway, we worked very hard. I was there for hours.'

'And?'

'I got a stiff neck from sitting so still. He says he wants some photos of me.'

'Uh-huh.'

'You know nothing about it. For working from. I'm not sure I've got any.'

'There's that wedding photo of you and Hugo.'

'That's about twenty years old – more, in fact, and

anyway I can't see Alexander going for that.'

'Why not?'

'I just can't. How's Jonathan?'

'Fine. I think.'

Agnes returned to her flat, and pulled down from the top of the wardrobe an old cardboard box, held together by yellowing strips of Sellotape. She opened it carefully and began to sift through its contents. That was the one, she thought, taking out a black and white image in a fancy cardboard frame and looking at it. For some reason it made her want to laugh, to see herself and Hugo looking like the epitome of fashionable Paris, surrounded by their friends, carefully arranged in front of the Hotel George V in deliberate poses of nonchalance. How young Hugo looked, she thought, in his longish dark curls and well-cut trendy jacket. She stared at the face, at the dark eyes that had promised so much. She looked at her young self, so full of hope for that short moment, only to be betrayed, dashed against Hugo's compulsion to destroy the things he loved most. She had been buried alive in wealth, violence and emptiness, and if it hadn't been for Julius, then a young curate in her village, she would probably still be there. Or dead.

She shuddered and looked at Hugo again. She wondered how long it would take before she would be able to see that face for what it was, neutrally, coolly. She wondered what Gabrielle saw when she looked at him now.

She stood up and went to the bathroom, where she stared into the mirror. The death of hope, she thought –

written in these lines. For the young Agnes, hope had become a purely religious state in those years of her marriage, a dogged act of faith against all the evidence. Poor Alexander, she thought, getting this ravaged version of myself – but then, it's the ravaged self he wants. For some reason.

The phone rang, suddenly, loudly.

'Yes?'

'It's St Hugh's hospital, we're ringing about Mrs Kathleen McAleer.'

'What about her?'

'We had a case meeting today, and would like to discharge her soon, but there's nowhere to send her. And she said to ask you. You see, if she could have some support she could go back home . . .'

'What sort of support?'

'She's regaining some mobility, but it'll never be what it was. And what with there being no family . . .'

'You mean, she needs someone to visit her, or live with her, or what?'

'Could you come in this evening and discuss it? Her social worker will be available at eight-thirty. She did suggest you. You live near her, apparently.'

'Yes. It appears I do. OK. I'll come to her ward.'

It took a long time, firstly waiting for the consultant, then finding the hospital social worker who'd got the notes from the meeting, and all the time Kathleen had sat there patiently. At one point she had turned to Agnes and said, 'Good times. Beers,' and Agnes had grinned back. In the end it was agreed that, if all went well, and if she could be transferred to a ground-floor flat in her block, Kathleen would be able to return home in a fortnight, and Agnes agreed that she would ask the sister-in-charge at her Order whether she could make it part of her duties that Kathleen had a visit twice a day. As the medical team departed, Kathleen suddenly grasped Agnes's hand.

'Thankyou thankyou,' she said. Agnes saw there were tears in her eyes. 'No workhouse, no more.'

'It would never be the workhouse, not these days.'

'Same difference,' Kathleen said.

It was dark when Agnes left the hospital, and she took the route through the new courtyard to her bus stop. It was a drizzly, misty night, and the building site looked like a lost city, the shapes of steel forming ethereal buildings against the sky, the cranes making ghostly towers. She saw a sudden, darting movement, and looked again. A human figure scurried along by the fence, and then vanished through a gap. Agnes quickened her pace and was just in time to see something large being flung far into the crater, and to hear it land, wetly, in the clay at the shallow edge on the far side. Agnes flattened herself against the boards as the figure turned, peered in her direction and then hurried off again, a scurrying shadow against the long bright windows of the hospital.

Agnes stared into the blackness of the pit, hoping to see – what? Another bone? A severed arm? Hoping, she thought, to see nothing at all.

She woke early the next morning. The spring sunshine filled her room, but her thoughts were still shrouded in the mist of the night before. She had a premonition that there would be more industrial relations problems at the hospital building site this morning, a feeling borne out by the evidence as she approached and saw four bobbing figures sitting on their oil drums again.

'What's happened?' she asked the nearest of the men.

'You don'wanner know,' he said, shaking his head.

'What have you found?'

''E found it. Mikey 'ere, didncha?'

'Bleedin' did. 'Uman 'eart.'

'A heart? Where?'

'Over there, weren'it. By Number Four.'

'We'd just had our breakfast.'

'An' the lungs an' all. Still attached.'

'What will you do now?'

'Call the police, Xcept, 'e won't.'

'Bleedin' git.'

'So we just sits 'ere, don't we?'

Agnes went straight to Amber Parry's ward but her bed was empty, with fresh new sheets smoothed across it in waiting for the next patient.

'Excuse me,' she tried to say to a hurrying nurse.

'Be with you in a minute.'

'Could you tell me . . . ?' she tried another.

'Back in a moment.'

'Perhaps you can help,' she said to the nurse on the desk at the ward entrance. 'I'm looking for Amber Parry.'

'Miss Parry was discharged this morning.'

'Where is she now?'

The nurse raised one efficient eyebrow. 'At home, I imagine.'

In fact, Agnes found as she came out of the lift in the basement, Amber Parry was in her little office, an airless cubicle with a tiny window, squeezed between the Pathology museum and a series of store cupboards. She looked up as Agnes put her head round the open door, and smiled genially.

'Ah, it's you. Have you heard? A heart this time.'

'Yes, but—'

'I did warn them.'

'Shouldn't you be at home?'

Amber smiled. 'There's far too much to do here. Of course,' she went on, 'it's all the proof I need.'

'But it's new, isn't it? It must be, to still be, you know, recognisable. It's hardly the result of digging up old graves, is it Miss Parry?'

'Well, new ones, then. It's all the same to me.' Amber's smile had a fixed, steely edge to it; the sort of smile you don't argue with, thought Agnes, turning to leave and almost bumping into Julia as she came running down the corridor.

'I thought you might be here,' Julia said, breathlessly, taking Agnes's arm and directing her back towards the lift. 'I've just seen McPherson. It's all rather odd.'

'What?'

'He was waving a piece of paper around and shouting at his secretary. It turned out he'd received a fax or something, but when they saw me they both went really quiet. But he was – I mean, unusually for him –

you know, really kind of panicky.'

'What was it?'

'He said, "I don't have to bother with these petty, small-minded, anonymous threats",' Julia mimicked with his trace of a Scots accent.

'Time to sneak round his office again?'

Julia nodded. 'I think so.'

'Have you heard about the new find?'

'On the site? Uh-huh. It's all round the medical school. A dissected body or something.'

'Not quite. A heart and lungs. Although that gives me an idea. To whom would you address yourself if you thought something might have gone missing from the mortuary?'

Julia opened her eyes wide. 'You mean, a body?'

'Something like that, yes.'

'The mortuary technicians, I suppose.'

The day felt fresh and warm after the subterranean corridors of the hospital.

'I knew it wouldn't work,' pouted Julia. 'Closing ranks. We're all trained to do it. Even the mortuary lads.'

'But don't you think he knew what we were on about? When I said, I had reason to believe that bodies had been tampered with, you saw his face.'

'Yes. He knew what you meant all right.' They walked on towards the new building. 'What *did* you mean?' asked Julia after a moment.

'Whatever they found on that building site this morning had been put there last night.'

'Oh.'

'And when I heard what it was, I fell to wondering where one might get hold of such a thing.'

'But who . . . ?'

'I have my suspicions. Still, let's see what McPherson's so upset about, shall we?'

Dr McPherson's office was locked. His secretary's next to it was open, and deserted. The two women stole in, and Julia began to leaf through a neat stack of correspondence.

'Be careful,' Agnes hesitated. 'We shouldn't just—'

'Shhh. It's not here anyway. It must be in his office.' Julia tried the adjoining door, which opened. She darted to the desk, which was covered in chaotic piles of papers, and began to rummage through them.

'Do you think—' whispered Agnes.

'Ooh, look,' whispered Julia. She held up a business card on which was a picture of a stiletto shoe, and the words, 'Make-A-Date Escort Agency'. Julia giggled. 'There's another,' she said. 'Oh, no it's not. Just a business card.'

'Let's see,' Agnes said, taking it. It was a small plain white card bearing the name 'Sisco Limited', and an address in Moorgate. 'I wonder what that is,' Agnes said, handing it back to Julia who replaced both cards carefully in the pile of paper, then cried out, 'Ah-ha,' and pulled out, with a flourish, a thin scroll of fax paper. Looking over her shoulder, Agnes saw, in large handwritten capitals, the words: 'YOU ARE DIGGING UP THE PAST. BEWARE.'

'Where's the number, quick?' breathed Agnes.

'What number?'

'Where it was sent from?'

'It'll be on the other page.'

'Quick.' Agnes riffled through the pile of papers. 'It's not here.'

'His secretary will have kept it.'

They carefully buried the fax in its original position in the stack of paper, and hurried back into the secretary's office. They could hear the sound of footsteps along the corridor. Julia looked at Agnes, and then, taking her arm, walked boldly out of the office, just as a young woman approached them.

'Excuse me, but are you Dr McPherson's secretary?'

'Yes. I'm Angela.' The woman smiled pleasantly.

'Sorry to bother you. We thought you might be in your office.'

'How can I help?'

'Um, Dr McPherson said he'd let me have a reading list. He said he'd leave it with you.'

'And you are . . . ?'

'Julia. Julia Hart.'

The young woman frowned as they followed her into the office. 'I don't recall anything – we've had rather a – a busy morning. I'll just check.'

Julia nudged Agnes, who looked down and saw a top sheet from a fax. There were two telephone numbers, and the words, 'Number of sheets including this: two.' While Julia chatted pleasantly with Angela, Agnes carefully folded the paper in four and slipped it into her pocket.

'Sorry, he must have forgotten,' Angela was saying.

'That's OK. I'll pop in later in the week.'

'Well,' said Agnes, as the lift doors closed behind them, 'this destination number must be the hospital's, I presume.' Julia looked at it and nodded. 'So the other is the source of the mystery fax. Perhaps.'

'Not perhaps, definitely,' said Julia. 'And it had better be worth it, as I've just committed myself to reading through McPherson's *Guide to Postgraduate Microbiology*.' She made a face. 'I hope she forgets to tell him.'

'So do I. I wonder how you track down a fax number.'

'Spend hours poring over phone books, I imagine. Still, it'll be more interesting than medical journals,' laughed Julia as they walked across to the hospital. 'There's your evening cut out, anyway.'

'Ah, no, not this evening. I'm – um – seeing Alexander.'

Julia stopped and looked at her, then resumed her even pace. 'Poor you,' she said. 'I'd prefer the phone books myself.'

Chapter Fifteen

'There,' said Agnes dismissively, dropping a strip of four tiny images of herself on to Alexander's table.

Alexander glanced at it and smiled. 'When I said photos,' he said, 'I didn't mean—'

'It was all I could get. London Bridge station, two quid. A bargain.'

Alexander leaned over and, picking up the card, examined Agnes's four faces one by one. 'Actually, it's not bad as these things go.'

'Don't be silly, it's dreadful. They always are.'

Alexander studied her. 'Was that on purpose, then – to choose something ugly?'

'Nothing I had at home was suitable. My wedding photo—'

'I'd have loved to see that.'

'It's horrible.'

'I quite like this one.'

Agnes looked over his elbow and nodded. 'Yes, I thought that was the best.'

'You look, sort of, amused. This hint of a smile, here round your eyes, like a private joke. Yeah, I like that.'

Agnes wandered over to the window. 'Mind you,' he went on, 'I could base the whole portrait on this one. You look like a crazed maniac. Like someone whose attic is stuffed with mummified corpses.'

'How do you know it isn't?' laughed Agnes, turning towards him, feeling her smile freeze at the look on his face, a look like hunger.

'Shall we start work?' she said, after a moment.

He blinked. 'Sure.'

Some time later she heard him say, 'We should take a break.' She put her hand to her neck and yawned, then slowly stretched and, slightly dizzily, stood up. 'What time is it?' she asked.

'Nearly eleven.'

'I had no idea.'

'Me neither. Do you want to have a look?'

She joined him by the easel, aware that the last time she had seen Alexander's version of herself it had been a mutilated travesty. But this one was different. The lines were bolder, the detail was stronger. She saw a tall, upright form in green and black, gazing somewhere beyond the viewer with an extraordinary softness of expression.

'You flatter me,' she said at last.

'No, not at all.'

'I look . . . vulnerable.'

Alexander, looking down at her, shrugged. 'It's still not right. It's better than it was, but there's something – missing.'

'Any chance of a cup of tea?'

'Sure.'

Agnes allowed him to busy himself with the kettle while she aimlessly paced the studio, feeling the circulation return to her legs. She paused in the shadows by one of the huge roof beams, a swathe of white muslin falling behind her, the light from the solitary spotlight glancing off the thin fabric, softening the edge of her face. She looked back towards Alexander, searching for him beyond the dazzle of the lamp. She heard him gasp.

'Oh my God,' he whispered. She could see him across the studio, beyond the lamp, she heard his steps approaching. 'That's – I knew it,' he breathed, suddenly next to her, grabbing a fistful of the muslin, arranging it behind her. She stood quite still. He dragged the anglepoise towards her, casting sudden clumsy shadows in all directions. She felt complicit; even when he bent and touched her chin, tilting her face towards the light, she felt as if she and Alexander were simply playing their parts in a pre-destined scene which was about to unfurl in some quite obvious way. He stood in front of her, gazing at her, while she breathed, too loudly, she thought. He went back to the lamp and tried to draw it nearer, but in doing so he pulled the plug from the socket. The darkness was immediate and close, so that when Agnes felt Alexander's hands on her shoulders, it seemed somehow normal. He brushed her cheek with his fingertips, and she gave in to a sudden recognition of yearning, to the overwhelming need to bury herself against his jumper, feeling him wrap his arms around her, feeling herself become small against him.

'Don't speak,' he whispered.

'All this time . . .' she said.

'You are a very surprising person,' he said, his lips against her neck. She opened her eyes to find the darkness was less black. She could see Alexander's profile in the night haze from the windows, and she traced her fingers across his eyelids, along the side of his face, until he grabbed her hand and bit it, gently. She caught her breath, aware of him smiling in the darkness as he brushed his lips against the inside of her wrist. She reached up and entwined her fingers in his hair, feeling, as their lips met, an electric, familiar sensation that jolted her back into her past, to a time when all this—

'What did you say?' he whispered.

'—when all this was possible,' she murmured.

Agnes opened her eyes, bleakly, then closed them again. It appeared to be late morning and she was in her own bed, alone. She opened her eyes again and looked around the room, taking in the empty whisky bottle and her clothes in a heap on the floor. The green shirt crumpled on the top made her heart ache.

The phone rang, and she heard the click as her answering machine swung into action.

'Darling, poppet. Where are you? Any news? I bet there is.' There was a giggle. 'Do phone me as soon as you can, I'm dying to hear Everything.'

Agnes groaned and lay back on her pillows. Almost immediately the phone rang again, and a tentative voice said, 'Agnes? It's Julius. Um, just making contact, you know. Wonder how you are. Had this feeling – doesn't matter. Whenever.'

Oh Julius, thought Agnes. You would have this feeling, wouldn't you? Just when you're the last person I could possibly speak to. She sat up in bed, her hand on her forehead, then slowly got up and stumbled to the bathroom, where she rummaged clumsily in her bathroom cabinet for some headache tablets. She ran a glass of tap water and dissolved one of the tablets, watching it fizz. She heard the phone ring again, and paused, waiting for the click of the machine.

'Why did you run?' she heard an anguished, male voice. 'Why?' She put down the glass and went to the phone, her hand poised over the receiver. 'Just when you – are you there? Just when I . . . And don't try telling me it's not your fault. Christ, if I'd thought—'

Agnes suddenly snatched up the phone. 'Alexander? Alexander?' She heard the dialling tone. 'I'll tell you why I ran,' she went on. 'Because the last time anyone made me feel like that was when I got married, and that was – oh God, can't you see? I ran because – because it was all a mistake,' she shouted against the electronic purring, remembering his kiss, how he had undone the buttons on her shirt, how she had, tentatively, explored the shape of his chest with her fingers. 'And then I ran,' she said into the phone, 'out of the door, and you followed me into the street, and that cab came out of nowhere and I cursed it as I jumped into it, and if you must know,' she said, her voice subsiding into a hoarse whisper, 'if you must know,' she said, dropping the receiver and collapsing on to her bed again, 'I came back here, finished off most of a bottle of whisky and passed out. Alexander,' she whispered, gazing blankly at the ceiling, listening to the soft whining from the telephone. 'Alexander. I ran because – of course – I can't.'

'Calling yourself a religious is not an excuse to beat yourself round the head,' Madeleine said firmly later on that afternoon. She was making a pot of tea in Agnes's tiny kitchen, and the whole flat had taken on an appearance of neat efficiency merely by her presence within it. Agnes covered her eyes with her hand, wondering why she'd let her in when she'd knocked on the door half an hour earlier, saying, 'Um, we've tried ringing you a few times – well, Julius has. He's a bit worried,' and Agnes had reluctantly dragged herself upright and opened the door. Now her fellow sister was handing her a cup of perfectly brewed tea.

'You look terrible,' Madeleine said.

'I've told you why.'

'You've just told me that something terrible happened last night and it was impossible because you're a nun and you're a terrible person. Or words to that effect.'

Agnes smiled weakly. 'That's about the truth of it.'

'Do you want to talk about it?'

Agnes shook her head and took a sip of tea. 'There's this man,' she said.

Madeleine was smiling. 'Look at you. Did you go to bed with him?'

Agnes opened her eyes wide. 'Of course not.'

'Well, that's something, eh? Or is it the thought of what you missed? Sometimes I think that's the worst feeling of all. Lust, eh? It's a bugger. I mean,' she went on, opening a packet of chocolate digestives, 'if just wanting it is the sin, then it's no worse actually doing it, is it?'

Agnes grinned, despite herself. Her headache was lifting at last, after its third dose of painkillers. She took a biscuit, looked at it, and put it back. 'You can't really think that.'

'You see, I've done all that,' Madeleine went on, 'mostly before I joined the Order, and then there was a rather difficult . . . overlap, shall we say. But in the end, you have to channel all that stuff, not ignore it. Using it as an excuse to hate yourself is going to get you nowhere, isn't it?'

Agnes sipped her tea. 'But it's much more difficult than that. When I became a nun—' she paused, remembering the madness of her marriage '—it was only through the religious life that I found any kind of stability or contentment – or sanity, really. And even in those times when it's difficult, or when you're thinking, is that all there is? – even then, it's still a source of joy and peace for which I am constantly grateful.'

Madeleine looked at her and smiled. 'Well that's fine, then.'

'If only it was. And where does it leave me and Alexander?'

'Where do you want it to leave you?'

Agnes reached for a biscuit and took a bite. She brushed

a crumb from her lap. 'I wish I knew.'

That evening, after Madeleine had left, Agnes lay on her bed and stared at her window. The tree outside, now coming into blossom, made soft woolly shadows against the sky. Agnes suddenly got up, put on her raincoat and went out.

She walked up to the Thames Embankment, then climbed the stairs on to London Bridge, joining the last surge of late commuters heading home. She stood by the railings of the bridge, peering down into the muddy shallows, then looked up, across the illuminated grid of the railway station, to the yellow rectangles of St Hugh's.

'Feelin' low?' Kathleen asked.

'Is it that obvious?' Agnes replied.

'Men, eh?' Kathleen giggled. Agnes tried to smile.

'Still, eh? Good times,' Kathleen added vaguely. Agnes stayed for a few more minutes, glad to see her friend in such good spirits. Then, leaving the brightness of the ward, she wandered aimlessly along the corridor, feeling the hospital, now so familiar, envelop her as if she were part of its workings. She hesitated at the staircase before choosing to go down, keeping going to the very bottom. As she set out along the grey concrete tunnel, she felt her despair return. She reached the mortuary and stopped in the corridor, waiting, listening. By the door was a stray orange plastic chair and she sat down, hearing the drone of the air conditioning in the pipes over her head, like a beating pulse. She thought how the hospital buried everything to do with death in its lowest reaches, whilst continuing its work with the living on the clean bright floors above. It's an illusion, she thought. Behind this door, a mere few yards away from where she sat, there was a body. Or several bodies. Departed souls, she thought. We all end up here in the end.

Suddenly, she heard movement behind the door, and instinctively bolted from her chair to the next doorway. She heard the door open, and voices, apparently finishing a conversation.

'But my dear, you are part of my plan.' That was clearly Stefan Polkoff's voice.

'Oh, you and your plans, Stefan,' she heard Alexander reply, and then Stefan laughed. She heard the door open further and, peeping out, saw both men leaving Polkoff's office, Stefan carrying something wrapped in a cloth. She watched them disappear round the corner, then followed at a distance, their conversation now out of earshot. They turned off towards a door which was labelled 'Emergency Exit', pushed the bar and went outside. She waited a moment, then followed them out, finding herself facing the courtyard between the old and new buildings. There appeared to be no one around. She crossed the courtyard to the building site and slipped behind the fence, peering round the edge of the excavated pit in the dim light. It was deserted. Emerging back into the lamplight of the courtyard, she saw a tall figure hesitating by the fence some way further along. It looked like Alexander. She turned to go, feeling foolish, but she heard footsteps approach behind her, and his voice say, 'What on earth are you doing here?'

'I could ask the same of you,' she replied.

'Well?'

'I was visiting my friend Kathleen on the wards. And you?'

'Just having a chat with my friend Stefan.'

'I see.' And what is he up to? she wanted to ask, but didn't.

'It seems to me,' Alexander said, 'that you haven't quite laid to rest the ghost of Gail Sullivan, or whatever her name was.'

Agnes looked at him. 'What do you mean?'

'It's as if you're still searching for something here.'

Agnes scanned his face, wondering what to say, how much to trust him. Not at all, she felt, even though . . . 'I'm – I'm sorry I ran away,' she heard herself say. 'Not that – I mean . . .'

'That's OK,' he said gently. 'You did what you had to do.'

They began to walk back across the courtyard, the new saucer-shaped lamps throwing long shadows ahead of them.

Agnes was thinking fast. Alexander clearly was party to some scheme or other that was being hatched by Polkoff. If she could throw some bait, without giving anything away . . .

'You know,' she said, conversationally, 'Dr McPherson received a very strange fax yesterday.' Agnes watched Alexander's expression closely.

'Who's he?' Alexander asked.

'He's the head of the new Genetics unit. He was made dean last year.'

'Oh, him. I've heard the professor mention him. And what was this fax?'

'It was some sort of threat about the new building. It's been built on church ground, you see, and people have got upset about it.'

'Which people?' asked Alexander. 'It's only a building.'

'I know. Strange, isn't it? Kathleen told me,' she lied.

'And why are you telling me?'

Agnes smiled at him. 'No reason. Just making conversation.'

He looked down at her. 'Do you fancy a drink? It's not closing time yet.'

For the second time that evening, Agnes found herself on London Bridge. The tide had come in, and the water was dark and circled in deep swirls. They walked uncertainly beside each other. Agnes looked at the river surging blackly beneath them and concentrated on keeping a distance between herself and Alexander. Things were different now.

'Here we are,' Alexander said, as they approached a pub on the north side of the river. 'We'll just catch last orders.'

They waited at the bar, strangely silent in the midst of the babbling crowd, then took their drinks out to a chilly patio that overlooked the river. The wind blew Agnes's hair across her face, and Alexander watched its movement intently. Suddenly he reached over and gently brushed it back.

'It's all so odd, my life,' he said.

'How's your mother?'

'They're moving her to the hospice tomorrow.'

'She'll be well looked after there,' Agnes said.

Alexander wandered over to the low wall. 'I love the river,' he said suddenly. 'That's why I chose Battersea. Partly, anyway.'

'Are you a Londoner?' she asked, for something to say.

'Yes. No, well, mostly. You know. Born here. Then I ran away from my horrible family as soon as I could and settled here.'

'Your accent isn't quite—'

'You can talk,' he laughed, suddenly, and Agnes laughed too. 'You still sound completely French.'

'Nonsense, my English is near perfect.'

He looked at her. 'I was working on you today, I mean, the painting. I'm really on to something now. Those photos—'

'Oh, those.' She laughed. 'If you can get something decent from those, you really must be a genius.'

'I am a genius,' he said, suddenly serious. 'At least, I would be if—'

'It's a human failing,' Agnes smiled, 'finding excuses for falling short of what we'd like to be. There's always something in our lives that we can blame – our parents, our schooling, our mistaken relationships. The past. "If only things had been different" – all that.'

She looked up and was taken aback by his expression, which had become distant and cold.

'You're just like Stefan,' he said, absently.

'What do you mean?' she asked.

'Sorry? Look, I'm in no fit state. If you've finished your drink, I'll walk you home.' It seemed to be a statement that required no answer.

At her doorway, she hesitated. 'You can – I mean, if you like, it's not late or anything,' wondering what it would be like to entertain a man in her flat, what it would be like to have that gaze pass over her paintings, her coffee cups, her bed, her chairs. She touched his hand. It was like ice. Not even looking at her he said, 'Some other time, maybe.'

She wanted to grab hold of him, to hold his face between her hands, to force him to meet her eyes, to ask him – what exactly? She felt his fingertips brush hers as he turned, and then he was gone, loping down the dark street, his long shadow juddering in the lights from the station beyond.

'I can't think what it was, Julia. I've racked my brains.'

'Obviously something you said,' Julia replied.

'Yes, but what? I was just wittering on,' Agnes said, wondering whether it was time to be honest with Julia.

'Well, what were you saying?'

'He'd said something about being a genius.'

'And you doubted him? That's it, then. If you weren't a nun, you'd know that Rule Number One is, always treat men who think they're geniuses as if they are.'

Agnes laughed. 'But it wasn't quite like that. I said how we can always find excuses for not being what we'd like to be, something in our past, you know, our family relationships . . .'

Julia was suddenly thoughtful. 'You know, I think he really is a suspect.'

'Hmm,' Agnes said. It was true that he'd been discussing something with Stefan, and that Stefan was up to no good. It was also true that whatever she'd said had upset him in some way. But why? Looking at Julia, she realised that her own feelings for Alexander were so complicated that there was no point even trying to explain them now.

'I told him about McPherson's fax,' Agnes said. 'He didn't seem to know about it.'

'Hmm. That doesn't mean he's not a suspect. Where was all this then?'

'Outside my flat. He walked me home.'

'Did you invite him up for coffee?' Julia smiled.

'He didn't want to.'

'If I didn't know better, I'd say you were disappointed.'

Agnes laughed. 'Hardly. Not me.'

'You're in love. It's obvious, poppet.' Athena poured a large glass of kir and handed it to Agnes.

'I spend the morning discussing it with Julia. I spend this lunchtime discussing it with you—'

'QED. One of the symptoms: desperate need to mention the beloved at all times.'

'Athena, I don't fall in love. After Hugo – don't look at me like that.'

'You're regretting having run away the other night, and just when you thought you might not run away, he doesn't give you the chance to find out.'

Agnes sighed. 'It's appalling.'

'Why? You're a passionate woman. It's normal.'

'You're a passionate woman,' Madeleine said, over a quiet supper in the house.

'So everyone says.'

'It's normal, to fall in love.'

'You as well? I thought at least you would—'

'Would tell you off? Would go on about the sins of the flesh, urge you to go and confess? Does it feel like a sin?'

'Yes. No. Only he's certainly untrustworthy and possibly violent.'

'I mean, sure, it's unbalancing, and at some point you'll have to resolve it. I'm not saying people like us can just go around having sexual relationships. But denying it is no help at all, is it? You could go to some priest and confess – and then what? Nothing's changed. Because you haven't addressed what's going on in you.'

'What *is* going on in me?'

'That's what you've got to find out.'

'Oh no,' groaned Agnes. 'I think I'd rather just confess.'

When she got home that night, there were two messages on her answering machine. The first was from Athena.

'Sweetie, I spoke to Jon, and you know you were asking about his RCA contact, before we got sidetracked into talking about lover boy? Well, he's coming for Sunday lunch, Doug that is, and you're invited too. One-thirty, OK? Super.'

The second message said, 'Hi, it's Julia, at four-thirty. I just heard that another weird thing happened. This morning, McPherson found an arm nailed to his office door. You know, like the abbot. A human arm. Weird, huh? Phone me.'

Agnes leafed through her notebook to find Julia's number and dialled it.

'Hello, I just got your message. As you say, weird.'

'We should meet.'

'Tomorrow's Saturday. Can you visit McPherson again?'

'If he's there, suppose so.'

'We've got to ask him who's got a grudge against him, go through the names.'

'Which names?'

'Well, Stefan Polkoff is obvious. And Amber Parry. And, I guess, Alexander.'

'You're on,' Julia said cheerfully. 'Meet you outside the library at ten.'

Agnes put down the receiver and stared at it for a while. She went over to her bed and lay on it, still fully dressed. She thought of Alexander the night before, striding away from her as if she had ceased to exist for him, when before, in his studio, it had all been so . . . She sighed. So delicious. She tried to feel relieved, because, if he had agreed to her invitation, anything could have happened. Anything, she thought, and her mind ran ahead of her through the various possibilities contained in the Anything, throwing up images of discarded clothes and breathless moments before she could catch up with it and say, Enough, Stop, This cannot be. 'No,' she whispered, 'This cannot be.'

Chapter Sixteen

'Here we go,' said Julia at ten-fifteen the next morning as they went into the shiny lifts of the new building.

'How do we explain me?' said Agnes.

'Like we said. It's time to come clean. Up to a point. This is fun,' giggled Julia, as the doors opened on to the first floor.

'You're sure he's in?'

'He was half an hour ago, I saw him go in when I came out of the library.'

Julia knocked and then put her head round the door.

'Hello,' Agnes heard Dr McPherson reply warmly. 'I heard you'd been here again.'

'The thing is, Dr McPherson,' Julia said, as Agnes followed her into the office, 'I haven't been totally honest.' Agnes watched Julia put her head charmingly on one side, her sleek hair sweeping her cheek, her smile warm and girlish. 'You see, with all these weird goings-on—'

McPherson made a dismissive gesture with his arm. 'Pah. Some nonsense. Silly students, no doubt.' He smiled welcomingly at Julia, then looked up at Agnes. 'And you are . . . ?'

'Sister Agnes,' said Agnes, wondering for a moment whether to try Julia's wide-eyed femininity but settling, sensibly she thought, for briskness instead. 'I'm a nun, I visit patients here. Julia and I have noticed that you seem to be the target of some kind of campaign.'

Dr McPherson blinked in surprise, his manner cooling visibly. 'And you think it necessary to come barging in here when I'm working and—'

'I know,' Julia said, 'it does seem silly, doesn't it?' Agnes watched her sit herself down opposite Dr McPherson and lean forward, looking at him through her eyelashes. 'It's just, we think it might be dangerous.'

Tom McPherson looked at her doubtfully, then burst out into brash, jovial laughter. 'Now really, young lady – ladies,' he added. 'I'm touched at your concern, but I have better things to do—'

'Are you allergic to penicillin?' asked Agnes suddenly.

'Wha – yes.' His eyes narrowed as he looked up at her where she was still standing a pace behind Julia. 'Is this some kind of jape?' He frowned, impatiently, waiting for Agnes to reply.

'Someone tried to get some to you, when you were prescribed antibiotics.'

'This is preposterous. Ridiculous. I mean, how could they? I would have . . . And how did you . . . ?' He collected himself. 'Now look. Someone's obviously got some kind of grudge, not surprisingly, given my current success in diverting funds – but that does not give you, a complete stranger, the right to delve into private details concerning me and my medical records. How did you find this out?'

Agnes and Julia exchanged glances.

'Do you know Stefan Polkoff?' Agnes asked.

'Yes.'

'And Amber Parry?'

'I think she may be behind all this, yes,' he replied. 'Unhinged, obviously. Stress of the job too much, won't adapt to change. And we're offering her a perfectly reasonable retirement deal, I can't see why she's so upset. I'm prepared to believe that such a person might be responsible for all this, and these faxes—'

'What did the second one say?' asked Julia quickly.

Dr McPherson pushed a piece of paper across to her, and she glanced at it and passed it to Agnes. Agnes read the words, HERESY WILL OUT. REPENT BEFORE IT'S TOO LATE.

'It's the same number. That it was sent from,' Agnes remarked.

'The local bureau,' McPherson replied shortly.

'You mean, you—'

'I checked it out, yes. The first time. I thought, if I was going to do this, where would I go? There's a fax bureau at that photocopying shop by the station. I went in and checked the number. It was sent from there. Both were.' Agnes and Julia stared at him. 'I'm not the idiot you take me for,' he added. He stood up. 'And I think you've wasted enough of my time.' The conversation had ended. Julia got up to go.

'Do you know Alexander Jeffes?' asked Agnes. Dr McPherson looked blank. 'He's a painter, he's doing the portrait of Professor Burgess.'

'Oh, that,' McPherson said. 'Good old Robert. Who did you say?'

'Alexander Jeffes.'

McPherson looked thoughtful. 'Jeffes? A portrait painter. Hmmmm. Are you sure it's Jeffes?'

'Yes.'

McPherson hesitated, then said, 'No, I've never heard of such a person.' He ushered them to the door, then said with false joviality, 'And if I were you, young lady, I wouldn't let my nosiness get the better of me.'

'We should have thought of that, checking that printshop,' said Julia as they walked across to the hospital.

'Mmm. He's keen on Burgess, isn't he?'

'They all have this silly camaraderie, those chaps.'

'Of course,' Agnes went on, 'the building was going to be a Surgery wing.'

'That's true.'

'And Alexander's lying. Hiding in doorways. Obviously, the name doesn't ring a bell with McPherson, but the face would.' They went through the revolving doors of the main entrance, and Agnes suddenly stopped still. 'Of course,' she said, the doors still thumping rhythmically behind her. She took Julia's arm, and said, close to her ear, 'Alexander must have changed his name. It's the only explanation.'

'But—'

'A long time ago,' she added, remembering that all his RCA friends knew him as Alexander Jeffes.

'But he didn't know McPherson a long time ago.'

'How do we know?' Agnes went on, unleashing Julia's arm and setting off along the corridor to the medical school. 'I mean,' she added, warming to her new idea, 'that would explain why Alexander was so keen to get the job. To be near McPherson. And if his name's different, then McPherson wouldn't know, unless he saw him. Hence the hiding in doorways whenever McPherson goes past. In fact, I bet you anything . . . Come with me.' She grabbed her friend's arm again and dragged her to the lift. They went up to the third floor and Agnes knocked boldly on the door of Professor Burgess's office. There was no answer.

'Right, where can we hide?' muttered Agnes, seeing the stationery cupboard across the corridor, and leading Julia in there. 'I bet you anything that McPherson is wondering about Alexander, now we've planted the idea in his head.'

They peered through the crack in the doorway at Burgess's empty office. 'I'm not quite with you—' Julia began, but Agnes suddenly shushed her. 'He's here,' she whispered, her face a picture of triumph as McPherson approached the professor's door. He tried the handle, but the door was locked. He looked around for a moment, then set off back the way he'd come.

Agnes and Julia sat on the floor in the cupboard. 'I knew it,' Agnes beamed. 'You see, once we'd mentioned it, he got curious. It explains everything. My artist friends said that Alexander was a strange choice for this work.'

'I thought he was a great catch,' Julia said.

'He's managed to convince them of that. He was

obviously desperate to get this job, for some other motive.'

'To be near McPherson. I thought you said he hadn't heard of him.'

'He appeared not to have.'

'And why's Alexander sending faxes—?' Julia began.

'No, he's not sending faxes. That I can tell. I wasn't sure, at his response to McPherson's name, whether he was lying. I thought perhaps he was. But when he said he knew nothing about the faxes, that was genuine.'

Julia looked at Agnes. 'Do you learn such things at Nun School – to tell when someone's lying, I mean?'

Agnes laughed. 'Something like that, yes. Come on, before we get locked in here.'

They sat on the wall outside in the spring sunshine, swinging their legs.

'What now, Boss?' Julia said.

'I don't know. It's all very odd. Even if Alexander has changed his name, and did know McPherson a long time ago when he had a different name—'

'It all sounds rather far-fetched,' said Julia, suddenly doubtful.

'Yes. It does.' Agnes frowned. 'Also, I'm sure Stefan's the one carrying bits of bodies around, not Alexander. Except, he was there. And there's Amber Parry . . .'

'Maybe she's the mystery fax-sender?'

'Maybe.'

'They're all in it together, then,' Julia said. 'There was a lot of bad feeling about the new building. Still is. It wouldn't surprise me if there was a campaign to get rid of McPherson.'

'No. And Burgess may be involved too.'

'Why Burgess?'

'Only that – no, perhaps not.'

'Hmm. Do you think they want to kill him?' Julia asked.

'I don't know. I'd say perhaps they just wanted to get him to leave, if it wasn't for the penicillin.'

'And that was Polkoff, that signature?'

'True. Yes. Or maybe . . . I know what we've got to do. I'm going to track down Alexander's old name – and you're going to talk to the Pathology department about the source for these human off-cuts: hearts and arms and bones and so on. OK? And if you can find out who had access to the mortuary, and whether grieving relatives have noticed bits of their loved ones are missing, that would be helpful too.'

'You know,' said Julia, as they got off the wall, 'this is much more exciting than revision.'

'Oh dear,' sighed Agnes. 'If you do badly, I'll blame myself.'

'That's OK. I'll blame you too.'

'We'll reconvene on Monday – lunchtime OK? That gives you a couple of days with your books.'

'OK,' Julia said.

'Oh, and – can you sign me into the swimming pool? I brought my things on the off-chance?'

Agnes ploughed up and down the laned section of the

pool, her face in the water, staring through her goggles at the deep blue undulating lines of the tiles. Alexander's past, she thought, coming up for air. She remembered his sudden change of mood on London Bridge two nights ago. And what had she been saying? About how people are so keen to blame their past for things not working out in the present. It explained everything, she thought, switching to backstroke, watching the cool water flick from her skin in silvery splashes. It explained why Alexander was eaten up with some deeply buried anger, paralysed by a cankerous self-hatred. And, she supposed, a need for revenge. Against whom? she wondered, finishing with a few brisk lengths of crawl. Dr McPherson? It seemed most unlikely that they would have a shared past, she thought, hearing in her mind McPherson's soft Scots accent, remembering Alexander's English tones.

She swam over to the steps and hauled herself out of the pool. She pulled her goggles from her eyes and almost bumped into Alexander who at that moment emerged from the changing room. They stood stock still about a foot apart and looked at each other.

'Hi,' he said, allowing his gaze to travel from her wet hair down to her plain black swimsuit and back again. She was suddenly conscious of the rings her goggles had left around her eyes.

'Hello,' she said. He was wearing fluorescent orange swimming shorts with pictures of Donald Duck all over them. She noticed the muscles of his thighs, his well-toned abdomen. 'I didn't know he was famed for his surfing prowess,' she heard herself say. Alexander looked blank. 'Donald Duck, I mean,' she added.

Alexander looked down at his shorts. 'Is he? Surfing? I've never looked that closely. How observant of you,' he said, with a trace of a smile. They stood as if rooted to the spot. Then Alexander said, 'I don't suppose you'd come out with me tomorrow night?'

Agnes sighed, and looked up at him. 'I'm not sure we're very good for each other.'

'It's a private view. An exhibition, set up by a friend of mine. You'd like it. It's about the self-portrait. Do you work out?'

'Sorry?'

'Only, your muscle tone – it's – I'm sorry, shouldn't really comment. Great, though. What do you think? Tomorrow, I mean?'

Agnes smiled at his flustered confusion. 'OK. Where?'

'St Katharine's Dock. I'll call for you. Seven o'clock?'

'OK.'

She went into the changing rooms, and stripped off under the shower. Yes, she thought, watching the hot water run in rivulets across her belly. Not bad for my age. Not bad at all.

'It ought to be easy,' Agnes said to Madeleine after Mass the next morning, 'to say no. I mean, just No.'

Madeleine stirred her cup of coffee and grinned. 'It depends on whether you're the kind of person who says Yes.'

'"No, I won't go to your private view." See, I can do it

now. "No, thank you, Alexander, I won't see you any more."'

'The difference being, he's not standing right in front of you wearing hardly anything at all.'

'I wish I could say that had nothing to do with it,' Agnes sighed, suddenly serious. 'I need help, Madeleine. Spiritual guidance.' She sat on a kitchen chair. 'In my prayers these days, there's a sort of blank space, a silence. A stubbornness.'

Madeleine sat down next to her. 'Who would you normally turn to?'

'Julius.'

'Oh. I see. Anyone else?'

Agnes shook her head. 'I've never been this bad before.'

Madeleine smiled. 'I find that hard to believe.'

'No really,' Agnes went on, 'last time there were mitigating circumstances; this time, it's just selfish, bloody-minded, egotistical, off-the-rails—'

'We all do it. And if you need to talk, I'm here.'

At one-thirty-five, Agnes pressed the intercom of Athena's mansion block in Fulham. Walking into Athena's flat a few moments later, she was once again assailed by delicious smells. Athena showed her into the lounge.

'Darling, this is Doug. Doug Trevithick. Doug, this is Sister Agnes. Now what can I get you?' Doug nodded at Agnes. He had wiry brown hair which was receding at the front, and tortoiseshell spectacles. Agnes glanced at Athena and noticed the tension that showed through her tinkling good manners.

'Oh,' Agnes said, 'er, a glass of white wine?' The lounge still looked temporary, somehow. It was as if Athena had made no impact on it; as if she didn't really live here.

'Jon's slaving over a hot stove, as usual,' Athena was saying. 'Has he always been like this?' She turned, charmingly, to Doug.

'The first time I met Jon,' Doug replied, 'was over a whole sheep roasted on a spit.'

'Typical,' Athena said. 'You'd never catch him making egg and chips.'

'Which is funny, really, for a boy from Sidcup.'

'Are you betraying my true roots?' Jon said, appearing in the doorway.

'Nothing wrong with Sidcup,' grinned Doug.

'Where is it anyway?' laughed Athena.

'You know where it is,' Jon said to her, and turned and went back to the kitchen. Athena smiled thinly and poured herself another glass of wine.

Doug turned to Agnes. 'I gather we're here to talk about Alexander Jeffes?'

'Well—' Agnes began.

'Funny boy. He was, anyway. Haven't seen him for years.'

'You were at college with him, Jon said.'

Doug pulled at one ear. 'Sort of. He laid into someone at the beginning of the summer term and got expelled. Or left, or something, it was all a bit unclear. Ended up in prison. So I only knew him for two terms. It was serious, though, the guy nearly died.'

'Why did it happen?'

'No one knows. It was another student, in the year above. A guy named Christopher Morton. There was lots of gossip afterwards, but Alexander disappeared.' Doug sipped his wine. 'What's he like now?'

'Um – well, he's doing portraits, commissions, you know.'

'Not bad.'

'He hates it.'

'That figures.'

'He's making lots of money.'

'Good for him.' Doug grinned. 'Funny business, Art.'

'So, when was this – incident?'

'Let me think, now – nineteen sixty . . . sixty-eight, I started, and it was the spring, so it must have been sixty-nine. Strange time to be at the RCA, that was, loads of upheavals.' Doug fiddled with his earlobe. 'I liked him, really. Alexander. There was something about him – about his work. Searching stuff, kind of vulnerable. And angry. Good, yeah.'

'Does the name McPherson mean anything to you?' Doug shook his head. 'Or Polkoff? Stefan Polkoff?'

'Blimey, yes. Polkoff did a series of lectures on anatomy for artists. Historical stuff too – Leonardo, that kind of thing. Good lectures. Yeah, they became close, he and Alexander. In fact, Alexander got a minimum sentence, people said, because Stefan spoke on his behalf in court. Sixty-eight, eh? I feel old.'

Athena stood up. 'I'll see how Jon's getting on.' She left the room in a swish of cream linen.

'Do you think,' Agnes went on, 'when he attacked that student, that it was about anything specific?'

'I don't know. He was always quite aggressive. It might just have been an off night. The guy he attacked told someone that he'd just got in the way when Alexander went into one. You know, like, it wasn't personal. He was always pretty unpredictable.'

Agnes nodded.

'He'd been to a funeral,' Doug went on, 'a day or two before. There were rumours that it was to do with that, him being more unstable than usual.'

Voices were suddenly raised in the kitchen. 'I thought we had lemons in the house. I specifically asked you—'

'Darling, it'll be just as nice without,' they heard Athena reply, then a few moments later she appeared in the doorway. 'Lunch is served,' she said, looking near to tears.

At ten-past four, Agnes finished a cup of tea and looked at her watch. 'I'd really better go quite soon,' she said. 'I'm going out again this evening, and I was hoping to catch an early evensong.'

'And where are you going?' asked Athena.

'An exhibition. Yes, with him.'

The two women were sprawled in the lounge. Doug had just left, and Jon had gone for a session at his gym in South Kensington.

'Are you – are you all right?' Agnes asked.

Athena drew her hand across her eyes. 'No, not really, poppet. I mean, he's lovely, but . . .' She stared at the carpet for a while. 'What he wants, and what I want, seem to be mutually exclusive. We're always clashing.'

'And what does he want?'

Athena managed a smile. 'I wish I knew. Men – they're not like other people, are they?'

Agnes walked all the way to Westminster Cathedral and caught the end of a service. Creeping to a seat at the back, she felt soothed by the cool marble pillars, relieved to become part of the milling, anonymous crowd. 'My soul doth magnify the Lord,' she began, thinking about her own, empty, stubborn soul. An image came into her mind of the wily hen of the folk tale, who escapes from the fox's sack and sews a large stone into it instead. The fox drags the sack home, unaware that he is carrying a lump of rock instead of a live, fluttering bird.

She arrived home exhausted at half-past six and flopped on to her bed. At five to seven she got up and checked her face in the bathroom mirror. She stared closely at her skin, at the pores, moles and stray hairs, the tiny veins in the whites of her eyes. This is me, she thought. Part of God's creation, an expression of Life itself, briefly existing in time . . . What am I for? she wondered. In church she had felt, once more, detached, as if God and all the saints were somewhere beyond her reach; as if she, with her soul of stone, had deliberately placed herself at a distance from them. She looked at the mirror again. A self-portrait, she thought, as the doorbell buzzed.

She grabbed her bag and went down. Alexander was on the front steps, and he rather awkwardly ushered her to the passenger door of his car.

'So,' she said, as they set off towards Rotherhithe, 'what's this we're going to?'

'You'll see. An old friend of mine, runs a gallery, got some American sponsorship deal for an exhibition on "The Self-Portrait". Might be good. You look – ' he turned slightly towards her – 'you look tired. Or is it deliberate?'

'I don't know what you mean.'

'Yes you do. No make-up, that sort of thing.' Agnes stared out of the window. It was dark, and the old industrial buildings of east London made an uneven skyline beyond the river. After a moment Alexander said, 'It suits you.'

Agnes turned to him. 'What suits me?'

'How you are now.'

'I don't need your judgement on how I look,' she snapped. 'You may have four scratchy photos of me, but you don't own my appearance, OK? A portrait of me is not the same as me.'

Alexander fell silent. Agnes tried to see his expression in the darkness. He seemed to be smiling, but it might just have been the beat of the shadows cast by the street lamps.

They pulled into a dingy car park. It had begun to drizzle. She followed Alexander over rough tarmac until they rounded a corner and were met by a blaze of light from two wide glass doors. A woman emerged from the hubbub of voices and came to greet them. She had a chic blonde bob and wore a long tunic dress in crimson velvet. 'Hi,' she beamed.

'Alexander,' he said, hurriedly, 'Jeffes.'

Agnes noticed the woman give him a funny look. 'Sure. Yes, Alexander. I'm Bridget,' she said, turning to Agnes warmly and offering her hand. 'Come in to my wonderful wonderful gallery.'

Agnes found herself in a sea of hats and outlandish hairstyles. Tall glasses of white wine bobbed precariously amongst them. Agnes wondered why Alexander should have been so keen to give Bridget his name when she clearly recognised him – and when it was quite obvious they were old friends. She stood in front of a large canvas smeared with thick layers of oil paint, whole tubes squeezed out into formless humps and ridges of brown and cream and dark grey. Agnes stepped back from it, and then a few more paces, until suddenly a likeness emerged, the face of a man brimming with life and good humour. It must be, thought Agnes, that Bridget knows Alexander under his former name, and that he was reminding her to call him by the new one. She looked around for Bridget, and was just making her way over to her, when she felt Alexander at her side. He took her arm.

'I want to show you this,' he said, leading her away from the gaggle of people to another room. 'Look,' he pointed. Agnes saw a gloomy, starkly realistic painting of a middle-aged man. His face was lined and anguished, with a profound sadness about his eyes.

'It's like looking at the man himself,' Alexander whispered, visibly moved. 'In fact,' he went on, 'it's like looking within him, or beyond him, or something. Distilled.'

'Who was he?' asked Agnes, reading the label which said 'Thomas Eakins, Self-Portrait, 1902'.

'American.' Alexander's voice was hushed. 'He's – I've always loved . . .' he turned back towards the painting. 'Can you imagine, seeing yourself like that? Being able to stare into a mirror and then portray what you see, with that degree of skill, of openness—'

'Of honesty,' Agnes said, looking at Alexander.

'Yes. Honesty.' Alexander met her eyes, then turned back to the painting. 'When I was a student, this was what I wanted. Now, when I look at it, I see what I've lost. This, and this one. Look, this is his wife. Can you see? She's looking at him with open dislike, or accusation, rather, yet there's a sort of acceptance there too. I used to wonder,' he said, scuffing his shoes against the polished floor, 'what sort of talent it would take to see so clearly and to paint what you see like that. Something more than technical brilliance. I mean,' he went on, 'there's all sorts of ways of representing a likeness.' He waved his arm vaguely towards the noise emanating from the central room. 'All that stuff. It's all valid, all interesting. But for me, the idea that there was an inner truth – that you could make something emerge just by seeing truly . . .' He broke off and laughed, briefly. 'You'd call it the soul, wouldn't you?'

'Not exactly—'

'But now,' Alexander went on, not listening, 'all I see is what I've lost.'

He stared up at the Eakins portrait, at the eyes moist with age and feeling, and Agnes saw his own eyes fill with tears.

239

'Maybe it is the soul,' Agnes said. 'Maybe you're right.'

'What do you know about it?' The old bitterness flared and died away.

'Nothing,' said Agnes, thinking of Little Red Hen and the fox's stone. They stood next to each other, staring at the floor.

'I've never met anyone like you,' Alexander said.

'It's not too late.'

'For what?'

She looked up at him. 'No, not that. I meant, it's not too late for you to be honest again.'

'Honest? Look where it got me, being honest. Last time I got two years. After that I shut it all down, decided not to care. Life's gone swimmingly ever since.'

'Has it?'

'Oh yes. Money, women, freedom—'

'Freedom?' Agnes allowed herself to laugh.

'OK. So I can't fool you.'

'Any more than you can fool yourself.'

They smiled at each other, a smile of complicity.

'Why did you attack that person at college?' asked Agnes hesitantly, reluctant to shatter the fragile moment.

Alexander took her chin between thumb and forefinger and tilted her head gently upwards. 'Never you mind,' he said. He held her gaze for a second, then said, 'Shall we join the party?'

Someone had put some music on the CD player, and Agnes felt dazzled by the noise and bright lights. Alexander melted into the crowd. Agnes could see only faces, laughing mouths, lips greasy with make-up, teeth biting into canapés. Behind these animated likenesses was suspended the still calmness of the painted ones.

'Enjoying it?' Bridget seemed to be shouting, her blonde bob still perfect atop the crimson column of her body.

'Ye-yes, very much.' Agnes found her voice.

'I'm exploring ideas of identity and self,' Bridget went on. 'There's a lovely man here from telly, we're discussing a series, it's sooo exciting. The zeitgeist,' she said, behind her hair, 'I've always been in tune with it. You ask A . . . Alexander.'

'What were you about to call him?' Agnes held her breath.

The green eyes were suddenly sharp, eyeing Agnes for a moment. 'I'm sorry, sister, top secret. He and I – well, let's just say I collected him a long time ago. Ooh, look, there's my lovely man just leaving . . .' Agnes watched her glide across the space, and reflected on the unsisterly uses of the word 'sister'.

'Do you want to go?' said Alexander, suddenly at her side.

'Yes, actually. I've had enough.'

'Me too.'

At the door, Bridget kissed him goodbye extravagantly, and stroked his nose with an elegant red fingernail. '*Ciao, carissimo,*' she said. 'Phone me.'

Outside the rain had stopped, leaving uneven puddles in the stony ground. Alexander walked fast, his head lowered. Agnes sensed his desperation.

'I can't take it,' he said. The gallery's lights threw out

long shadows behind them. 'Where did we leave the bloody car?'

'It's over there,' Agnes said, peering across the unlit wasteland, trying to keep up with him.

'I could have been – I should have been up there with – and all those shallow stupid fucking bastards – they all know that. They like failure, it reassures them. Bastards.'

'The only person who cares about your failure is you.'

Agnes heard the rage in his voice. 'Fine. Well, that makes it all OK then, doesn't it? And now you're going to tell me it's not too late, aren't you? As if I could start to see again, as if I could look at myself the way Eakins looked at himself.' He stopped, breathless. They were on the edge of the car park, by the graffitied wall of a derelict warehouse.

Agnes, fearful of his anger, of what it recalled, said, 'And what would happen if you did – look at yourself, I mean?'

'I'd probably kill myself. Or someone else.'

He set off again, more slowly, and Agnes followed him, keeping to the wall.

'Bridget said she collected you,' Agnes said, lightly.

'Yeah. All her men, butterflies pinned to a board.'

'The thing is, you're killing yourself anyway. All this hatred, all this blaming your past—'

She was unprepared for the response. Alexander stopped short and grabbed her by the shoulders so that her back was against the wall. 'What about my past?'

'It's obvious . . .' Agnes felt her knees weaken as the old fear returned in the face of his rage, remembering

Hugo, whose anger, once provoked, would take an inevitable terrifying course. She swallowed hard, telling herself, again, this is Alexander, not Hugo.

'What else did she say?'

'Wh-what?'

'Bridget. I saw you two talking. I realise now – God, I'm an idiot. All this time you've been pretending to care about me, and I'm fool enough to believe it, and then to drag you along here right where you want to be, into circles of people who know me – from before . . .'

Agnes braced herself against the wall.

'What did you ask her?' Alexander hissed.

'Nothing.' They glowered at each other.

'What was it? About my name? That must have been it. She didn't tell you, did she, the bitch . . . ?'

'I asked nothing, she told me nothing.'

'God, I've been a fool. Treachery – and there you are, skulking around the hospital, going on about this Tom McPherson, and me playing right into your hands by asking you to sit for me.' He let go of her, suddenly, and walked away, then turned. 'And the irony of it is, oh God, the irony is – ' he laughed harshly, loudly – 'that that painting was all about honesty. About you and me being true to ourselves. And all the time you were bloody lying.'

'Stop this, Alexander,' she said firmly, taking a step towards him. 'It's ridiculous,' she said, feeling the ghost of Hugo recede. 'I don't know what you're talking about.'

'Oh yes you do. You can see into my soul,' he hissed, leaning towards her, 'but then, I can see too. I can't help seeing. And I know when you're lying. And your lie is worse than mine. Yours was a deliberate betrayal, when I was at my most vulnerable, and you . . .' She could feel the warmth of his breath against her face. 'You lied,' he whispered, then turned sharply away and strode off into the shadows. She heard him start his car, saw the headlamps cutting two searchlight beams across the puddles, heard the engine noise fade as he drove away.

She stood by the wall, fuming with rage. How dare he strand her here in this wasteland in the middle of the night, stuck here with all his stupid pretentious friends tinkling away around the corner? She set off towards the distant yellow mist of the main road, striding fast in her fury. She should never have agreed to come, she thought, risking his stupid childish tantrums, his crazy violence. Because of course, she thought, gritting her teeth, she had lied. Of course she'd lied. How dare he be right?

Chapter Seventeen

'But why didn't you go back to the gallery and phone a cab?' asked Julia, at lunch in the canteen the next day.

'I don't know. I didn't trust that Bridget, I think. The idea of falling on her mercy, arriving back into that party . . .'

'So did you walk?'

'Yes.'

'And weren't you mugged or anything?'

'I didn't see a soul until I got to civilisation, and then it was just the late-night City boys. Anyway, I probably looked pretty weird myself. I'm sure I was muttering things as I walked along, now I come to think of it, I was so angry.'

Julia chewed thoughtfully. 'He really is the violent type, then, our Alexander. Or whatever his name is.'

'I think he felt betrayed.' Agnes rubbed the back of her neck.

'Are you trying to justify his violence?'

'Violence is too strong a word. He just gets angry.'

'But male anger—'

'And anyway, it was partly my fault.'

'Listen Agnes, these days women don't have to feel responsible if men are violent to them.'

'But if I hadn't—'

Julia was shaking her head. 'Male violence is men's problem, OK? Not ours.'

Agnes looked at Julia. 'If I'd known that when I was your age, I wonder how different my life would have been.'

'Oh, very different,' Julia replied, delicately moving slices of discarded tomato to the side of her plate. Not very different at all, thought Agnes, reaching across and helping herself to them.

'Anyway,' Julia said, 'to business. I bumped into McPherson today, quite by chance, and so I asked him who he thought might have nailed an arm to his door.'

'Good for you. And?'

Julia pouted. 'I think we've blown it there. He was decidedly frosty; rushed off to a meeting or something. It's quite obvious he doesn't want us to know any more. Like, why someone might want him out of the way.'

'It must be tied up with Alexander. When he mentioned him, Alexander, I mean, he said "this Tom McPherson". Tom. I've never used his first name, but there's Alexander using it as if it was normal to him.'

'Yup.'

'And now McPherson's being cagey too. It must be about this name business.'

'I don't suppose you got anything done on that.'

'You suppose wrong,' said Agnes, 'though we're none the wiser. I phoned a few places this morning, and managed to establish that very few people who change their name bother to enrol it – because you don't have to – and sure enough, when I phoned the Public Records Office they had no trace of Alexander.'

'Much progress we're making.'

'However, I spoke to a friendly policeman I know – who gave me some tips.' Agnes grinned as she recalled Lowry's voice on the phone. 'Well, I don't know, Sister. DIY post mortems, state-of-the-art surveillance work – and you still don't have a corpse to show for it. It's not how we go about things in the Force, I have to tell you.'

'What tips?'

'Official records, he said. National Insurance, tax, medical records—'

'And how do we get into them?'

'Any ideas?' Agnes leaned back in her chair.

'Not as such. We could just break into his house and nose around.'

'Do they teach you house-breaking at medical school these days?'

Julia laughed. 'We could try his studio, seriously.'

'Well, maybe,' Agnes said. 'And how about the old bones and things?'

'Right. The first bone was old, could have come from anywhere. It was human, but it seemed to have been dumped on the surface, not dug up. The second one was obviously from a butcher's – an ox leg or something. The arm was steeped in formalin, and had been nicked from the dissecting room.'

'And the human heart?'

Julia picked up her fork and put it down again. 'Um – fresh, you know – stolen, probably, from – from the mortuary.'

'Hmm. Not very nice – I mean, for the relatives, or whoever—'

'The Path labs said no one's been able to trace the source, no one's noticed, not even the technicians. But if it was a routine post mortem, you could just sew the body up and we'd all be none the wiser.'

'So someone with access to all this has been raiding the labs for their own purposes – to frighten McPherson, presumably, and hold up the building.'

'Polkoff.'

'It has to be, hasn't it?'

They wandered out of the medical school into the afternoon sunlight. Julia squinted up at the bright sky. 'What shall we do now?'

'Well, we should keep tabs on Stefan and Amber,' Agnes replied. 'Or rather, I will. You've got your books to read.'

Julia sighed. 'OK.'

'And Alexander.'

'I don't suppose you're too keen on seeing him again,' Julia said.

Agnes smiled brightly. 'Oh, I've had worse. See you tomorrow? Lunchtime?'

'Same time, same place, Boss.'

Amber Parry was sitting calmly at her desk in her cupboard of an office, somewhat swamped by large stacks of files and papers. She looked up as Agnes popped her head round the door.

'How nice to see you. Could you be a dear and fetch some tea from the machine – my hands are rather full, as you can see.'

Agnes returned some moments later with two cups of tea. 'In fact,' Amber went on, 'I was just thinking about you.' Agnes sat down on a worn swivel chair. 'Oh, do be careful – that one's got a foot missing and tends to tip at awkward moments. It's all they'd give me.' Amber's face seemed smoother and pinker, her eyes brighter.

'How's the new medicine going?' asked Agnes.

'Oh, much better, thank you. Stefan said I look ten years younger, the other day, when he brought me my new pills.'

'Stefan?'

'Yes, he's so sweet, he passes the pharmacy that way, it's easier for him.'

'Oh. And – er – how's your job?'

Amber looked suddenly furtive. 'We'll see,' she said. 'Things may change soon.'

'I looked up the archives. The abbot's curse, all that. It's interesting, isn't it?'

Amber looked closely at Agnes. 'Yes. It is interesting. More than interesting.'

'What's that?' Agnes asked, conversationally, indicating the heaps of files.

'Oh, just research. If you must know,' she lowered her voice, 'things are going missing. Photos, papers, that sort of thing. It's all part of it, the wrongness. No one respects the past, people just steal it. And even that poor girl, Gail—'

'What about Gail?'

'Well, I was going through these, and found two missing, and then I remembered, she'd come and asked me for some documents to do with the new building, and I'd lent her the files, though there was nothing of importance in them because the Powers-That-Be sit very tightly on all that. And then of course, she'd died so I never got them back. In fact, I wondered whether you'd be able to—'

Agnes thought of the key that Mark had given her, that was sitting in a drawer at home waiting for her to visit the flat. 'Yes. I can have a go at finding them, if you'd like.'

'That would be so helpful, dear.'

'Why would Gail have wanted to look at the files?'

'I really have no idea.' Amber opened another box file and began, lovingly, to riffle through its dusty old papers.

Agnes stood up. 'Just one thing – these human remains that they've found on the building site – what do you think?'

Amber continued to arrange sheets of paper on her desk, smoothing them out as she went. 'I wouldn't know about that dear. Maybe the abbot's curse still has influence.' She smiled, briefly, brightly, at Agnes, then went back to her files.

Agnes left her, absorbed in the crinkling of old paper, the handling of history.

The building site seemed to have grown, with signs

extending along the newly dug pit, saying 'Danger. Deep Excavation.' Bob Bryant's hut was in the same place, however, like a seaside chalet balanced on a crumbling cliff face. He greeted her cheerfully.

'No more corpses this time. Not just recently.'

Through the little window behind him, Agnes could see the cranes dipping their iron necks up and down.

'No more strikes, either?' she asked in reply.

'A few stiff words from head office. Works wonders. Lazy sods'll try anything.'

'But human remains?'

'That's what I thought too. But these are reasonable people, here. They want the job done same as we do. Them doctors, the big cheeses, came down, had a chat. No problem.'

'You mean, no one's going to follow it up. Even though—'

'No point, lady. Someone bears a grudge, insider, obviously. It's not as if it's murder, one of them said. "Just proceed as usual," he said.'

'I see. Well,' said Agnes, in the narrow doorway, 'you must be relieved.'

'No skin off my nose either way, lady. But, yes, relieved.'

'And these big cheeses – might one be called Dr McPherson?'

Bob Bryant nodded. 'Yup, that was it. Mac something. And the other was a little guy, but very, you know, above himself. Snooty.'

'Professor Burgess?'

'That's it. Professor-and-don't-you-forget-it Burgess.'

Walking back to her flat ten minutes later, Agnes had the impression that her mind was functioning in a fog. Nothing made sense. In one corner there seemed to be Polkoff and Parry, both of whom were against the building. In the other there was McPherson, who was doing very nicely out of the new building; and Burgess too. And, of course, Alexander, who was connected to McPherson in some way. And now it turned out that Gail Sullivan, who had died so tragically, had borrowed some files to do with the new development.

At least that part of it was accessible, she thought, taking the key from the drawer and going out again.

Agnes pushed hard at the door to Gail's flat. Unopened post had piled up behind it, and Agnes picked her way past it into the hallway. The flat was small, and papered in uneven grey and off-white. Agnes glanced through the letters, which were mostly unpaid bills. There was a note from the landlord confirming that, as agreed by Mark, he would be clearing the flat at the end of the month. She went through the hall to the living room. The furniture was sparse and gave the impression of belonging to no one at all. There was a chest of drawers, and Agnes opened one or two, finding only jumpers and underwear.

She glanced around the room, looking for the files described by Amber. There was a small bookshelf, on which was arranged a handful of shabby paperbacks. Next to them were two A4 document wallets. Agnes went over to them and opened one. It contained the architects' plans for the St Hugh's extension. The other contained some correspondence between the developers, who seemed to be called Avalon Limited, and the hospital Trust. Slipped into the front of this one was a set of forms from the Land Registry in Telford for application for copies of the register entries concerning the site. She had started to fill in her name and address, but had got no further.

This must mean, thought Agnes, that Gail had been about to send off for details concerning the transfer of land. A photocopy of the site of the development was with the forms. There was also a press cutting about the Stott Institute agreeing to fund a new Genetics wing at St Hugh's, dated nearly two years earlier. Agnes was just closing the file when she noticed a slightly crumpled piece of paper tucked in behind the others. She pulled it out and saw it was a handwritten letter addressed to the Stott Institute. 'Re, the St Hugh's Development,' it said. 'I am writing to inform you of gross malpractice in the financial handling of this building which you have so generously sponsored.' Agnes could barely make out the words in the scrawl. 'I am writing anonymously because of my position in the hospital itself, but I think it important you know that the ownership of the land is in question, and that people have not declared interests who should have done. I can say no more.'

Agnes held the letter in her hand. Her first thought was that it was out of keeping with everything she knew about Gail. Her second thought was that this was not Gail's handwriting. She scanned the room, looking for anything that Gail might have written, and her eye fell on a wall calendar pinned to the peeling paintwork by the bookshelf. The few, sparse entries were written clearly in blue biro, nothing like the thin black ink in front of Agnes now. Looking at it again, she noticed it was a photocopy. Where was the original, she wondered, putting it carefully back in the file; and who had written it?

Agnes put the files and the landlord's note to Mark into her bag and left, reflecting, as the door slammed behind her, on how the flat bore no imprint of its occupant, as if Gail had come into existence and left again without making a mark. She wondered whether, in God's scheme of things, it mattered.

By the time she went to bed that night the fog had developed into a raging headache. She lay on her bed, and through the pulsing pain was aware of images of Alexander. She found herself wondering, vaguely, whether two people could suffer the same headache at the same time.

She wasn't aware of having slept, but some time later stirred at a sound, a strange whirring noise coming from within the room. As she turned on the light, she realised that it was the fax machine that had sprung to life, the paper rolling crisply through the printer. She went over to it. The first thing she saw was a picture, a rough representation of a woman's body – the Rokeby Venus, she realised, as it emerged fully from the machine, and the printer noise stopped. She pulled it out and looked at it more closely. It was a roughly drawn copy, the naked form of a woman lying with her back to the viewer, holding a mirror. But a dagger had been drawn, plunged grotesquely into the back of the woman, with caricatured drops of blood dripping from it; and the face of the woman, the face in the mirror in photographic detail, was Agnes's own.

Agnes put the fax down shakily and went over to the window. After a moment she went back and picked it up and stared at it for some time. She picked up the phone and began to dial Julia's number, then stopped and replaced the receiver again.

She glanced again at the fax, at the face in the mirror which was recognisably one of her passport photos. Only Alexander, she thought. Only Alexander had those pictures. She looked at the sender's number, and then leafed through her notebook and checked it against the number from which McPherson's faxes had been sent. It was different, although the exchange was the same. But then, she thought, looking at her clock and finding it was fourteen minutes past midnight, the local fax bureau at the station would be closed.

She ran her hands through her hair. It didn't make sense, she thought. Why on earth would Alexander bother? It had almost certainly been Polkoff, or perhaps Amber, who had sent the others. And now here was Alexander joining in. The idea made her feel ill.

She imagined Alexander standing by the window in the shadows of his studio, in the darkness of his thoughts. With sudden certainty she saw that he would be too caught up with his own unbearable guilt, his need to blame someone else for his actions, to do anything as measured and deliberate as sending a threatening fax. On the other hand, she thought, those pictures, the reference to the Rokeby Venus – how had she come to receive this, if it wasn't via Alexander?

She imagined Alexander and Stefan together, old friends, sharing a glass of wine in the studio, confiding in each other their plans – for what? for intrigue? for murder? and Stefan borrowing, or perhaps stealing, one of her photos. For if Polkoff had enough mischief about him to scatter human remains on the building site, it would be an easy step from that to fax machines.

She got back into bed and lay down. She found herself engaged in a formless dialogue with God, pleading on Alexander's behalf in some half-imagined crazy courtroom scene. She lay awake in the darkness, arguing the case for the defence, for a long time.

The next morning was dull and drizzly. Agnes woke abruptly with the dawn. Her limbs ached and she felt weary, but she got up, pulled on her clothes from the day before, and went straight out. She walked to St Simeon's church, arriving just before seven-thirty, and sat on the low wall outside, turning her face up to feel the drizzle against her cheeks. She closed her eyes, and when she opened them again a moment later, Julius was standing there.

'A visitation,' she said.

He smiled. 'I was about to say the self-same thing. Come in.'

He led the way to the Lady chapel, and Agnes sat

quietly in a pew while he busied himself in preparation for the eight o'clock mass. Then he came and sat next to her.

'Anything in particular?' he asked.

She shook her head. 'The usual,' she replied.

'Pride, Lust, Avarice, Envy,' he began counting them out on his fingers. 'What are the other three?'

'No,' she laughed, taking his hand, 'be serious.'

He looked at her gravely. 'You look tired,' he said. 'Is this story you've been telling yourself any nearer to ending?'

She sighed. 'Either I'm right, in which case it is; or I'm wrong, and there is no story, and it's all just a jumble of coincidences like the rest of life, with no beginning or middle or end, just a chaotic list of events bearing very little relation to each other.'

'In other words, you're right.'

She looked up at him and laughed. 'No, I mean it,' he went on. 'Why else would you still be embroiled in it all?'

'Because I'm stubborn, and vain, and too attached to my intellect, and . . .' She took his hand again. 'Julius – there's this man who seems to be involved in it all. And I – and I've – it seems to be very difficult for me not to care about . . .' She let go of Julius's hand and fiddled with her fingernails. 'The painter,' she added.

'I see. And are you in danger from this person?'

'I don't think so. Perhaps,' she added, unable to lie to Julius.

'When are you going to inform the police about your story?'

'I don't know. When I know whether it's a story or not.'

They sat in silence, side by side. 'How would you feel, Agnes,' Julius said after a while, 'without your story?'

Agnes met his calm, clear gaze. 'I would be – without my story there would be silence. And I'm frightened of the silence.'

Julius sat quietly for a while. Then he said, 'There's no need to be frightened of it. It's where God—'

'That's just the point.'

'The God of love and forgiveness—'

'For those worthy of it.'

Julius looked at Agnes and she stared at the floor, tears welling behind her eyelashes. He took hold of her hand and held it tightly. Behind them, footsteps echoed in the church as the early morning worshippers arrived for mass. Agnes got up to leave. At the doorway, Julius said softly, 'Come back soon.'

She looked up at him and nodded, then went out of the church gates into the street, lifting her face to feel the rain splash against her skin again.

At nine o'clock she knocked on the door of Professor Burgess's office. There was no answer. She was about to knock again, wondering why people always did that, when she heard voices raised in indignation, approaching.

'. . . Can't think what the fellow's playing at.'

'There must be some explanation, Professor. Probably this illness in the family he told me about. I'll get him on the telephone now.'

'I specifically said half-past eight; it's so nearly finished. And I wanted it hung in pride of place at my leaving party,' puffed Professor Burgess as he came into view, with Mrs Holtby at his heels. They nodded absently at Agnes, and each disappeared into their own office, only to emerge a few moments later.

'No answer? I told you,' spluttered the professor. 'That's two sessions he's missed now.'

'There was only his answering machine, I'm afraid.'

'Did you leave a message?'

Marjorie Holtby faltered. 'I'm not very good at those things.'

'Where's his number? I'll let him know in no uncertain terms . . .'

Alone in the corridor, Agnes smiled at Marjorie. 'These unreliable artists. Terrible.'

'Oh, I know,' said Marjorie, going back into her office. 'And we were so impressed with his – his professionalism. He wore a suit, you know, at least to start with. Funny colour, mind you, sort of muddy beige.' She sat down mournfully at her desk. 'But now he's vanished altogether.'

'When?'

'Well, he was due to see the professor yesterday evening, and didn't turn up. And now this morning. It's all we need. I'm trying to sort out the invitations for his leaving do too; there's all these people from the Trust I've been asked to invite, and it's so rude at the last minute like this—'

'Can I get you a coffee? I'm just going . . .'

Marjorie looked surprised, then pleased. 'Would you?

How kind. The professor has his black with two sugars. And white for me, I have my sweetener.'

Agnes paused by the professor's door just long enough to hear the message he was gruffly recording on Alexander's answering machine.

'Right,' said Julia over their sandwiches in the canteen at lunchtime, 'I've made up a list. Medical records – pretend to be a GP? Credit card agencies, pretend to need a credit record and phone his bank—'

'What are you on about?' Agnes asked.

'Ways of getting his old name, of course. Alexander's. Look.'

'And how do we phone his bank without his bank account number?'

'We get that from here, of course, silly. They must have records of paying him.'

'What if it's just by cheque, or cash?'

Julia sighed. 'National Insurance, that's another. Pretend to be from here and say we need his number for payments.'

'Pretend to be from – that's not bad. Except,' said Agnes, thinking fast, 'we can't ask for his proper name. So we can't get his number if it's under the old name.'

'Hmmm. You're right.'

'What was the first one – pretend to be his doctor?'

'Yes, and phone the Family Practitioners Committee or whatever it's called, say we've lost his records . . . OK, don't look at me like that.'

'Let's check with Personnel anyway. There might be a starting point. And otherwise—'

'Otherwise, we break into his house.'

'Or studio. You see, this evening, Professor Burgess is meeting him there.'

'For the painting?'

'That's what I thought. Only, the painting is here. And anyway, on Alexander's answering machine, Burgess has left a message about picking something up, because he needs the money. He said ten o'clock,' Agnes said.

Julia thought a moment. 'Those two are always swapping stuff around between them. I wonder what it is.'

Only one way to find out, thought Agnes. To Julia she said, 'By the way, Mark sends his love.'

'Mark – Mark Henderson?'

'The very same. I wish you'd make your mind up about him.'

'But he's seeing Marisa Giles, didn't he say?'

'Oh dear, I'm out of touch. We didn't actually talk about all that, in fact.'

'What did you talk about?'

'I sought him out this morning. We shared a cup of mid-morning coffee. I wanted to ask him about Gail.'

'Oh. Gail.' Julia made a face.

'I'm helping him sort out the flat clearance, you see. We talked about Professor Burgess, who was surprisingly nice when Gail died, wasn't he?'

Julia nodded. Agnes went on, 'Did you know that Mark knew Tom McPherson?'

Julia frowned. 'Yes, he was his personal tutor.'

'McPherson knew about his dilemma before anyone else did. Even, it seems, before you.'

'How odd,' Julia pouted. 'Still, that's all over now, isn't it?'

'Yes. It is.'

'Unless you think it has any bearing on all this. Though I can't imagine—'

'No, no, none at all. It was just something Amber Parry told me.'

'Oh, her. Mad as a hatter, apparently. Anyway, when are we going to break into Alexander's studio?' Julia said, her interest renewed at the prospect.

'Let's start with Personnel, shall we?'

Agnes was, once again, floored by Julia's audacity. 'Would you have an address for Alexander Jeffes, the painter?' she asked sweetly, popping her head round Gillian Taylor's door. 'We, that is the medical students, would like to give him a presentation. Perhaps in your files?'

Gillian looked puzzled. 'Which painter?'

'The famous Jeffes. He's doing the portrait of Professor Burgess. Surely it would go through your systems?'

'Oh, him. No, that was a private arrangement through that department's own budget. Can't you just do a presentation here?'

Julia looked crestfallen. 'We were hoping to make it a surprise. Still, you're right. Thank you so much.'

Out in the corridor, Julia looked at her watch. 'I said I'd meet Fiona for some clinical practice – and we've got nowhere. It'll have to be burglary,' she grinned.

Maybe, thought Agnes, watching Julia's departing form. Maybe.

She decided to see whether Marjorie had heard from Alexander yet and, heading for Professor Burgess's office, she passed him leaving the pharmacy. He didn't see her. This gave her an idea, and she knocked on the pharmacy door.

'Last time, I promise,' she said to the same young woman, who huffed impatiently. She checked the most recent prescriptions. There was nothing either for, or collected by, Professor Burgess. Then she turned back some pages and ran her index finger down the columns for April, looking for that signature again. There it was, next to a new prescription for Amber Parry, where it said 'Collected By'. And now that Amber had told her, Agnes could see that it said 'S. Polkoff'. She turned back to the week of Gail's death. Polkoff had collected Amber's Nifedipine, as she had already ascertained. She found the Tipp-Exed signature and studied it carefully. An initial 'P', two 'f's at the end, an 'l' – but that wasn't an l, even under the white paint she could see there was no upper loop for the l, but instead a lower one, like y, or g. And if the beginning letter wasn't a P but a B . . . Burgess, she thought. The long 's's looked like 'f's, but in fact, Burgess.

So Burgess had collected Tom McPherson's prescription and obscured the evidence. And, she thought, Burgess and Polkoff had very similar handwriting. Very similar indeed.

She slipped out of the door of the pharmacy, and saw, approaching her, the fast, teetering gait of Marjorie Holtby. Agnes put on her best smile.

'Any luck?'

'None at all. The professor is very angry, I'm afraid.'

'I'm sure he could do without added stress. It can't be good for him, for his health, I mean,' said Agnes with concern.

'Do you know, I was only reading about that at my niece's the other day. Stress-related illness, they call it.'

'And with this sore throat that's going round . . .'

Marjorie laughed. 'One thing you can say for Professor Burgess, if he's suffering from stress, he jolly well lets you know about it. Buttoning it up is not for him. Roars with rage, quite makes me jump, sometimes. But he's never ill. Doesn't hold with medicine. It's always the way, isn't it?' Her hand went to her throat and she swallowed. 'Sore throat, did you say? There's always something, isn't there, and with this do on Friday night. Oh dear, that reminds me, I must phone the caterers, we've got a vegetarian in, apparently.' She teetered away along the corridor.

'You're late. You said before lunch.' Kathleen had her arms folded across her chest.

'Sorry. Got waylaid.'

'And no chocolates?'

Agnes looked suitably sheepish, she hoped. She moved Kathleen's empty lunch tray and sat down on the bed. 'Mind you,' she said, 'chocolates are for invalids. And you hardly qualify these days.'

'Another week, they said.' Kathleen grinned.

'How's the walking?'

'Crooked. Falling over lots. But I like my wheels.'

Kathleen indicated a shiny new wheelchair by the side of the bed. 'My nephew. Don't know where the money come from, don't ask. But it's mine.'

An hour later, Agnes left the hospital. The air was pink and crisp in the setting sun, but nothing could alleviate her unease. She had phoned Lowry from a call-box for instructions on breaking and entering: 'If anyone finds out, Sister, I'll have sacrificed my whole career, plodding as it may be, for one crazy nun.' Now she had to find a hardware store to pick up a few necessary tools before the shops shut. And then it would be time to visit Alexander's studio. If Burgess didn't get there first.

Chapter Eighteen

A fog had fallen with the night, and now, as Agnes walked the deserted streets of Battersea, she breathed in its dampness. The four columns of the old power station loomed in the distance as she turned the corner into Alexander's street. As she approached his warehouse building, she could see, through the shadows, someone rattling the door and then disappearing inside. The door was still open when she reached it. She hesitated, then went in. She paused at the bottom of the staircase. She could hear steady footsteps receding above her. She listened hard, and concluded that whoever the footsteps belonged to was heading for Alexander's studio on the top floor.

In the distance she could hear bells chiming ten o'clock. Burgess, she thought. As if in answer, she heard his voice, way up above her, shouting, 'Jeffes, you bloody fool. Open the door.' There was the noise of him rattling the handle, then his voice came again, 'It's your money too, you idiot. You may not care, but I do. Open the bloody door.'

Why was he so sure that Alexander was in, Agnes wondered.

'If I don't sell them tomorrow, we're stuck,' he shouted, kicking the door. 'I want them off my hands. You stupid bloody bastard.' There were a few more kicks aimed at the door, then a pause. After that came the sound of footsteps descending. Agnes ducked behind the staircase, sheltering in the dank space by the mailboxes. Burgess came down the stairs and went out into the night, his breath in the chill air merging with the fog.

Here goes, thought Agnes. She crept up the stairs to the top, got out from her bag a torch, miniature screwdriver, wire, and a few other bits and pieces, and got to work on the single heavy lock on the door. A few moments later she pushed open the door into the studio and closed it silently behind her.

She blinked in the darkness, and for a few moments listened to the traffic rumble. Then she flicked on her torch and shone it swiftly round the studio. She could see an empty whisky bottle lying on its side in a sticky pool; an overturned chair; some burnt-down candle ends. She took a few steps and the beam of her torch caught her own image, the half-finished canvas on the easel. She stared at her portrait in the pale yellow light. It was, oddly, like looking at a mirror. No, that wasn't it. It was like seeing a very close relative, a twin sister. She shivered, slightly. To work, she thought, wondering where to start. She remembered the antique bureau with its little set of drawers, one of the few pieces of furniture with any kind of storage space, she thought, going over to it. She flicked through the papers piled on it: invitations to gallery openings, invoices from suppliers of artists' materials, lists of auction

lots – 'to Mr Jeffes', 'A. Jeffes Esq', 'Dear Alexander' . . .
Where was this other name, this former, real name?

Her eye fell on a large brown paper package, on which
was scrawled, 'Professor R. Burgess.' That was what he
was shouting about, then. She picked up an ivory-handled
paperknife and quickly slit it open under the sticky tape.
She pulled out what appeared to be a collection of black
and white photographs and laid them out along the top of
the desk. In the dim light she could see the female form,
endlessly repeated, mostly naked. As she shone her torch
along the line of images, she realised that these were very
old photographs. The thin beam of light picked out the
grainy contrast in ghoulish detail, as she saw women lying
prone on brass bedsteads, or facing the camera with rolling
eyes. One was lifting up a rough nightdress with a shocking,
vulgar gesture. What was it about these bare beds and
institutional garments? thought Agnes, reminded suddenly
of a time long ago when, as a child, she had had an
operation to remove her tonsils in a country hospital just
outside Paris. That was it. These women were patients,
not models. These photographs were medical ones, taken
by men exploring new pathologies not just of the body but
of the mind. Agnes's torch scanned their worn faces,
searching for some account in the dulled eyes. She imagined
these women incarcerated as insane – hysterics, they'd
have called them – endlessly examined in the name of
medical science, observed and recorded and photographed.
And now, she thought, bought and sold too, remembering
Burgess's words outside the door – valued as commodities
long after their miserable lives had ended.

That must be how Burgess and Alexander knew each other, long before the painting commission was ever suggested, thought Agnes. It explained why Alexander had got the job at all, to the surprise of people like Jonathan. Why did Burgess want these 'off his hands'? she wondered. And where were they from? She remembered what Amber Parry had said, and saw in her mind Burgess pillaging the old hospital archives for things to sell, and Alexander, with his talent for making money and his connections in the art world, realising their value.

She slipped into her bag the smallest of the photographs. Between its tattered edges it showed a woman lying on a bed facing a wall, her grubby nightdress lifted up around her waist. Then she carefully put the others back into their envelope and stuck the tape down again, matching the fragments of paper where it had torn at the edges, and put the envelope back where she had found it.

She pulled at a drawer, surprised to find it opening easily. It contained a roll of parcel tape, a piece of string and two gummed-up paintbrushes. She tried another which was stuffed full of papers. They seemed to be bills, fuel and rent and so on; all paid, she noticed, seeing the banker's stamps, wondering why she expected Alexander to be lax about such things. And all addressed to Mr A. Jeffes.

Maybe that is his name, she thought, easing out another drawer. What have I got to go on? McPherson behaving oddly at the mention of his name, when everyone in that bloody hospital is behaving oddly and no doubt always has done? Bridget letting something slip? Probably some silly pet name like Fishface or something – no wonder he was embarrassed at the idea that someone else might find out. But as the third drawer opened she remembered Alexander's fear and violence when faced with any mention of his past. I am right, she thought. She looked down and saw a few sparse papers. An insurance claims form, totally blank. A railway season ticket, expired. And a letter from the Department of Social Security, Contributions section. Dear Sir, Re. Self-Employed National Insurance Contributions . . . It was addressed to Mr Andrew Jeffreys, trading as 'Alexander Jeffes'.

Agnes could hear the blood thumping in her ears. She scanned the form for more details. On the tear-off slip he had written his date of birth; 14 September 1946. She memorised this, then was just about to put the papers back when she heard footsteps on the landing and keys jangling. She switched off her torch, bundled the papers back into the drawer, closed it as quietly as she could, picked up her bag and – where the hell to hide? She remembered the couch with its quilt, and in the darkness rushed over to it and flung herself behind it under the drape, as she heard the door open and heavy footsteps enter the room.

'Bloody lock bloody buggered,' she heard Alexander's voice, thick with drink. 'Buggled – b-burgled or what?' He staggered across the room and switched on the anglepoise lamp. She imagined him surveying his studio for signs of damage. 'Nothin' – nothin' bloody nicked anyway. Bloody Burgess, 'spect.'

She heard him straighten the overturned chair and flop

on to it. Then he stood up again and went over to the sink. She heard a drink being poured. She held her breath as he approached the couch and flung himself down heavily on to it. There was silence apart from his hoarse breathing. Her mind scanned the possibilities fast. The most obvious was to stay here until he went out again – which might not be for hours. Or until he passed out, which judging by his state was more likely. What she wanted to do, she realised, was to emerge and confront him. To say – what, exactly? To say, I can save you from yourself. She sighed inwardly, annoyed with herself for churning out the same schoolgirl fantasies when stuck in a farcical situation hiding behind a creaky old sofa on which snored a drunken and possibly homicidal failed artist. Her annoyance gave way to an urge to laugh, which in turn made her think, of what am I afraid? She couldn't think of an answer. The worst that could happen if she emerged would be that she'd have to own up to breaking and entering. It was all too funny, really. Although, there was the risk he might be violent, but then, what the hell? He was drunk. She had never feared drunken men. Hugo, at his most terrifying, was always stone-cold sober.

She crawled out from behind the sofa and looked at Alexander. He was asleep. She found she was grinning absurdly. He looked dishevelled, unshaven and oddly young. His clothes appeared to have been slept in for a week. She looked across at the door, which Alexander had left swinging open. It was quite ridiculous, she thought, still kneeling on the floor. I could just walk right out of here and . . .

'Wha – wha' you doin' here?' Alexander had opened his eyes and was now staring at her as if at a vision.

'Oh, I was just passing, you know.' Agnes tried not to laugh.

'Drinkin' for days 'cos of you. And Mum. Not long now.' He closed his eyes, then opened them again. 'Didn't meanter be so . . . leaving you there like that.' He felt the floor by his couch, picked up a bottle and swigged from it. 'I was very very angry. Very angry 'deed.' He stretched out the bottle to her. 'Have some. Whisky. Glass somewhere, think.'

'No thanks,' said Agnes, 'I was just leaving.'

He closed his eyes with utter weariness. 'We could've been – always do it, you know. Ruin things. Always a stupid bastard.' He was asleep again.

Agnes got up. She stood over him for a moment, then touched his forehead with her fingertips. Then she picked up her bag and left. Outside the streets were eerie in the fog. Agnes was surprised to find it was only just after eleven. She caught the 344 bus to London Bridge. When, something after midnight, she lay down to sleep, she saw his dishevelled, troubled image drifting across her mind, heard his name, Alexander. Alexander.

Andrew Jeffreys, thought Agnes, waking the next morning, feeling extraordinarily hungry and craving, for some reason, bacon. The fog had cleared, and the air was fresh with spring and sunlight. Agnes wandered down to a scruffy old café just off Borough High Street and ordered eggs, bacon and tomatoes with three slices of fried bread, something she'd always viewed as a delicacy, however flabby, however badly cooked, ever since her arrival in this country.

As she savoured each mouthful, she reflected on the events of the night before. She checked her bag to see if the photograph was still there, proof that it had all really happened. It was, but she didn't want to risk taking it out with her greasy fingers. Andrew Jeffreys, she thought. All I know about him is that he is in some way connected to Tom McPherson. Andrew Jeffreys, she thought, remembering, suddenly, the first conversation she had had with Alexander, when they'd talked about Lent in the canteen at St Hugh's. She looked at her watch, which said nine-twenty. I can be at St Catherine's House by ten, she thought.

At ten-past ten she walked through the doors of the Office of Population, Censuses and Surveys in Kingsway. She found herself part of a swarm of people, some alighting confidently on the bookshelves, some hesitating, staring uncertainly at the red leather-bound volumes, unsure where to begin.

Agnes had walked down Kingsway repeating to herself, 'September 1946, London', and now she chose the aisle of shelves marked 'Births, 1938–1946', went to Sept 1946, and pulled down the book labelled 'J–L'. Jedd, Jefferson, Jeffrey, Jeffreys. One entry, Andrew R. Born London. Mother's maiden name, Robinson. She closed the book and replaced it on the shelves. Then she went to the green bound books of the marriage section and, starting with 1945, looked up Robinson. December 1945, P–R,

September 1945, P–R, June 1945, P–R, March 1945, P–R, December 1944, P–R, thumping each volume down on the desks, thumbing through the pages, scanning down the columns of Robinsons to find one paired with Jeffreys. September 1944, P–R, June 1944 . . . Agnes paused, aware of the constant bustle around her, the large books removed, checked, replaced. 1944. The war, intervening in people's lives, postponing some things, hastening others. She turned to 1939, thumbed through March, June, September. In December 1939, she found Robinson. Daisy M. married Jeffreys, London. She looked up Jeffreys, found Richard D., married Robinson, London.

Richard and Daisy, parents of Andrew. Feeling slightly dizzy she returned to the Births section. Now for it, she thought. She took out from her bag a scrap of paper she had scribbled on some weeks ago, when, with Julia, they had looked at McPherson's personnel file. It had on it a date; 18 April 1953. 1953, M–N. Mc, Mac, Macintosh, Mc – McPherson. Tom S. Mother's maiden name, Robinson. District, Edinburgh. It could all be a coincidence, she told herself, returning to the green files. Again the endless leafing through the books, 1953, 1952, 1951, maybe they didn't even marry, she thought, but then, the husband's surname . . . June 1950, Robinson, Daisy M., married McPherson, London. June 1950, Joel McPherson married Robinson, London. And the infant Andrew was at some point moved up to Scotland where his brother Tom was born three years later. It explained the slight blurring of Alexander's accent, she thought. She imagined him aged seven, stubborn and hostile, maintaining his English accent as best he could, doggedly refusing to merge into this new life, hugging to himself the fragments of the old life in which he'd still had a father; his real father.

She emerged into the noon sun, the traffic racing round the curve of Aldwych. She blinked up at the stately buildings. An old hatred, she thought, enough to murder for, festering slowly through the Scottish childhood, the early move back to London, the change of name, the career. Or perhaps, she thought, not quite enough to kill for. When does hatred become murder, she wondered, remembering all Alexander's 'if onlys'. 'I could have been great, if only . . .' She slipped back inside St Catherine's House, asked a direction of the clerk at the desk, and then set off across Kingsway towards the Strand. Entering the courtyard of Somerset House a few minutes later, she thought for a moment she must be in Paris, remembering how in her country the Napoleonic architecture which housed various government departments gave everything an air of pompous importance. The probate registry was tucked away in one corner. Agnes hesitated in front of the polished wooden shelves, the soberly dressed men and women checking through the lists of wills in solemn silence.

'Can I help you, madam?' asked a uniformed commissionaire.

'Um. Yes, how do you . . . I mean . . .' Agnes remembered Doug's words. They'd started college in 1968, and the violent incident was in 1969. After a family funeral.

'Yes,' Agnes said to the waiting commissionaire, 'I'd like to look up 1969.' Once more she found herself thumbing pages of leather volumes, this time to find McPherson, Joel. And there he was, died in York, March 1969, probate 5 August 1969, executors . . . and an amount, £143,515. A sizeable amount. Agnes filled in a reading request slip and waited for them to bring the will out to her to read. She was making calculations in her mind. Daisy remarried 1950, Alexander born 1946 – four years. Idly she picked out the books for 1947, 1948, scanning the lists of names under J, until she found, Jeffreys, Richard, died London, August 1948, leaving £5,213. Not bad for those days, she thought. Alexander's father would have left everything to Daisy; if she'd remarried, it would, she supposed, have become part of the new household's assets, unless she'd put it in trust or something, which seemed unlikely given Alexander's frequent references to money. Her thoughts were interrupted by someone bringing out Joel McPherson's will for her to read.

She sat down and began, 'The Last Will and Testament of . . . I, Joel McPherson . . .' It named executors, disposed of some possessions in detail, a collection of watercolours to the city museum, his mother's jewellery to his surviving sister. And then came the main estate, his house, his sizeable investments, all to go into trust, the income of which was to be paid to his wife Daisy, but on her death to pass to 'My only son, Tom'.

'My only son, Tom.' Agnes breathed in sharply at the brutality of the words. How violence begets violence, she thought. Whether deeds or words.

A church bell tolled as she stumbled back across the courtyard. The sky had clouded over and the air was heavy. She went into the nearest sandwich bar and ordered a large black coffee, which she stirred repeatedly, even though she didn't take sugar. I might have got it wrong, she tried to tell herself. Perhaps this Joel McPherson did only have one son, Tom. Perhaps it wasn't the same Joel McPherson who had a stepson called Andrew, a silent, anguished little boy who grew up into a distant, anguished young man. Or perhaps I've missed something out, perhaps Daisy left her money separately, perhaps everything was all right . . . 'To my only son, Tom.' It was the words. The money was secondary.

She drained her cup of coffee and ordered another and a smoked salmon sandwich. Outside it began to rain. Agnes squeezed lemon juice between thin slices of brown bread and realised that she still had work to do. She wrapped her hands round her coffee cup, trying to warm herself against the chill that had come upon her at the prospect of Daisy's imminent death.

'You again?' said Kathleen, chomping on her battered cod supper.

'You'll be seeing even more of me once we've sprung you from here.'

'What d'you want?'

'Well, seeing as you asked – now you're mobile and all that—'

'Ah. Spying.' Kathleen waited.

'I thought it would be a good excuse for you to practise getting about on your crutches.'

'Not crutches. Bad job. Wheels is faster.'

'Wheels, then.'

'What'll you be wanting to know?'

'I wondered if you could pay a visit to Amber Parry. There's a few things I think she might help me to understand.'

Agnes got home at half-past seven. She dialled Alexander's number and waited while it rang, endlessly. She counted fifteen rings and then rang off. She went over to her desk and leafed through various papers until she found his home number which he'd given her – when was it? It felt like months ago. She dialled that number, and heard a recorded message:

'You have reached the home of Alexander Jeffes. Please leave your message after the tone.'

She hung up and stared thoughtfully at the phone. Then she dialled the same number, and at the tone she spoke. 'Alexander, it's Agnes. Look, you must finish that painting of the professor. You must, OK? He wants it unveiled at his party on Friday: that gives you two days. Do it in the middle of the night if you have to, but just do it.'

She hung up, put a hand to her cheek and realised she was blushing. Then she dialled Julius's number. 'Hello, it's me. Have you eaten?'

'You need a night off, do you?' Julius was smiling in spite of himself.

'If you can call discussing Jesuit theology with you a night off, then yes.'

'And I'm to call mulling over your latest obsession a night off too, am I?'

'You know I always protect you from my obsessions,' laughed Agnes. 'I promise only to discuss the ontological proof of the existence of God.'

'How very dull.'

'And maybe Madeleine would like to come.'

'Madeleine's living in at the project for a week. They're short staffed.'

'Oh.'

'Am I to view your obvious relief charitably?'

'You should be flattered that I want you all to myself.'

'Agnes, my life is littered with people wanting me all to themselves.'

'Yes, but they're not me.'

'Hmm.'

'I'll see you at the Maharani in twenty minutes.'

'Make it half an hour.'

Late that night, she dialled Alexander's number again. She got the same message at his home, the same endless ringing at his studio. As she put down the receiver, the phone rang.

'Did you just try me?' Alexander sounded hoarse and weary.

'Um – yes.'

'Why are you nagging me?'

'You know why. And it's not nagging.'

'Are they going crazy, Burgess and his harpy?'

'Yes.'

'Fuck them. I've been with my mother all day. She barely recognised me.'

'Why have you phoned me back?' Agnes asked.

'Tell me, was that you in my studio the other night, or some kind of whisky dream?'

'It was me.'

'Uh-huh. Weird, eh?'

'Suppose so.'

'What day is it?'

'Wednesday. Well, it's five past midnight, so technically, Thursday.'

'Fine. Thursday. I'll finish the picture tonight. Tell him to leave his office open. I don't want to see the bastard.'

'OK.'

'And I want you there.'

'Me? Why?'

'Just be there, OK?'

'What time?'

'Ten. Tonight. OK?'

'OK.'

Agnes replaced the receiver wearily. Another crazy night with Alexander, half-brother of Tom McPherson. Alexander, in whom this shared destiny had nurtured a terrible hatred. And then on Friday night there would be Burgess's drinks party, where the portrait would be unveiled, in front of – Agnes put her hand to her forehead at the thought of Tom McPherson and Alexander coming face to face. Is that what he was planning, she wondered? Was all this drunken turmoil just a front to some well-ordered plan? Either he was someone on the edge, whose disordered life reflected inner chaos – or he was incisive, deceitful and, therefore, capable of anything. It annoyed her that, even now, she couldn't tell which.

Chapter Nineteen

The next morning, Agnes woke early and opened her window. The dawn was damp and fresh, cut through with birdsong. She settled down to pray, aware of a surprising sense of peace descending on her, as her dialogue with God quietened into breathing. She felt like a warrior-monk, arming herself for battle. 'Lord, by your Cross and Resurrection you have set us free,' she murmured, going into the shower.

She spent the rest of the morning at her desk in Julius's office, causing him, on her arrival, to raise an amused eyebrow and dump a large pile of correspondence on her desk. At noon an image flashed into her mind of the medical school canteen, of Julia sitting with her sandwiches, waiting for her. She stood up, returned the slightly reduced pile of papers to Julius's desk, and mussed up his soft white hair.

'So soon?'

'I hope I'll be back for good in a week or so.'

'That would be nice.'

'So?' Julia's tone was belligerent.

'OK, OK.'

'I waited for you yesterday as well.'

'I was doing research.'

'You really are playing detectives, aren't you?'

'It's not a game—'

'—doing the lonesome private investigator bit.'

'It was boring old leafing through—'

'And what have you found out?'

Agnes looked at Julia, saw her indignation, her youth, her perfect teeth. 'Julia – when's your first exam?'

'That's not the point.'

'When is it?'

'Monday week.'

'And how do you feel about it?'

Julia swung her hair. 'Fine.'

'It's just—'

'You mean, I should be working, not playing detectives with you?'

'Don't you think—'

Julia stood up. 'You mean, when you needed me, for breaking into offices and chatting up McPherson, then we were all in this together, and now you're on to something on your own I've become the little girl medic who has to do her homework—'

'It's not like that. Listen, you know tomorrow night Burgess is having a drinks party to unveil his painting? Can you wangle an invite?'

Julia softened a little. 'Yup. I expect so. Maybe Mark—'

'I thought he was seeing Marisa Giles.'

'It's gone rather complicated. I'll see what I can do.'

'Good. I'd like you to be there.'

Julia sighed. 'And I promise to do my homework between now and then.'

Passing the wards, Agnes popped her head around Kathleen's curtain. Kathleen was sitting up in bed doing a crossword, which she discarded at once on seeing Agnes.

'Ah, you, good, good,' she said. 'Spoke to Amber. Wheeled down to see her this morning. Lift, everything. Lots of news, like you said. Stealing things they are.' Agnes sat down next to her. 'Old photos,' Kathleen went on. 'All gone. Burgess. She hates him, she does.'

'Does she know why? Why they're being stolen, I mean?'

'Money. Root of all evil, look at nephew, eh? Amber said all money these days.'

'But Burgess is doing it secretly.'

'That's what I say to her. If they wanted to, sell the whole flamin' lot under our noses. Not secret.'

'So it must be for a personal reason,' said Agnes, 'not hospital policy. I mean, if they're closing it down, no one's going to notice if the whole photography collection has vanished. If it's all going to end up on a rubbish tip anyway . . .'

'Mmmm. Poor Amber.'

'Did she seem upset to you?'

Kathleen looked at Agnes, and shook her head. 'Odd, no. If it was me, hoppin' mad I'd be.'

'She seemed rather jolly when I last saw her.'

'Something up her sleeve, I bet.' Kathleen cackled

loudly. 'Revenge. I would. And that Polka – Polka Dot—'

'Polkoff.'

'Yes, him.'

'What did she say about him?'

'He's the only one what understands, she said. All darkly, she said it.'

Agnes smiled. 'Did she say why?'

Kathleen shook her head. 'Plotting something, those two, that's what I think. Gotta fag?'

Agnes passed her a packet of ten that she had remembered to buy on the way from the church. 'Though heaven knows where you'll be able to smoke them – even the day room has become a non-smoking area.'

Kathleen held the pack to her ear and shook it. 'Down the pub,' she said.

Leaving Kathleen, Agnes went to see Marjorie Holtby, to pass on Alexander's request that the professor's door be left open.

'I can't do that, what does he think—'

'Or . . .' Agnes hesitated. 'Or, you could leave me a spare key. I'll be here too.'

Mrs Holtby looked relieved. 'I'd far rather do that. We can't be too careful these days.'

As Agnes took the key, she said, 'You wouldn't happen to know if the professor had a key to that medicine cupboard in Gail Sullivan's room?'

Marjorie frowned, thought a moment. 'Not that I know of. No, of course he didn't, because the other week when he needed one I had to talk the girl into lending me hers.

And she was all sniffy about it too. I'm afraid I really must get on . . .'

Agnes went and sat on the wall outside the new building. A ginger cat was zig-zagging its way across the courtyard, dodging in and out of the groups of passing students. Agnes watched it make its way eccentrically across to the building site fence, which it scaled in one leap and then padded purposefully along until it was out of sight. She was aware that something was taking shape in her mind, and that the questions which hovered there, questions which for so long had been vague and disturbing, were becoming specific and focused. It was like the woodland mist clearing before a duel; but in this case, she thought, a duel with more than two sides.

She got out her notebook from her bag and turned to a page and stared at it for a while. Then she turned to a fresh page and wrote down the names 'Polkoff' and 'Burgess'. Under Burgess she wrote, 'Money'. Under Polkoff she wrote a question mark, followed by the name 'Amber'. Then she wrote 'Gail', and 'McPherson', and then 'faxes'. She looked up at the courtyard again, at the milling groups of people, then turned her head towards the building site. The cat had returned and was now balanced neatly on a fence post, contemplating the clumsy cranes moving to and fro. Agnes imagined herself perching there next to it, staring down into the churning mud. She turned back to her notebook and wrote 'Alexander', then frowned and chewed the end of her pen. After a few more minutes, she got up and left.

* * *

'I thought you said next week.' Julius looked up from his desk.

'Um, it's just . . .'

'Oh, I see. What can I do for you?'

'Do you have any friends among the local Anglican clergy?'

'Some of my best friends are Anglicans,' grinned Julius, reaching for his address book. 'Here. James Liddell, vicar of All Saints, that's the one down towards Rotherhithe.' He scribbled the number down on a scrap of paper and passed it to Agnes. 'So your murder suspect is a Protestant? It doesn't surprise me.'

'That's enough of that,' grinned Agnes from the doorway.

Twenty minutes later, Agnes was talking on the phone to James Liddell.

'You mean the demolished church at St Hugh's?' he asked. 'They got rid of that some time ago. But you see, it belonged to the hospital, technically anyway.'

'And the burial ground?'

'What burial ground?'

'Wouldn't there have been a graveyard?'

'Not that we know of. It was a tiny city church squeezed between the old hospital buildings.'

'Ah.'

'Redundant churches is one thing, digging up graves is quite another.'

'Yes, I see. Where might the parish records be now?'

'I'm pretty sure they'd have gone to the borough archivist for storage. Either that or the diocese. If you hang on a minute I can give you the numbers.' A moment later he came back and Agnes took down the phone numbers. 'Give my regards to Julius, won't you?' said the Rev Liddell.

At a quarter to nine that evening, Agnes was standing in front of her bathroom mirror, pulling at her hair, debating whether to wash it now or wait for the drinks party tomorrow. She was tired, and she had a headache from having spent the afternoon in the cellars of the borough library going through the burial records of a redundant Southwark parish. The result of her researches was that she now felt enormous sympathy for Stefan Polkoff. If the burial records she had unearthed turned out to be connected with him, and she was almost certain they were, then it would explain at least some of his extraordinary behaviour. So much suffering, she thought, pulling at her hair. To be human is to suffer, she thought, deciding not to wash her hair after all.

She went over to her wardrobe and absently picked out some clothes, seeing in her mind with sudden startling immediacy a little boy, uprooted from his home to start a new life with a new father, tearfully hugging close to him the memory of his old life like a favourite bear. She found she was standing in front of her wardrobe clutching her green silk shirt with tears streaming down her face. She put the shirt back, picked up from the floor her old black lambswool jersey and grey leggings, washed her face with cold water and left.

She arrived in the deserted office corridor of St Hugh's

at twenty to ten, and unlocked the professor's door. The room was dark. As she switched on the light by the desk, she glanced down at the professor's papers, neatly ordered, at his in-tray, its emptiness befitting someone who was about to retire. Mrs Holtby had left a few letters for signature, and Agnes idly read the top one, then stopped and read it again. It was addressed to a finance company, to their Pensions Management Division, and marked Confidential.

'Dear Mr Padgett,' Agnes read. 'Further to our telephone conversation I confirm that I will soon be receiving sufficient monies to continue the Super Plus pension scheme as planned. I regret very much the hiatus in my payments over the last academic year, and am pleased to tell you that this will not occur again. It will therefore not be necessary for you to cancel this scheme, nor, more importantly, that of my wife, Myra, from whom I wish all details of this correspondence to be kept secret. I hope I can trust you to understand this point. I look forward to seeing my pension fund mature as planned at the end of this financial year.

Yours faithfully, etc.'

Agnes flicked through the other three letters, which were routine correspondence confirming speaking engagements at various dinners. She heard footsteps approaching along the corridor, and quietly replaced the letters. She went over to the window, and turned to see Alexander.

'Hi,' he said. He had shaved, and his hair was combed. He was wearing the scruffy black jumper of their first meeting.

'Hi.' They grinned, foolishly, at each other.

'Have you looked?'

'I was waiting for you,' Agnes replied, following him to the easel on which rested the large canvas of the professor's portrait. She saw thin paint in delicate brushstrokes, a neat white background intersected by the angles of the door-frame, the desk, the glass cabinets behind the professor. The face was bland, fleshy peach in colour, the darting reflections in his spectacles the only life about it.

'Well?' asked Alexander, looking hard at her.

Agnes wandered over to a cabinet full of antique surgical instruments. 'Is that why you asked me to be here tonight?'

'What do you mean?'

Agnes slid open a glass door and took out something that looked like a giant hairpin, made of ivory with a carved handle. 'Because you knew what I'd say.'

'You mean, it's crap.'

She put the instrument back and came to stand next to him at the easel. 'I'm no artist, but . . .'

'It is crap.'

'No, that's not what I mean.' Agnes took a deep breath and went on, 'I like these lines. I like this table edge, the way the light falls on it. I like the angle you've made with his hand by these books. I like the window, there – but . . .' She looked up into his eyes and was taken aback by the profound yearning she saw in them. She swallowed and went on, 'You've allowed him no life. All the life is in the things around him.'

Alexander walked over to the window and stared out

into the night. There was a distant rumble of thunder. 'I can't afford to see,' he said.

'Why did you ask me here, then?'

He turned, and she was aware of his gaze as he looked at her for a long moment. She heard the shudder of more thunder. Finally he shook his head and turned away. 'I don't know,' he said.

Suddenly, Agnes saw clearly, as if a lightning flash had lit up the whole room like a vision, that she had one chance. One last chance to make contact with Alexander, to break through his anguish, his defences. Her eye fell on his case of paints which he'd placed on a stool next to the easel. Calmly she reached for it and took out a tube of white paint. She held the tube for a moment while she considered the portrait, then took a brush and, squeezing a large dollop of paint on to it, proceeded to paint out the face of the professor in clumsy thick brushstrokes. Then she picked up the black tube and managed to do a caricature of spectacles and a little moustache before Alexander reached her and with some violence wrenched the brush from her hand.

'What the fuck . . . ?'

She stared at him, triumphant, breathing hard. He looked at the damage.

'You little – you fucking stupid . . . I've got to show this tomorrow.'

'You've got nothing to lose,' Agnes said, breathlessly.

He stared at her, searching her face. Slowly he collected himself. 'Tomorrow,' he said. Then, looking at her again, he added, 'You're right. Nothing to lose.' His smile was dangerous, and she shivered openly as he grabbed her wrist again and placed the brush in her fingers. 'Go on, then,' he said. The thunder sounded nearer this time.

Hesitantly, Agnes put cartoon dots for eyes in the spectacles frames, and clown-like eyebrows above them. Then Alexander joined in, adding some spiky orange hair, stepping back to look at what they'd done. Agnes put her brush down, and waited. He began to laugh, and she smiled, and he laughed some more, and said, 'Still, it's a better likeness than before,' and she laughed too, and taking up her brush put in two neat white fangs hanging from the professor's upper lip, and Alexander, giggling, added crimson blood dripping from them. 'I shall call it,' he said, between chokes of laughter, 'I'll call it, "The Modern Surgeon".'

'No,' giggled Agnes, 'call it, "Portrait of the Artist".' Alexander made a dracula face, shaped his hands into claws and stalked theatrically across the room, just as a clap of thunder erupted loudly, shaking the windows. They both stopped giggling and looked at each other.

'Right then,' he said, suddenly serious. 'To work.'

He took out a series of photographs and began to sort through them. One fell to the floor, and Agnes noticed, before Alexander absently scooped it up again, that it was her image, three times, the fourth having been cut out and removed. 'Here,' Alexander said, handing her a photograph of Professor Burgess. 'Hold that.'

He rushed over to the canvas and began to paint a wash of white paint across the ruined section. 'Talk to me,' he said.

'What?'

Alexander was making hurried brushstrokes, selecting a new colour, working fast. 'Tell me what you see. Him, I mean.'

'The professor?'

'Go on,' Alexander began to fill in the background with dark shadows.

'I see a man at the height of his career, a certain gravitas—'

'Don't be so bloody charitable. What do you really see?'

'OK. A hollow man, a fragile sense of self shored up by his utter dependence on those around him.'

'Better.'

'An unacknowledged dependence. Like most men,' she added.

'OK, OK. What else?' Alexander chose a new brush.

'Right. I think he's very aware of status. And it's important to him to be connected with people in a way which advances his own interests. In fact,' she said, seeing a truth, 'a Freemason.'

'Aha,' smiled Alexander, working at a shade of yellow around the face.

'Money is very important.'

'That's obvious. What about his sexuality? Anything kinky?'

Agnes giggled. 'Am I the person to ask?'

Alexander stopped his furious painting for a moment. 'I think you are.'

'OK. He's straight, not gay. Married, but – oh, you

know these products of the English public school. I expect he pays someone to spank him from time to time.'

'I knew you'd know.'

'And I see someone who's broke, who's teetering on the verge of ruin. A desperate man.'

Alexander put down his brush and stared at her, hard. She watched him, aware of wanting – of wanting something beyond her reach. Slowly, Alexander took up his brush again and started on the professor's hairline.

The thunderstorm abated. Agnes wandered over to the desk and sat in the professor's chair. Somewhere a church clock chimed midnight. She leant her head on her elbows and closed her eyes.

'Some help you were,' a voice whispered into the back of her neck. Agnes, waking, sighed sensuously, then blushed on seeing Alexander. He smiled.

'You went to sleep.'

'I didn't – oh, no.'

'Shows you trust me, anyway.'

Agnes rubbed her neck and wondered whether she looked ghastly.

'Come and see my masterwork,' said Alexander. He took her hand and led her to the easel. She gasped in astonishment. The same rigid lines were there but now they served as a grid, each one leading the eye to the subject at their centre: a tall, pale, yellowing man suspended in menacing shadows, his brow furrowed, his spectacles slightly askance, his expression preoccupied.

'It's him,' breathed Agnes. 'But he won't like it.'

'I know,' grinned Alexander.

'What's that he's holding?'

'That surgical thing you were fiddling with.'

'What is it?'

'I've no idea. Some kind of instrument.'

'But if you don't know what it is?'

'It shows he's a surgeon.'

'It might be – it might be a special kind of hook used in the eighteenth century for removing stones from riding boots, for all you know.'

'All the better. It's a clue.'

'Don't be silly, how can it be a clue without meaning?'

'Because the viewer will attribute a meaning to it.'

'And what will Burgess say?'

'He'll say, "Why am I holding an old riding boot hook?"' laughed Alexander. Agnes giggled. Outside the sky had turned a light grey, and she realised she must have slept for hours. Alexander was still holding her hand, but now he let go and went to the window which he opened wide, breathing in the damp silence of the dawn. He turned back to her, elated.

'You see?' he said. 'I can still paint.'

Agnes looked at him as he stood framed by the window, flushed with honesty, and with a wave of compassion she remembered the boy he had been. Andrew, she thought, reaching out to him, realising as he came towards her that it was not Andrew the boy that she wanted but Alexander the man, this man, these arms that enfolded her, the warmth of his body, his lips against her hair, her fingers exploring the angles of his chest, the muscles of his back, her lips finding his. 'Alexander,' she murmured, knowing it to be true, gasping at his touch as the years of yearning fell away, as Hugo receded into a past she had at last escaped.

She broke away from him, went over to the door and locked it.

'What, here?' murmured Alexander as she returned to him.

She began to unbutton his shirt.

'You're—' he said, watching her expression of delight.

'Shh,' she said.

'I never thought . . .' he said.

'I said Shh.'

'I don't see how this can be right – for you, I mean,' he murmured into her neck.

'It's a long time since anything felt this right,' whispered Agnes, realising as she said it that it was absolutely true. He was different from Hugo – his body, his touch, his kiss, all new – and she was allowing him to awaken her, to rename the self that Hugo had entrapped by naming first.

He spread their coats on the floor, and drew her down on top of him.

'This has no future,' he murmured.

'—the human condition,' she said, shivering against the warmth of his skin. 'I mean—'

'Shh,' he said.

Later she was woken by a rumbling noise. She reached out for him, amazed to find he was there, real, flesh and blood next to her.

'Thunder,' she murmured.

'Cleaners,' he replied. They sat up and looked at each other. 'We should have gone to your place,' he said, getting up and rummaging through the discarded clothes.

'If we'd gone to my place it would never have happened.'

'If we'd gone to your place,' he said, coming over to her and kissing her neck, 'we could just be starting all over again. As it is . . .'

Agnes lay on his coat, giggling. 'As it is . . .'

'Come on, get dressed.'

They unlocked the door and went out into the corridor. They could hear the sound of hoovering several offices away.

'What about the painting?' Agnes said.

'I don't know. I could just veil it and leave it.'

'The paint's not dry.'

'True. Can I lock it away somewhere?'

'I know where we can store it. And you'd better leave a note here to say it's finished.'

Kathleen was drinking tea, and appeared to be completely unsurprised at the appearance of a large canvas, behind which struggled Agnes and Alexander.

'It's only till this evening,' Agnes explained. 'I thought you wouldn't mind.'

'Stand it by the window, there. I'll tell the nurses it's a present from – ' she eyed Alexander appreciatively – 'from my lover.'

'Right, well . . .' Alexander stood there awkwardly,

and Agnes saw the old furtive look return. 'I'll pick it up for the grand unveiling, then. I'd better be off now – um . . .' He sidled past the bed, looked briefly at Agnes and then left.

'Nice,' said Kathleen, patting her bed for Agnes to join her.

'You mean him?'

'Mmm. Nice night?'

'Well . . .' Agnes smiled.

'Hope you used something.'

'What?'

'Safe sex. I know all about it.'

Agnes blinked. 'Oh. Yes. We did, yes.'

'Lot of nonsense, safe sex. It's always a dangerous bugger, always has been, always will be.'

Agnes felt a wave of relief at being able to admit to someone, anyone, the reality of the night before. The time for denying it would come soon enough.

Kathleen was looking at her with compassion. 'Tricky, eh?' she said.

'It has no future,' Agnes said.

'Didn't look like he wanted one,' said Kathleen.

'That makes two of us, then,' Agnes replied.

It was nearly nine when she left the hospital and walked to London Bridge, finding herself adrift in the hurrying waves of city commuters. The tide of the Thames was out and she descended a flight of stairs under the bridge on to the river bank itself. She wandered along aimlessly, watching the black mud cling to her shoes, crunching glass and weeds and tin cans underfoot, wondering what she had done. She had never broken her vows before; the authorities of her first convent might dispute that, but her own vows, the ones she had made to God when she first joined the Order, she had always kept. With what relief she had submitted herself to the will of God, to find that all her self-destructive impulses could be viewed with compassion, could be turned around and channelled into her spiritual life. It had been a liberation. And now, for reasons she could barely begin to understand, she had deliberately, joyfully even, broken her vows. Joyfully. She picked up a gnarled old stone. It was entrapped in sticky tendrils of river weed which left black trails on her sleeve. She felt her heart clench. She threw the stone into the reaches of the river, flung herself down in the mud, and wept.

Chapter Twenty

Much later that day, Agnes let herself into her flat. She was dishevelled, mud-stained and hungry. She opened her fridge and a couple of cupboards; then, finding nothing to eat, went out again. She bought milk, a loaf of bread and some eggs, went home and made a four-egg omelette which she devoured, still in her coat.

When she'd finished eating, she went to her mirror and stared at her face. It was streaked with mud. She felt strangely glad about this. It reminded her of a medieval altar piece, the marks of the sinner. Sackcloth and ashes. It occurred to her that she had to get washed and changed, ready for the drinks party at St Hugh's. The idea of seeing Alexander again struck her as completely unreal. It all seemed so long ago. She had spent all the intervening hours walking eastwards along the Thames, leaving the river bank as the tide came in, turning towards the docks with their peculiar mixture of affluence and dereliction, and now she realised she was physically exhausted. Good, she thought, welcoming the numbness. There would be plenty of time for anguish later.

She put her coat aside for the dry cleaners, undressed

and went into the shower. The warm water splashed against her skin, recalling his touch, the heat of him next to her, inside her. She shivered. What made all this so difficult, she thought, was that try as she might, she could not feel regret. She soaped her arms, thinking, I have sinned, knowing it to be true, but finding suddenly a soaring joy, as if what she had done had been an act of healing, of redemption; of love. She had never felt anything like it before.

She chose her clothes carefully, happily, picking out her one good dress in black silk, applying some subtle make-up, a touch of lipstick, and at the last minute, digging out a jewellery case from the back of her wardrobe and finding a string of pearls that Hugo had once given her. As she fastened them round her neck, she thought: the only explanation must be that I have gone completely mad.

The reception was in a conference room in the medical school. Agnes had never received an official invitation, but her years of experience of walking into a room as if she was entitled to be there served her well. She arrived deliberately late, so that she could merge with the guests. She was inordinately relieved to see that there was no sign of Alexander, or of his painting. Marjorie Holtby skittered up to her.

'Oh, good, I do hope – only I thought, you'd know—'

'The painting? It's in safe hands. It wasn't quite dry, but Alexander is going to bring it with him.' Agnes smiled reassuringly.

'Is he back from Luton, then?'

Agnes felt her mouth go dry. 'S-sorry?'

'I thought you'd know. His mother died today.'

Agnes put a hand against the wall to steady herself.

'Professor Burgess has invited the dean to unveil it,' Marjorie was saying. 'I suppose we'll just have to carry on without him.'

'Without McPherson?' Agnes said, weakly, realising that the two brothers would have met at the hospice by now.

'McPherson? No, no, the former dean. He's an honorary fellow of the School, retired now. Professor Hamblin. But I expect Professor McPherson will be here too. Do excuse me a moment.' Marjorie waved to someone and picked her way across the room. Agnes stared at the faces around her, her mind racing ahead to the inevitable moment, the arrival of . . . or perhaps, she thought, neither of them will come, and the painting will stay on Kathleen's ward, and the evening will prove embarrassing but at least not fatal. She remembered the Pharmacy book, the penicillin, Gail's files – and realised that even if this particular evening didn't prove fatal, it would be merely a postponement.

''Ere, have a drink.'

Agnes looked down, dazed, and saw Dawn Scott handing her a glass of wine.

'Thank you,' Agnes said, taking the glass and gulping a large mouthful. 'I'm glad they invited you,' she added, feeling her mind clear a little.

'They can't avoid it. I always end up 'elping organise them, you see.'

'Who are all these people?'

'Mostly Trust. Some are teaching staff. That's Antony Wright, over there, nice geezer, diabetic. Physiology, 'e is.'

'I've been meaning to ask you – when did you get your plans of the new building, the ones on your wall?'

'Mmm, now let me think. They'd been up in the office, and when someone replaced them, we said—'

'We?'

'Me and Gail. We both wanted them.'

'Ah. I thought so,' Agnes said.

'Not like her to stick her neck out like that.'

'This was when you shared an office?'

'Yeah. Anyway, in the end, the architect bloke said we could 'ave one lot. And she was ready to fight me for them, I can tell you. That's why I got the old ones, and she got the new ones. Though God knows what she did with them.'

Agnes surveyed the crowd of people. 'Any idea why? Why she should be so keen?'

'Nah. S'funny, because it weren't like 'er at all.' Dawn took a gulp of wine. 'I've got this theory, you know. Like, she'd been a nobody, right? Just a typist, all that. Then she gets her promotion, finds something she wants to do, and it makes her feel part of something. So, with the building, she sort of gets involved, looks at the plans, that sort of thing. Once she even went to see McPherson, she said.'

'What about?'

'She wouldn't say. But it was something about the

building, 'cos she had the files out on her desk.'

'When was this?'

'Not long – not long before she died. Ooh, look, Professor Burgess seems to be enjoying himself.'

Agnes looked across and saw the professor talking to a very glamorous young woman who was wearing a flimsy chiffon jacket over a tight strapless mini-dress.

'Look where 'is eyes are lookin' – just 'cos she's taller than 'im,' Dawn giggled.

'Who is she?'

'Haven't a clue. Trust, probably. Uh-oh, better go. There's the caterer looking for 'er cue. See ya.'

Agnes saw Julia appear at the far end of the room with Mark in tow. Julia was wearing a wide cream floating skirt and a floppy velvet hat. She smiled across at Agnes, then winked. Agnes grinned back.

'Am I forgiven?' she said, approaching Julia.

'For having my best interests at heart? Of course.' Julia turned to Mark. 'Sister Agnes here has been encouraging me to return to my coursework instead of getting distracted.'

'And what's been distracting you?' Mark asked.

'Never you mind,' Julia replied sweetly, tossing her hair. Agnes felt a brief moment of pity for Marisa Giles. 'I'm impressed by Professor Burgess's companion,' Julia went on. The glamorous young woman had just brought him some canapés, and the professor picked an olive from the top of a wafer-thin open sandwich and popped it into her mouth. Julia and Agnes exchanged glances of mock disgust.

'I'll get us some drinks,' Mark said, and vanished towards the bar.

'Well?' Julia said, once he had gone.

'Right. The main thing to know about this evening is that – oh, here we go.'

'What?'

'Tom McPherson has just arrived.'

'And?'

Agnes drew a deep breath. 'When Alexander appears, with his painting, assuming he does – McPherson is likely to explode into little tiny pieces.'

'Are you sure? Why?'

'Because they go back such a long way that a room the size of this one is simply not big enough to hold them both. Thank you Mark,' Agnes added, as he handed her a glass of white wine.

'Young Henderson,' boomed a voice behind them in a deep Scottish accent. 'And the charming Julia.' McPherson appeared, glanced at Agnes and went on. 'Sorry I missed the revision tutorial this morning. Called away suddenly, family matter.' Agnes watched him closely. His brash good humour seemed odd for a man so recently bereaved. 'All set for your exams, then?' he was saying. 'Great things are expected of you, my boy.'

'Oh, well, I hope, um—'

'Nonsense, boy, you'll do famously. Good, good. Now, no lingering here and putting away the drink, eh? Early nights, I think.' He winked at Julia, who smiled politely, then hailed someone across the room and departed.

'Stupid prat,' Julia said.

'He's all right,' Mark replied.

'"Great things are expected of you, my boy,"' she echoed, imitating his Scottish swagger. 'They all know I've been getting consistently higher marks than you have.'

'I'm sure he meant—' Mark began.

'And as for him,' Julia went on, indicating Professor Burgess who was approaching them, 'he can barely walk straight.'

'Mark. Mark Fender – Henderfield. Ready for the grand unveiling? Though what that painter will have made of me, God only knows. Moment of truth, what? Now where's that girl . . . ?'

He passed on by, and Agnes noticed Polkoff standing by the door watching him closely. Someone came and spoke to Polkoff, who then fished in his pocket for something to write with. Various bits of paper scattered from his pocket in the process and Polkoff bent down to pick them up. The room had filled up, and white-aproned waitresses were distributing canapés on trays.

'I'm going to circulate. See you later,' Agnes said, spying Amber Parry engaged in animated conversation with someone.

'So, you see,' Amber was saying, 'the male midwife of the eighteenth century wasn't so much an interloper as an – oh, hello there. Sister Agnes, this is Shirley Ingrams, she's from the Trust. We've been agreeing on the importance of an historical perspective.'

Agnes shook the business-like hand that was offered. 'Are many of your colleagues here?' she asked conversationally. She watched as Shirley Ingrams scanned

307

the room, seeing her eyes pass over the professor's new acquaintance, before she turned to Agnes and said, 'Do you know? I seem to be the only one.'

Amber was saying something, and Agnes nodded vaguely before moving away. She stood at the edge of the room, leaning against the polished oak panelling, trying to think, knowing with sudden conviction that Alexander was about to arrive. She saw Polkoff across the room watching the door, saw his face brighten, turned to where he was looking and saw Alexander's canvas being brought in by two porters, Alexander behind them in a dark grey, superbly cut suit, supervising the arrangement of the easel with professional nonchalance. He nodded a greeting across to Polkoff, then scanned the room briefly – for sight of her, she wondered – but appeared not to see her. Good, she thought, wondering why she felt breathless.

Marjorie Holtby was now with them, and the crowd of guests had arranged itself in anticipation. Professor Burgess was shaking Alexander's hand, then introducing him to the young woman, who simpered at him ridiculously, Agnes thought. Mrs Holtby was talking to a frail, nattily dressed elderly man, presumably the former dean. Agnes looked round for McPherson, but there was no sign of him. The people by the easel were now grouped formally, and Marjorie Holtby knocked on the table for silence. Antony Wright introduced Professor Hamblin, the former dean, who then stood up.

'Ladies and gentlemen,' he began in a thin, reedy voice. 'I have been invited to unveil this painting. It should need no introduction, as its subject, our esteemed colleague, is standing right here. I am therefore not going to make a speech, other than to thank you all for inviting me, and to wish him well in his retirement. And now it is my pleasure to show to you this tribute to Professor Robert Burgess.'

He pulled on the cloth, which fell to the floor. There was a shuffling silence. Burgess was peering round from the dais to try to see his own image, and Agnes heard Julia giggle. Marjorie Holtby was staring at the painting open-mouthed. Polkoff suddenly stood up and ostentatiously began to clap, and with a wave of relief the whole room joined in. Professor Burgess looked a little confused, then beamed, and murmured to Alexander who was standing behind the easel. Alexander stepped forward, his eyes fixed on a point in the crowd. Agnes followed his gaze and saw Tom McPherson, who was staring horror-stricken at the dais. Alexander's voice rang out into the hushed crowd.

'She's dead. You know she's dead.'

McPherson paled. His mouth opened and closed again. Suddenly he turned, fighting through the bewildered crowd to get to the door and out into the corridor. Alexander bolted after him, and Agnes followed as he disappeared down the stairs after McPherson.

'Alexander,' Agnes cried, cursing her heeled shoes, kicking them off and hurtling down the stairs behind the two men. She could hear shouting at the bottom of the stairs, and a door slamming, then silence. She reached the ground floor, pushed open the door and walked outside in stockinged feet.

She was in the courtyard in front of the new building.

There was silence apart from the patter of rain. She allowed her eyes to get used to the dark, straining to hear which direction the two men had taken. She heard a distant shout from the building site, then a voice calling, 'Andy! What the hell do you think you're doing?' Agnes paced silently across to the building site fence. She saw a darting movement behind a crane, heard a voice saying, 'This is a bloody dangerous game, Andrew.' She slipped inside the fence, feeling the rough ground under her feet. Lamps swung from the cranes, shedding uneven beams of light here and there, and Agnes saw now the figure of Tom McPherson on the far edge of the building site, heading for the opposite fence. She was aware of movement near her, and realised that Alexander was crouching only a few feet away from her, poised as if for attack; and in his hand, glinting in the sparse beams of light, was a pistol. She recoiled into the shadows, pressing herself into the fence, and whispered,

'Alexander.'

He started, but didn't move.

'Alexander,' Agnes whispered again, and 'Leave it, Andy,' McPherson's voice echoed across the pit.

Alexander whispered out of the corner of his mouth, 'Get the hell out of here.'

'Not while you're likely to fire that thing,' Agnes whispered back.

'Who else is with you?' McPherson shouted.

'No one,' yelled back Alexander. 'It's you I want and you I'm going to get.'

'You'll be lucky,' McPherson sneered. 'You've

310

never—' A shot rang out, echoing metallically across the pit. 'Oh my God,' they heard McPherson cry. 'Andy – why?'

'She died.'

'I know. Of course I know.'

'You couldn't even be bothered—'

'For God's sake, she was my mother too.'

'You didn't even—'

'I was there this morning. They said you'd gone. She was in a coma.'

'She'd still have known . . .'

'The nurses said they'd phone me. In the end—'

'In the end you couldn't give a damn, could you?'

'You know that's not true.' A stone clattered into the building site as McPherson shifted position.

Alexander said quietly, 'She held my hand. All the time, right until the end, she held on to me. I watched her go. I breathed with her breathing . . .' He stifled a sob.

'And who paid for her nursing care, eh? At least I looked after her, which is more than you ever—'

'You never cared for her. You and your gold-digging father—'

'So that's what this is about is it? Money? Just because her will—'

'How come you've seen her will?' Alexander's voice seemed to ricochet off the huge metal cranes. There was a silence, then they heard McPherson moving along the edge of the pit. His voice when he spoke was nearer.

'Listen, Andy, it's been a long day. We're both upset. Let's just go home, shall we?'

Alexander levelled the pistol towards the voice. McPherson appeared briefly in the light from a lamp which swung from one of the cranes, then vanished again. Alexander stared into the darkness. There was a long silence. Agnes took a deep breath, then sidled along the fence towards Alexander. 'You're mad,' she whispered.

He turned towards her. She was just a string of pearls glinting against velvety blackness. He turned back, his eyes scanning the pit for signs of McPherson.

'What do you hope to gain?' Agnes said.

'You wouldn't understand,' he hissed.

'Maybe, but—'

'Just go away. I'm not worth it.'

'Tell me, did Polkoff introduce you to Burgess?'

'Yes. Why?'

'Some time ago? So you could help Burgess sell off some stuff that didn't belong to him?'

'So?'

'So, when the portrait was mentioned, Burgess returned the favour by giving you the commission.'

'I don't see what—'

'It's a nice pistol.'

'One of Stefan's. Now go away.' There was a sudden crack of wood in the pit beneath them. 'Just get the hell out of here,' Alexander hissed, aiming at the sound. A gust of wind swung one of the lamps, and in the swaying beam McPherson reappeared. Alexander fired, McPherson shouted something, then vanished. Agnes waited, her back pressed against the fence, watching Alexander crouched as still as a cat. In the distance a door slammed; they

312

heard a woman's giggle. Then, near them, there was a rustle. Alexander took aim again, scanning the site. Agnes closed her eyes, hardly breathing, as another shot rang out.

'Damn,' Alexander said.

Agnes could bear it no longer. She marched up to him, treading on something sharp as she did so, and put out her hand.

'Give me the gun.'

'You really are crazy,' he said.

Someone was running, fast, they heard laboured breathing, Alexander grabbed Agnes, flung her to one side and fired again. The running continued, unevenly, into the distance, then stopped. Alexander took a few stumbling steps towards the pit. 'Oh my God,' he whispered, 'Oh my God. Agnes?' He began to sob, standing alone at the edge of the pit, his face wet with tears. Suddenly there came from further away the sound of a human cry, hoarse and eerie, followed by a sickening, squelching thud. Alexander paused uncertainly at the edge of the pit, then, still weeping, fled silently through the fence.

A few minutes later Agnes pulled herself out of the excavation. She had jumped down on to the scaffolding and ducked under some planks of wood, and now emerged smeared with mud, one foot sticky with, she thought, blood, but wasn't going to stop to find out now.

She skirted the fence towards the far edge of the excavation. There was no one in sight. It was darker here, with fewer cranes, and a deeper, half-flooded pit. She strained her eyes into the darkness, knowing what she was going to see, trying to make out the uneven shapes of the heavy plant, the JCBs, the mountains of gravel and sand. Something deep down caught her eye, and she peered over the edge. A large mound, wet and shiny, appeared to be floating, bobbing in the muddy water. She stared some more. At one side of the object she could just make out the detail of a hand. A human hand.

Afterwards, she was amazed by how normal it had been. She had left the site and walked, she was pretty sure she had walked, although why she hadn't run, God only knew, perhaps it was the foot injury which turned out to be quite bad, she had walked back to the party. It was after midnight now, and there were just a few stragglers left, Polkoff and, surprisingly, Amber Parry, and Julia and Mark who were in deep discussion sitting in one corner, and some people whom Agnes didn't recognise. McPherson and Alexander, of course, were nowhere to be seen, and neither was Burgess, although his companion of the evening was still there, perched on the edge of a chair and talking loudly, with a lot of laughter, to a rather bewildered middle-aged man in a navy suit. They looked up as Agnes appeared, she must have shouted or something, and she remembered wanting to laugh at their horror-struck faces, although she was covered with mud and one foot was dripping blood, so their reaction was hardly surprising. She was cross, then, when no one moved, even though she was sure she was making herself clear, that someone was dead and lying in the building site, until at last Julia, bless her, took charge, came over, whispered 'Police?' to which Agnes had nodded, delegated Mark to dial 999, and galvanised everyone else to the building site.

The ragged party had converged on the site, and someone had thought to find a torch in the Pathology lab; Polkoff, it must have been, because he'd been making creepy faces in the dark corridor on the way, by pointing the torch beam upwards under his chin and grinning. At the side of the pit, Agnes had taken the torch and directed it into the depths, and there it was, the rounded, bobbing form. It looked larger than a person this time, but the hand was clearly visible. Then the police had arrived, and proper procedure had been carried out with ropes and stretchers and then an ambulance had appeared, and at last the body, for body it clearly was, was raised from the pit and laid down on the concrete path face down, leaking muddy water into a great puddle around it. They all waited, and then an official person stepped forward and gently turned the body over. Everyone stared; at the pasty cheeks, bloated with water, the eyes bulging and staring, the filthy, twisted face. Despite all this, it was, quite recognisably, Professor Robert Burgess.

Chapter Twenty-one

In the hours that followed, the building site became a confusion of noise and light, of cars and sirens, radios and headlamps. Police officers swarmed, asking questions, taking statements, gathering in huddles to confer, asking more questions. Who saw him last? Was he drunk? Who was he with? Why might he have come outside? In the midst of it all Agnes was aware of Burgess's young companion, pale and tearful, shivering in her tiny dress. Yes, she was the last one to have seen him alive, yes he had been drinking. Yes, she was with him when he left the party.

'Any idea why he left, miss?'

'Well, you see, oh dear, it's all so awful, he suggested we . . . oh dear.' She dissolved into tears and was wrapped in a blanket and escorted to a waiting police car.

More questions – how did Burgess seem, who else was at the party? Agnes heard the name 'Alexander Jeffes', and turned to see Marjorie talking animatedly to a woman police officer.

'And Professor McPherson, he's gone too, it was all most peculiar, although I'm sure nothing to do with this terrible . . .' and then, quite unexpectedly, Marjorie burst into loud, snuffling tears. Agnes looked up to see Polkoff standing on the edge of the chaos, wrapped in a beautifully tailored winter coat.

At last a body bag arrived and the body was loaded up and driven away. 'Morning post mortem,' Agnes heard. 'Eight o'clock job.' Someone thought to notice that Agnes's foot was filthy and still bleeding, and she was led away to Casualty to have it cleaned and bandaged. The sky was just beginning to lighten when Agnes joined Mark and Julia in the deserted canteen. They were slumped wearily at a table, drinking cups of tea from the machine. They looked up as Agnes approached.

'At last you're here,' Julia said, going to get her some tea.

'How was it?' Agnes asked Mark.

Mark chewed at a fingernail. 'OK, I think. Though I was scared. But then, after all, as far as Burgess is concerned . . . I just told the truth. All I knew about the party. Luckily I was with Jules nearly the whole time.'

'They won't connect this with Gail?' Julia said anxiously, returning to the table.

'I hope not,' Agnes said. 'What did they ask you?'

'About the party,' Julia replied. 'About McPherson, why did he run away, where might he have gone, why should he have been upset, who was Alexander—'

'What did you say?' Agnes asked.

Julia looked at Agnes. 'Not much. There's not much I could say, is there?'

'No,' said Agnes, thinking about her own statement.

No, she had no idea what was going on between Alexander and McPherson, she didn't know anything about them, it was only chance that she was at the party . . . Agnes wished she was better at lying.

'Did they ask about hearing gunfire?' she said suddenly.

'Gunfire? No. Why, was there—?'

'The music was up very loud in the party,' Mark interrupted.

'Who was firing? At Burgess?' Julia was wide-eyed.

Agnes shook her head. 'It's all very complicated, and I have to say, I don't understand it all. I think a lot depends on this post mortem result. I mean, maybe it was an accident, that's what they seemed to be saying, isn't it? He was drunk, he might have just fallen in. More tea?'

They sipped their sugary tea, trying to get warm. As the sky grew lighter people appeared in the canteen, and a clattering started up from the kitchens. From time to time Mark or Julia would say something like, 'Old Burgess, eh?' or 'I still can't believe it.'

After her third cup of tea, and with the pain in her foot sharpening as the shock wore off, Agnes began to see events with a certain clarity. She decided to look for her shoes, and wandered back to the conference room. The police had swarmed over it earlier; now it was deserted. Agnes looked around, at the discarded paper plates with their half-eaten delicacies, at the empty glasses and occasional spills on the floor, the chaotic array of chairs; and the portrait which gave to its surroundings a certain dignity, particularly as now it had become the definitive image of Professor Robert Burgess, deceased. It was an astonishing work, thought Agnes, wondering if she would ever see Alexander again.

She heard voices approaching; one low, the other high-pitched and apparently distressed. She put her head round the door and saw Stefan Polkoff approaching, pursued by Burgess's young woman.

'Do you think I've incriminated myself?' she was wailing to Polkoff. 'I've only told them what I know.'

'I can't imagine they'd see you as the murdering type,' Polkoff drawled, coming into the conference room, then, seeing Agnes, went on, 'What does our resident guardian of people's souls think? We've just returned from a session with the Old Bill, and now this young woman thinks it's only a matter of time before they discover her true, evil nature.'

'Well, I hardly think—' Agnes began.

The woman lifted a pleading face to Agnes. 'I was the last one to see him alive; they got really heavy,' she said. 'It's all my fault, I'm such a silly girl. A silly, silly girl.' She dabbed at her eyes with the back of her hand.

'You haven't seen my shoes, have you?' Agnes asked Stefan.

'I can't say that I have,' he replied. 'I'll keep my eyes peeled, as they say.'

He wandered around the room, then bent and prodded some rubbish on the floor, a discarded serviette. He straightened up, scanned the room, then turned to go. 'Well, what a swell party that was.' He passed the portrait and considered it a moment. 'I always knew he had it in him. Some talent, wouldn't you say?' He allowed his gaze to alight on Agnes, then left.

'I don't know what I'm going to do,' the young woman whined.

'Come and have a cup of tea.'

Agnes led her new companion down to the staircase, where she found her shoes tucked away on one of the steps. Returning to the canteen, she found to her relief that Julia and Mark were still sitting where she'd left them. She introduced them to the young woman, then said, 'And you are . . . ?'

'Trisha. Trisha Slaithwaite. I'm a temp.'

'Ah. In which department?'

'Pharmacology. Only since Tuesday, and I was supposed to finish today. Demob happy, that's what it was. Why I misbehaved, I mean.'

Julia brought her some tea, which she sipped at.

'You didn't really misbehave,' Agnes said.

Trisha looked at her with big, childlike eyes. 'Oh, but I did. All that, you know – allowing him to – poor old geezer.'

'Allowing him to what?'

Trisha blushed. 'I weren't thinking. Too much to drink, and then he's all over me. I only recently finished with my boyfriend, I s'pose that was it, getting my confidence back.'

'It's perfectly natural. How did you get invited?'

'Oh, you know, the others – we just went along. I thought it'd be a laugh.'

'So what happened outside?'

Trisha looked quickly at Agnes, then took a gulp of

tea. 'I've already told them coppers all this. He said he wanted some air. I knew what he meant, I shouldn't have gone. 'E were well tanked up. And then, once we were outside, he goes over to where all them fences are saying Keep Out, and there's me sayin' do you think we should, trying to get 'im back inside, and 'e's pawin' at me, and then—' She broke off and her eyes, which were red with drink and exhaustion, watered. 'I left 'im there, you see, that's why it's my fault. I'd had enough, 'is great big hands all over me, ugh – I went back to the party. And – ' she choked back a sob – 'he must have tripped, fallen in. Oh dear me . . .' She began to cry.

Agnes put a hand on her shoulder. 'Did you tell the police all this?'

'Oh yes, I had to, didn't I? Even though they'll think—'

'They'll think nothing of the sort. Don't be so silly. The best thing you can do is go home and get some sleep, tell your agency – I assume you came from an agency? – and next time you feel the need to reassure yourself with the attentions of a man, choose a little more carefully.' Agnes stood up. 'Now, let's find you a taxi home.' She escorted Trisha from the canteen, returning a few minutes later with three more cups of tea.

'You didn't like her, did you?' Julia said.

'I'm – I'm not aware of holding a view,' Agnes replied.

Julia stirred her tea thoughtfully. 'It must be because her self-esteem depends on being fancied by men.'

'What must be?'

'The reason you didn't like her,' Julia said.

Through all her weariness, Agnes began to laugh.

'Did I make a joke?' Julia asked.

Mark grinned, yawned and stretched. 'Drink up, Jules. We need some sleep. Though at this rate, there won't be any exams to sit next week.'

It was still dark when Agnes let herself into her flat. She felt numb with tiredness, but her mind was racing. She sat down with her notebook and scribbled furiously, then stared at what she had written for a long time. It was only when she got up to go to bed that she noticed that there was a curl of paper lying on her fax machine. She went over to it and pulled it out. It was another version of her photograph. This time the face was superimposed on to a hastily scribbled figure of a nun, complete with habit; and the figure was hanging from a gibbet, the noose around her neck. Underneath it said, ASK NO MORE. She checked the time it had been sent: 3.44. Her clock said 5.02. The fax must have been sent not long before she arrived home. The sender's phone number was the same as last time.

Still holding the paper, Agnes went over to the window. A chilly dawn was just breaking over the rooftops. She closed the curtains, screwed up the fax and threw it across to the waste-paper basket, then undressed and went to bed. She fell immediately into a deep, dreamless sleep.

Agnes woke to the sound of rain against the window. She got up, looked at her puffy eyes in the mirror, put on the kettle, pulled on some clothes. After a quick cup of tea she left for the hospital.

Even though it was Saturday, St Hugh's was abuzz with chaos and rumour. The office staff were nearly all at their desks, or at least all at each other's, chewing over the events of the night before. Agnes had only to spend half an hour in Dawn Scott's office to hear from the constant traffic of people a range of views as to what had occurred.

'It was an accident,' one young woman said, but was interrupted by a porter.

'Murder, obviously. A man like that.'

'An accident,' the girl went on. 'He was drunk, he was trying to entice some bird over there, he fell in.'

'What have the police said? I bet when they do those tests—'

'Autopsy,' Dawn broke in.

'—they'll find some other cause. How could he drown in just a few inches of water?'

'People do, you know. There was that toddler the other day—'

'That's different. A baby. Nah, we're talking about a man with enemies.'

'Who? Go on.'

'Well, it stands to reason. A man like that. You don't get so far in life without people wanting—'

'If that was true, there'd be no one in any high position anywhere – they'd have all done each other in, wouldn't they?'

'You only have to read the papers, don't you? Take that bloke what buried all them women under the floorboards—'

'Nah, 'e was a nutter, that's different too.'

Agnes left quietly, reflecting, as she crossed the courtyard, on the everyday nature of murder, pausing momentarily by the building site, its fence now gaping where Burgess had been winched up the night before. It is time for Tom McPherson to tell me what he knows, she thought, ascending in his shiny lift to his newly carpeted corridor.

'I thought I might get a visit from you today,' he said, as she showed her face round his door. 'Sit down.'

She sat opposite him and waited.

'You seem to know my half-brother Andy. You were there last night.'

'Yes.'

'I now realise that you knew more than you were letting on last time we met.'

'With respect, Dr McPherson, if you'd been prepared to listen—'

'Yes, well, that was then. Now he turns up again with murderous intent – I had no idea this Alexander Jeffes that you mentioned . . . and with a gun too.'

'Do you know where he's gone now?'

'I rather thought you could tell me that, you being his moll.'

Agnes straightened her shoulders. 'Now look,' she began, and her mind flashed up a picture of herself stepping into the path of Alexander's gun. 'If I hadn't—'

'All right, that may have been unfair. All I know is, last night I ran for my life and I don't care if I never set eyes on him again.'

'And do you think you will?'

'Andy has plagued me on and off for years. He resented my father all his life; nothing the old man could do would get through to him. Andy is someone who hardened his heart against people at a very young age. I can't see him changing now.'

Agnes nodded, chewing her lip. 'Did the police catch up with you?'

'Yes, they were here when I arrived this morning.'

'And what did you tell them?'

'About poor old Burgess? What was there to say? As it is, I'm hardly thinking straight – my mother died yesterday, as you may have gathered.'

'And what about the attempt on your life?'

McPherson fingered his beard. 'Let me be honest with you – Sister – um . . .'

'Agnes.'

'Agnes. Last night was most peculiar. I arrive back from my mother's death-bed. I then see my long-lost half-brother, whom I had never suspected of being in the hospital all this time. Then he tries to kill me. Meanwhile, old Burgess flings himself at a floozy, misses the floozy and ends up face down in that trench out there. I told the police what I could. I left out the Andy stuff because, in all honesty, I don't wish the boy any harm. No one heard gunfire except you and me – and we, I assume, haven't told anyone.'

'Someone else must have heard – Burgess and his floozy for instance. And anyway, it seems to me, Dr McPherson, that you're in great danger. Apart from your crazy half-brother, there's also the fact that someone tried to kill you once—'

'With penicillin, so you said. At least, that is what I inferred from our previous meetings with that charming girl. And do you think it was someone other than Andy?'

'If it was, and if it was connected with Burgess—'

'But who would have a grudge against us both?'

'Perhaps you might have some idea about that. Presumably, it's something to do with this building. And those weird faxes you've received would suggest that.'

'Well, there is Polkoff. I imagine it's him sending these things, don't you?'

'Yes, actually, I do.'

Tom McPherson looked genially across at Agnes. 'Shall I get us some coffee?'

'You see,' McPherson said, coming back into the room a few moments later, 'Polkoff's a bit of a nutter if you ask me. He's obsessive about that jumbled old collection of pickled bits of tissue. He's managed to convince that old trout, what's her name – Parry – that I'm the devil incarnate. But they're harmless – eccentric, I'd call them, hardly dangerous.'

'So what do you think the police will find out when they cut open Burgess?'

'I fear, Agnes, they will find a silly old man who drank too much and fancied his chances.'

'And you don't think you're in any danger?'

A shadow darkened McPherson's features. He shook his head. 'If I am – it is not immediately apparent.'

* * *

The drizzle of the morning had cleared, and the courtyard was bathed in spring sunlight. Agnes went and sat on the wall by the library. She frowned. If Burgess's death was an accident – and if Alexander had been threatening to kill McPherson on and off for years – then she might still be wrong. Because, she thought, noticing the succulent buds on the magnolia tree in the centre of the courtyard, it could still be a coincidence. There might not be a murderer. In the distance, she saw a man with long black hair, wearing a scruffy jumper, loping towards the new building. She felt the blood rush to her face, only to see, as he came nearer, that it was someone else.

What would she tell Julius? That she had agreed to sit for a painter, knowing what it would involve? That the more she had found herself wanting this man, the deeper she had become involved, until inevitably . . . Inevitably, she thought, that's what people always say. 'It was inevitable.'

The thought occurred to her that all the events of the last few weeks might just be a series of haphazard happenings unconnected with each other, and the only reason she had seen a pattern in it was to excuse her own behaviour, the story she had chosen to weave around her own desire.

'Hi. Sorry, I didn't mean to startle you.'

'Oh, hello, Julia.'

Julia settled down comfortably next to Agnes. 'I thought I'd find you here.'

'Mmm.'

'What's new?'

'I've seen McPherson. Alexander is his half-brother and tried to kill him last night. Meanwhile, Burgess drowns in a pit of filthy water, apparently by accident.'

Julia was looking at Agnes strangely. 'Right. Fine. Anything else?'

'What else? Oh, just that I'm in love.'

Julia laughed. 'No really—'

Agnes was gazing at the magnolia tree. She turned back to Julia. 'OK. We know that Alexander wants to kill McPherson. We know that Polkoff has got it in for McPherson too. It's something to do with the building. We know that Burgess behaved very oddly around Gail's death, with the cover-up and everything. But Burgess appeared to have relinquished his connections with the new development.' Agnes remembered the letter she'd found in Gail's files, the nervous handwriting. 'Although—' she began.

Julia interrupted, 'Do we think Alexander did the penicillin trick?'

'No,' said Agnes with certainty. 'We don't. Although that doesn't mean McPherson is safe from him. I can't see Alexander being all calm and courteous at the funeral, let alone when the will – oh God, the will.' She jumped to her feet.

'What?' Julia hurried to keep up as Agnes began to stride across to the main entrance.

'McPherson knows what's in his mother's will. Alexander has yet to find out. And my bet is – ' Agnes paused for breath – 'that particular explosion could cause a crater the size of Australia. McPherson's such an arrogant sod. The silly man believes that Alexander won't harm him, though given the evidence . . . he's really in very great danger indeed.'

Leaving Julia, Agnes went straight to her community. She was relieved to find Madeleine in.

'I'm supposed to be sleeping, I did a night shift at the Project last night,' Madeleine yawned, as Agnes started opening cupboards in the kitchen in search of lunch. 'How's the crisis?'

'So you and Julius discuss me?'

'Julius? No, of course not. All I know is, you were heading for one last time I saw you, and I didn't think you were likely to avert it, the way you were behaving.'

They settled down at the table and said grace over bread and cheese. Agnes munched in silence for a while.

'At least you're not off your food,' Madeleine remarked.

Agnes grinned, then sighed. 'What would you say if someone came to you and said, they had fallen in love with a man, and – and yes, had made love with him, and it was wonderful, and it won't ever happen again, and it felt healing and wonderful and not awful at all – and that the man was capable of murder and might well carry it out? I mean, how would you stop him killing someone?'

Madeleine looked at Agnes with compassion, at the tears welling up in her eyes. 'Who is he likely to kill?' she said gently.

'His brother. No one else. You see,' Agnes went on, 'if I don't stop him it will be for ever on my conscience, won't it? Given that I know that he might, I must prevent it happening, else I'm—'

'Guilty,' Madeleine said quietly.

Agnes looked at her gratefully. 'Yes, guilty.'

'But not of the murder.' Madeleine sighed. 'You poor confused woman. You're feeling guilt and you've just displaced it on to this murder business, when it's all about your feelings for this man, and the fact that you can't regret it. But why should you regret it?'

Agnes stared at Madeleine. 'Because – because, well, obviously – I've never broken my vows before.'

'But it was wonderful?'

Agnes sighed deeply. 'I can't begin to tell you. You see, with marrying Hugo, he was so – so warped, really, only I was too young to see, so I'd always thought sex was like that, and pleasure was all confused in my mind with – oh God.' She scrunched her hair in her fingers. 'But this was so – such *tendresse*, such *plaisir*, so generous. So simple, really. I wish I'd never found out.'

'No you don't.'

Agnes looked at Madeleine, who continued, 'You're the one using words like healing. You've got to see this as a good thing.'

'But—'

'Denying it's happened is no good. Pretending it was terrible, sinful – none of that is going to be any good to you at all. You've got to view this as a starting point.'

'For what?'

'That's what you've got to find out. A new way of being. That's what these things usually lead to. But hating yourself isn't going to help, feeling guilty, all that.'

'I don't feel guilty,' Agnes admitted.

'You've got to drop all this going on about him being about to kill someone.'

'He *is* about to kill someone.'

'Psychologically, it's an interesting metaphor.' Madeleine got up and put on the kettle.

'He is,' Agnes said. 'It's real. I've got to stop him. Surely it can't be God's will?'

Madeleine came over to Agnes and placed a hand on her shoulder. 'That's just it. You believe yourself to be this man's salvation, the agent of the Lord in saving him. You argue that it can't be God's will that this man kills someone, so therefore it follows that it is entirely up to you, Sister Agnes, to prevent it, because you alone know what might happen.'

'But I am responsible.'

Madeleine sat down opposite her. 'If there's a famine in Africa and you fail to give money to the aid agencies, it's not as if you've personally caused people to die, is it?'

'You could have saved lives by giving – so by not giving, you are, indirectly, causing more deaths.'

'That's not murder, though, is it?'

Agnes shook her head. 'But this is one person who I know might kill, in all probability will kill—'

'Short of following him around, what can you do? And that's just the point I'm making. You've displaced all these feelings to do with him on to this murder idea.' Madeleine covered a yawn with her hand.

'I'm sorry, I ought not to keep you from sleeping.'

Agnes stood up. 'When all this is over I'll be back at the project too.'

'When all this is over you should go on retreat for a very long time.'

'You mean, "get thee to a nunnery".'

They grinned at each other. 'Something like that,' said Madeleine sleepily.

The next day Agnes went to the eight o'clock mass at Julius's church, slipping away at the end to avoid speaking to him. At noon she went to mass at Westminster Cathedral. At three she attended chapel at her Order. She heard the familiar words ring emptily like a bell tolling in a vacuum, her own liturgy of numbness. But gradually, as the day wore on, she felt a lightening of spirit, felt the tightness round her heart dissolve. She began to breathe more easily.

It was evening when she made her way back home. She glimpsed the webbed roof of London Bridge station edged with the darkening sky, and it seemed to her to have an extraordinary beauty. She began to think it possible that she might be worthy of God's love after all. If I am to continue in the Order, she thought, then stopped. The idea of leaving the Order was intolerable. She stood in the street, reflecting on everything that the religious life had given her, thinking how her obedience to her Order had been tested over the years, but her faith had never faltered. How could it? she thought. In her submission to the will of God she had managed to quieten, if not silence, the most destructive of her inner voices. In taking her vows, she had set herself free. No, it would take something far

333

greater than this episode with Alexander to make her falter from her chosen path. Of course, she thought, setting off again, the aftermath of Alexander still had to be sorted out, and there was still the process of confession and reconciliation to go through to remake her vows. But, breathing in the crisp evening air, she felt ready to trust in God's will.

At nine o'clock the next morning, Marjorie Holtby was sitting at her desk, ashen-faced, with blue shadows around her eyes. She looked up absently as Agnes came in carrying two cups of tea, then looked down again. Agnes saw she had Professor Burgess's desk diary open in front of her. She placed a cup of tea by her elbow. Marjorie looked at the tea, then looked again at the diary. At last she said, in a faint voice, 'I really don't know what to do.' She gestured vaguely to the appointments neatly written down. 'He'll be expected to – people will be waiting.'

Agnes stirred some sugar into her tea, handed it to her, and waited while she took a sip. 'Let's get on the phone, shall we?' she suggested gently. 'Right – who's this, first appointment?'

'The external examiner.'

'And where will his phone number be?'

Ten minutes later, Marjorie had settled down with a list of names and phone numbers, and was working through them. 'I have very sad news to tell you, I'm afraid, there was an accident at the hospital on Friday night . . .' Gradually the tremor in her voice subsided and the old efficient sharpness began to return.

Agnes idly flicked through some papers on the desk, wondering what to do next. A business card caught her eye. It had the name 'Sisco Limited', and the same address in Moorgate. She scribbled down the details on a scrap of paper. 'That reminds me,' she said to Marjorie between calls, 'could you tell me which temping agencies this hospital uses?'

Marjorie wrote down two numbers, and then, as an afterthought, a third which she said was one they had previously used but which had gone downhill. 'Some of these girls just don't know how to set out a letter properly any more.' She was interrupted by a phone call from a Detective Sergeant Watts. She listened, nodded a lot and then rang off.

'They've had the post mortem results. They say it looks like death by drowning, with high blood-alcohol levels.'

'An accident, then?'

'They don't tell you anything, do they? He said the water was quite shallow, but there were no bumps on his head or signs of a struggle. He said they'd be in touch . . . Oh dear, I just can't get over it.' Marjorie began a contained weeping, dabbing at her eyes with a lace handkerchief. Agnes rested a hand on her shoulder for a moment, before leaving discreetly.

That afternoon, Agnes finished filling in the Land Registry form that Gail had started, enclosed Gail's photocopied plan of the site, and posted it off. She read through the correspondence in Gail's files concerning the purchase of the site. There were two letters disputing the value of the land, sent from someone called Dick Montgomery, Managing Director of Avalon, who seemed to feel that the consortium, which included the Stott Institute, was offering a price that was far too low.

Just after two o'clock Agnes set out for Companies House, where she looked up two companies, Sisco Limited and Avalon Limited. The directors of Avalon Limited turned out to be Dick Montgomery and someone called Roland Van de Meer. The directors of Sisco Limited were Myra Burgess and Marjorie Holtby. She looked up a few more details, then returned to her home soon after four o'clock to phone some temping agencies.

'Hello, Skills Search, how can I help you?'

'I was wondering whether you have a Trisha Slaithwaite on your books – medical secretary, she works as a temp.'

There was a pause and a tapping of keyboards. Eventually the voice came back on, 'No, sorry, no one of that name. Can anyone else help?'

'Not really. Thanks for your help.'

The second agency was the same. Agnes tried the third.

'I'm trying to get in touch with Trisha Slaithwaite.'

There was the muffled sound of a hand over the mouthpiece. 'Lady here asking for Trisha. What shall I do?' The young woman came back on the line. 'Trisha's due to pop in this evening. Shall I get her to phone you? Can I ask who's calling?'

'It's a personal call, I'll give you my number.'

For the rest of the afternoon, Agnes sat quietly at home, reading the *Spiritual Exercises* by St Ignatius of

Loyola, making notes and sometimes just staring into space. At five-thirty, the phone rang. A prim, slightly northern voice asked for Agnes. 'I'm Trisha Slaithwaite,' the voice said.

'Oh, thank you for phoning back. I'm helping St Hugh's Hospital sort out their Personnel and I wondered whether you could tell me when you'd last worked there.'

'St Hugh's, now let me see. My last job there must have been early this year – January, maybe February. I had to help some woman in the medical school who fussed about how I set out my letters. And their typewriters are terrible. And, now I come to think about it, I left a timesheet there and never got it back and you lot argued about my money. Sorry to be blunt.'

'You haven't been there recently? You didn't attend a party in honour of Professor Burgess?'

'Now that's the name – it was his PA who was so – I'm sorry, I shouldn't be rude. No, I haven't set foot in the place since then.'

'You've been very helpful, thank you.'

Agnes stared at the phone. Two Trisha Slaithwaites? Both medical secretaries? It seemed most unlikely.

That night she dialled Alexander's home number but hung up as soon as she heard it ring.

'So McPherson reckons it was an accident,' Julia said in the canteen next morning.

'He just told me,' Agnes replied, 'that the word was out that it was accidental death. He also told me that his mother's funeral is the day after tomorrow, and

337

the name of his family solicitor.'

'Why?'

'Because I need to know what's in his mother's will.'

'And Alexander's still a danger to him, then?'

'I fear so.'

'He should tell the police.'

'He doesn't want to incriminate Andrew, I mean, Alexander. If the police get involved he'll face firearms charges.'

'Hmm. But isn't McPherson in danger from someone else?'

Agnes carefully removed a teabag from her mug. 'Frankly, I don't think he is.' Julia looked at her, and she smiled. 'How's the revision?'

'Oh, OK. I'd hoped to be let off the hook on Surgery at least, but they've wheeled out some retired examiner or other, so it's business as usual. First exam in less than a week.'

'How's Mark?'

Julia grinned. 'Lovely, actually.'

'Good. I'm glad.'

'And are you still in love?'

'As to that, there's a short answer and a long answer. The long answer is that in the last day or two I think I've caught a glimpse of how God's love expresses itself throughout Creation, in different forms, and how – it's difficult this – if we are attentive to God's love, we can experience love without attachment . . . Oh dear, you're looking blank.'

'What's the short answer?'

Agnes sighed. 'The short answer is, yes. I'm still in love.'

They wandered back to the library together. The glass doors of the new building reflected the magnolia tree; but just as Agnes was about to remark on this, they swung open, flashing sunlight, and revealing a stretcher on which lay a figure covered in blankets. The stretcher was picked up and propelled fast toward the hospital Casualty entrance. Agnes and Julia looked at each other, then ran after it, arriving breathlessly at the admissions desk.

'Wh-who was that?' Julia almost shouted at the nurse.

'Who was what?'

Julia pointed down the corridor to the departing stretcher. The nurse looked down at her paperwork. 'McPherson,' she said. 'Dr Tom McPherson from across the way. Allergic reaction to a drug, maybe penicillin.'

'Definitely penicillin,' Julia shrieked. 'Oh my God.' She turned to Agnes. 'And after everything you said – we're too late.'

Chapter Twenty-two

'There's nothing we can do here,' Agnes replied, watching Tom McPherson being wheeled towards the theatres. 'However – ' she took Julia by the arm and set off back to the new building – 'his office will be deserted.'

They crept into his secretary's office, which was empty, and then into his own lair. Agnes went straight to the desk.

'Ha. There we are,' she said.

Julia saw she was pointing to a half-drunk cup of tea.

'You surely don't—'

'Take careful note, Julia,' Agnes said. 'Very rarely in this life will you see such clear evidence of God's order amidst the apparent chaos. Look. The cup of tea, still warm, I expect – don't touch. Half-way through drinking it, poor old McPherson feels his throat constrict, swelling, you know all that better than me, I imagine. Now look – his work – some medical paper, I think – flung down, his pen still oozing ink – those books pushed to the floor in the panic in which he calls his secretary. And now look – the saucer actually contains all the evidence we need. Tell-tale white powder, just a few grains.'

'It might be sugar.'

'He doesn't take sugar. Anyway, this is powdery, crumbled up.'

'But who—'

'Anyone could have watched Angela get the tea, interrupted her on a pretext and slipped the stuff in. It's a clumsy job, but it's done the trick.'

Julia flopped into McPherson's chair. 'We'd better let the police know.'

Agnes shook her head. 'I think, in this case, McPherson won't thank us for involving them.'

'You mean, you know who . . . ?'

'Yes. I do.'

They found themselves outside, blinking in the sunlight. Julia said, 'I was thinking the other day, remember, when I was seeing Alexander? How he asked me about Gail's death. More than once.'

'When was that?'

'When did I stop seeing him? It must have been—'

'The second of May,' Agnes said, without thinking.

Julia looked at her. 'Yes. About then.'

They ambled towards the library. 'Only,' Julia went on, 'he was talking about drugs overdoses and things then.'

'Yes, you told me at the time.'

Julia looked at her again. 'Yes. So I did.'

'I'm doing my best,' Kathleen said. 'Off out of here at any excuse. Watching, waiting. It's just, not knowing what I'm s'posed to look for, difficult, you know?' She paused and thought a moment. 'Saw two people snogging yesterday. No one we know.'

Agnes smiled. 'In a couple of days it will all be clear.'

She passed Amber's door on the way out. Amber was fastening up her large red duffle coat and pretended not to see her.

'Going already?' Agnes said cheerily.

'Oh. It's you. I'm – I'm not very well, actually.' She fumbled with a toggle.

'Another funny turn?'

'No. I mean, yes. It's just—' she turned tearful eyes to Agnes. 'I had no idea it would be serious. Not this serious. I didn't mean . . .' She dashed the tears from her eyes, pulled her hood over her head in defiance of the hospital's furnace heat, and marched awkwardly away down the corridor.

'How's it going?' Madeleine's voice, at ten o'clock the next morning, was carefully modulated warmth and sympathy.

'OK,' Agnes replied. 'It's ages since I've read the *Spiritual Exercises*.'

'You're – you're doing that now?'

'Yes. I'm very impressed by his approach. I hadn't realised how contemporary he appears. This idea of the moment, of the presence of God. It's very now, isn't it?'

'Um, yes. It's a while since I've looked at St Ignatius. And how's the rest of – I mean . . . ?'

'Oh, all the lust and murder?'

'That, yes.'

'Well, I've had an interesting letter,' Agnes said, glancing at the Land Registry Office copies which had arrived that morning, and which gave details of the property company responsible for St Hugh's new development. 'I'm just waiting to visit a lawyer. And then I'm off on my retreat. If you lot can spare me.'

Madeleine started to laugh. 'You really are – you're – all I can say is, I'll miss you.'

Agnes's reading was interrupted by another phone call that day.

'Hi, it's Julia. Just to say, McPherson recovered. He hadn't received a fatal dose.'

'No.'

'You don't sound surprised.'

'No. Julia – are you around tomorrow?'

'Sure, why?'

'Alexander's going to hear the will at their solicitor's. If anything's going to blow up, it'll blow up then.'

'I'll be in the library. It's become my second home.'

The next day, at three in the afternoon, Agnes rang the bell of Griswold & Co., solicitors, in Bedford Row. The large Georgian door opened gracefully, and she went inside. After a few moments, Alexander drew up in a taxi, with Polkoff at his side. Both men went into the building. About ten minutes later, Alexander stormed out of the door and stood in the street, staring blindly at the passing cars, his arm half raised as he tried to hail a taxi. Agnes appeared in the doorway.

'For God's sake, Alexander, you can appeal, you heard what Mr Griswold said, you can make a claim against the estate . . .'

'That's not the fucking point, is it? The point is, she was still scared of him. Even after his death, he still had a hold over her.'

'But when she's not even buried—'

'I shall go to her funeral when I've avenged—'

'You'll be locked up before her funeral at this rate.'

'Leaving everything to Tom. Christ, I can't bear it—'

'He's in hospital, penicillin overdose.'

'I know. It's up to me to finish the job. Where's Stefan?'

Polkoff emerged from the door, and taking Alexander's arm, began to lead him away. 'I'll deal with this,' he said to Agnes.

'That's just what I'm afraid of,' Agnes replied, as Polkoff hailed a cab and followed Alexander into it, slamming the door. They sped off – towards the hospital, Agnes concluded, jumping into another cab and issuing directions. The taxi lurched slowly through the London traffic, and by the time she reached the hospital, Stefan and Alexander were nowhere to be seen. She went straight to McPherson's ward, and found him sitting on his bed, fully dressed, reading a newspaper.

'Hello,' he said, looking up.

'I went to see your lawyer, as you'd arranged.'

'And?'

'It was just as you said. The will. And Alexander wants to kill you.'

'It's nothing new, believe me.'

'How's your health now?'

'They're about to discharge me.'

'But a murder attempt—' Agnes said.

'Oh, we spent all morning talking to a charming young woman from CID. She's probably still around somewhere.'

Agnes sat down next to the bed. 'When did you know about the will?'

McPherson sighed. 'She told me before she died. She was very guilty for Andy's sake, but she felt she couldn't do otherwise.'

'Didn't she think what it would do to him?'

'She felt powerless, she said, but she had to respect my father's wishes. And she had nothing of her own to leave.' McPherson folded his newspaper neatly in four.

'Have you mentioned Andrew to the police?' Agnes asked. 'They could arrest him, you know, you'd be safe—'

'Do you want that?' McPherson said, eyeing her steadily.

'No. But I don't want you killed either.'

'It's very nice of you. But don't worry, I've got an appointment with Polkoff this evening. I think that might sort everything out.'

'Here?'

'Yes.'

'Don't go.'

'Why ever not?'

'You really do think you're immortal, don't you?'

'No. Just one step ahead of my fellow mortals. Ah, here's my consultant,' he said, as a bespectacled man with a shiny pink face appeared and started to close the curtains around the bed.

On her way out, Agnes passed a pay phone. She dialled Alexander's numbers, but got no reply. Then she went to the basement of the hospital. Polkoff's door was locked; listening at the door, she could hear nothing.

'Damn,' she thought, heading for the library.

'Well, at least *you're* where I expected you to be,' she whispered to Julia who was half hidden behind a huge pile of books. 'Alexander wants to kill McPherson, because, as I suspected, his mother respected the wishes of his stepfather in her own will. Stefan is with him, which doesn't help. McPherson has got a meeting with Polkoff this evening.'

'And I've got an exam for which I know about three per cent of the stuff.'

Agnes looked at the pile of books, at the other students similarly occupied around them. 'You're right,' she whispered, 'it isn't fair on you.'

Julia sucked the end of her biro, then whispered, 'It's a very public way to kill someone – I mean, if Alexander comes here.'

'My fear is that Alexander is past caring.'

Agnes left Julia to her books and wandered aimlessly back to the hospital. She began to feel suffocated by the endless corridors, the dry heat, the fluorescent hum. She also felt completely useless. The clock at the main entrance said ten past five as she went out through the doors, taking deep breaths of the cool evening air.

What I really ought to do, she thought, is to find Alexander and put a stop to all this. Then I'll only have one murderer to deal with, not two. She paced the streets near London Bridge, feeling weak with fear at the prospect of the coming evening. The idea of going back to the hospital unarmed seemed foolhardy. Perhaps, she thought, it would be best to tell the police, who were already, after all, aware of some of the events in the hospital. But then Alexander – how long, she asked herself, am I going to be able to save Alexander from himself?

Reaching the station she fought her way through the rush-hour bustle to the call boxes. She dialled Alexander's number again, and to her amazement he answered.

'Oh, um – it's Agnes, listen—' she began.

'It's no good. It's all arranged.' His voice was weary.

'Why him? Why kill Tom? It's not his fault.'

'If they'd never had him – it would have been – don't you see—? I wish he'd never been born.'

'What time did Stefan say?'

'Nine.'

'Don't go. Can't you see? He's using you.'

Alexander gave a dry laugh. 'No, on the contrary. I'm using him.'

'You'll get arrested. It's crazy, a hospital, people around everywhere, the police around too—'

'I don't care.'

'Well I do – Alexander, please—'

There was a slight pause, then Alexander said, 'It's too late.'

Agnes hesitated. She heard Alexander say, 'Agnes?'
'What?'
'Nothing.' There was a silence, then he hung up.

'Damn, damn, damn,' Agnes said to the dialling tone.
Nine o'clock, she thought. She headed for home, to grab a
bite to eat, to reflect, over a glass of Armagnac, on the
evening ahead. She wished she was braver. The thought
of what was to come, the collision of two people harbouring
evil intent, filled her with dread. Her task was to prevent a
murder but still to catch a murderer. She poured another
drink, watching the reflection of the icon of St Francis in
the curve of the glass. Evil, she thought, is never simple.

At eight-fifteen, Agnes was standing by the library entrance
of the new building. The library windows threw crisp
yellow angles across the paving stones, and Agnes thought
of Julia, still battling with her revision. She wished she
was here. Further along the building, McPherson's light
stood out alone against the darkened windows. Agnes
wrapped her cashmere scarf tighter round her neck against
the cold and waited for that window to go dark too.
People came and went in ones and twos, mostly students
leaving the library, their odd words of conversation making
little clouds in the night air. A colony of starlings twittered
in the distant trees. At just after a quarter to nine,
McPherson's light went out. A few minutes later, he
emerged from the building, crossed the courtyard and
went through the door into the hospital. Agnes followed.

The basement of the hospital, even at night, maintained
a constant, throbbing hum. Agnes trod the corridor silently,

following the ceiling's coiled tubing, the grey viscera of water pipes and electric cables, glad of the soft soles of her trainers. In her pocket was a sharp kitchen knife and a battery-operated personal alarm. The memory of Alexander's pistol flashed across her mind, but she dismissed it. She saw McPherson disappear around a corner. Reaching the door of the Anatomy lecture theatre she paused, her ears straining for sounds above the background hum. Nothing. She went on her way, slowly, one silent foot in front of the other. She thought she heard footsteps, echoing hers, and was just about to turn round when someone grabbed her from behind and dragged her into a room. She smelt formalin, was aware of smooth fabric across her face, at the same moment realising that her aggressor must be Stefan Polkoff. The crook of his elbow was across her mouth, so she bit, hard, into it, and he dropped his grip so suddenly she stumbled.

Polkoff turned the key in the door. 'Alexander said you'd be here,' he said, eyeing her and rubbing his arm.

Agnes returned his gaze. 'If you wanted McPherson dead, why didn't you do it yourself?'

Polkoff smiled. 'Me? Oh, I'm not a killer.'

'Perhaps you can tell me then,' she said, 'what that syringe was doing in your pocket on Friday night?'

His hand darted to his desk on which lay a silver liquor flask. He unscrewed the lid and took a swig from it. Agnes smelt whisky. 'What syringe?' he said, wiping his mouth with the back of his hand.

'I had this memory, the next day,' Agnes went on, 'just as I took the torch from you, a sort of glint in your jacket pocket. I imagine that it was some preparation of Burgess's that he never got a chance to use, that he'd collected from the pharmacy that day.' Polkoff had carefully screwed the lid back on, but now he unscrewed it again. 'Though I don't quite understand why you should cover for him.'

Polkoff's mouth was wet with drink. He produced a neatly folded handkerchief from his pocket and dabbed at the corners of his lips. She felt suddenly like a headmistress who has called in a delinquent, possibly dangerous schoolboy.

'It seems strange,' she went on, 'after all Burgess had done.'

'Wha-what do you mean?'

'I mean, with that land. The new building land.'

'What do you know about that?'

Outside there was a shout, then silence. Agnes listened hard. She looked at the door. The keys were nowhere to be seen. I haven't got long, she thought, and her calm began to ebb away.

'What I mean is,' she went on, 'that although it was McPherson who authorised the digging up of the land, it was Burgess who had acquired it. Wasn't it? It was he who had bought it, with no respect to its history, to what it might contain?' Polkoff stood awkwardly in front of her, his shoulders hunched, staring at the floor. 'You knew,' Agnes went on, 'that they were both involved, and you played one off against the other, pleased that Alexander became involved, helping Burgess reveal to the Stott Institute that there had been wrongdoing in the finances of the building, once he had nothing to lose.' Agnes softened her voice. 'I suppose you hate them both.'

'No regard for history,' Polkoff muttered, not moving. 'Not the land, not the collection, nothing. All sold off.'

'But when you used human remains – wasn't that a bit—'

He lifted his head sharply. 'It was symbolic.'

'Of what?'

Polkoff frowned, his eyes darkened in his sallow skin. He said nothing.

Agnes, keeping her voice gentle, said, 'It's not as if it was a burial ground, is it? Just a church. They're allowed to re-use church land as long as there are no graves.'

Polkoff was staring at her, his eyes like embers.

Agnes stood up and paced towards the door, then turned. 'But there was one grave, wasn't there? One secret grave. A Stan Polkoff, died 1941 in London, in the parish of St Hugh's as it then was. And his wife, a good churchgoer, persuaded the vicar, who was a family friend, to bury him in the tiny church garden, secretly. And he complied, partly, I imagine, because he was a good man; and also because Mrs Polkoff was pregnant.' Polkoff was standing in front of Agnes like a waxwork, his glassy gaze fixed on her. 'And the reason it had to be secret, it being the war, was that Stan Polkoff, or Stanislaw, to give him his proper name, was Jewish.'

Polkoff's voice was a growl coming from deep within him. 'Those bastards . . . the site was razed. And Burgess, with his greed . . . and then McPherson . . . And I couldn't tell them, I couldn't tell them why . . . my father . . .' the last word came out as a sob. Polkoff sat down heavily.

'Was he murdered?' Agnes asked.

Polkoff nodded. 'They married in 1937, in Belgium. She was half-Flemish, he was Polish-Jewish, a refugee. Her mother was a Londoner, and this was the only place they felt they belonged. They lived quietly near Bermondsey market. But – ' he faltered ' – the past will out. Some local gang got wind of him being Jewish. One night they came for him . . .'

Stefan was sitting very upright, his face now composed. He reached for his flask again and drank from it. At length he said, 'I never knew him. Never met him. But she showed me the site of his grave.'

They sat in silence for a few moments. Agnes thought she heard footsteps, briefly, some way away. Polkoff said, 'How did you know?'

'It's all in the parish records. Well, just a name, that's all. But that was enough to piece together your story.'

'My history,' Polkoff said. 'I can't forgive them, you see.'

'But using Alexander – that's pretty unforgivable too, isn't it?'

Polkoff looked at her. 'We're old friends,' he said quietly.

'Did he give you my number for those faxes?'

'Yes. And the photo.' Agnes felt suddenly cold. 'He said you were getting too close—'

'Did he?'

'Maybe it was my idea. I can't remember precisely.'

There was silence again, broken by sudden running footsteps and a male voice, 'Stop! No, Stop!' and then more running and a door slamming.

'Alexander,' Agnes breathed. She jumped up and tugged furiously at the door, then whirled on Polkoff who was also standing, and cried, 'The keys! Open this door for God's sake!' He shook his head. 'Someone's about to get killed,' Agnes shouted. Her eye fell on a small rack of shelves to the right of the door. She saw a ring containing two keys. She grabbed the keys and tried the larger of the two. At the same moment Polkoff tried to stop her. She pushed him away and turned the key in the lock. It was the wrong one. Polkoff jumped forward and seized her wrist, trying to get the keys away.

'Don't you see—' Agnes gasped.

'Let him kill him,' Polkoff whispered. 'Let Alex do it. I got him here this evening, I told Alex he'd be here.'

Agnes struggled to try the other key in the lock. 'Did you invite him to discuss the building with you?'

Polkoff was muttering, 'He knows I know, you see. I found out today that he'd survived. It's Alex's turn now. He'll avenge us both. Give me those keys . . .'

Agnes tried to grab them in the other hand and they fell to the floor. Polkoff stooped to retrieve them, and Agnes hesitated. In that second she heard a shot and a man's cry. She brought the edge of her hand down hard on Polkoff's neck, and he groaned and fell sideways. She grabbed the keys, unlocked the door and was out in the corridor, locking the door behind her.

All was quiet again. The door to the Pathology museum was slightly ajar. Agnes paused outside, listening, then crept in and stood by the staircase. The place was in darkness, apart from a shaft of moonlight which fell across the central well of the staircases. A sudden scuffling above her made her jump. She strained her eyes in the darkness. Across the gallery she could see a flickering torchbeam; then there was the sound of someone running, and Alexander's voice above her.

'It's over. Once and for all . . .'

There was more running directly overhead, then a scuffle, a thump, a groan. The light went out and the torch clattered down the stairs, landing at Agnes's feet. She heard a voice saying, 'It'll do no good – it won't make any difference now,' and Alexander was laughing an eerie, hysterical laugh; then there was a crash, a shout of pain, and McPherson fell backwards down the staircase in a series of rhythmic thumps, slithering to the floor in front of Agnes. She backed away into the shadows.

In the silence, McPherson stirred. And then, illuminated by the moon, Alexander appeared at the top of the stairs, his pistol in his hand, his teeth bared in a ghastly grin of triumph. His voice came in short, breathless bursts.

'I can't tell you how long I've waited for this moment.'

McPherson opened his eyes, and sat up, staring upwards at his brother. 'Andy – you wouldn't . . .'

'I would,' Alexander replied. 'I will.'

McPherson began to struggle to his feet, but at that moment Alexander shouted 'Now! NOW.' There was a shot, a cry, a cloud of plaster dust raining down in the silence. Agnes looked up and saw a bullet hole in the ceiling. Alexander suddenly slumped on to the top step, letting the pistol fall to the ground. Agnes could hear his choking sobs, as she realised that he must have aimed deliberately to miss.

It was time to take action. 'Alexander,' she whispered, aware of McPherson in the shadows. She backed towards the half-open door, so that Alexander would see her there. He looked down and began to descend the stairs with his eyes fixed on her as if she might vanish at any moment. As he came level with her, he murmured, 'I couldn't do it.' He stumbled out of the door, and she heard his footsteps fade along the corridor.

Agnes reached for the lightswitch and realised, to her annoyance, that it was not in the obvious place by the door. She wondered where Alexander's pistol had fallen, hearing McPherson circling beyond.

'Dr McPherson,' she called out. 'Why did you poison yourself with penicillin?' She could hear his footsteps. 'And why did you send yourself threatening faxes?'

'You are a silly girl. It was Polkoff, those faxes.' His voice came from the shadows.

'The first ones were. He even sent a couple to me. But it gave you the idea.'

'This is all a little fanciful. Two minutes ago I was in fear of my life, and now you come in here accusing me of all sorts of nonsense—'

'You killed Burgess. And you killed Gail Sullivan.'

There was a pause. McPherson's reply, when it came, seemed far away. 'This is slanderous rot. Of course I didn't kill them. There are two post mortems to back me up.'

Agnes moved silently towards the voice, then spoke.

'In Burgess's case, you hired a girl from an escort agency to lure him to the site. Did she get extra money for being an accessory to murder? And in Gail's case, she helped you herself.'

In the silence, Agnes heard a key turn in the lock behind her. She went on, 'Let's start with Burgess, shall we? Before the party, both you and Burgess prepare yourselves for battle. He, with some drug, something he sneaked out of the Pharmacy earlier that day, evidence of which Polkoff destroyed before the police could get to it.'

'It's not the first time he's tried to kill me.'

'And you, with your so-called Trisha Slaithwaite, who wasn't Trisha Slaithwaite at all but a call-girl who assumed the identity of a temp who left her time-sheet here a couple of months ago. And your weapon proved the stronger. All she had to do was lure Burgess to the building site, and you did the rest. It was all complicated by Alexander – Andrew – turning up and trying to kill you too, but you managed it.'

'You could never prove it, even if it were true. He was drunk. He drowned. It's simple.'

'He was drowned. There's a difference. Held down, by you, I imagine. Unless you got poor old so-called Trisha to do that too. She seemed guilty as hell.'

'There were no signs of a struggle.'

'He was too drunk. Practically passing out before you even started. Your Trisha made sure of that.'

McPherson seemed to have moved further into the shadows, and now he took on a tone of bluster. 'What you forget, my girl, is that Robert and I were colleagues. We had projects in common, we respected each other.'

'A loyalty based on self-interest and greed. And it soon came apart. Burgess wanted that Surgery wing very much. He had no intention of retiring early, particularly as he couldn't afford to. In fact, he was in dire financial straits. Did you know he was a Lloyds Name? He'd lost out very badly a year or two ago, it seems. And then, along you come, presenting him with an offer he can't refuse. Together you'll set up a company, draining the last of his savings, and acquire the church land, then sell it on to your funding body at a vastly inflated price, agreed by you, rubber-stamped by the committee. I imagine you get a cut too. In return he agrees to go gracefully. That way you get your Genetics wing, and he solves all his financial problems in one go.'

'We had nothing to do with the property company.'

'Avalon Limited? Which, it turns out, is owned by Sisco Limited. And the directors of Sisco Limited, at least in name, are Myra Burgess and Marjorie Holtby.'

'I still don't see why this means anything.'

'Poor old Andy had a spoilt little brother, didn't he? It's plagued him all his life. And you are spoilt, aren't you? And the land value didn't quite match up to your expectations. And you didn't have the influence over Stott and Co. that you thought you'd have, despite getting your stooge in the company to argue. Which didn't matter so much for you, as you had your empire all sewn up. But for poor old Burgess, now ruined, and desperately selling off whatever he could get hold of, it was disastrous. So he became a dangerous man – dangerous because he had nothing to lose. It got to the point where he realised he could make your little deal public. He'd be in trouble, but no worse than before. Whereas you . . . well, it didn't bear thinking about.'

'He tried to kill me. That prescription—'

'Oh, yes, that was his first idea. He did intend to kill you. But at the same time, he was about to set in motion the revelations that would have damaged your career irreparably. Assisted by Polkoff, who was enjoying the fall-out, and who had agreed to send an anonymous letter. And so Burgess had to be stopped. Just as Gail Sullivan was stopped.'

'Now look, that really is far-fetched.'

'I'm not saying you killed her. But you were the agent of her destruction. When Mark Henderson confided in you about his little dilemma, you had a little chat with her. I imagine you told her a few home truths, that this glittering young medical student was never going to settle for a life with her. Am I right?'

'Any tutor would have done the same. I had his interests at heart.'

'But then she, a bit unhinged perhaps, plans her revenge, on you. And she picks up on something slightly odd about the new building too, and she does some research. And meanwhile, Amber Parry gets hold of a copy of an anonymous letter written by her friend Stefan, and passes it to Gail thinking it will help their cause.'

'Amber Parry?'

'Yes, poor Amber, who was upset about losing her job, who felt that you were, as she saw it, dismissing the past. And so Gail is about to contact the Land Registry when you have another go at her. And whatever home truths you went for that time – perhaps evidence of Mark's affair with Julia? – were enough to break her heart.'

'Sentimental claptrap.'

'And she decided to kill herself. And Mark too.'

'That might have happened anyway.'

'Yes. It might. And you weren't to know that in her panic she would swallow the penicillin intended for you by Burgess.'

McPherson's voice shook slightly. 'All this is neither here nor there. It may have been suicide, but the inquest concluded natural causes, and anyway she was cremated.'

'I'm afraid I didn't quite trust your so-called post mortem. Yes, I know it was Burgess who authorised all that, having realised that the penicillin dosage would raise some questions. But you were quite concerned too, I gather, at the time of the autopsy. So, you see, I did my own.'

'I don't – this is quite ridiculous . . .' spluttered McPherson.

'And she's still in a freezer, should she need to give evidence even at this late stage.'

Agnes suddenly saw a glint of metal, and realised, too late, that McPherson must have picked up Alexander's gun. She ducked into the darkness, as a shot rang out and a bullet whistled past her, splintering into one of the huge glass jars behind her. Glass and formalin spilled on to the floor as another shot was fired, again hitting one of the cases. Agnes heard the dripping of fluid and something slithering on to the polished floor. Silently she trod backwards and ducked behind the next display case. He fired again, splintering the case nearest to her.

'You're mad,' she cried.

He fired again, shattering more glass, flooding the floor with preserving fluid. The smell of formaldehyde was unbearable but McPherson had stopped firing. Agnes picked her way in the darkness across to the staircase. She heard his quick step, and whirled to see the pistol glint a few feet away from her. She ducked behind the ironwork of the steps as he lurched towards her, then there was a crash as he slipped and landed heavily on his back. The gun rattled as it fell from his grasp. She darted to pick it up, only to see it slide along the floor towards the door, which opened slowly. In the doorway stood a figure, who now bent and picked up the gun and aimed it at McPherson.

'You. Up,' Agnes heard Kathleen say.

McPherson stood up gingerly. His silhouette was gaunt in the yellow light flooding in from the corridor. There were voices, and Julia appeared with Stefan Polkoff and two policemen.

'Bloody hell, Agnes, we could hear gunfire from miles away,' Julia said.

Not taking her eyes off McPherson, Kathleen jerked her head in the direction of the police officers, and McPherson wearily walked towards the door. Agnes looked at Kathleen, who was upright, elated. Julia brought Kathleen her wheelchair as McPherson was led away.

They emerged, dazed, into the corridor, Kathleen in her chair, Julia, Agnes and Polkoff behind her. They heard an outside door open some way away, and then saw someone walking towards them. The others watched as Agnes began to move towards him. They watched as both figures slowly approached each other, as Alexander enfolded Agnes in his arms, burying his face in her hair, Agnes clutching fistfuls of his jumper, leaning into him with utter weariness. She turned to go, and Alexander pushed at the door and led her out, out into the dawn that was just breaking across the sky.

Chapter Twenty-three

'So it's all just snooping, really, this detective work,' Athena laughed, pouring more coffee.

'Absolutely. Just snooping. Not too much milk, please,' Agnes said.

'And all this was only the night before last?'

'Yes. I've been sleeping it off. And hiding from people. And there was the funeral yesterday.'

'It's a bit more dangerous than the snooping I do, though,' Athena said, closing the window against the morning drizzle.

'Yes.'

'I mean, pistols everywhere.'

'Mmm.'

'Have I said the wrong thing?'

'I brought some almond croissants, they're in that bag there.'

'And what became of the man?' Athena put the croissants out on a plate and brought it to the table, licking sugar from one finger.

'That's what I was trying to tell you,' Agnes said, thinking about the burial of Daisy McPherson, the two brothers at the graveside, Tom haggard and panicky, Alexander weeping openly but strangely peaceful – and the police standing guard over both.

'You mean—?'

'He was arrested. Yesterday.'

'Oh no. Why?' Athena asked indignantly.

'Oh, just a small matter of firing guns all over the place, missing his brother by sheer luck, and on the second occasion causing several thousand pounds' worth of damage to the medical school—'

'Hmm. What's going to happen?'

'Well, Stefan's working like crazy to sort it out, hiring lawyers, pleading mitigating circumstances. He's stricken with remorse. And Tom's trying to get the charges dropped. I guess he knows he's facing a life sentence, he's got nothing to lose. But if that doesn't work—' Agnes put one hand over her eyes. 'With his record? Attempted murder? Several years, I imagine.'

'That's terrible.'

'It's such a waste. He was going to go away and everything, make a fresh start. Before they came for him he'd been talking to your Jonathan.'

'Oh, I wouldn't know about that.'

'That bad, huh?'

'All I can say is,' Athena sighed, 'at this rate I'll be back in boring old Gloucestershire by the end of the month.'

'That's a shame. I like Jon.'

'So do I. I suppose that's just it – if we'd really fallen in love, at least I could be full of passionate hatred for him now, instead of affectionate regret. No, poppet, it's definitely over.' She laughed loudly. 'Men, eh?'

Agnes sighed. 'As you so truthfully say. Men.'

'And what will you do now?'

Agnes stabbed at flakes of almond on her plate. 'It's all a mess. I should go back and work with Julius again, but he doesn't know the half of it. I've got serious work to do with my Order – and with my own conscience. The first thing I'm going to do is go on retreat.'

'How lovely. Can I come with you? We'll eat lettuce leaves together, and chant soothing mantras and have aromatherapy massage . . .'

'I think perhaps you haven't quite got the idea, Athena.'

'Retreat?' Kathleen was indignant.

'It's only a couple of weeks.'

'You said you'd spring me from here.'

'Don't you shout at me until you've heard what I've got to say. You're out of here on Monday, that's two days' time, OK? It's all arranged. I'll be there to settle you into your new flat. And while I'm away I've organised a rota from the Order to help until I get back.'

Kathleen looked sullen. 'Holy Sisters, eh?'

'Yes, Sisters, like me.'

'You're different.' Kathleen stopped pouting and broke into a peal of laughter. 'It'll take more than a couple of weeks for you to confess all your sins.'

Leaving Kathleen some time later, Agnes went to find Julia. The blank, shiny corridors of St Hugh's had become unfamiliar to her, as if she'd never set foot in them before; as if it had taken merely a few cleaners with mops to bleach out all trace of her. She went tentatively to the canteen and was relieved to see Julia sitting alone at a table.

'I was hoping you'd be here,' Agnes said, sitting next to her.

'Why?'

'There's no need to be hostile.'

Julia's eyes flashed with anger. 'If I'd known that getting involved in all this was going to mean Mark being sent down—'

'Now hang on—'

'Before you came along, Mark was protected by Burgess and McPherson. One's dead, the other's charged with murder, and Gail's body is going to be used as evidence . . .' Julia's voice cracked and her eyes filled with tears. 'He's just waiting for the knock at the door.'

'If we hadn't intervened—'

'Not *we*—'

Agnes sighed. 'OK, if I hadn't intervened, Alexander would have killed McPherson.'

'So we've just traded your man for mine. Yours was going to be the murderer. Now mine is.'

'He's not my man,' Agnes said very quietly, tracing a coffee ring on the table top.

'I've been such an idiot,' Julia said. She stood up and, without looking at Agnes, slowly crossed the canteen and disappeared out of the door. Agnes watched her go and leaned her head wearily on her hands.

* * *

That evening, Agnes went to St Simeon's and knocked at Julius's door. He was sitting in semi-darkness in his office, under windows which were indigo with the last of the day. He looked up as she came into the room.

'Ah, there you are, Agnes.'

She sat down, unable to speak.

'Is the story over, then?'

She nodded, swallowed, shook her head.

'Of course, it never is,' he said.

Julius, she wanted to say, it's much more serious than you can ever know. I am still miles off course. She stared at the crimson swirls of the carpet.

'Agnes,' he said, staring at her hard, 'you may be adrift, but you don't have to drown.'

'I – I want to go on retreat.'

'Ah.'

'I'm sorry.'

Julius's blue eyes twinkled. 'What for?'

'I really will come back and work with you and live up to the tradition of my Order, and be—'

'And be good?'

She nodded, tears welling in her eyes.

Julius came and sat next to her. The room was dark, flecked with yellow from the street light outside. After a while he said, 'What will become of him?'

She looked up, trying to make out his expression in the darkness. 'Of – of Alexander?'

Julius nodded.

'Who knows when it will come to trial?'

'It must be terrible.'

'But you don't know—'

'What don't I know?'

'The worst.'

'Or, in this case, the best.'

She took his hand, and fiddled with his fingers. 'Was it so obvious?'

Julius smiled. 'To me, yes.'

'I'm not seeing him until we know.'

'And does it make any difference?'

She shook her head. 'No. No it doesn't.'

On Sunday, Agnes met Athena for lunch in the same fish restaurant.

'Well, that's that, then,' Athena said. 'Our two affairs started and finished since we were last here. And a murder or two. Doesn't time fly when you're having fun?' She took a large swig of white wine.

'What will you do?' asked Agnes.

'Well, thanks to your man, Jon has decided to run away. He's found a gallery in the States interested in buying Alexander's work, just on the strength of those two portraits, yours and that old professor.'

'Oh, yes, mine.'

'Do they allow them to do art in prison?' Athena asked doubtfully.

Agnes smiled. 'Perhaps. Although, I don't know what strings Polkoff has pulled, but there's talk of dropping charges.'

'Even better. They can both go away after all and lead

the life of Riley in New York, I suppose.'

Agnes looked at her closely. 'So, you do mind?'

'Poppet, I'm too old to mind.' Her eyes watered and she refilled her glass.

'I'll miss you,' Agnes said.

Athena stared at her. 'Oh, gosh, didn't I tell you? I'm staying here. It's all happened so fast. Do you know Jon's friend Simon? He runs a gallery at the back of Bond Street? No, of course you don't. Anyway, yesterday I was minding the gallery for him for some reason, and all these people came in asking me things and I sold them loads of paintings, and some of his peculiar lumps of stone too. So he's offered me a job, and I'm going to rent Jon's flat until I can find somewhere of my own . . . What's so funny?'

'Just the thought of you selling art.'

'Darling, it's easy-peasy. Only this morning I sold three to this sweet American couple who said they wanted something modern. Well, Jon was always going on about the – now, let me get this right – ' she screwed up her eyes in concentration – 'the modernist legacy, reclamation of form, the new austerity. So I just trotted out that sort of thing. Hope I got it the right way round. They showed me photos of their condo – apparently they all have swimming pools in Florida. And their grandchildren too, Barry and Topsy, really sweet.'

Two days later, Agnes sat in the office with Julius. He was typing, she was checking over the details of various retreats.

'Didn't your Provincial suggest one for you?' he said.

'Mmm. Yes, she did. I'm just browsing.'

'Ignatian spiritual exercises, you need.'

'I know. Ooh, look, here's one. The first prayer session is at five in the morning, and there's no food after mid-day.'

Julius came over and took the leaflet out of her hands. 'Agnes, I want you to go on one where the first session is no earlier than eight and you have three square meals a day.'

'But—'

'These tough ones are for very sane people. These retreats where you don't eat after midday aren't for people who are going to glory in their hunger pangs – they're for people who won't even notice them. Oh, Agnes, don't look so horrified. On your retreat, I want you to learn to like yourself better. Otherwise, the last few weeks – the way you've been . . .'

Agnes began to unfold a paperclip. 'You mean, it'll happen again.'

'Unless you learn to accept God's love for what it really is.' He laughed. 'Hark at me,' he said. 'To hear me you'd think I'd got the hang of it myself.' He looked at his watch. 'What time do we have to be there?'

'Three-thirty. We'd better go.'

Once again, Agnes found herself in the crematorium gardens, this time with Julius at her side as they ambled along past well-trimmed lawns and endless flowers.

'Well,' Julius began. 'That's that.'

'Poor Gail,' Agnes said, 'become a suicide.'

'For the best I suppose.'

Agnes nodded. 'Yes. In a way,' she said. She was carrying a small bunch of white roses, and now she stepped off the path and arranged them on the grass. She looked at them, then bent and adjusted one, and returned to the path. Julius took her arm and they walked on towards the gates.

Alexander shouted down from his studio. 'Push the door, it's open.' Agnes looked up at the shock of black hair against blue sky, the window flashing sunlight against sparse white clouds. She climbed the dark staircase, and arrived dazzled and breathless at the top as Alexander let her in. All was white and bright and full of June birdsong. She turned to him and they looked at each other.

'How's it been?' he said at last.

'Oh, OK. When's your flight?'

'Six o'clock tomorrow morning. I won't sleep.'

'No. Neither will I.'

'You could come and see me off.'

'I'm doing that now.'

'For ever?'

'For ever and a day,' she laughed.

'Agnes, I want you to know—'

'Are you going to show me my painting, then?'

'Y-yes, of course. I was hoping to give it to you, but it's part of my portfolio.'

'I'd rather you kept it.'

She followed him across the studio. The canvas was leaning against the wall, surrounded by packing material. He stood back while she looked at it.

'What do you think?' he said.

After a moment she said, 'Does it count as hand luggage?'

'What?'

'On the plane.'

'Don't be silly. The agents pack it all up for us and send it on.'

'Mmm.' She stared at the painting some more. A warm breeze gusted against the open windows.

'Well?' Alexander said.

She turned towards him. 'It could have been nude. I'd be no less exposed.' He smiled uncertainly. She went up to him and touched his cheek. 'I like my painting very much,' she said.

'I want you to know,' he began, 'that – you've – you've saved me.'

'Oh, nonsense,' Agnes replied. She started to laugh. 'I've never heard anything so—'

'Listen to me,' he said sharply. 'I realise now I'd wanted to kill Tom for years. You know, even when he was born, and everyone expected me to be glad I'd got a little brother . . .' He swallowed, then said, 'And then, with my mother, and the will and . . . And yet, when it came to it, I didn't. It wasn't that I couldn't, because there he was, at the foot of those stairs . . . but I made a choice. It was like, in that split second, I changed my whole life. And now it's passed, and Tom's alive, although . . . Well, anyway, if I hadn't met you . . . And now, I'm starting my life all over again.'

They were standing very close together. Agnes spoke quietly. 'You made the decision. It wasn't me. You saved yourself, or if not you, then—'

'Then God, you'll say.'

'Yes, I will.'

'I can't believe, you see. Not in Him.'

'OK, but if anyone's going to take the credit, it isn't me. Just because we—'

'Because we what?' He smiled, stroking her head. She shivered and looked up at him.

'And have I changed your life?' he asked.

She laughed. 'Me? My life keeps sweeping me up in tidal waves of change, and none of it I understand. I'm going on retreat at the end of next week, in search of calm and quiet.'

'And will you find it?'

She wandered over to the window and looked out. 'What time is it?'

'Nearly two.'

'I must go, I told Kathleen I'd be there by now.'

'Will I see you again?'

She smiled at him. 'If I'm going to fill my life with calm and quiet, then the answer must be no.'

He smiled back. 'Is that your answer, then?'

She laughed. 'I have no answers.'

At six the next morning Agnes woke suddenly, opening her eyes to see her thin curtains already dappled with the early sun. An aeroplane roared across the sky, the noise fading slowly into the rumbling traffic. Agnes stared at the ceiling for a while, then pulled the covers around her and went back to sleep.

MILK AND HONEY

A PETER DECKER WHODUNNIT

FAYE KELLERMAN

'Faye Kellerman establishes herself as a unique voice in crime fiction. The central character of Peter Decker is unforgettable' James Ellroy, author of *The Black Dahlia*

Sergeant Peter Decker is driving through a modern housing estate late one night when he discovers an abandoned toddler wearing blood-stained pyjamas. No one claims the curly-headed girl and Decker and his partner, Marge Dunn, resolve to find her parents as soon as possible.

Noticing bee-stings all over the child's arm, they go on a hunt that takes them to a honey farm set in the barren scrubland surrounding Los Angeles. It's a tough landscape, the people work hard and have little time for city folk, so the two detectives aren't surprised when no welcoming party is there to receive them. Nothing, though, has prepared them for the incredible stonewalling from the locals, nor for the grisly sight that greets them in the farmhouse. But Decker and Dunn are professionals to the core and, delving deeper, find themselves stirring up a gruesome mystery far more lethal than the ordinary hornets' nest . . .

Some reviews for Faye Kellerman:

'A tour de force that shouldn't be missed . . . a stellar performance' *Publishers Weekly*

'Excellent story of rape and murder' *Time Out*

'Irresistibly plotted' *Financial Times*

FICTION / CRIME 0 7472 3430 2

More Thrilling Fiction from Headline Feature

FAYE KELLERMAN

'WIFE OF THE MORE FAMOUS JONATHAN
BUT . . . HIS PEER' *TIME OUT*

GRIEVOUS SIN

Minutes after Sergeant Peter Decker witnesses his wife give birth to their first child his policeman's instinct tells him something's wrong, something the doctors are not telling him. He is right, and in the midst of his wife's trauma he begins to suspect something else is awry in the hospital. The disappearance of a new-born baby, together with that of the nurse in charge of the post-natal unit, confirms once again that Decker's instincts were correct – but this time *he* is the professional best qualified to deal with the potentially tragic crisis, a task to which he takes with a vengeance.

The early signs look bad – the missing nurse's burnt-out car, together with some charred remains, are found in a remote ravine. But as Decker and his partner Marge delve deeper, they start to uncover the network of family tragedy and betrayal that led to the frantic kidnapping of an innocent baby girl.

'Faye Kellerman creates powerful, unhingeing characters and her narrative leaves you sweaty-palmed' *Jewish Chronicle*

'Painfully touching as well as taut with suspense'
Mystery Scene

'A marvellous melange of complex family feuds . . . satisfying denouement' *Scotsman*

'Tautly exciting' *Los Angeles Times*

'The most refreshing mystery couple around' *People*

FICTION / THRILLER 0 7472 4118 X

More Compelling Fiction from Headline

Written in Blood

Caroline Graham

'Graham has the gift of delivering well-rounded eccentrics, together with plenty of horror spiked by humour, all twirling into a staggering *danse macabre*' *The Sunday Times*

It is clear to some of the more realistic members of Midsomer Worthy's Writers' Circle that asking bestselling author Max Jennings to talk to them is outrageously ambitious. Which is why Gerald Hadleigh, who knew Jennings many years before and for whom the prospect of seeing him again is the most appalling he can imagine, does not challenge the proposal. But, astonishingly, Jennings accepts the invitation and before the night is out Gerald is dead.

Summoned to the well-heeled village, Chief Inspector Barnaby finds that, despite the fact Hadleigh lived within a stone's throw of most of them, the polite widower was something of a mystery to his fellow group-members: as witnesses to his final hours they are little help. But the one thing they all agree on is that on the night of his murder Gerald was a deeply troubled man. The obvious cause of his distress was their guest speaker. So why did the wealthy and successful Max Jennings travel to Midsomer Worthy to talk to a small group of amateur writers? And, more to the point, where is he now?

'A wonderfully rich collection of characters . . . altogether a most impressive performance' *Birmingham Post*

FICTION / CRIME 0 7472 4664 5

A selection of bestsellers from Headline

OXFORD EXIT	Veronica Stallwood	£4.99 ☐
BOOTLEGGER'S DAUGHTER	Margaret Maron	£4.99 ☐
DEATH AT THE TABLE	Janet Laurence	£4.99 ☐
KINDRED GAMES	Janet Dawson	£4.99 ☐
MURDER OF A DEAD MAN	Katherine John	£4.99 ☐
A SUPERIOR DEATH	Nevada Barr	£4.99 ☐
A TAPESTRY OF MURDERS	P C Doherty	£4.99 ☐
BRAVO FOR THE BRIDE	Elizabeth Eyre	£4.99 ☐
NO FIXED ABODE	Frances Ferguson	£4.99 ☐
MURDER IN THE SMOKEHOUSE	Amy Myers	£4.99 ☐
THE HOLY INNOCENTS	Kate Sedley	£4.99 ☐
GOODBYE, NANNY GRAY	Staynes & Storey	£4.99 ☐
SINS OF THE WOLF	Anne Perry	£5.99 ☐
WRITTEN IN BLOOD	Caroline Graham	£5.99 ☐

All Headline books are available at your local bookshop or newsagent, or can be ordered direct from the publisher. Just tick the titles you want and fill in the form below. Prices and availability subject to change without notice.

Headline Book Publishing, Cash Sales Department, Bookpoint, 39 Milton Park, Abingdon, OXON, OX14 4TD, UK. If you have a credit card you may order by telephone – 01235 400400.

Please enclose a cheque or postal order made payable to Bookpoint Ltd to the value of the cover price and allow the following for postage and packing:

UK & BFPO: £1.00 for the first book, 50p for the second book and 30p for each additional book ordered up to a maximum charge of £3.00.
OVERSEAS & EIRE: £2.00 for the first book, £1.00 for the second book and 50p for each additional book.

Name ....

Address ....

....

....

If you would prefer to pay by credit card, please complete:
Please debit my Visa/Access/Diner's Card/American Express (delete as applicable) card no:

Signature .... Expiry Date..............